...y come, boys!"

Shepherd turned at the sound of the voice, looking left, then right. The fighting seemed to be coming from all sides, yet in the excitement no one manned the front of the sod-walled saloon. He ran to his old position and flung open the door.

Indians on horseback completely filled his field of vision. On frothing horses, brightly painted savages brandished knives, spears, rifles, and clubs. They screamed like crazed animals and rode straight at him.

Shepherd's knees weakened, and he fell to the floor. His arms were paralyzed with fear, and he stared at the door, wishing it shut. He would die under the hooves of a charging horse.

Dixon glanced about and saw Shepherd on his knees in front of the open door. Thinking him wounded, Dixon ran to his side. He looked up and locked eyes with a Comanche not twenty yards from the door, bearing down on him at full speed.

BOOK YOUR PLACE ON OUR WEBSITE AND MAKE THE READING CONNECTION!

We've created a customized website just for our very special readers, where you can get the inside scoop on everything that's going on with Zebra, Pinnacle and Kensington books.

When you come online, you'll have the exciting opportunity to:

- View covers of upcoming books
- Read sample chapters
- Learn about our future publishing schedule (listed by publication month *and author*)
- Find out when your favorite authors will be visiting a city near you
- Search for and order backlist books from our online catalog
- Check out author bios and background information
- Send e-mail to your favorite authors
- Meet the Kensington staff online
- Join us in weekly chats with authors, readers and other guests
- Get writing guidelines
- AND MUCH MORE!

**Visit our website at
http://www.pinnaclebooks.com**

BLOOD RED RIVER

Walter Lucas

PINNACLE BOOKS
Kensington Publishing Corp.
http://www.pinnaclebooks.com

PINNACLE BOOKS are published by

Kensington Publishing Corp.
850 Third Avenue
New York, NY 10022

All Kensington Titles, Imprints, and Distributed Lines are available at special quantity discounts for bulk purchases for sales promotions, premiums, fund raising, educational, or institutional use. Special book excerpts or customized printings can also be created to fit specific needs. For details, write or phone the office of the Kensington special sales manager: Kensington Publishing Corp., 850 Third Avenue, New York, NY 10022, attn: Special Sales Department, Phone: 1-800-221-2647.

Pinnacle and the P logo Reg. U.S. Pat. & TM Off.

First Printing: December, 2000
10 9 8 7 6 5 4 3 2 1

Printed in the United States of America

This novel is dedicated to

Daddy
Mom
Lary
Memo

I wish you all were here to see this.

One

The buffalo bull jumped as a thunderclap echoed across the plain. Bright red blood shot from his nostrils. The bull grunted and shook his shaggy head, slinging a crimson arc across the grass.

"Die, you woolly son-of-a-bitch!" Billy Dixon muttered under his breath.

The bull took two shaky steps and fell to the right, sides heaving as he struggled to breathe. Soon the movement stopped.

A cow approached and sniffed at her fallen comrade. Her eyes rolled in fright and confusion. She started to bawl, attracting the attention of the others grazing nearby. Dixon quickly reloaded, sighted, and fired. The cow dropped to her front knees, afflicted with the same massive bleeding from mouth and nose.

A young bull raced across the plain toward the main herd. He ran with a peculiar, rocking gait that characterized the American bison. Others took his cue and followed, quickly blending into the rolling black and brown sea. Slowly at first, then with increasing speed, all the buffalo broke into a swaying gallop until the sound of rolling thunder filled the valley.

Dixon lowered the barrel of his Sharps .50-caliber rifle and watched the buffalo run. His gaze followed the herd to the horizon, and still he saw no end to the beasts.

What had spooked the buffalo? After years of being

hunted, the mere scent of an Indian was known to panic a herd. Was that why the young bull had bolted? Dixon gazed around him. Was he being watched? He quickly glanced at his horse, a black gelding named Jack. The animal got skittish near Indians—so did his owner. Jack looked relaxed.

Dixon sighed and stood. Anything could have set off the buffalo. Wolves, coyotes, mountain lions, even other white hunters. Sometimes the fool animals just took a notion to stampede for no reason.

He looked over his kill. Thirty dead buffalo lay at the bottom of the draw. Not as many as he wanted, but not bad for the first day.

He bent and retrieved his cartridge belt, draping it casually over his left shoulder. He also picked up a dark brown leather bag that held shell casings, then walked the twenty yards to where Jack was staked. After pulling the picket from the ground, he looped the straps of the casings bag over the saddle horn and stepped into the saddle. Dixon studied the land.

From a distance the Texas plains looked flat and featureless. Looking closer, he saw dips and small valleys with plenty of room to hide Indians.

Lush grass, normally green, had yellowed under the relentless sun and a spring short of rain. Antelope, prairie chicken, and quail wandered about in plain sight. A hunter's paradise.

Dixon grabbed his hat as he was caught in a sudden gust from the southwest. The wind blew constantly on the plains. Some days, it was only a breeze, others, a moaning, wild thing able to topple a man.

Satisfied he could easily find his way back, he turned the gelding home, eyes scanning the land for sign of movement. There probably wasn't an Indian within a hundred miles of where he sat, but a man just couldn't be too careful.

* * *

The next morning, he stared into the campfire, his Sharps cradled in one arm, a buffalo robe draped over his shoulders against the chill. One bullet, one buffalo. That was his goal. Dixon realized the goal was unattainable. Even the best marksmen he'd ever seen missed, but the effort improved his aim and forced him to be patient.

"My God! I'm as stiff as a bloody piss-proud cock."

"Mornin', Charley," said Dixon.

Armitage shuffled into Dixon's line of vision and sat by the fire, shivering. "Nice robe, Billy. It seems to be colder here on the plains."

"Nothing to stop the wind." Unfortunately, the wind blew from the Englishman's direction, and the smell of yesterday's work hung heavily in Dixon's nostrils.

The skinner nodded his agreement, then looked around, absently scratching his chest. "Where's the cook?"

"Out yonder, I suppose. I heard him moving around earlier."

"That man was royally drunk last night, wandering about the camp singing those asinine songs, and drinking toasts to every bloody thing he saw. He even toasted the hides we took yesterday. Bloody fool probably passed out and has been eaten by wild animals."

"Well," Dixon said, pulling the robe closer, "wherever he is, I wish he'd get back. I could use some coffee and breakfast."

"Too right!"

A shout rang out from the other side of the hide wagon, followed by a short scream. Dixon leapt to his feet and tossed the Sharps to Armitage. He pulled his pistol from its holster and ran, fearing the worst. He rounded the corner of the wagon and braked so short Armitage bumped into him.

"Dammit, Billy, why don't you . . . ?" Armitage stopped as Dixon pointed.

Frenchy sat in the middle of the creek, eyes wide and mouth agape as he tried to catch his breath.

Dixon lowered his weapon. "Damn! It ain't even September, and here you are taking a bath!"

Armitage laughed. "Perchance, you'd like some Castile soap and lilac water for your ablutions."

"You know, Mr. Armitage, that there creek water looks a mite cold."

"I agree, Mr. Dixon. I fear our friend's ballocks have been sucked up to his Adam's apple."

Frenchy glared at the others. "Fu . . . f-f-for God's sake, g-get me out of here!"

Dixon and Armitage each grabbed an arm and lifted the cook from the creek. Frenchy stomped back to camp and stripped off his wet clothes. The others returned to the fire.

Frenchy reappeared wrapped in a blanket, carrying his long underwear on the end of a stick. He stabbed one end of the pole into the ground as close to the flames as possible without setting the clothes alight. Huddling beside his homemade clothes hanger, he pulled the cork out of a bottle of gin and took a long drink. The glass neck clicked against his chattering teeth. Without a word, Armitage rose and started making coffee.

Dixon reached for the bandolier used for his rifle and slipped three-inch shells into loops. "Well, Frenchy, you gonna make us wait forever?"

Frenchy grunted. "Ain't nothing to tell."

"Do tell. We thought you were killed and scalped, what with all that hollerin' and such."

"Well, I wasn't."

Armitage carried the coffeepot to the fire and hung it on a hook over the flames. "There, that should do the job," he said, sitting back down. Then he turned to Frenchy. "Come on, old fellow, give us the story."

Frenchy looked from one to the other. "There really ain't no story to tell. I was just crossing the creek to do my morning business. Then these here big, flying wasp or hornet things attacked. Plumb backed me into the creek."

"You mean to tell me you were chased into the water by bumbly bees?"

"Hell, no, they weren't no—"

"I can just see it," Dixon interrupted. "People'll ask, 'Now, what's happened to Frenchy?' and we'll say, 'Why, he went to shit, and the bees ate him.' "

"They wasn't no goddam bees, goddammit! Them son-of-a-bitches was as big as my thumb!"

Armitage sat straight up. "How many were there?"

"Why?"

"If I were attacked by a horde of the beasts, I'd run, too. How about you, Billy?" He gave Dixon a slow wink.

Dixon nodded. "I reckon so. So how about it, Frenchy? How many was there?"

Frenchy shifted uncomfortably. "Some, I guess. Not so many as a horde."

"Some ain't a number. Was there fifteen? Twenty? A hundred?"

"Not quite."

"Well, then, was there five of 'em?"

Frenchy felt his face get hot. "If you gotta have a number, they was maybe one or two." He saw the wide grins on both Dixon's and Armitage's faces. "Oh, all right, there was just the one. There—I said it. One big-ass hornet chased me into the creek."

The others broke into laughter. They replayed his story, adding buzzing sound effects and screams of fright. Angered, Frenchy jumped to his feet; the blanket fell to the ground. They stared at him, then laughed even harder.

"I say," Armitage said, wiping tears from his eyes. "That water must have been very cold, or maybe it's just hiding from the bumbly bee."

Frenchy looked between his legs, then grabbed his

underwear and the blanket. "Kiss my ass!" he growled, stomping back to the shelter followed by sounds of merriment.

The rising sun burned off the earlier chill and everybody relaxed. Frenchy's humor improved as the temperature rose, and by breakfast, he was laughing at the morning's events.

The meal consisted of fried buffalo hump, coffee, and biscuits liberally smeared with hunter's butter. Unlike cow's butter, this spread was made by roasting the bones of a buffalo until blackened, then breaking them open and scraping out the cooked marrow.

"Good breakfast, Frenchy," Dixon said, wiping his mouth on the sleeve of his dark blue cotton shirt. He dropped the empty plate by the fire, refilled his tin coffee cup, and retrieved the Sharps.

Weapons maintenance was a lifesaving task on the prairie. The constant wind blew dust and dirt particles into everything, but the breech mechanism of the rifle seemed particularly susceptible. He carefully examined and cleaned the surface of the Sharps, then the barrel, and finally the stock. Satisfied with its condition, he slipped the rifle into the saddle scabbard.

Ammunition had to be checked also. Dixon always started with manufactured bullets. If he used all of what he brought initially, he'd reload the half-inch-diameter slugs until the opportunity presented itself to buy new ones again. He traveled with the primers out of the rounds to prevent accidental discharge. Each day's hunt started by loading primers into the base of the shells.

The combination of the big lead slug and almost two hundred grains of black powder produced a bullet capable of killing a buffalo bull over a quarter mile away. Targets could be hit at distances up to one thousand yards. On the other hand, if Dixon was careless, this same lethal combination delivered a recoil sufficient to knock him off his feet.

"Billy?"

"Yeah, Charley."

"Do you think we'll have Indian trouble?"

Dixon picked up his coffee cup and sipped slowly. "Cain't say. Leastways, you cain't blame 'em none. Indians need the buffalo more'n we ever will. If they go, you and me just have to find respectable work, but the Indian dies."

"Oh. Then do you think we're morally wrong?"

"Jesus, Charley, what's got into you? It ain't a matter of morality. If I don't shoot 'em, Wright Mooar or Emanuel Dubbs will. This is a hard business, without sentiment. It's dollars against tenderheartedness, and dollars win." Dixon paused to sip again, then grinned. "Now, if the red man takes exception to that, he's welcome to try and stop it."

"Shit, don't talk about that!" Frenchy looked around, half expecting a painted savage to appear. "Yes, sir, I could just go all damn day long without that kind of talk. I heard tell they do frightful things to a man and . . . well, I just don't want to think about it."

"Agreed," Dixon said, emptying his cup. He dropped it next to the plate and picked up his saddle. "We got buffalo to hunt. We'll deal with the other when, and if, we have to. Now, I've been thinking it wouldn't hurt to hire another skinner. That way we can kill more and still get them skinned and staked. That all right with you?"

Both men mumbled assent, and Dixon proceeded to his horse. He tossed the saddle over the gelding's back and talked as he did the rigging. "I make the wind to be from the south, southwest, so I figure to travel north and east of here about five or six miles. I'm going to shoot enough buffalo to keep you both busy for a couple of days. Then I'll take the light wagon back to the Walls."

Armitage frowned at Dixon's back. "If you shoot that many bloody animals, we'll be skinning day-old buffalo. I hate dealing with an old carcass. They're a bloody pain in the arse."

Dixon swung into saddle. "Relax, Charley. The more you skin today, the less you have tomorrow. Besides, just think of it as money on the hoof. I'll see you boys directly."

He waved as he rode out of camp and back onto the plain. The enormous herd was within two miles. Keeping a safe distance between himself and the buffalo, he kept pace with the animals until he found what looked to be a good shooting site at the top of a small rise.

He staked Jack at the bottom of the hillock, out of sight of the herd. Climbing to the top, he stood and gazed at the thousands of buffalo grazing about three hundred yards away. He quickly scanned the surrounding country looking for wolves, other hunters, and Indians. Satisfied, he dropped the cartridge belt and lay belly-down in the grass. He loaded a round into the Sharps, sighted on a large bull, held his breath to steady his aim, and squeezed the trigger.

The buffalo dropped, soundlessly at this distance. Dixon selected his second kill as he threw open the block on the rifle and reloaded. Weapon again at his shoulder, he fired.

The second bull leapt into the air and ran a short distance before collapsing. Dixon ignored him. By the time the second buffalo fell, the Sharps had barked a third time, and a large cow had immediately gone to its knees.

His fourth shot killed a calf as it bawled over its fallen mother. The fifth missed completely. The now-spooked herd broke and ran.

He ran down the hill to Jack, mounted, and rode until he found high ground again about a quarter mile away. He quickly climbed the ridge, dropped to his belly, and peeked over the top.

Below him, a small group of buffalo grazed, separate from the main herd. He dropped his cartridge belt and casing bag, lay down, and went to work again. This pattern of kill and pursue ran through the morning and past noon.

Finally, he decided to call it a day. His shoulder ached, and he was almost out of rifle rounds. He'd lost count of the number of buffalo he'd killed, but he did try to keep them in a line.

He backtracked the trail of bodies until he heard the familiar jingle of one of his wagons. Topping a rise, Dixon saw his skinners approaching.

"You must've strung buffalo for ten miles," Frenchy complained, reining the mules to a stop. "How much farther we got to go?"

"Not more than a mile or so. Follow me."

Dixon and his crew continued until they arrived at the carcass of the cow he'd shot shortly before. Frenchy drove the wagon a few yards past the buffalo and stopped. The skinners dismounted and walked back to Dixon's kill. Armitage carried a three-foot stick called a "prichell." One end was sharpened. The other had a nail driven through it. He dropped the stick next to the cow.

Frenchy grabbed its front left leg, Armitage the back. "Ready, Charley?"

Armitage nodded, and both men pulled until the cow rolled on its back. Frenchy caught the right foreleg as it swung by, effectively balancing the animal. Armitage picked up the prichell, jabbed the nail into the buffalo's skin, and forced the sharpened end into the ground. This maneuver made access to the animal's belly easier and kept its legs out of the way.

Being nearest the head, Frenchy removed his sharppointed ripping knife and, starting just under the chin, cut through the skin. He continued the cut over the chest and along the belly until he reached the middle. "This here cow's fresh enough. We ought to be able to peel her like an orange."

"Indeed," Armitage answered, taking over and slicing through the skin over the rest of the belly and to the tail. "But on the morrow, those that are left will stink and be as stiff as that prichell."

Frenchy moved to the right front leg, cutting a ring around the ankle just over the hoof. He split the skin along the inside of the leg until he met the centerline. Armitage followed suit. Each man replaced his ripper with a skinning knife featuring a wide curved blade.

Armitage started with the hind legs, drawing the skin off the muscle. When necessary, he sliced through the thin, white membrane binding it to the animal. Frenchy cut a ring around the cow's neck, pulling the hide down from the centerline. He worked opposite the prichell.

"Son-of-a-bitch!" Frenchy cursed as he removed skin along the side and belly. "Damn hide's almost too fresh. I keep losing my grip from the blood."

Frenchy moved to the front legs and skinned them. Armitage finished the first phase by pulling the skin to the ground. He tucked the loosened hide under the cow's backbone, rose, and grabbed the legs on the skinned side.

Frenchy pulled the prichell free and moved beside his partner. Stabbing the carcass with the nail, he let the animal's weight drive the point into the earth. Both men worked down the second side. Soon, the hide remained only on the animal's back.

They bunched the newly skinned hide against the body. While Armitage held the buffalo's legs again, Frenchy removed the prichell. Armitage released his grip. The body flopped over to the right. Each man grabbed hold of the hide near the head and pulled back. Slowly, they stripped the skin away. The job ended when the tail skin slipped off.

Dixon knew the cow was about as big an animal as the men could handle without the wagon. On larger buffalo, a rope was tied to the hide just at the neck, the other end to the hind axle of the wagon. The team would be started, and mule power stripped the dead buffalo of its skin.

Frenchy wiped bloody hands on the hide's shaggy hair and stretched it out on the ground. A skin like this weighed sixty pounds uncured, but about half that when dry. He folded the hide into quarters, smooth side in, and carried it to the wagon to be later staked out using small wooden pegs.

Dixon shifted in the saddle. "I got to run. You got your rifles, don't you?"

"Sure do," Armitage answered, trying to clean red-stained hands on his coveralls. "We plan to keep a sharp eye out for wolves with two or four legs."

"Good. Then I'm off. I expect to see you boys in about three days."

Two

Kiowa war chief Lone Wolf quirted his horse and leaned closer to the animal's lathered neck. His right hand gripped the short whip, while his left struggled to retain a hold on his reins and the leads of two pack-horses. Glancing to the rear, he saw their pursuers close behind.

Fools, he thought bitterly. *Why do they chase us? Could they not see this was no war party?* He wore no paint, his men's faces were washed clean. But these were soldiers sent by the Great White Chief. All they knew of the Kiowa was how to kill them.

An angry hornet buzzed by his head, followed by a sharp crack.

Another crack, a grunt, and an empty saddle. He tried to see who fell, but there was too much confusion.

More shots.

A bullet shattered the sandstone next to his face, stinging him with bits of rock and molten lead. He lost his grip on the rope to the pack animals. As the two mustangs fell farther and farther behind, he tried to rein in, but was swept along by the other riders.

He raced along the riverbed until a narrow cut in the bank allowed him to lead the rescue party to level ground. After a quick glance over his shoulder for signs of pursuit, he stopped. Walking his jaded pony back to the riverbank, he watched as the soldiers gathered the abandoned horses. One carried the remains of his son, Tau-ankia. The other, his nephew, Gui-tain.

Bitter tears of rage and frustration ran down his cheeks. The purpose of the mission had been to find the bodies of their warriors and take them home. Now that was impossible. The dead, and those who had died trying to rescue them, were to be left behind.

"We will come back," he said quietly, as much to himself as the others, "with a mighty army. It is time to drive the whites from our lands."

He wheeled his horse and galloped across the east Texas countryside. Unlike their original journey's purpose, they were now on the hunt. They rode until forest turned into farmland.

The war party left the cover of the woods and silently trotted across the field. The freshly plowed furrows muffled the sound of the horses' hooves. About four hundred yards to the right, a man, dressed in dark pants and a white shirt, plowed behind an old horse. His back was to them.

Lone Wolf pointed. Boy and White Goose broke ranks and charged at full gallop. War honors varied among the Kiowa and Comanche, but counting coup held the most prestige. A coup involved the warrior physically touching his enemy. First coup could be received only by contact with a living opponent. The remaining three levels counted whether the man was dead or alive. The greatest coup was killing a man in hand-to-hand combat. It was also the most hazardous.

Boy, like many in his tribe, preferred using a coup stick, a long slender rod. Riding past the fleeing farmer, the young warrior struck him across the shoulders. White Goose followed immediately with a war ax. He claimed second coup and the kill with a vicious chop to the base of the white man's neck, nearly severing his head. Both warriors continued toward the farmhouse.

Lone Wolf signaled again, and the younger, inexperienced warriors pulled away, screaming war cries. He allowed them to get about fifty yards away before kicking his pony into a lope. At seventy-five yards, the older men charged, their howls joining with the others.

The scene at the farmyard was bedlam. Chickens ran in all directions. An old man lay between the house and barn with three arrows in his back. Another arrow killed a barking dog. Lone Wolf watched as a skinny, gray-haired woman doubled over the lance driven deep into her stomach, her cries lost amid the general noise.

He pointed to the barn and shouted, "High Forehead, take some men and look in that house. I will check the smaller one." He dismounted and ran to the farmhouse.

War ax at the ready, Lone Wolf kicked the door open and found himself staring down the barrel of a pistol. He had faced firearms before, but never one just a few feet from his nose. He marveled at the size of the hole in the barrel. At any second, a red flower of flame would burst forth, chasing a large lead slug, and remove the top half of his head. He wondered if it would hurt, if he would hear the sound, if he would go to the Happy Hunting Ground with only half a head.

Then he wondered why he was still alive, and his gaze shifted from the weapon to its owner. He saw two very wide, brown eyes; then the frightened, tear-stained face of a young white woman. The pistol shook in her grip. Behind her, two small boys tried to hide in her skirts. One cried, but the other just stared at him.

Lone Wolf made no move. The woman shifted the pistol from him to her own head. Then she aimed it at her children and back to him. He knew she was trying to decide who to kill first. Movement at her waist caught his attention, and he found himself staring into the eyes of the boy who'd been crying.

His stomach clutched and twisted, driving the wind from his lungs. The boy's eyes were as black as Tau-Ankia's. They even had the same shape.

Lone Wolf heard the call of the eagle, smelled burning cedar, and found himself back at home. Before him stood Tau-Ankia as a small child. Tears ran from his eyes, and he clutched tiny hands to his mouth. Lone Wolf knew something was very wrong, for the Kiowa teach their infants not to cry.

Lone Wolf was again in the farmhouse, facing the terrified woman and her children. He avoided looking at the small boy, afraid another vision would occur. The sight of his lost son opened old wounds, and a familiar ache began. What had the vision meant? What was he to do?

He heard footsteps approach, and Bear Mountain stood in the doorway. Lone Wolf's body effectively barred his entrance, but not his vision.

"A woman," Bear Mountain said, arching his eyebrows. "This is good. We have scalps and now a woman for sport, and there, two little scalps as well. Maybe I'll use their hair for my son's first scalp pole."

"We must leave."

"Leave? Why? This has been an excellent raid. Not one shot was fired by the whites. The young men have counted coup and taken hair. A celebration is called for, but you want to leave?"

"There is a strange medicine in this lodge." He pushed Bear Mountain outside and closed the door. "We cannot hurt these people. We must leave now." He looked into the distance. "I don't like the feeling of this place or these people. I've had enough problems with the spirits, and I will not incur their wrath for the sake of scalps."

Bear Mountain sighed. "I don't understand what's

happening, but I will abide by your wishes. What do we tell the others?"

"Nothing," Lone Wolf replied, watching his men celebrate their victory. In the distance, White Goose bent over the fallen farmer. "I see White Goose is taking his prize. Good." Then louder to the others, he said, "I want to make sure none of these whites goes to the Afterlife. Cut off hands, heads, feet, or what you will. Open their bellies; split their heads. Bear Mountain, go help White Goose."

As the members of the war party began the methodical mutilation of their victims, Lone Wolf turned again to the farmhouse. Impulse told him to run inside and kill all of them, but the small boy's eyes haunted him. To kill that child would be like killing his own son. What did it mean when the enemy looked like the People?

Later, that night, he stared into the campfire ignoring its crackle and pop. The burden of leadership weighed heavily on Lone Wolf's mind. Another incident like the one at the farmhouse and his men would desert him. He couldn't blame them. What use was a war chief who couldn't bring himself to kill the enemy?

Maybe the vision was real. Maybe not. They would soon be on the plains. Then, among the true enemies of his people, Lone Wolf would test his medicine again. He almost pitied the first white buffalo hunter they found.

Three

"Four hundred pounds of flour ought to do it," George Eddy, bookkeeper for the Rath & Company store, muttered to himself. He carefully added the entry to his list, then folded the paper. As he rounded the shop counter, he was met by Andy Johnson.

Johnson was a large man with a barrel chest, broad shoulders, and narrow hips. The man radiated strength. He had a ruddy complexion, red hair, and sported a superb handlebar mustache, thick and Nordic as his accent.

"Dem boys 'bout got that wagon ready to roll. You got your list together?"

Eddy waved the paper. "Right here, Swede."

"I need for you to add to it," Johnson said. "I need Ryan to make me a new blade."

"For the sod plow?"

"*Ja*. Tom, he done sharpened the old one as much as he can. Soon there'll be nothing left. If you want me to finish the wall to the shit house before it gets cold, I got to have the new blade, by damn."

Eddy nodded, fished a pencil stub from his pocket, and penciled in the request at the bottom of the order. He took the paper, folded it, and handed it to Johnson. "How many hides are we shipping?"

"We only got the two wagons. We loaded dem up

as high as they would go. Dem fellers in Dodge can count them."

"Two wagons? Charlie Rath ain't gonna like that."

Johnson shrugged. "Oh, well, we will just have to beat Fred to them next time."

The Swede's offhand approach to business irritated Eddy. The hunters bartered hides for supplies at Adobe Walls. The real profit lay in Dodge City, where the hides were bought by agents from New York City and England. Undelivered goods could not be sold.

"You said the wagons are stacked high."

"*Ja,* high as they would go. Dem boys is plumb up to their asses in buffalo skins."

"Who's driving? We got good drivers?"

"I know Shorty Scheidler is on one team with his brother, Ike. The other team has a new man and that young one, Bat Masterson."

From the north came a series of shouts and the jingle of harnesses. Johnson turned and ran out the door. Eddy followed him into the clear morning light. Six fully loaded wagons pulled away from Leonard's store, headed north. He looked back as he heard his own teams approach.

The Scheidler brothers waved as they drove by. He returned the gesture, then hailed the second wagon. Masterson smiled and shouted something lost amid the rumble and rattle of the freight wagons.

Dust was minimal at Adobe Walls. The small post sat in a shallow valley covered in thick buffalo grass. But there had been little rain since their arrival in March, and the rich greens were starting to yellow. Without moisture, the grass would disappear, leaving behind dirt to be lifted with each breeze or kicked up by each passing horse and wagon.

Eddy licked his lips. He could almost feel the grit that would work its way into the flour and cornmeal.

As he stepped through the doorway of the Rath & Company store, he saw his clerk, William Olds, stagger across the floor under the weight of a fifty-pound sack of flour. Olds's wife, Hannah, followed close on the clerk's heels.

"William Olds, you had just better listen to me!"

"Leave me alone, Hannah," Olds gasped between steps. "I can handle it."

Eddy thought Olds gaunt. Everything about the man was thin. His narrow, hollow-cheeked face perpetually wore a pensive expression. Brass glasses, fragile frames surrounding thick lenses, made him a blue-eyed owl. Thinning blond hair was grown long on one side and combed over to hide a pink pate. He was short, with rail-thin arms and legs, and had translucent skin almost as white as the flour he struggled to carry.

"Mark my words, you stubborn jackass, you're going to hurt yourself!" Hannah shouted in an alto voice that probably reached Fred Leonard's store.

Olds grunted a reply as he waddled through the doorway leading to the restaurant his wife ran. Hannah leaned against the counter, arms crossed.

She stood close to six feet tall. Her dark brown hair was piled on top of her head, held in place by a deadly-looking array of pins and combs. Large of breast and hip, with wide shoulders, she exuded an intimidating power and strength, but for all that, she had a weakness for small animals—human and otherwise. Her face, ruddy and raw from life on the plains, usually showed a smile. Now, as she stared at the empty doorway and chewed on her lower lip, she looked as pensive as William.

"What am I going to do with him, George?" she said.

"I don't know, Hannah. You know how Bill—"

"William."

William. They insisted on William. Not Bill or Billy or Will or Willy, just William. Eddy sighed. "You know how William gets," he said. "Seems to me that since we got into Indian country, he's been trying, and doing, more. Maybe he feels he needs to be more manly out here on the frontier."

"He's plenty man enough for me," Hannah snapped. Her expression hardened as though cast in iron. Eddy raised his hands in surrender. "I ain't saying he ain't," he replied quickly. "I work with the man day in and day out. He more than pulls his load, but it ain't me you got to convince. The only one around here who don't think Bi—uh—William's a man, is William."

Hannah's gaze softened. She smiled and patted Eddy's hand. "I know, but I worry about him. You watch. He's going to hurt himself out here. I don't know what I'd do without him."

"Lord willing, you won't have to."

The day's chores complete, Eddy made his way to Hanrahan's saloon for the weekly meeting of the Adobe Walls Merchants' Association. He was content with a bellyful of Hannah's cooking, and looked forward to good company.

Stepping into the dark saloon, he blinked for several seconds until his eyes adjusted to the gloom. Poorly lit on the best of days, its interior was draped in shadows deepened by the few lamps scattered through the establishment.

At one table, without the benefit of faint yellow light, sat Johnson and Bermuda Carlyle, a Myers and Leonard employee, each squared over his side of a checkerboard.

"It's in their blood, I tell ya. They cain't help it." Carlyle moved a red checker to the edge of his opponent's side. "King me, Andy."

Johnson set a checker on top of the one Carlyle had just moved. "I say you're wrong. Dey can change."

Eddy moved to the table and sat in the remaining chair. Hanrahan's was so dark, he could barely distinguish the colors of the game pieces. "What're you boys arguing about?"

"Redskins," Carlyle answered, then pointed to Johnson. "He thinks if'n you take one of 'em and dress him up white, he'll act white. I believe once a Injun, always a Injun. They cain't help it."

"Don't listen to him, George. He don't know his asshole from his elbow, by God. You got to do more than change his clothes. You have to teach him to read, to believe in *Gud i Himmel*. Den you will see."

Eddy stood. "I'm going to leave this argument where I found it." He walked to the bar, where Shepherd polished glasses. "Evening, Oscar."

"How do, George? What are they fussing about?"

Eddy glanced back at the table. Carlyle punctuated an argumentative point with his index finger. Johnson looked ready to bite off the offending digit. Curiously, the men's voices never rose above conversational volume.

"Indians, Oscar. The Swede thinks if we dress up the red man and send him to school and church, he'll change his ways and live like a white man."

"Never happen."

Eddy looked back at the barkeep. "Oh?"

"Hell, look at the niggers. After the War Between the States, they got forty acres and a mule, but nothing changed." Shepherd paused as he set down one glass and started polishing another. "Nothing changed at all," he continued. "They're still lazy, thieving, no-good niggers. Indians are just red niggers."

Eddy couldn't follow the logic of Shepherd's argument, but he didn't want to argue. "I suppose."

"Something riding you, George? Most of the time, you're all piss and vinegar."

A small smile tugged at Eddy's lips. "It shows? It's really foolish, but any day now the new manager of the store will be here."

"So? You think he aims to let you go?"

"Don't know." Eddy shrugged, then shook his head.

"No, not really. What bothers me is that I've been running things here and haven't had any problems."

"When Hanrahan went to town, he thought I was mad at being left behind. I just didn't want to be left in charge. While that old fart hoots and hollers and gets himself laid, I got to put up with you."

The grin on Shepherd's face removed any sting the comment may have had. Eddy smiled back. "Yeah, you're probably right. Keeping books is enough work for one man to do."

"Damn right, hoss. How about a beer? I got some cold Kirmeyer."

"Why not, Oscar? After all, I will soon be a man of few burdens."

Both men looked up as Fred Leonard entered the saloon. Leonard, co-owner of the Myers and Leonard store, was an English gentleman who dressed the part but didn't act it. Eddy liked him, and couldn't think of anyone he knew who didn't.

"Evenin', Fred."

"Good evening, Oscar. I trust you're doing well."

"Fair to middlin'. You drinking beer?"

"Not tonight, but I will have a cup of coffee."

"Just so happens I got a fresh pot."

Leonard faced Eddy. "Good evening to you, too, George. How are things at Rath & Company?"

"Hoppin' like a toad. Judging from the load you sent to Dodge, I guess you're a mite busy yourself."

"Indeed," Leonard replied, nodding.

Eddy turned as the saloon's door opened. The newest patron was Tom O'Keefe, the blacksmith. O'Keefe stood no taller than William Olds, but any resemblance ended there. He was shaped like a wedge, with shoulders almost twice the width of his hips. Thick muscles bulging up from his shoulders and chest hid any trace of neck he may have had.

O'Keefe pounded the bar. "Goddammit, Shepherd!"

he growled. "Where's my beer? Get off your lazy ass! Move, man, move! I don't pay you to visit."

Shepherd laughed at O'Keefe's imitation of Hanrahan. "Kiss my butt, Tom. I get enough grief from the old man when he's here." He slid a bottle of Kirmeyer's across the bar. "How's the smithin' business?"

"Right good. This country's pretty rough on wagons. Most everybody comes by with something busted." O'Keefe took a long drink, then faced Leonard. "How're you, Fred?"

"Well, thank you."

"George, I just finished supper at Mrs. Olds'. Man, can that woman cook. We had fried chicken, biscuits, and gravy."

"Don't tell me that." Shepherd groaned. "I haven't got to eat yet. My belly's emptier than a bummer's pocketbook."

"Listen, Oscar," Eddy said, "we'll watch the shop. You run next door and fetch you a plate of vittles."

"Yes, indeed, Oscar. By all means, have your dinner. I'm sure we can manage until your return."

Shepherd untied the apron at his waist and started around the end of the bar. "Now, if you boys are sure. I don't want to be the cause of any trouble. Hanrahan would hang me from the ridgepole if he—"

"Go on," O'Keefe interrupted. "Hell, if it'll make you feel any better, bring the plate back."

"Huh? Oh, yeah. I could do that. You need anything, Fred?"

"No, thank you, I've eaten. Mr. Keeler prepared dinner earlier. I believe it was something brown in a bucket."

Shepherd's face wrinkled in disgust. "You know, Fred, you really shouldn't eat that old man's cooking."

Eddy moved to the only table in the bar equipped with its own lantern. He scratched a match across the tabletop, raised the lamp's glass chimney, and lit the wick. After lowering the chimney and blowing out the match's flame, he sat.

"Gentlemen?" he asked with opened arms.

"I need another beer," O'Keefe said, belching. "How about you, George?"

"Fine by me, as long as it's cold."

Leonard placed himself across the table from Eddy. O'Keefe sat to Eddy's right. The remaining chair stood empty, to be refilled by Hanrahan upon his return.

Eddy tapped his bottle on the table. "I now call this weekly meeting of the merchants of Adobe Walls to order. Any old business?" He looked at the other members. "No? Then we'll proceed to new business. Who's got the cards?"

"I do," O'Keefe answered. "Last time we played with yours, George, I like to lost my pants."

"I am cut to the quick," Eddy protested, placing a hand over his heart. "Fred, surely you cannot let such a wound be inflicted upon my character."

Leonard squirmed as his stomach gnawed on dinner. "We would never accuse you of anything nefarious, old boy. But it does seem that your cards like you much better than ours do." A gurgle served as punctuation.

Eddy peered closely at Leonard's face. "You don't look so good, Fred. You know you really shouldn't eat that old man's cooking."

"Really." A gurgle, a twist, another gurgle.

"Yeah, really. Speaking of not looking good, how about we split the wagon trains from now on? Charlie Rath's gonna jump my butt if I don't get more hides out."

Leonard rubbed his aggrieved stomach and replied wearily, "Yes, yes, whatever. I wonder what that old devil fed me tonight."

O'Keefe stood and walked behind the bar. He returned with a small brown bottle.

"Here, drink this tonic," he ordered. "Go on, now, drink it down. You'll feel better."

Leonard uncorked the bottle and emptied it in one long draft. He closed his eyes against the acrid taste that threatened to expel itself from his body. His stomach heaved once, and suddenly, he belched. Not a mere mortal belch, but a gaseous eruption of air from the very bowels of his soul. A noxious blast of fumes reverberating through space like a cross between a thunderclap and a braying jackass.

"Sweet Mary, Holy Mother of God!" O'Keefe whispered in awe, crossing himself.

Four

The inside of the tipi was hot and close. Quanah longed to be out in the night, but his business with Isatai required privacy. He inhaled deeply on the pipe and felt smoke work its way down to his lungs. Exhaling, he passed the instrument to his companion.

"I've been thinking."

Isatai accepted the pipe and smoked before replying. "You are always thinking, but that's what I like about you."

"Tell me again why we must have a Sun Dance. The Comanche have never felt the need to gather like this before."

"That's why we must," Isatai replied, leaning forward. "The buffalo are disappearing. People are afraid. The tribe is split. The old men are as old women. They want peace with the whites and to move to the reservation. We must change these old women back into warriors. Warriors want war."

"But why a dance? Can we not just hold a council meeting?"

"When I ascended to the house of the Great Spirit, He told me we have acted foolishly and forgotten the Comanche are one people. He said, united, we could no more be destroyed than can the buffalo when they stand as a herd, but divided . . . divided we are as easy to kill as a lone cow."

Isatai paused and regarded his friend. "We both know there are too many buffalo to kill. So where have they gone? Tell me, Quanah, do you know?"

Quanah watched Isatai's face glow in the firelight. He wasn't sure if the shine came from the fire or from within the prophet.

"No." Quanah squirmed under the medicine man's gaze. He didn't like to be put on the spot. "I've heard the stories of animals stripped of their hides and tongues, but I don't believe there are enough white men to kill all the buffalo."

"And you're right. The Great Spirit has shown me many wonderful things. Soon you will see them for yourself, but first, we must dance."

"What will we do if the others won't join us, or worse, if they don't believe your magic?"

Isatai smiled. "My magic is real enough, but for those who are blind, I've brought some of the white man's whiskey. A few drinks and their eyes will see."

"I don't like using the white way to convince people. They must come to us on their own."

"Oh, they will, Quanah. You must understand I want nothing more than to open the eyes of our warriors. The whiskey just makes it easier. Once they have seen the truth, their hearts will take them on the warpath."

"Yes, but to what end?"

Isatai frowned. "End? Why, to the only end possible. The buffalo will return, the whites will be gone, and we will have avenged the deaths of our relatives. You ask many questions. You are a different kind of Comanche."

Quanah gazed at the shaman. Short, stocky, with a large chest, Isatai radiated Comanche. His eyes, black as a moonless night, stared from a face richly blessed by the sun.

Quanah knew he looked different. Taller than most, he had a leaner build. Slate-gray eyes, a gift from his white mother, sat in a strong face. No matter how much he stayed in the sun, his skin remained lighter than the rest. He stood out. Perhaps that was what Isatai required, someone different to lead them to victory.

"I have had dreams," Quanah started quietly. "I dreamed of honoring my father, but he died when medicine could not heal his wound. I dreamed of hunting and going to war with my brother. The white man killed him with sickness. I dreamed of sharing my honors with my mother and sister. Like the others, they are gone, stolen by the whites and, for all I know, dead." He pointed to the roof of their shelter, his voice rising. "My wishes and desires have disappeared through a smoke hole. I want to fight, not dance. These whites owe me more than the deaths of my father and brother. The white man owes me for killing my life!"

The next morning as Quanah raised the flap of the tipi and stepped into the light, he sensed change in the air. On an earlier morning, he'd stepped from his lodge with that same feeling.

His father, Peta Naconi, had been the chief of his band. But the chief's death left Quanah and his brother open to abuse by those in the band who resented their white blood. His brother's death, a short while later, left Quanah brokenhearted. When the white soldiers kidnapped his mother and sister, not only was he devastated, but a slow anger began to burn deep within him.

He became the fastest runner, the best horseman, and the fiercest of fighters. He became a warrior and a man in his sixteenth summer. He became more Comanche than the full-bloods.

By his twenty-fifth summer, he had two wives and several horses. He was a chief and enjoyed the reputation of a fearless and ruthless warrior. Though he was respected by the members of his band, Quanah knew the Wanderers were not considered one of the warrior bands like the Antelope-eaters. He liked the way those men looked and carried themselves, so he packed up his wives, Weckeah and Chony, and left for the village of the Quahadis.

Outside the main ring of lodges, he instructed his wives to raise their tipi. He rode in alone. The Antelope band had many families, and all looked strong and healthy. Scalps hung from lances at almost every tipi. Curious faces watched him. He sat straight in the saddle, face set in what he hoped was a sternly dignified manner. First impressions were very important.

An older warrior dressed in a breechclout, leggings, and moccasins approached Quanah. His hair was black, parted down the middle and braided on either side. Ebony eyes sat above a large, aquiline nose. One stripe of yellow and one stripe of red on each high cheekbone served as the only ornamentation on his body.

"I am Brown Bull of the Antelopes," he said in a rich baritone voice.

"I am Quanah, Wanderer band. I've heard the Antelopes are strong and not afraid to take the war pipe."

Brown Bull smiled, pleased. "Stay with us, then, and judge for yourself. You'll be my guest. My brother, Bent Arrow, will tend to your horse. Come inside. There's cool water to drink, and we'll eat and smoke."

Several weeks later, Quanah and Brown Bull partook in a raid on the Navajos, during which several members of their party were killed. Among the dead was Bent Arrow. Having grown close to both brothers, Quanah shared Brown Bull's grief. Bent Arrow's death reminded him of the loss of his own brother.

Brown Bull came to Quanah's tipi the night before the war party left on a revenge raid against the Navajo.

"My brother's death has left me with no one to help my family if I am killed. With no hunter, my wife will starve, as will her parents. Become my brother. I will share all my possessions with you, as I did with him."

Quanah sat and looked at his friend. The offer was a great honor, but also a great responsibility. If Brown Bull died, he inherited Blue Running Water as a wife, and her parents as a social obligation. Still, he knew the arrangement would ease Brown Bull's journey to war. Furthermore, should he die, Brown Bull would take good care of Weckeah and Chony.

"I accept," he said.

With those two words, Quanah became Quahadi Comanche.

Now he stood again at the entrance of a tipi, surrounded by family and friends. Other clans' lodges stood on either side, their ranks seeming to stretch to the horizon in a giant circle. For the first time all the bands had come together as one tribe.

The Wasps came from the south. Northern Yap-eaters settled next to their plains cousins, the Buffalo-eaters. His old band, the Wanderers, camped here, too. Isatai and his magic had brought them together.

Thousands of fires cooked breakfast. Buffalo meat sizzled on spits over open flame. Paunch pots boiled stews and soups. Camp dogs ran from lodge to lodge, begging bites. The delighted shrieks of children chasing the dogs, and each other, accompanied the aroma of the food. The children also begged for bits of meat or stole berries from baskets before being shooed away.

Quanah drank in the sight of so many of his people. How could the whites withstand an army of this magnitude? For the first time since meeting Isatai, he felt a chance existed to prevail over the white invaders. The Comanche could win alone. Combined with the forces of the Kiowa and Cheyenne, they would surely be invincible.

"Quanah!" boomed a familiar voice.

The warrior turned and waved to Brown Bull. "How are you this morning, big brother?"

"Well, but I suggest you eat a hearty breakfast. You've been selected to kill the buffalo for the center pole of the Sun Dance lodge."

Quanah stared at Brown Bull. "Why me? There are many other warriors with far more experience."

Brown Bull shrugged. "I am just telling you what I was told."

Quanah wondered how much of the choice was Isatai's doing, but said nothing. He and Brown Bull retired to the elder's tent and ate and discussed strategy for the hunt.

Breakfast over, Quanah dressed for the occasion in his best buckskin shirt, beaded leggings, and new moccasins. He parted his hair down the middle and braided each side. Weckeah wrapped each braid in beaver. She then painted a white stripe down the part. A single yellow feather hung from his scalp lock.

Brown Bull helped with the war paint. "First, a line of black under the eyes, since you will make war on the buffalo," he said, applying color with his fingertips. "Besides, the black helps with the glare of the sun. Next, we put a stripe of red for the blood you will spill. Finally, white because it looks good."

Quanah decorated his horse with white and yellow paint circles, red handprints, and feathers. He checked his bow and selected three of his straightest arrows. He had no intention of using more than one, but the kill was far more important than the number of arrows needed.

Prepared, he rode to the herd, followed by warriors from all the bands. Once there, he dismounted and crawled to the top of a small hill.

The buffalo lay exactly where he'd expected. Breakfast eaten, the animals lounged about chewing their cud. Some slept; others watched as calves played. The range, dotted with woolly brown lumps, yielded nothing satisfactory until his gaze fell on a magnificent bull.

He raised his bow to tell the others he'd selected a buffalo. The warriors moved forward to watch the show. Inveterate gamblers, they were soon betting on which buffalo he'd selected and whether one shot would do the job. He ignored the action around him. He had a job to do.

Brown Bull wished him luck as he mounted. Quanah nodded his thanks, then rode to meet the buffalo. He skirted the herd to approach upwind. His plan was to get as close as possible to prevent a long chase. The backup plan was the long chase.

He walked the pony toward the herd. Several buffalo stood and moved off, the bull among them.

He kicked his mount into a lope; the buffalo moved faster.

He nocked an arrow to the bowstring and kicked his horse into a full gallop.

The bull was now in full flight, but the mustang closed the distance quickly. Legs locked around his horse, Quanah drew the bowstring back. He approached from the right, sighted on a spot between the hip and last rib, and let the arrow fly.

The arrow disappeared into the beast's flank, piercing its heart. The great bull dropped in its tracks.

The other warriors quickly descended on the downed buffalo and gutted it. The empty carcass was stuffed with grass and impaled on the center pole of the Sun Dance lodge.

Quanah stood and stared at his kill atop the pole. One arrow, he thought. It took just the one. Pride swelled his chest.

"You have done well."

Isatai's voice startled him. The medicine man had the unnerving habit of appearing from nowhere. "I didn't hear you approach," Quanah said.

Isatai laughed. "Perhaps the spirits carried me here."

"Perhaps I wasn't paying attention," Quanah replied, turning to his friend. Isatai's face reflected amusement.

"You are a strange one, Quanah. Others regard me as a prophet of the Great Spirit, yet you remain stubbornly unimaginative."

"I've told you before I'll do whatever I must to assure my vengeance on the whites. Don't expect me to believe a dance will accomplish what the bow and lance has failed to do."

He turned and watched warriors fill the spaces between the perimeter poles with brush.

"Your magic is impressive," he continued. "It will sway the hearts of those who don't know they want to fight. I need no visions, flaming arrows, or spirits to make war."

As Isatai walked off, Quanah heard him mumbling about "white blood." A quick retort came to mind, but was dismissed. The old ways of the Comanche hadn't prevented the white man's coming or the death of the buffalo. Maybe now it was time for new blood, different blood to lead the People.

That evening a feast was held in celebration of Quanah's kill. He and Brown Bull danced through the night reenacting the hunt and kill with Brown Bull taking the buffalo's part.

Quanah stumbled home, exhausted but in high spirits. He crawled into his bed, only to find another gift from Brown Bull, Blue Running Water. As she drew back the buffalo robe, he felt his exhaustion melt away.

Quanah awoke alone. He stretched luxuriously like a great cat, feeling every muscle tighten in response. Blue Running Water's scent lingered in his nostrils, and he lay back contemplating the previous night's pleasures. His sister-in-law had been unusually aggressive, urging him on to higher levels of ecstasy until, spent, he'd begged off. She'd then curled up next to him, and he'd fallen asleep basking in the warmth of her body.

An impatient bladder interrupted his reverie. He tossed aside the buffalo skin blanket and reached for his breechclout.

"Quanah?"

Brown Bull's voice called from outside the lodge. Quanah stepped from the tipi, squinting against the bright morning light. He smelled wood smoke and cooking meat.

"What a day," he said.

Brown Bull chuckled. "It would seem Blue Running Water has worked her magic on you. It's good to see you relaxed and smiling again."

"I have no choice. She left me little else but my smile."

A horseman galloped into the middle of their camp and slid to a stop.

"The scouts are leaving!" he shouted, pointing at the Sun Dance lodge.

Quanah ran to the lodge, followed closely by Brown Bull. Four mounted warriors waited in front of an ancient medicine man. The old man wore a hat with two buffalo horns and shook a tortoise-shell rattle. His voice wavered and cracked as he sang a buffalo hunting song. Finished, he raised skinny arms to the sky.

"The spirits are pleased that the People have gathered here," his old voice rasped. He pointed to the riders. "Now you must find the herd. Go and seek the buffalo!"

Shouting war cries, the scouts wheeled their ponies and dashed away in a boiling cloud of dust. Quanah and his fellow tribesmen cheered until they rode out of sight.

"We are off to a good start," he said to Brown Bull.

The older warrior nodded. "Yes, we are. Come, let's eat. We will need our strength these next few days."

After breakfast, Quanah wandered the camp visiting people he knew. He heard a commotion at the north end of the encampment, and turned to see an approaching dust cloud.

A gray wraith appeared from the dust. It had a huge nose and wore a hat of green willow leaves. More leaves grew from its body. In one hand, it carried a club of willow branches. The other bore a shield. The phantom howled as it rode. Voices of other apparitions joined the cry.

People lined up in front of their lodges to witness the coming of the mud men. These were the clowns of the Comanches. No sooner had they arrived, than their leader chased one of the camp dogs. Accompanied by the cheers and laughter of the onlookers, the clown wove his horse from left to right behind the frightened mongrel.

Not to be outdone, the remaining mud men chased each other in circles. They held mock combat with club against shield. Pretending to be injured, several hung from their horses. Each action brought roars from the spectators. Suddenly, one of the mud men rode behind a watching warrior and smacked him resoundingly in the middle of the back. The surprised Comanche sprawled face-first into the dirt.

Cries of delight changed to shrieks of panic as the clowns turned on the crowd attacking members at random. Women grabbed their children and dived through lodge doors. Warriors ran and ducked, trying to avoid blows from the gray mounted men.

Quanah started to run for shelter, then was knocked flat by a clout to the side of the head. Anger flashed like gunpowder. He leapt to his feet. His right hand grabbed the mane of the clown's pony. The left caught the mud man's wrist in mid-swing.

"Quanah!" Isatai barked. "Quanah!" he repeated

after being ignored. He waited until the warrior's angry eyes met his. "You know the rules. You can run, dodge, or hide in a tipi, but you cannot strike back."

With a grunt, Quanah shoved the clown away. He was answered with a sharp blow across the shoulders. The next swing of the club found empty space as Quanah dropped to the ground and rolled to one side. He jumped up and ran to Isatai.

The mud man spun his mount, but after seeing Quanah standing next to the shaman, decided not to attack. He stood his horse on its back legs, sounding his war cry as he waved the willow club over his head, and charged off in search of easier game.

"That hurt," Quanah complained, rubbing the left side of his head.

"I don't doubt it," Isatai replied with a wry chuckle. "At first, I thought he took your head off."

The warrior grinned. "He almost did. When will they stop?"

"Soon. They'll want to get back to the creek to wash before the sham battle. The enemy camp is prepared, isn't it?"

"We finished last night. I've already informed the scout where to find it."

"Good." The shaman faced his friend. "Very good. I've ensured us a spirited battle. There are some bottles of whiskey at the stream for the clowns. My followers have others that will be available before the fight."

Quanah shook his head. "I don't like this, Isatai. We're using too much of the white man's way. Our warriors should be inspired to fight, not driven to it by liquid madness."

The medicine man stared long and hard at Quanah. "You worry too much about matters that don't concern you. Perhaps you would do better to worry about what you will do with the warriors I send you."

The rest of the day was spent in celebration of the

upcoming dance. The scouts returned to say they'd found the herd, actually senior hunters dressed in buffalo robes. The "buffalo" were herded into a make-shift corral and ritually slain.

Then followed a feast, the entire tribe sharing food and drink. Old men told tales of past glories; young men bragged about what they had done and what they hoped to accomplish. As the whiskey bottles were passed from man to man, talk grew wilder. Elegant speeches turned into screaming tirades against the white man. Each drunken warrior became a prophet predicting the rise of the Comanche nation over all people, the impending demise of the whites and their allies, and the return of all the buffalo.

Besotted warriors stumbled to the creek to don war paint. More whiskey made the rounds until, reeling, the warriors mounted a sham attack against a mock white village made of tree trunks and brush.

As the sun dropped low to the west, Quanah and Brown Bull sat outside the latter's tipi, smoking.

"I don't know what to think," Quanah said. "The warriors were ferocious. I saw fear in the eyes of the women and children, and knew they weren't sure the fight was a sham."

"Isn't that good?" Brown Bull asked.

Quanah leaned back and watched the stars. "My blood screams for the scalps of whites, yet I saw men who acted like animals. They fought recklessly. That was Isatai's firewater. I want warriors, not mad dogs, next to me in battle."

"I don't understand you, Quanah. Don't you have medicine to protect you from our enemies' arrows? Haven't you fought wildly, knowing you're invincible?"

"It's different!" Quanah cried. He got to his feet and paced. "My medicine is a gift from the gods. The whiskey is a poison sent by the white man to destroy us. You should have seen them. The gallant warriors, so powerful in battle. Invulnerable to a man, until their bodies spewed up the poison. Then they lay there clutching their bellies and groaning like old women. I should lead men such as these? The future of the People is carried in the shaking hands of the mindless?"

Brown Bull stood beside his brother. "The young want a prophet. To them, Isatai speaks for the Great Father. You must be careful, Quanah. There are many warriors among the Comanche who would take your place at the shaman's side."

A slow smile spread across Quanah's face. "Not among the Wasps. Those old women have gone home." He clasped Brown Bull by the upper arms. "More than once I've thanked the spirits that you are my brother. Again your wisdom has made me see the truth and tempered my anger." Turning to look at the campfires in the distance, he continued. "I'll hold my tongue among the others, but tonight, after the common dance, Isatai has to get rid of the whiskey."

"And if he doesn't listen?"

"If Isatai insists on killing the People with the white man's drink, he won't live to witness our death throes!"

Five

Dixon left Old Man Keeler's restaurant with an ominously rumbling stomach. He knew he should have gone to Mrs. Olds', but the damage was done.

Keeler's place was part of the Myers and Leonard compound consisting of the eatery, stables, the goods store, and a hide yard surrounded by a ten-foot stockade fence. The north and south walls were fifty yards long, flanked east and west by seventy-five yards of cottonwood trunks.

The compound was empty except for Fred Leonard and his employees. Disappointed, Dixon decided to try his luck at the saloon. Even if he didn't find any help, a cold beer sounded good.

To keep his eye sharp, Dixon liked to gauge distances, then pace them off. He guessed he stood about 120 yards from the saloon. His last step hit 125.

The thick sod walls of Hanrahan's kept the place cool and dark. Inside, Shepherd talked to a man Dixon didn't know. The stranger, in his early twenties, wore his dark hair long like a hide man. Dixon approached one end of the bar.

"Hell's bells! If it ain't Billy Dixon," Shepherd greeted him.

Dixon's stomach rumbled. "Afternoon, Oscar. You got some cold beer?"

"Coming right up. You ain't been gone long. No buffalo?" He set the beer on the bar.

"Nope. Too many." Dixon's stomach lurched, and he broke wind mightily.

"Son, what crawled inside you and died?" Shepherd asked, waving his hand in the air.

"Old Man Keeler."

"You should know better than to eat his cooking." He reached behind the bar and picked up a small brown bottle. "Here," he said, handing the vessel to Dixon. "Drink this before the beer. When you think you're fit for company, I'll be at the other end of the bar."

Dixon removed the cork and drank. The liquid burned its way down his throat, leaving behind the acrid taste of alcohol and licorice. The bitters tasted awful, but his stomach settled. He continued to drink, emptying the bottle. Then he picked up his beer and joined Shepherd and the stranger.

"Thanks, Oscar. That seemed to help."

Shepherd smiled. "Don't mention it. You know Jackson Miller?"

The stranger offered his hand and Dixon shook it. "I don't believe we ever met," Dixon said.

"No, sir, we ain't, but me and my brother heard about you back in Dodge."

"You a hunter?"

"Hunter, skinner, cook, hide man." Miller grinned. "We just got the two of us."

Dixon nodded. "Well, Jackson, I got more buffalo than my men can handle. I need a skinner, and I'll pay top dollar."

Miller frowned. "It sounds good, but I got to wait on LeRoy. He'd skin *me* if I wasn't here when he gets back."

"How long's he going to be gone?"

"I dunno. Maybe a week, maybe two."

"All right then, you come work for me for, let's say,

ten days. I'll furnish your grub and pay you two bits a hide. That's cash. You're looking at over ten dollars a day. I don't know about you, but to most men a hundred dollars for ten days' work is good wages."

"To hell with *him,* Billy," Shepherd said. "Take me."

"You got a deal, Mr. Dixon." Miller laughed. "Lord knows we can use the money. When do we go?"

"Soon's you finish that beer." He turned to the barkeep. "Oscar, will you tell his brother when we'll be back?"

"Sure, Billy."

As Dixon emerged from the bar, he noticed the weather had warmed considerably. "I got a couple mules at Myer's corral. You'll be riding Joe. He ain't mean, but he can be contrary."

"How far we got to go?"

"Day, day and a half's ride southwest."

"Think we'll see any Injuns?"

Dixon shrugged. "Mayhap. You can't expect to work in Indian country without seeing Indians."

"Me and LeRoy's talked about maybe joining another outfit, a bigger one. It don't sit well with him 'cause he wants to be his own boss, but I don't like it just the two of us alone. It ain't that I'm scared . . . but then again it's . . . you know what I mean?"

"Yeah, I do. I get this feeling when there's Indians close. I'm all itchy and can feel the hair raise up on my neck."

Miller nodded. "Uh-huh. That's it!" he said excitedly. "That's just the feeling. You feel all jangly and cain't sit still."

"There's something about the red man that makes a horse jittery. Ever see that? It doesn't bother mules much, but it'll devil a horse. Now, mules ain't stupid. They may not know what's bothering that horse, but they'll watch him close. You and me are like my gelding, and your brother's like Tobe and Joe. Trust your feelings, and make sure LeRoy keeps an eye on you. You do that, and you should be all right."

"That feeling ever let you down?"

Dixon stopped and stared into the distance. "Every season, one or two of us lose our scalps." He turned to Miller. "If it's your time, nothing in this world'll save you."

Dixon and Miller rode Dixon's mules back to the north bank of the Canadian River, where the hunter had left his wagon. Dixon then drove the rig to the headwaters of White Deer Creek and struck across the plains to his camp.

At sunset, they stopped for the night in a flat-bottom draw to conceal their fire. Miller talked about life with his brother and asked Dixon questions about hunting. Dixon enjoyed the young skinner's company and told him about buffalo, Indians, and the work of bull skinners. Finally they slept under a cloudless star-studded sky.

Dixon roused Miller as the sun peeked over the horizon. They hitched the team and struck out as soon as they could see land clearly. The prairie was smooth, and they made good time. The day warmed as the sun climbed toward noon.

"Billy, I'm starvin'!" Miller complained, rubbing his stomach.

Dixon smiled at his companion. He supposed young Miller wasn't used to going to bed with a belly full of jerked buffalo and water and then having no breakfast. He'd learn.

"Won't be long now, Jackson."

"We close?"

"Close enough to smell wood smoke."

Within minutes, Dixon spotted the camp. As they neared, the odor of drying hides overpowered everything else. He saw his men had been busy during his absence. Staked hides lay in long rows to the north and east to take advantage of prevailing southwest winds. When the winds shifted, as they had this morning, the stink was indescribable.

Armitage and Frenchy sat near the fire, the latter stirring a large pot set over the flames. They rose at his approach.

"Good day to you, Billy."

"Charley. You boys look like you been busy."

"Too right, we have, but the weather's been kind, and we've had no trouble with interlopers."

"Good." Dixon drew the wagon to a halt. "I want you to meet Jackson Miller. He'll be skinning for us a few days." He turned to Miller. "Jackson, this here's Charley Armitage, and that large gentleman over by the fire's Frenchy. Whyn't you hop down and fix yourself a plate? Whatever Frenchy put in that pot's gonna be good."

Miller scrambled from the seat, and Dixon moved the wagon behind its larger companion. He unhitched the mules, hobbling them near the stream, then returned to the fire and watched as Miller attacked a plate of stew.

"Poor blighter," Armitage said, slowly shaking his head. He looked at Dixon. "How long has it been since this lad ate?"

"Last night. Course we just had jerky and water."

"That was nothing." Miller grinned around a full mouth and chipmunk cheeks. "I been eating LeRoy's cooking all this time, and he cain't cook. I ate at Adobe Walls, in that woman's place, and thought I'd died and gone to the angels. But this here stew"—he held out his plate for more—"is better'n that."

Frenchy beamed at the young man like a proud father.

"You eat all you want, son," the cook said, refilling Miller's dish. "There's plenty here, and I can always make more for somebody who appreciates it."

"Now, Frenchy, you'll have Miller thinking we don't like your cooking." Dixon gave Armitage a slow wink.

"Indeed," the Englishman agreed. "Why, I know, I've always held your culinary abilities in the highest regard."

Frenchy's gaze traveled from one partner to the other. "You know it ain't just cooking I'm talking about."

Armitage raised a finger to pursed lips. "Ah . . . I see now. Billy, I believe he's speaking of the incident."

"What incident?" Dixon frowned, then smiled. "Do you mean *the* incident?"

"Indeed I do, Mr. Dixon."

Frenchy groaned. "Oh, shit, here we go again."

"Are you saying, Mr. Armitage, that Frenchy feels he's been wronged?"

"Indubitably, Mr. Dixon."

"Well, we can't have that. Can we, Mr. Armitage?"

"Indeed not, Mr. Dixon. We must rectify the matter to the satisfaction of all parties concerned."

"Agreed. And I know just the man to do it."

"Really? Whom might that be?"

"Jackson, Mr. Armitage."

Miller froze, the spoon inches from his mouth. "Who? Me?"

"Capital idea, Mr. Dixon!" Armitage slid closer to Miller, draping his arm around the younger man's shoulders. When he spoke again his voice was low. "You see, Jackson, Frenchy, Mr. Dixon, and myself have been involved in a matter of some delicacy. None of us can offer a clear opinion as to whether I or Mr. Dixon have injured Frenchy by our actions."

"Now, wait a minute," Frenchy interjected. "There ain't no need to be rehashing the past. I ain't even sore no more. So why don't we let those dogs lie."

Dixon grinned at the cook. "Can't," he said. "Charley's got a point. We need to take a close look at what happened that day and see if you have an apology comin'."

"No, we don't. It's all forgot, Billy. Put back where it belongs. This here boy don't need to be dragged into it."

"Nonsense, old boy. We must resolve matters. Now I shall relate the tale to Jackson, and we will all abide by his verdict. Agreed?"

Dixon nodded. "Sounds fair to me. How about you, Frenchy?"

"What about me?" Miller blurted out. "I ain't about to get sucked into no mess that might get me kilt!"

"There will be no bloodshed involved," Armitage reassured the young man. "Now, you relax while I tell you about the Great Bumbly Bee Incident."

The following morning's breakfast over, Dixon picked up his saddle and Sharps rifle. Miller followed him.

"You going hunting?"

Dixon nodded. "Yep. While I'm gone, you and the others pack up for the day. I told Frenchy which direction I'm headed. You'll take both wagons, and come the same way."

"Oh."

Looking across the gelding's back, Dixon noticed Miller still there. "Somethin' you need, Jackson?"

"No, sir. Not really. I . . . uh . . . Well, I just wanted to thank you for the job and all. They was some fine vittles last night, and I thought I'd bust a gut hearing about Frenchy and that hornet."

Dixon smiled. "Frenchy is one suffering soul."

"He sure got drunk last night. I was hoping it wasn't my fault, what with me coming in and taking a share of the hides."

"Wouldn't of mattered whether you were here or

not. Frenchy gets like that most nights. He's reliable as hell during the day."

Miller slid his hands in the front pockets of his dungarees and looked at the horizon. "Sure is a fine mornin'."

"Yessir, it is." Dixon grunted as he tightened the cinch on the saddle.

"On a day like this, I bet a man could see plumb to Kansas."

"I reckon so. I like any day with six hundred yards of visibility." He slid the Sharps into its scabbard. "The only bad part is the Indians can see me."

"Whenever me and LeRoy hunt, one shoots while the other watches his back."

Dixon removed makings from a vest pocket. "Yeah, I thought of maybe taking Charley or Frenchy along, but it'd still leave one man alone." Tobacco poured, he moistened the edge of the paper with his tongue and sealed the cigarette. He ran his hands along the edges of his pockets. "Shit! Jackson, you gotta match?"

Miller shook his head. "Don't smoke. I never could get the hang of rollin', but I got a chaw."

Irritated, Dixon flicked the useless cigarette into the grass and mounted up. "I got to ride."

"Alrighty, Billy. Good hunting!"

Dixon rode up on the plains into a steady wind. He made his way straight toward the herd hoping to make his kills close to home. The hunting area he chose had no hills, so he staked Jack about a mile from the buffalo and proceeded on foot.

Dixon approached the buffalo slowly in a straight line. The herd seemed to be grazing peacefully, but he knew better. Buffalo were wary and nervous animals always prepared to run. Sentries stood at the fringe of the herd. Anything out of the ordinary, sight, sound, or smell, would spook the guards and panic the rest. He'd started stalking at six hundred yards, but a strong breeze assured further closure before the first kill. The wind would drive his scent away from his prey, cover what little noise he made in the tall grass, and help to muffle the sound of his shot.

At four hundred yards, a sentry snorted and pawed the ground. Dixon knew this was just a gesture of nervousness and indicated flight rather than fight. He fell to his hands and knees and crawled across the prairie. Two hundred yards later, the guards again shifted. This was as close as he would get.

He chose a very large bull as his first target. Lying on his stomach, he raised the Sharps to his shoulder, elevated his aim to allow for distance, and pulled the trigger. Through the cloud of white smoke, he saw the bull jump and run followed by the others.

"Son-of-a-bitch!"

He grabbed his ammunition and gave chase. After fifty yards, the wounded buffalo collapsed. Dixon dropped back to earth and replaced the spent cartridge. Up on one knee, he sighted another bull, hoping this was the leader, and fired.

The animal immediately stopped running. Bright red blood ran from its mouth and nostrils and within a few seconds, it fell, only to be passed by the remaining buffalo.

Dixon chased the herd trying to keep downwind. He saw an old cow in the lead, and swore at himself for not paying closer attention. His concentration was such, he almost stepped on the second downed buffalo before seeing it.

The bull snorted, rising to its forelegs. One black horn slipped between Dixon's legs. With a short toss of its shaggy head, hunter and rifle flew in separate directions.

Flat on his back, the air driven from his body, Dixon grappled at his holster trying to pull his handgun. Every movement was accompanied by grunts as he fought to refill his lungs. The pistol finally free, he raised his head and looked into the red eyes of more than a ton of murderous, wounded buffalo. The bull's sides heaved as it tried to pull air into its ruined lungs, each gasp punctuated by scarlet mist from flared nostrils.

Dixon topped a small hill and saw his wagons in the distance. He hailed Armitage and walked toward them leading his horse. His limp had gotten progressively worse, but the pain of walking couldn't compare with what he felt when astride Jack.

Reaching the lead wagon, he tied the horse to the back. He stiffly climbed onto the box next to Armitage. Frenchy and Miller ran over from the other rig.

"You okay, Billy?" Frenchy asked.

"I reckon so. Seems that one of the bulls I shot was paying me more mind than I was him. Bastard horned me and pitched my ass most of ten yards."

Miller's eyes widened. "You bleedin'?"

"No. If he'd gored me, he'd of taken my balls and left me to bleed to death. He just threw me and stood there staring at me with those blood-red eyes."

"What was he doing?"

Dixon knew he had Miller's undivided attention. "Now, I was winded, but good, from the fall. I'd already shot this bull through the lights, and he was trying to breathe through lungs that didn't work. I'd suck a breath; then he'd suck a breath. It was almost like he was watching me breathe." Dixon drew his revolver. "I slipped my Colt from its holster." He held the weapon at arm's length. "I drew a bead and shot him right through the left eye."

"Capital shot, Billy!" Armitage exclaimed.

Frenchy offered his hand. "Capital, my ass! That was a hell of a shot."

"That's all well and good," Miller said. "But what did the buffalo do?"

"Why, he fell over dead. To tell the truth, I was about half scared to shoot him again. The first bullet just pissed him off."

Armitage asked, "So, Billy, how many head today?"

"Just two, both bulls. They're laying just on the other side of that rise I came over. I figure we can skin them out and call it an early day."

As Frenchy and Miller returned to their wagon, Dixon removed his hat and took out the photograph kept in its crown. He looked at the only thing he had left of his mother. Like the woman, the image was pale and delicate. He gazed into her eyes, trying to will living memories back, but even the sound of her voice eluded him. Without the portrait, he probably wouldn't remember what she looked like.

"Rather a close shave today, wouldn't you say, Billy?"

Dixon looked at Armitage and saw him eyeing the photograph. "I suppose so," he replied, tucking the picture back into his hat. "Hunting's a dangerous business. You're always takin' a chance with buffalo, wolves, or Indians."

"Yes, indeed. However, you almost died out here today."

"It ain't the dying part that bothers me, Charley. It's the dying alone I don't like."

The sound of chirping birds woke Dixon. He lay on his bedroll contemplating the sky as it changed from royal blue to azure. The sun crept over the eastern horizon, and molten light flowed across the prairie.

He was content. He'd chosen this life and enjoyed it with abandon. True, there were dangers, but they came mostly as wild animals and Indians, either of which a bullet stopped. The greatest threat came from his own kind. They were slaughtering the buffalo here as in Kansas. With them gone, farmers and townsfolk would cover the prairie, leaving no room for the un-tamed man—red or white.

He threw back the blanket and rose to his feet, grunting with pain. A bruise ran from his groin to his right knee. He looked up and saw Armitage watching him.

"Mornin', Charley."

"Billy. Leg a bit stiff?"

Dixon grinned. "Like a tree trunk."

"Maybe you'd do better to rest for the day."

"Cain't, Charley." The hunter winced as he swung the injured limb. "Damn, that's sore!" He hobbled around the campfire. "Jackson's time's about up. I intend to keep him busy."

A shapeless, blanket-covered object groaned. Then Frenchy's head appeared. He lay on his back and flailed his arms and legs like a turtle. His clothes, stiffened by blood, buffalo dung, and sweat, refused to bend. Finally, with a roar like a bull during rutting season, he heaved himself into an upright sitting position. Frenchy wasted no time gaining his feet, and walked in a determined, if unsteady, manner toward the water barrel. Once there, he plunged his head inside.

The ritual amused Dixon. In all the time he'd known the skinner, Frenchy's capacity for drink, and his subsequent recovery, still amazed him. Dixon had about decided Frenchy needed help when the shaggy mane erupted from the barrel in a spray of water. Small waterfalls cascaded down his beard and plunged into the dirt at his feet.

He sniffed and coughed until he'd hawked up enough phlegm to deposit by the wagon wheel. Still clearing his throat, he removed the tin cup hanging on the water barrel and filled it. Frenchy took in one gulp, swished it around, spat it out. Then another. The remainder of the cup, he drank.

The skinner reached into the wagon and pulled out

a clear bottle filled with crystaline liquid. He pulled the cork and drank deeply for several seconds. He shuddered and twitched, eyes blinking rapidly.

"Whoa!" he whispered, then louder; "Gin'll do it for ya."

His body shook as violently as a freezing dog. Replacing the liquor bottle in the wagon, he ran large hands through dripping hair and turned to face the others.

Frenchy grinned. "Mornin', everybody."

Dixon smiled in return. "Why, good morning, Frenchy. How are you?"

"Better . . . now."

"Good. Maybe you can rustle up some breakfast. I'd like to start a little early today."

Armitage pointed to the still-sleeping Miller. "Poor lad's worn out."

Dixon shrugged. "This winter he'll get all the rest he needs or wants."

While Frenchy cooked, Dixon walked and stretched until most of the stiffness in his leg was gone. He refilled the loops on his cartridge belt, packed some jerky for a snack, and saddled Jack.

Returning to the fire, he saw Miller was awake. He was wrapped in a blanket, stocking feet almost in the fire.

"Mornin', Billy," Miller called. "Beats me how it can be cold in the middle of the summer."

Dixon smiled and noted the breeze was from the north. He scanned the sky, but saw only blue.

"Something wrong?" Armitage asked.

"Nope. Just looking for clouds. The wind doesn't usually make it down here off the plains."

Armitage nodded. "True. Could be a storm moving in."

"I hope not. I don't mind the wind, but I hate to get wet."

After breakfast, Dixon rode up to the prairie. Here

the wind blew steadily and had a cold bite. He turned up his collar and rode on, determined to make his kill for the day.

The herd had moved, and it took the better part of an hour to locate a decent shooting site. As he dismounted, he sensed a change in the air. Glancing up, he saw the sky was yellow-white. He looked north. The horizon was reddish-brown. Clouds of dirt billowed into the air, pushed by the wind, changing the sky from blue to tan to yellow.

"Aw, shit, Jack! A dust storm."

Cursing soundly, Dixon climbed back in the saddle and made for home. He was almost to the breaks when the storm struck.

The wind slammed into him, rocking him in the saddle. An envelope of dirt cut his visibility to a few feet. This was what he dreaded. If he couldn't see, neither could Jack, and there was nothing to stop the horse from breaking a leg in a prairie-dog hole or falling over a cliff.

One hand on his head and the other on the pommel, he eased the black off the prairie and down a gentle slope into the breaks. Free of the gale, Dixon removed his dust-covered hat and sighed, blinking rapidly to clear the dirt from his eyes.

"Well, Jack, that was a waste."

Jack seemed to agree as he snorted and nodded his head. Dixon reached down and patted the animal's neck.

"Let's head to home, boy."

The gelding moved off immediately, as eager as his rider to escape the blustery conditions of the open prairie. The wind whistled over Dixon's head, reminding him of the blue northers that appeared from nowhere in the winter. Many frontiersmen had been caught off guard by these sudden, intense storms that usually brought heavy snowfall. Sometimes men trapped in the open froze to death. Others, Dixon among them, found protection inside the carcass of a freshly killed buffalo. He shuddered at the memory and prodded Jack along with a gentle kick to the flanks.

He quickly reached the small stream he had come to think of as Dixon Creek. He ambled along the waterway until his campsite came into view. Charley Armitage sat in the big wagon's box. Miller rode shotgun. Behind them, Frenchy tossed a sugar sack, with what Dixon guessed would be lunch, into the seat of the small wagon and climbed aboard. The Englishman flicked the reins and started to turn the team, only to draw up sharply.

"What the bloody hell are you doing here? Already shoot your lot for the day?"

"No, sir," Dixon replied, dismounting. "Big wind's blowing in from the north. Looked like half of Kansas flying across the prairie. Hell, I couldn't see past Jack's nose, so even if I'd shot rockers, you'd never find the carcasses."

"Oh. What do we do now?"

"Nothing, I reckon. I was going to give Jackson another day's hunt, but seein's how that got shot to hell, I guess we'll head back to the Walls this morning."

"Some of these hides is dry enough to take," Frenchy said. "Maybe you can carry a load in."

"Could at that, but yesterday, I saw rain falling north of here. Now we got that wind, may be bringing in a gully-washer."

Dixon turned and loosened the cinch on Jack's saddle. "Canadian's hard enough to cross on a good day. I don't reckon to see my wagon, mules, and hides sent to hell-and-gone in no mad river."

Six

Lone Wolf sat by the campfire, lost in thoughts of men, buffalo, and how to regain the look of leadership he'd lost at the farm. It had been three days since his vision, and he was no closer to an answer now than he was then.

"Do you feel all right?"

He looked up into the worried eyes of Bear Mountain. Lone Wolf's preoccupation with the vision showed in the wary glances he'd seen from his men and the concern in his friend's voice.

"Yes, I feel much better. I had no bad dreams. Nothing to interrupt a good night's sleep."

"We were troubled by your silence all day today. Some of the others want to take you home to a medicine man."

"That's not good. Have the men gather around my fire, and I'll speak to them."

He watched as Bear Mountain assembled the war party. Most came willingly, but some wore grave expressions. He now realized how close he'd come to losing them. Anger rose in him, not at the warriors, but at their leader, who'd allowed himself to be frightened by a vision of his own making. The time had come to make amends.

"We are close to our homes. You have seen the herd, have tasted the flesh of what was given to us by the spirits." He turned and stared into the darkness. "Did you hear them?" he continued. "Boom, boom, boom, like small thunder. That was the white hunter."

A voice came from the group. "But I heard shots behind us."

Lone Wolf faced the speaker. "True, White Goose. And you will hear shots in front of us and from both sides. We are in their midst! These white men are like a sickness that will kill all the buffalo if we do not act."

Murmurs of assent rose from the war party. Lone Wolf paced, gaining confidence and strength from his men.

"We left home to find our dead, but the spirits stopped us with the help of the white man's soldiers. I was sent a vision at the farm that death there would mean the death of the Kiowa. The image haunted me until we arrived here. With the sound of the first rifle, I knew what the spirits want of us."

"Tell us, Lone Wolf!" cried Bear Mountain.

Others began to shout.

The chief paused, marshaling thoughts, allowing tension to build.

"The buffalo!" he shouted. "The buffalo are a gift to us from the Great Spirit. No matter how many soldiers and farmers we kill, the buffalo will still die. If the buffalo die, we die."

He paused again, watching the anxious faces of his men.

"What to do?" he continued. "So many hunters spread over so great a land can't all be found. I have seen some of their groups. One will have many men, many rifles. We will leave them alone. I've also seen small groups with three or four hunters. We will take those. Then we ride and strike, again and again, until they all flee. This is what the Great Spirit wants."

The warriors rose and shouted, brandishing spears and rifles. They chanted Lone Wolf's name and began to dance around the blaze. He raised hands high to silence them.

"Before we kill any hunters, we must show the Great Spirit we understand His wishes. Each of you who has a trophy from the farm, bring it to the fire. Offer it."

The warriors gathered about, tossing clothing, jewelry, trinkets, and scalps into the flames. They sang war songs and danced by firelight.

Lone Wolf used hand signals to direct his men. Below, he saw two white men. To the right of the camp, Kiowa warriors crept from bush to bush. The plan was to capture, not kill.

With everyone in position, Lone Wolf gave the signal. One warrior, who had managed to hide in the wagon, rose and jumped on the first white man. The hunter's companion shouted and ran for the weapons stacked near the fire. He was too slow. Another warrior tackled him from the brush. Lone Wolf stood on the ledge overseeing the scene, and shook his head.

Too easy, he thought. *These hunters are no challenge at all.*

Descending the slope, he joined the others. Warriors flanked the prisoners. Lone Wolf looked into his captives' faces. The first, with yellow hair and blue eyes, looked terrified.

"Look at this one," Lone Wolf said. "His eyes are like the lakes in spring. I wonder if they would stay blue if I plucked one out."

The war party laughed.

Lone Wolf chuckled. "Maybe I'll wear it around my neck." He looked at the other man. "This man is trouble. He is afraid, but his dark eyes burn with hate. I think he's a warrior. Breaking him will be good medicine."

White Goose pointed. "Look, Lone Wolf, the

yellow-haired one pissed himself. Do you think he knows what you said?"

"These men do not speak our language. They understand nothing but killing buffalo." The chief curled his upper lip in disgust. "We might as well start with Yellow Hair. I bet his scalp he screams before we ever cut him."

"I'll bet he screams when we take his clothes off," Bear Mountain said.

"That's a wager—" Lone Wolf stopped as movement caught his eye.

He shouted a warning as the dark-haired captive pulled a knife from behind his back. His guards quickly moved away to avoid the slash, but the prisoner instead came around and buried the blade deep into his partner's chest.

The man with yellow hair gurgled. Bright red blood bubbled on his lips, and he slumped to the earth. The guards quickly wrestled the other white man to the ground.

"Fools!" Lone Wolf shouted. "I told you he was dangerous." He approached his prisoner. "Dark Eyes, you will not escape as easily as your friend."

Lone Wolf had the captive taken a few yards from the main camp. There he was stripped and tied spread-eagle to four small stakes driven in the ground. A large fire was started, and the war party danced about its flames.

The chief broke ranks and squatted near his victim. "The gods themselves gave us the buffalo. From even before the time of my father's father, the Kiowa, the true People, have hunted here. We lived well until the white eyes came."

He stood and circled the prisoner. "You must understand, Dark Eyes, that we are a hospitable people. We welcomed you and your kind. You repaid us with bullets, whiskey, and hungry children." He shook his head. "Now you will be the beginning of retribution."

Lone Wolf withdrew his knife and drove it deep into the man's thigh. He pulled the blade down toward the knee feeling the scrape of steel against bone. Dark Eyes squirmed and grunted in pain, but never cried out.

"Good. Very good. You show much strength and courage. The longer you take to break, the more powerful the medicine will be for me." Lone Wolf sighed. "Unfortunately, you will break, and then you will die. My only regret is that you will die and never understand why."

Dark Eyes broke late in the afternoon as the sun painted the sky orange. His screams sent chills of adrenaline running down Lone Wolf's spine. This one was strong. He'd endured hours of torture, and still had the strength to shriek as the flames burned away his genitals. Tremendous medicine came to all of them. The visions were vanquished. Lone Wolf was back.

"They are still fresh," Bear Mountain said, rising. He held a handful of dirt. "This soil has not yet dried. He's close."

Lone Wolf regarded the wagon tracks disappearing in either direction. "Which way?"

Bear Mountain pointed at hoofprints in the soft ground. "South."

"So what is to the north?"

"The Canadian. I have heard talk that the whites have built a village there." Bear Mountain nodded to the south. "That way is Dark Eye's camp."

Lone Wolf thought a moment, then quickly remounted. "White Goose," he called. "You follow this trail. The rest of us are going back to Dark Eye's camp."

The war party moved off, taking a semicircular route to avoid being seen. Back at the camp, they stopped at the base of a ridge on its eastern edge, scrambled to the top, and scattered among the rocks.

The warriors basked in golden sunlight and grew lazy and sleepy. They talked gently among themselves or dozed. The time passed easily for Lone Wolf who, half asleep, thought of happier times with his people.

On days like this, the men lay about the village enjoying the life their skills had made. Women did their work, daughters at their side. Little boys splashed in the river, naked brown bodies glistening with water. Their older brothers practiced the skills they would one day use to live as their fathers did now. All this the white man would stop.

Lone Wolf stretched sun-bronzed arms and yawned. *Things will be better when the whites are gone,* he thought. Glancing into the distance, he saw White Goose approach.

"Wake up, children," he said. "There is a goose in the camp."

As Lone Wolf walked to his scout, the others stirred.

"He is close," White Goose said.

"Does he suspect?"

The scout shook his head. "Not at all. I stayed near enough to hear him singing."

"Good." The chief turned back toward the ridge. "Everyone find a good spot. Our hunter is coming. You older men have probably seen this before, but I want the young ones to pay close attention."

The wagon emerged near the base of the ridge, its metal clinking and clanking as the mules pulled against the dead weight of the vehicle. It continued its passage, then pulled up short.

"See that?" Lone Wolf said quietly. "He sees his camp, but senses something is wrong. He can't tell you what, but the feeling is there just the same."

"What could he see that would bother him?" Boy asked. "We left the camp almost the same as we found it."

Lone Wolf shrugged. "Who knows. Maybe it's too quiet, or he misses the wood smoke. Maybe he smells the rotting bodies of Dark Eyes and the other one."

The hunter flicked the reins, and the wagon resumed its course. Drawing closer, he slapped the reins hard on the mules, and they broke into a run.

"He has seen the yellow-haired one." Lone Wolf shook his head. "This one is no warrior. See how he blindly charges in. We could have men hiding all around him, and he would be trapped."

The wagon slid to a stop at the edge of the campsite. Its driver leapt to the ground and ran to the first body. He stood and shouted. Lone Wolf guessed it was Dark Eyes' white name. The hunter continued to yell as he searched. He suddenly stiffened, turned, and retched.

Lone Wolf chuckled. "I believe he found Dark Eyes."

The hunter reeled about and pulled his pistol. He looked up the ridge, then turned slowly, peering intently.

"Do you think he knows we're here?"

Lone Wolf saw the apprehension on Boy's face. "No," he replied calmly. "He suspects, but is too frightened to act. Watch."

He clambered on a boulder and shouted, "Hey, white man, you better run away!"

As the hunter scrambled backward toward his wagon, the remaining members of the war party stood in the open shouting insults and chanting. The white man reached his team and cut the traces on one of the mules. He climbed aboard and kicked the animal hard, quickly disappearing into the distance.

Lone Wolf sighed and walked back away from the edge. "Now we wait."

"But he is getting away!" Boy cried.

"He'll be back. White men are funny that way. They run away now, but then they return to bury their dead."

"Why wait until he comes back? We could take his scalp now."

"That is true, but whites never return alone. He will find another camp of hunters to help him."

Leaving Boy to ponder his last remark, Lone Wolf found Bear Mountain and instructed him to send a scout to watch the trail. The chief then found himself a soft patch of grass and lay down for a nap.

When he awoke, the sun rode low on the horizon. He stretched and rose, looking for his lieutenant.

Bear Mountain sat patiently at the edge of the ridge. He looked up as Lone Wolf approached. "Soon it will be dark," he said. "Do you think we should make camp? Maybe he won't be back tonight—or ever."

"Perhaps. We will wait until the sun has truly set."

Boy appeared, breathless with excitement. "Lone Wolf, they are coming!"

"Our hunter?"

The young warrior nodded. "And others."

"How many?"

"Buffalo with Holes in His Ears says three times as many as us."

"What? Come on, let's see what our white man has brought us."

Light from the setting sun bathed the area in blood. Near the base of the ridge came a large party of men. They rode horses. Distance and gathering gloom made an accurate count impossible, but Lone Wolf knew the group was too large to be successfully attacked by his small war party.

The riders approached slowly. Many displayed rifles. They stopped at the camp and began the process of collecting goods and dealing with the bodies. Then they divided, with the leading unit setting off at a trot, followed by the wagon. The remaining men took positions at the rear.

Lone Wolf turned on his heel. "Get to your horses.

Boy, run and tell Buffalo with Holes in His Ears to follow the white men. We'll catch up shortly."

"Are we going to attack them?"

"I don't know, Bear Mountain. Probably not." Lone Wolf smiled. "But they do have a lot of nice horses."

Seven

Eddy stepped through the doorway into the restaurant portion of the store. He'd been following the aroma of biscuits and fresh-brewed coffee. Sunlight from the north-wall window revealed Hannah Olds as she prepared bread for lunch. Eddy watched her rhythmically assault the dough on the flour-coated tabletop. As she worked, she hummed a Negro spiritual, keeping tempo by thumping the dough. He marveled at the woman's contentment in such godforsaken country.

"Good morning, Hannah."

She jumped at the sound of his voice, quickly glancing over her right shoulder. "Oh . . . good morning, George. I didn't hear you come in." Hannah reached for a flour-sack towel. "Just let me get this off my hands, and I'll get you a cup of coffee."

"Don't bother yourself. I can get my own. No sense in cleaning up just to wait on me."

"Why, thank you, George," she replied, returning to her task. "I was about through anyway. Are you eating breakfast?"

Eddy nodded as he poured the black liquid in a cup. "Yes'm, believe I will. I could smell those biscuits of yours clean across the store."

"I've got eggs. One of Jim Hanrahan's men found some prairie-hen nests. I'll slice up some bacon, too."

Eddy sipped at the scalding coffee and shook his

head. "I haven't had eggs in almost a month. You have any wild-plum preserves left?"

Hannah grinned. "I've got one put back for family, son."

"Thanks, Ma." Eddy laughed, then asked, "Where's Pa Olds this morning?"

"He's on the veranda," the cook answered, tilting her head toward the open back door.

Coffee cup in hand, Eddy stepped out the west side of the building. Looking to his right, he saw the dry sink Hannah used to wash the restaurant's dishes.

Next to it sat Olds, his chair tipped against the wall, front legs off the ground. Small boots locked their heels to rungs under the seat. He had an open book sitting in his lap. A badly rolled cigarette hung from the left corner of Olds's mouth.

"Mornin', William."

Olds's gaze rose from his reading. Smoke drifted into his left eye, which slammed shut in self-defense. He quickly removed the cigarette.

"Ah, dammit!"

He then lost his balance and pitched forward, rolling out of the chair as its legs slammed to earth.

Eddy stifled a laugh as the diminutive man kicked free of the seat and got to his feet. He glared at the bookkeeper with a one-eyed, squinting, almost piratical expression.

"I suppose you thought that was funny."

"Thought never crossed my mind, William."

"It's not like it couldn't happen to anybody."

"True."

"After all, smoke gets in a man's eye—"

"Most anything could happen." Eddy avoided looking directly at the miniature buccaneer.

Olds wiped a tear away and regarded his friend suspiciously. "Did you have any legitimate reason to come out here?" he asked, brushing dirt from the bottom of his trouser legs.

"I just come to fetch you for breakfast . . . Pa."

"Pa? What's this Pa foolishness?" Olds looked up to discover he was alone. He quickly followed Eddy into the restaurant, and found him seated next to Andy Johnson.

"I'm telling you, by damn, he better not be thinking of changing things," the Swede argued.

Eddy sighed and sipped his coffee. "What do you think we can do? He's Charlie's partner."

Olds poured himself a cup and joined the others. "I don't like it one bit. We came here, built this place ourselves, and got it up and running. Now, this new man is supposed to just ride in and take over?"

"Dat's right," Johnson said. "We done the work. If he wants to be boss, he needs to be like Fred Leonard. Come down here and sweat with the rest of us."

Eddy agreed. Though technically in charge, he'd always regarded the others as equals. They were a group of people who did their jobs neither wanting nor needing supervision. He spread his hands on the table and stared at his ink-stained fingers.

"Look," he said. "Let's just wait until the man arrives. I think it only fair he gets a chance to prove himself."

Further discussion was interrupted by the arrival of breakfast consisting of fried eggs, bacon, and biscuits dripping with homemade jam.

"We got company."

Fred Leonard stepped out through the store's double doors and glanced in the direction Carlyle indicated. "Perhaps it's a hunter bringing in hides."

The clerk shook his head. "Most of them's to the south. These folks are coming from Dodge." A large wad of chewing tobacco distended his left cheek, distorting his speech.

"Well, it certainly can't be the wagon train. They've had barely enough time to arrive there."

" 'Sides"—Carlyle deposited a large spray of brown juice in the dirt—"from what I can tell, looks to be just one wagon and an outrider."

"That may be Charlie Rath's new man." The shopkeeper walked back inside. "Call me if you need me, Bermuda."

"Yes, sir, Mr. Leonard."

He was trying to decide if the canned tomatoes belonged next to the fruits or vegetables when he heard the familiar rattle and clink of a wagon drawing to a stop followed by an effusive "Oh, my God!" Smiling, Leonard walked to the door again, but stopped in the shadows to observe unseen.

James Langton was just as he remembered. A slight, sandy-haired, overdressed, somewhat effeminate young man reminiscent of the fops Leonard had left behind in England. Langton was dressed in knee-high, polished riding boots, beige cotton-twill trousers, a dark green velvet waistcoat, and matching dress coat with tails. Lace puffed from pockets, peeked from cuffs, and poked small holes along the edge of a handkerchief held in his right hand. He sat astride a superb chestnut mare. Even four days' trail dust couldn't hide the fine lines of the animal.

As Langton slid off his horse, Carlyle's face was a stone mask. His only comment on the sight before him was another spray of spit.

"Isn't it just magnificent?" the young man asked. "I mean, really, just look at it. Charles had said the conditions here were rather primitive, and you can just imagine what I thought. But this is so . . . so big." He ran over to Carlyle and offered his hand.

Leonard smothered a laugh as Carlyle stared at the offering. The clerk finally took the hand, but gingerly, as though it might burn him.

"I don't know where my manners are. Really. Just

because we're stuck out here in who-knows-where doesn't mean we have to forget how to be civil. Does it? My name is James Langton."

Spit. "Carlyle. Folk hereabout call me Bermuda." Spit.

Leonard saw Langton's nose wrinkle in distaste. "Yes, you are, aren't you? May I ask the whereabouts of Mr. Eddy? After all, it was he I thought would be meeting me."

Before Carlyle could answer, Leonard stepped into the light. "George is down at the Rath & Company store."

"Fred? Fred Leonard, is that you? Well, it must be, mustn't it? I remember now. You and Charles Myers have an establishment here as well." Langton looked around again. "I suppose all this is yours," he said. The hanky fluttered like a lace moth as he waved his hand.

Leonard nodded. Carlyle spat.

"Oh. Then where is my store?"

The clerk pointed down the compound wall. "That there wall runs to the south. 'Bout three hundred yards away is Rath's place. There's two buildings between us and them, but yours is the last soddy in the bunch."

"Soddy? Do you mean as in sod? As in dirt? Oh, my God."

Leonard noted the last "Oh, my God" lacked the enthusiasm of the first. Langton made desultory fare-wells and instructed his teamster to follow him.

Carlyle again made a deposit into what was quickly becoming a small pond of brown liquid at his side. "He sure don't make the sun shine for me."

"No? He seems to be a rather personable young man."

"He *seems* to be a Nancy-boy."

"I don't know, Bermuda. Mr. Langton may not be the most masculine man you will ever meet, but I have a feeling that when the time comes, he'll measure up."

"Well, I wouldn't want to stake my life on it." Spit. "Course he does ride a nice horse."

"Indeed he does."

Carlyle shook his head. "I wonder how George is gonna take him."

Eddy watched Langton's back as they drove toward the store. Though he'd never met Langton, he'd heard the talk in Dodge City. Some said Langton preferred the company of other men, and had bought such favors from young boys. Others claimed to have knowledge that he was the most notorious ladies' man in town.

The bookkeeper paid no attention to gossip. Prior experience taught him that talk was usually worth the price paid to hear it. But he did know a few things about the new manager himself.

Langton came from Milwaukee, Wisconsin, and arrived in Dodge City in 1872, about the time the town was incorporated. He didn't work, but was never without money. He dressed well—too well, by some—and ate in the finest restaurants, mingling with the cream of Dodge society.

"So why would he come here?" Eddy murmured to himself.

The wagon pulled to a stop and Eddy climbed down. He hurried into the store while Langton dismounted.

"William!" he called.

"Yeah, George," Olds replied, coming in from the restaurant.

"Come meet the new man in charge."

"Wonderful."

Eddy and Olds walked outside as Langton stood and stared at the store.

"I suppose this is it," the manager said in a tone that begged contradiction.

"Yes, sir, and this is my clerk, William Olds. His wife, Hannah, runs the restaurant."

"How do you do?" Langton walked to the building and picked dried grass from its side. He turned to Eddy. "It really is made of dirt, isn't it? When I first arrived in Dodge, I remember seeing some of this type of building. Never lived in one, though . . . until now." He tossed the turf aside, carefully wiped his hands on his handkerchief, and suddenly smiled. "Oh, well, one must do what one can with what one has. Agreed?"

Eddy was at a loss for words, but Langton seemed not to notice. The shopkeeper continued to examine the building. He indicated the roof, using the lace material as a pointer.

"Is that dirt as well?"

"Not really," Eddy replied. "We laid sod on top to turn water, but underneath it's got a layer of poles and brush."

"I see. So what keeps the whole thing from crashing down on us?"

"There's a ridgepole that runs the length of the store. The roof poles are attached to it. If you're really interested, you'd do better to talk to Andy Johnson. He built the place."

"Alone?"

Eddy shook his head. "No, sir. Everybody around here helped with the heavy lifting, but Andy's the man who knew what to do. He did our store and Hanrahan's saloon next door."

"I shall have to meet this builder of dirt houses then, won't I? William? It is William, isn't it?"

Olds nodded.

"Good. William, will you please assist Mr. Hollinger with the wagon?" The frilly cloth flapped at the teamster.

"Did you bring more supplies?" Olds asked.

"Oh, no. This wagon is carrying my belongings and

my bed. Wouldn't do to sleep on the ground, now would it?"

"If you say so, Mr. Langton." Olds walked to the back of the wagon.

"Good man." Langton turned to Eddy and spoke in a low voice. "He's not very large. Do you think he'll be able to do the job?"

The slur irritated the bookkeeper, who said sharply, "William has yet to fail any task I've given him."

"Please don't misunderstand me," Langton quickly replied. "Far be it for *me* to question the masculinity of any man. It's just that I have some very heavy pieces of furniture, and I don't want them damaged." He saw the anger in Eddy's face. "Or William," he added.

"Yes, or William," Eddy echoed.

The man had no idea what kind of people it took to build and maintain a home in such wilderness. As small as Olds was, ten Langtons couldn't replace him. Eddy took a deep breath.

"While William is unloading your stuff," he said, "why don't we take a tour of the store and the rest of our fine community?"

"Why not?"

"This is the main door. Now, if you'll just follow me . . ." Eddy led the way inside.

"Seems rather gloomy to me."

"It's not so bad once your eyes get used to the dark. We have lanterns, but most of the time we work by the light of open doors." Eddy swept his arm in an arc. "This is the store proper. We've only got about four hundred fifty square feet of space to work in, so we use lots of shelving. Over in the northwest corner are sacks of feed, corn, flour, and the like. The really big bags get stacked on the floor."

"And William can carry these?"

"He sure can. I've seen him tote a hundred pounds of corn out the door. In the middle here, we put the barrels of dry goods. They're in a circle to save space."

"What's in them?"

"One's got beans, another has pickles, still another's full of crackers." He led Langton to the south end of the store. "Now, here we keep liquor, medicinals, guns, and powder."

"I see." The hanky waved at the south wall. "This isn't made of dirt."

"No, sir, it's not. We built a partition here of cut lumber."

"That much is obvious. Why?"

"To give the Oldses some privacy. After all, they are married and—"

"Yes, yes, spare me the details." Langton stared around him, absently fluttering the lace material. He stopped and pointed. "Over there, in the . . . uh . . . southeast corner, is that another room?"

"Yeah. It's the bastion."

"Isn't a bastion designed for defense? I wasn't aware you'd had any trouble with the savages."

"We haven't. Frankly, after we built the main store, we decided there wasn't enough room for ample supplies and us. We added it as a bedroom."

"And that is where you sleep?"

"Me and Andy Johnson."

Langton arched an eyebrow. "Really? Together?"

"What?" Eddy, who'd been distracted by trying to remember what filled an empty spot on his shelves, quickly glanced up. "Hell, no! I mean . . . no, sir. My cot's on the south wall, and the Swede keeps his on the east. The room's plenty big. Lots of room. Yes, sir, that room must be twelve-by-twelve . . ." He stopped at the amused look on Langton's face. Through tightly compressed lips, he said, "If you'll follow me, we'll head back across the store and into the restaurant."

Langton laughed and brushed past Eddy. "Let's continue exploring. Now, is that the back door over there in the . . . ? Let's see . . . that's north."

"No, sir, that way is south. The back door is in the west wall."

The manager placed a fist on his left hip. "I am just so bad with directions. Really, I am." While he spoke, the handkerchief danced in cadence. He sighed deeply, then smiled at Eddy. "Of course, *you* are here, as well as William and that other man. I'm sure even Mrs. Olds can help to keep me on course, aren't you?" Langton waved his silken banner at the back door. "Onward, Mr. Eddy. Let's take to the great out-of-doors."

"Yes, sir."

A low sod fence enclosed the area of the backyard, making a smaller version of the Myers and Leonard corral. The sight of the fence reminded Eddy to check the incoming wagon train for Johnson's plow blade.

Virtually empty, the Rath & Company hide yard boasted a water pump and a four-foot rick of hides. This stack and the small load sent to Dodge represented all the business done to date. Eddy wasn't worried, because he'd heard about the numbers of buffalo. Soon their yard would be filled to capacity.

Langton pointed at the rick. "Are those buffalo skins?"

Hides, you ignorant bastard! Eddy thought, but said, "Yes, sir. We don't have many now, but the hiders have been gone less than a week."

The manager approached the stacked pelts. He stopped about ten feet away. "Oh, my God. What is that horrible smell?" He brought the hanky to his nose as though the small piece of lacy silk could dispel the odor. "Is it those skins?"

Eddy grinned. "Probably so. Most days, the wind here blows from the southwest and carries the stink off. On a calm day like today, it just sort of lingers waiting on the unsuspecting to come along."

"How poetic, Mr. Eddy." Sarcasm cut through the handkerchief. "Let's move on before I'm ill. How awful!"

"Surely you've smelled curing hides before."

"Why should I? I wasn't in the stinking skin business."

Langton's answer baffled the bookkeeper. How could the man live in Dodge the past two years and *not* have smelled them?

Eddy crossed the yard, followed closely by Langton. Stepping over the wall, he proceeded toward Hanrahan's. Suddenly feeling alone, he stopped and turned. About twenty feet behind Langton was busily sniffing at his coat.

He hurried to Eddy's side. "Tell me, does this smell?" He thrust a sleeve forward.

Eddy detected horse, leather, and maybe a trace of lilac. He shook his head. "No. I mean it doesn't stink. Sometimes when you get close to hides, that odor'll stick in your nose. Could last two, three days."

"Days?"

The stricken look on Langton's face was more than Eddy could bear. He coughed to cover a chuckle, and quickly turned on his heel. "This first building is the saloon I told you about. We could stop by and have a beer."

"Perhaps later. I would have thought everything would be closer together."

Eddy shrugged. "When me, Charlie Rath, and the others got here, Fred's store was almost done."

"I thought you were part of that massive wagon train that left Dodge."

"No, sir, that was at the end of March. We came down about a month later. Like I was saying, Fred was mostly done, and they'd already started work on Tom O'Keefe's blacksmith shop. When Charlie saw the size of the Myers and Leonard compound, he decided to come over here and build one just like it."

Langton turned and looked at the Rath & Company store. It paled in comparison to the stockaded Leonard place. He glanced at Eddy. "What happened?"

"Hell, I don't know. First, we got a late start. Then, by the time we got through cutting and laying sod, there was talk of the buffalo showing up any day. Charlie decided we needed to get ready for business. He said the rest could wait."

"Do you intend to finish the wall?"

"It depends. You got to understand, Mr. Langton, when those skinners start coming in, we will all be very busy. I'd be willing to bet money that we'll have thirty thousand or more hides ready for shipment by July."

"That's astounding! Do you really think it possible?"

"Why not? I saw it happen in Dodge."

Langton started walking back to the Rath & Company store. Eddy followed him. "Didn't you want to see the rest?" Eddy asked.

"Not now." The lace handkerchief rippled in the wind. "I've seen saloons and blacksmith shops before. I believe I'll tidy up and go meet the competition."

"Christ Almighty!" Carlyle swore. "Here he comes again, Mr. Leonard."

Leonard didn't have to ask who "he" was. The shopkeeper watched Carlyle spit in the dirt and stomp through the store, exiting through the back door. Seconds later, Langton walked in. Incredibly, the man appeared freshly bathed, though Leonard knew there were no tubs at Adobe Walls.

He sported black pantaloons and matching ankle jacks. Leonard would have bet not one of the half boots' ten lace holes had been missed. Langton had replaced the green claw hammer with a navy coat, the only difference being the color. To finish the outfit, he wore a gold brocade vest, white shirt, and the usual lace.

"Good afternoon, Fred." The hanky shifted to the left hand as Langton offered the right.

The strength of Langton's grip surprised Leonard. "James, how are you?"

"Fine, though facilities here are most primitive." The lace, back in the right hand, danced to Langton's speech.

"One does as one can," Leonard said dryly. His simple dress of brown trousers, brogans, and white shirt seemed shoddy when compared to Langton.

"Too true, Fred, but you seemed to have done well. Why, this place is just huge!"

"Not really. We're mostly comprised of yard. Our store is really not much larger than your own."

"I suppose. Now, tell me, how big is it?"

The shopkeeper sighed, not really in the mood to act as guide to a popinjay. "The stockade runs two hundred feet north-to-south by about one fifty east-to-west. Besides the store, we have a restaurant and stables in the southwest corner."

"Stables? Really? Could I board my horse there?"

"Certainly."

"Good. How much?"

Leonard waved a hand. "No charge. We're a small group. Trade between the shops is usually just that."

"How quaint."

"James, there are a few matters you should know." Leonard slid onto a stool beside the store's counter. "My shop has three employees. O'Keefe's one, and two for the saloon. You have the largest crew with five. Combined, we make eleven souls totally dependent on one another. On any given day, we may get one to a dozen buffalo hunters through here, but they're transitory. Should the Indians attack—"

"If the savages attack, I shall hide in my earthen bastion until help arrives."

Leonard spoke slowly. "There is no help."

"What?" The handkerchief fluttered as Langton paced. "What do you mean no help? Why, there must be help! What about the Army? Colonel Dodge himself said we should come down here and reap a harvest. Surely he wouldn't leave us to the devices of—of—them!"

Leonard watched as Langton worked himself into a lather. He noticed that under stress, the newcomer lost many of his affectations. "James?" he said calmly. "Listen to me." Langton quieted. "The '68 treaty set this land aside for the Indians. It's one thing for old Irving to tell us that coming down here is a good idea. It is entirely another for him to risk the lives of his command rescuing men from somewhere they shouldn't be in the first place."

"Oh. Then it's just . . . us?"

Leonard nodded.

"I see. In that case, I suppose we should make plans and such. Why don't we have dinner?"

"Good idea. Let me wash up, and we'll head to your store."

"No, no. I'm going to have to eat there every day. Let's eat here. My treat. I want something exotic."

Leonard's stomach churned in protest. "I can promise you a meal to remember."

Eddy walked into Hannah's restaurant. Everyone but Langton had gathered at one of the tables. No one spoke, but they all had their heads turned to one side. Eddy listened. From across the store came the sound of moaning.

"What's that?"

William grinned. "Langton, George. Seems he had dinner with Fred Leonard."

A slow smile spread across Eddy's face. "Old Man Keeler."

The men laughed, but Hannah clucked and shook her head. "I can't imagine what that man does to his food. But you, George Eddy, should have warned Mr. Langton."

"Me? First and foremost, I didn't know he was going to eat there. Secondly, Fred is as aware of Keeler's cooking as the rest of us. *He* should have warned him."

The room grew still as Eddy retrieved a coffee cup from the shelf and filled it. A low groan came from the bastion. "He sure sounds poorly. Anybody given him any bitters?"

"Let him suffer. He'll be better by morning." Olds stood and stretched.

"That's easy for you to say. He's sleeping in the same room as me."

"*Ja,* he is. And he's almost sleeping in mine bed, by damn. Besides, with the noise he is making, you are not so far away."

Olds absently scratched at his chest. "You're probably right. Let's get him some Hostetter's. Course he's already been outside a couple of times. A good dose of bitters might just do him in."

Eddy stood. "All the more reason to try. Alive or dead, he'll at least be quieter."

"I believe I'll leave the cure to you gentlemen," Hannah said, getting to her feet. "Come to bed when it's done, William." She glanced through the doorway. "And please, try to show the man some sympathy."

Olds looked at his wife. "Why, Hannah, we are most sympathetic." The skeptical look on her face put him on the defensive. "Well, we are," he argued. "Who here hasn't suffered at the hands of Old Man Keeler?"

"Come along, men," Eddy ordered. "Into the bastion. Our patient awaits."

"God help him," Hannah muttered, watching the men leave.

Eddy stopped at the store counter and picked up a small brown bottle. "Here's the plan. Make polite noises, give him the bitters, go to bed."

"What if he won't drink?" Olds asked.

"What?"

"You've seen him. He's such a dandy, I don't think he'll drink any of it."

"In that case, we'll turn to the second plan."

"Und dat would be?"

"We make polite noises, *give* him the medicine, and then go to bed. Now, come on before he hears us."

Langton lay in bed dressed in a nightshirt that hung past his knees. He clutched his stomach, knees drawn almost to his chin. He looked at Eddy. "Help me," he pleaded.

The bookkeeper shook his head. "I suppose this is partly my fault. I should have warned you not to eat at Fred's place." He smiled and held up the Hostetter's bottle. "Nothing like a good dose of bitters to cure what ails ya."

Langton groaned as he straightened his body. He managed a weak smile. "Really, I'm better. I think I'll be just fine without the medicine."

"Nonsense," Olds said. "You need the bitters to settle your stomach, or you'll be up all night."

"Ja, dat's the truth," said Johnson. "I know. I ate there once myself. Never did I feel like that before. My stomach, it danced all night long."

Langton scanned each determined face. He doubled back up. "I'm dying, you know. I'm dying at the hands of that wretched man, and now you want me to take poison." A tear ran along his nose. He sniffed.

"Oh, don't be such a baby," Eddy said. "Nobody's dying, and Hostetter's ain't killed anyone I know."

"But it tastes so bad!" Langton moaned.

"Ah-hah!" Olds declared. "The truth at last."

Eddy removed the cork and offered the bottle. "Come on, Mr. Langton, just drink it down and we can all get some sleep." Langton stared at the bottle and shook his head. "Don't force our hand," Eddy added.

As the shopkeeper buried his head under a pillow, Eddy sighed and handed the flask to Olds. "Andy, you take the legs; I'll get his hands. William, I want you to hold his nose. When he comes up for air, empty that bottle into him."

Johnson jumped on the bed, effectively pinning Langton in place. Eddy pulled the clutching hands from the pillow and held them against the bed. He nodded to Olds, who snatched up the pillow and placed the vial near Langton's sealed lips. When nothing happened, the small man pinched his employer's nose tightly.

Langton tossed about, but couldn't free himself of Olds's grip. His mouth popped opened for a breath, and the clerk quickly forced the bottle inside. Eddy would never have believed that four ounces of liquid could take so long to drain.

The manager was forced to swallow or suffocate. He took the medicine. Hands and legs free again, he sat up. "Oh, God! How awful!" He glared at the other men. "You are not very nice people."

"How do you feel?" Eddy asked.

"Better, I suppose. My wrists hurt where you held them, though." He looked at Olds. "And my nose."

"Sorry, Mr. Langton." Olds stared at the ground, shuffling his feet. "But you needed to take the medicine. It was for your own good."

Langton sighed and looked at the ceiling. "When you put it that way, I suppose . . ." His eyes grew wide. "Oh, my God!" He leapt to his feet and bolted from the room.

Eddy gave chase only to find an empty kitchen, the back door standing open. Looking outside, he saw a faint white figure disappearing in the distance.

Olds appeared in the room. "Where is he?"

Before Eddy could answer, Johnson burst through the doorway with the same question. The bookkeeper stepped outside, followed closely by his coworkers. He pointed to the west. "Looks to me like he's headed for Hannah's privy."

Through pursed lips, Olds asked, "Really? You think the bitters did that?"

"Can't say. I never heard of Hostetter's having that effect on a body." He looked at the sky. "Nice night, though."

Johnson nodded and grinned. "And quiet, too."

Eight

"What are you looking for, Quanah?"

"Water." Quanah lay back. A cedar screen separated his sagebrush bed from the dance floor.

Isatai saw the haggard look on his friend's face. He hoped Quanah could last through all four days. "Have you had a vision yet?"

"All I envision is you bringing me a gourd full of cool water."

"I can't. You're not allowed to eat or drink until the dance is over. You can have some slippery elm bark to chew on, and when you bathe in the creek tonight, no one would notice a small drink."

"Where did you get these rules? My mouth is full of dust, and my belly is empty."

"You must do as I say." Isatai looked around. Satisfied no one could overhear, he continued. "When this is over, I want to be able to point at you and say, 'Quanah did his share to revive the power of the tribe. Now let him do his share again and lead the war party.' A small vision would help."

Quanah sat up. "Vision? You told us this dance was about strengthening the tribe, not visions."

A small sigh escaped Isatai's lips. "We are about to face a terrible enemy. The whites are like ants. The more you stir the nest, the more that come out."

Quanah grimaced. "That is the most truth you've said so far."

"Then don't you see? These warriors will fight, but to defeat so many will take extraordinary power, conviction, and inspiration. How much better do you think they will be if you say the Great Spirit told you to lead our people to victory?"

"Please, Isatai, the dance is tiring enough. The People make war because that is our way. They will be inspired, but not by dreams. Rather, it will be the sight of me holding a white man's scalp."

The shaman persisted. "You must make the others look to you for leadership. There can be no war without a war party. Remember, Quanah, a coup doesn't count if there's no one there to see it."

As Isatai walked off, the warrior lay back down. What did that speaker of spells know about counting coups? His idea of warfare was to stand on a hill and pray.

Quanah slowly climbed to sore, tired feet. He saw young men standing about, watching the dancers shuffle around the center pole of the lodge. Snatching up his coup stick, he vaulted the low wall. As he raced around the perimeter of the lodge, Quanah struck each resting warrior with the staff, then ran to the center pole.

"Ha!" he called. "I am a Navajo dog!"

The drums fell silent. Quanah slowly turned his body, looking at each man in the Sun Dance lodge. Most just stared back dumbly.

"I am an old woman who has counted coup on the Comanche," he continued, a sneer on his face. "You call yourselves warriors. You would chase the white man from our lands. Do you think the Great Spirit talks to those who crawl at a Sun Dance?"

He ran to one dancer and struck him across the chest with the coup stick. He saw anger grow in the man's eyes as the welt rose on his body, but the warrior stood still.

"Weakling." Quanah spat the word as though it left a bad taste in his mouth.

He ran to another, and as he raised the stick, the young man cringed.

"Coward!" he screamed.

He ran to a third and swung the rod. It stopped inches from the third warrior's head. He'd caught Quanah's wrist in mid-swing. Quanah pulled free and turned to the others.

"This is a warrior," he said, pointing to the third man. "I saw no fear in his eyes. He will help to drive the whites away." Quanah pointed to each man in the lodge. "If you want to be worthy of the name warrior—dance. I will take warriors with me. The rest of you can go home and suckle."

The drums restarted, and the dancers attacked the floor. They whirled and jumped, calling war cries, begging the spirits to acknowledge their new efforts. The beds emptied, until the dance floor was full.

Quanah turned back to the third warrior. The anger in the man's eyes had been replaced by amusement. Quanah smiled. "Thanks, Brown Bull."

"You're welcome, little brother. I just hope you can control this hornet's nest you stirred up."

"Control isn't important, yet. What I want is this kind of spirit when we ride to the other villages. We will gather warriors by the hundreds."

Exhausted, Quanah climbed back over the low wall and lay down. Sleep was all he desired. Sleep and a drink of water. Sleep and a drink of water and something to eat. He groaned. He'd settle for rest.

"Wake up!"

"Go away. I can't eat or drink, but you won't take my sleep!"

"Quanah, wake up. We must talk."

"Leave me alone, Isatai. I can't wake from something I haven't had. If you want to talk, speak. I'm sleeping."

He heard his companion sigh deeply, and warily opened one eye. The dejected look on Isatai's face was more than he could bear. He sat up slowly.

"What is so important?"

"I'm going to try to have a tribal meeting called tomorrow night."

Quanah groaned. "Couldn't this wait until after the dance?"

"No, we must recruit warriors while they are still under the power of the dance. Hearts will cool in another day."

"I suppose you're right, but no whiskey."

"Why? We have—"

"No!" Quanah interrupted. "The young men wanted whiskey to help them dance, but the old ones said it's poison. They live on the reservation. They know. We need warriors, true, but without the peace chiefs, the warriors will not fight. It is the elders we must convince to take the path to war."

Isatai sat down and rested against the partition wall. "That's true," he said, then began to rub his temples. "My head hurts. I think it comes from wanting my people to be free of the whites." Quanah said nothing, so he continued. "Have you ever been to a reservation? The Indians try to be white and they fail."

"I will never be a white man," Quanah answered, "though their blood is in me. Yet, I feel a change in the People. I will fight it, but I'm afraid I can't change them back."

The medicine man rose to his feet. "You dance and pass the word to the others. You will see the Comanche come to life as the sun renews their spirits."

A large fire burned in the middle of the Sun Dance lodge, sending smoke drifting through walls and out the great hole in the roof. Despite the ventilation, a haze remained behind, and Quanah had difficulty recognizing faces across the room. On one side, he knew the peace chiefs sat, forming a great semicircle. Opposite them rested warriors of good reputation. Young, unrecognized men, like Isatai and himself, surrounded the elders. Unable to locate the shaman, Quanah sat with friends from his band.

Murmuring voices stilled as flame flared in the first pipe. No one spoke while the Great Spirit was invoked to appear. During the entire ceremony, the only sound heard was the crackling of embers.

The elder who'd called the meeting started the proceedings. Others would follow in rank, until all who wished to speak did so. Those with no standing in the tribe would not be allowed to address the council unless asked. Quanah wondered who championed Isatai's cause.

A chieftain rose dressed in fringed buckskin. "I am Ten Bears of the Yap-eaters," he said in a strong voice that belied the wrinkles on his face. "I once met with many white men who spoke for the Great Father in Washington. We smoked and made peace. They gave me a medal."

He turned slowly, displaying a large bronze disk.

"I tell you this so you will know it's true. We signed a piece of paper and moved onto the reservation. I don't like the reservation. We have no buffalo, and in the winter, no food. The children go hungry, the women weep, and men who were once mighty warriors drink the white man's whiskey and do nothing.

"The time has come for change, but the whites are strong with many soldiers. I long to be free to roam as the eagle does. I want to see the babies fattened on the meat of buffalo. I want to see my people happy again. I want many things, but I have no way of telling you how to get them. My hopes lie with this council."

Ten Bears sat.

The quiet following the speech was no surprise to Quanah. Council meetings ran under strict rules. The foremost of these forbade interrupting the speaker. After the speech, the others took time to consider what they'd heard and to formulate an answer. When ready, the next in line responded or declined to speak. No one went out of turn. Quanah remembered a story his father told him of a chief who had let the remaining members wait half a day before speaking.

Another chief rose, aged, but younger than Ten Bears. Unlike the vast majority of his fellow tribesmen, this speaker had hair on his face.

"My name is Black Mustache of the Antelopes." His voice sounded like dry leaves blowing across sand. "My band is split. Those who live on the reservation have no hope. I see the others. They look well fed and happy.

"I am ready to roam the plains again. I fear the white man's soldiers will chase me down and kill the women and children. There are too many whites for the Comanche to kill them all. They are like flies. We must join with others and make a great war party that can stand against any army!"

Black Mustache paused long enough to pull a Navajo blanket over his shoulders.

"I have friends among the Cheyenne who tell me their northern bands are gathering with the Lakota and Shoshone. We can do the same. Comanche, Kiowa, Kiowa-Apache, Arapaho, and Cheyenne united as one tribe. How this is to be done and who will lead, I don't know, but there is one who does. I want all of you to hear from a young man I know."

Black Mustache regained his seat. The new speaker approached. Quanah strained to see his face hidden in the shadows. He did see the man wore nothing but a red loincloth. A matching blanket was draped across his left shoulder, its edges reaching to his knees. He wore a band of German silver on his right arm just above the biceps.

"I am called Isatai," he said. "Some of you know me. I have been to the place where the Great Spirit lives, and what I am telling you is true."

Isatai walked to the center of the floor by the flames. Quanah saw two scarlet stripes ran the length of his right jawbone to the chin.

The shaman continued. "I have seen the Wichita and Caddos. They wear the white man's clothing and use his tools. Their warriors scratch in the dirt like birds. They have all become old women. This is what the white man wants.

"After seeing the Wichita, I saw the future of the People. I wept. The Great Spirit came to me and led me to His tipi. He told me how to save the Comanche." Isatai circled the fire. " 'First,' He said, 'you must make a dance. Bring the People together, and show them how powerful they are. Then you must gather warriors and drive the white man away. If this is done, I will bring the buffalo back in more numbers than before.' "

Isatai paused for breath. He continued. "I asked Him how can we force the whites out, for as Ten Bears has said, they have many soldiers. This is what He gave me."

The medicine man quickly raised his right arm. In his fist was a flaming arrow. He dropped the arm and brought it up again. A second arrow had joined the first.

"Look closely," he ordered, holding the weapons out so their heat could be felt. "These are real. They will pierce the heart of an enemy or burn down his lodge." With a flourish, the arrows vanished.

Isatai began to gag and cough. Several seconds later, he spat an object into his right hand. It was a new cartridge. He repeated the performance until five shiny, brass bullets were clenched in his fist. He tossed one to an old chief.

"There you are, Ten Bears. That is your solution to the whites. I can cough up wagon loads of bullets for our rifles." He swallowed the remaining ammunition. "I can raise the dead, but I won't need to. The Great Spirit's last gift to me was a magic yellow paint. With this paint, the white man's bullets will not break our skin. His guns will be useless, and he will die!"

Isatai walked through the ring of warriors and chiefs to the chants of mostly younger men. Quanah decided the meeting was basically over, and joined his friend, walking out of the Sun Dance lodge. As if on cue, others rose and followed. Many stopped at fires and collected flaming brands. Before long, Quanah and Isatai found themselves at the head of an impromptu parade of lights.

Nine

Eddy couldn't remember the last time he'd touched a woman, but there was one here now. Each time he stroked her bare thigh, she moaned in pleasure. Her gaze ran the length of his body, stopping just below the belt line.

Blue eyes wide, she said softly, "Oh, my. No wonder they call you The Tennessee Stud." She lay back against the pillows. "We can't let all that go to waste. I think it's time for Mama to saddle up."

Her voice was smooth as silk. Eddy grinned like a boy left alone in a candy shop. He rolled over on top of her, and she promptly tossed him out of bed. With a grunt, he landed face-first on the floor.

"What the—?" He raised on forearms, spitting dirt out of his mouth. "Dirt floors in the Dodge House?"

A loud snore startled him. He leapt to his feet, but didn't see anyone. In fact, he couldn't see at all. Terror squeezed his heart. *I'm blind! The fall did it. And it was that whore's fault!* Another snore like a dull saw through timber. He backed across the room, tripping and crashing to the floor again.

"*För Gud's skull!* Who's dat? You better speak up or, by damn, I shoot you between the eyes!"

"Andy?"

"George?"

"What're you doing in Dodge? And how did you get in my room?"

Johnson chuckled. "Hoo boy! Dat must have been some dream. George, you stupid shit, we are still at home."

Eddy felt sure his blush glowed in the black room. Mumbling obscenities, he got to his feet, brushing soil from his long-handle underwear. He knew there'd be hell to pay in the morning. The Swede would tell the whole trading post.

Groping in the darkness, he found his lamp and a match. The dim light showed his overturned cot and the trunk pushed to one side. At least he now knew what had tripped him.

He reached for the bed and froze. A low groan floated across the room. Turning up the lamp, he saw Langton lying across the huge four-poster bed he'd brought from Dodge. Much to Eddy's discomfort, the sound was identical to the moan the woman had made in his dream. An unwanted image appeared of his hand on Langton's thigh.

"Damn!" he muttered. Now he didn't dare go back to sleep.

He tossed and turned for a few more minutes, then gave up and got up. After a quick breakfast, he grabbed William, and the two started moving the crates of rifles.

Eddy took the back end of the case while Olds carried the front. Together they moved across the room, depositing the box atop a stack of similar containers.

"Wonderful! Just wonderful." Langton waved his tiny silken cape at Olds. "William, will you please get Mr. Johnson?"

Olds looked at Eddy, who nodded. Olds said, "Yes, sir, Mr. Langton."

Eddy watched Langton prance about the store, holding his hands in front of him as though measuring space. Occasionally, he stuck his thumb out and made humming noises. The whole exercise was a mystery to the bookkeeper. Presently, Olds return with the Swede.

"Good morning, Mr. Johnson. How are you?"

"Fine, tank you, Mr. Langton. You maybe needed something?"

Langton's head cocked to one side like a dog. "Of course, I need something." He turned and pointed to the counter. "Now, over here is our counter. What I want is a gun case on either side. Can that be done?"

Johnson nodded. "Sure can, Mr. Langton. We're a little short of cut lumber, but I can use shipping crates for what I need."

"Excellent!" Langton faced his employees. "Another matter comes to mind. We are a small group of people a long way from home. We will need to depend on each other, as well as the other permanent inhabitants here, for survival. Such being the case, I feel that conventional formality . . ." His words trailed off as he saw the blank looks on his companions' faces. "Let me put this another way. I want to be friends. Don't think of me as a boss, but more as a coworker who has the ability to fire you."

Blank faces changed to looks of consternation. Langton sighed. "No, that's not right either. Since we're all stuck here together, you may call me James." The three returned a collective "Oh." Langton quickly added, "Privately, that is. After all, appearances must be maintained for those people not a part of our little family."

Eddy glanced around the store to make sure only family was present. "All right, Mr.—uh—James. If you don't have anything else, we'll just get to unpacking these rifles, so the Swede can get right on those gun cases."

"Yes, indeed. Very good, George." Langton quickly stuffed his hanky in a pants pocket. "Now, if you gentlemen will excuse me, I have another matter to attend to."

"Amazing recovery," Eddy said, watching the manager leave. "After last night, I'd thought he'd spend the day in bed."

Johnson yawned and stretched. "He was all night with the moaning and groaning, and you dancing with a woman in your cot. It is amazing I slept at all."

Eddy cursed inwardly as he felt the blush crawl up his neck and across his face. Left speechless, he was saved further embarrassment by Hannah's arrival.

"What have you three been up to now?" she asked.

William straightened, a rifle in each hand. "What do you mean, Hannah?" he asked. "We're just unpacking guns."

"Then why did I see poor Mr. Langton galloping across the hide yard to the privy?"

Eddy grinned. "I suppose the boss ain't quite as recovered as he acts."

"He sure put on the good show, by golly."

"After all," William said in his best Langton voice, "appearances must be maintained."

The rest of the day was spent in performing the endless chores Langton thought up between trips to the privy. With each journey, the manager's mood seemed to grow fouler, his temper shorter. As Eddy tried to make sense of a group of figures in his ledger, Johnson stormed through the store's front door.

"It won't work!"

"What, Swede?" Eddy asked, looking up from his books.

"There ain't no way to fix up dem gun cases he wants." Johnson pulled a large blue kerchief from his back pocket and mopped his sweaty neck. "Most of the wood in the packing crates is just no damn good."

The bookkeeper sighed. "Then do what you can. As soon as the hides start coming in, we'll be too busy to worry about gun cabinets anyway."

"Good enough for me, George."

No sooner had Johnson left than William appeared.

"What are we going to do?" the clerk asked. "That man has had me rearrange the shelves time and again. There are only so many ways to stack canned tomatoes."

"I know. I know," Eddy replied, closing his ledger. "He's had me doing much the same, but what can I do?"

Hannah Olds stuck her head through the restaurant doorway. "William, you and George have got to see this."

Eddy and Olds stepped into Hannah's domain, which, as usual, was empty. Eddy hoped business would improve when the hunters started bringing hides in on a regular basis. Hannah had moved to the back door, and the two men joined her.

Langton stood near the northwest corner of the hide yard. Bent at the waist, he seemed to be holding something in his outstretched right hand.

"What's he doing?" Olds asked his wife.

"He's trying to make friends with that Yella."

"That dumb shit."

"William, watch your mouth!"

"Yes'm. Sorry."

"What do you mean 'friends'?" Eddy queried, raising on tiptoe.

"He's been out there holding a piece of buffalo jerky for that dog. Told me he has a way with animals."

Olds chuckled. "If he gets crossways to that mongrel, he'll learn a thing or two more about animals. Yella will take the meat and the hand holding it."

Eddy remembered the huge golden dog had appeared during the construction of the store. Whether a stray from a hunting party or an Indian camp, no one knew, but it hung around the post living on scraps and what it could kill. Once two hunters had teased the animal by holding a piece of antelope meat out of its reach. The dog attacked the man holding the flesh. Since then everybody left Yella to his own devices. Everybody, that is, until Langton.

The store manager waggled the desiccated meat at the dog in the same irritating manner he waved his handkerchief. Suddenly, Yella lunged for the prize, only to snap jaws on empty space. Langton had deftly lifted the morsel out of reach. Yella's hackles raised, and he began to advance. Langton's voice carried across the yard.

"Don't take that manner with me. I am the master here."

In response, Yella's teeth bared, and a low rumble came from his throat.

Langton tossed the meat on the ground. "Oh, bother it all! Take it, but don't expect any more." The hanky appeared and fluttered at the dog. "Now, go on and do whatever it is you do."

The shopkeeper turned and walked toward the store. Eddy saw Yella gulp the jerky down and start to run at Langton's back. Before the bookkeeper could shout a warning, Langton spun. An old '49 Pocket Dragoon appeared in his hand and barked once. Yella dropped in his tracks, a .31-caliber crimson dot in the middle of his forehead.

Langton walked back to the dog's body and shouted, "You ungrateful son-of-a-bitch!"

Fred Leonard stood by his horse, holding his saddlebags. He'd been arguing with Carlyle about going to Dodge City.

"Bermuda, it doesn't matter what you say, I'm still going."

Carlyle spat his opinion in the dirt. "I ain't saying you oughtn't go. I just think it'd be better for you to wait for the train. It ain't good for a man to travel alone. What would you do if Injuns was to jump you?"

Leonard pressed fingers into tired eyes. "Come now, you know better. There has been a steady stream of traffic from here to Kansas, and no one has seen an Indian, much less been attacked." He tossed the bags on his horse and stepped into the saddle. "I want to conduct my business and be back before the end of the month." He smiled and continued in a softer voice. "You needn't worry about me, Bermuda, I'll be fine."

"It ain't you I'm worried about," Carlyle replied, depositing more tobacco juice in the sand. "You get yourself scalped, I got to train me a new Englishman to run this place."

Eddy awoke to a sunbeam slithering across his face like a warm, pulsating leech. A throbbing head and pasty mouth bore testament to a long night of beer and cigars. He sat on the edge of his cot and dragged his swollen tongue over cracked lips. Still wearing yesterday's clothes, he stood and walked to the restaurant.

He stepped through the back door and urinated on the unfinished sod fence, relaxing as his bladder shrank to its normal size. From this vantage point, he saw the entire layout of the post.

Directly to his north lay the saloon. Part of O'Keefe's blacksmith shop was visible off the tavern's northwest corner. Farther north, and to the east, Eddy saw the south wall of the Myers and Leonard compound. Ten-foot-tall stockade walls lent the complex an air of impregnability, unlike the short, now-wet, and somewhat soggy structure before him.

Eddy cursed silently as he fumbled with his fly buttons. He stepped back into the store and drew a dipper of water from the bucket. The bookkeeper rinsed out his mouth and spat the remaining water through the open doorway. He rubbed at his teeth with a finger.

"They've invented a brush to do that for you, you know."

Eddy glanced at Langton, seated at the employees' table with the Oldses and Andy Johnson. Dressed immaculately as usual—down to his handkerchief— Langton made Eddy feel even grubbier.

"Do tell, James," Eddy replied, removing the finger from his mouth. "I've heard of such being sold in the main store in Dodge." He changed the subject. "Be nice to see a little rain."

"*Ja,* dat's the true," said Johnson. "By the time that plow blade gets here, the ground will be too dry to cut decent sod, by God."

"Mornin', folks."

Eddy looked toward the source of the new voice. "Good morning, Joe. You here for breakfast?"

Plummer nodded. "Yep, soon's I get my order filled."

"Leaving us so soon?" Langton asked from behind his silken wall.

" 'Fraid so, Mr. Langton. I gotta lot of buffalo to hunt yet. If we don't get some rain soon, I'm scared the herd's gonna move on early."

"Just like I say," Johnson said. "Soon the grass will dry up. Then we have no sod, no buffalo, and no reason to sit here and sweat."

Eddy walked from the kitchen into the store proper, followed closely by Plummer.

"Let's see, I need flour, bacon, coffee, and sugar," said Plummer. "And something else . . . oh, and a box of cigars for Dave." The hunter paused. "You reckon that train will get here today?"

Eddy shrugged. "Could be, Joe. You aiming to stay?"

Plummer took off his old hat and ran his fingers

through oily brown hair. "Naw, I got to git. Done wasted two days here."

"You go ahead and eat. I'll fill this and load your wagon. Maybe you can get Hannah to make a midday meal for you to take along."

"Won't need it. I'll be home by noontime. Figure them boys'll be taking a siesta or maybe dancing a jig on a flint hide. Either way, we're spending the rest of the day on the hunt."

Eddy offered his hand over the counter. "If I don't see you before you go, have a good trip."

"Thanks. I'll see you again in a month or so." Plummer turned to walk back to the restaurant.

"You seen any sign of Indians?" Eddy called after the hunter.

Plummer snorted. "Hell, no! Don't reckon to neither. Them redskins is sittin' on the reservation. They ain't about to fool with a full-armed hunting crew."

After a quiet day and quieter evening in Hanrahan's, Eddy stepped through the smoky saloon's door and into a fresh evening breeze. He pulled out his pocket watch, checking the time by the light of the building's doorway.

"Eight-thirty," he muttered. "Eight-thirty, and it's dark."

To the west, atop the bluffs, twisted juniper trees were set aflame by the rays of the setting sun. He shook his head. Life in a valley was almost unreal. As God painted the heavens in reds and oranges, Adobe Walls sat in darkness. The entire matter befuddled a plains man.

The sound of an approaching wagon interrupted further rumination. This wasn't the jingle-jangle of a team walking in, but the thundering rattle of full flight. Echoes from the surrounding valley walls confused Eddy as to its location. He backed toward the safety of the saloon's sod walls.

The vehicle exploded into view from the south,

slewing around as it passed the Rath store, and sliding to a stop ten feet from the bookkeeper. The driver jumped to the ground. Eddy recognized Joe Plummer's face as he raced through the door.

Eddy followed the hunter inside. Plummer staggered to the bar and leaned against it sobbing. Shepherd's expression showed both concern and curiosity. He looked at Eddy, who shrugged.

"Joe?" Shepherd said softly. "Joe, you all right?"

"Damn, Oscar!" Eddy swore. "Any fool can see he ain't all right." Eddy walked over to Plummer. "What happened, Joe? Was it Indians?"

The hunter nodded.

"Oh, shit!" Shepherd reached for a bottle of whiskey and three glasses. "Jesus! Shit! Goddam son-of-a-bitches!" The bottle rattled against the rims of the glasses as he poured.

Tom O'Keefe burst into the room, breathing heavily. "Where's the crazy—" Looks from Eddy and Shepherd stopped him in midsentence. He noticed Plummer standing at the bar. "What's happened?"

"Don't rightly know, Tom," Eddy answered, "but it's got something to do with Indians."

"They're dead!" Plummer shouted. He spun around. "That's what happened. Them red devils done killed Dave and Tommy." He covered his face with filthy hands. "Poor boys was cut up something fierce. I ain't seen nothing like that in all my life."

O'Keefe slid into an empty chair. "My God!"

Eddy took another chair, and Shepherd came from behind the bar to join the others.

"Come on over here, Joe," the bartender said. "Sit and have a drink."

Plummer sniffed, wiped his eyes, and shuffled to the table. He dropped wearily into a chair and took the proffered glass from Shepherd.

The room lapsed into strained silence. Finally, Eddy

asked the question he knew was on all their minds.
"Do you know what happened?"

Plummer shook his head, grabbed the whiskey bottle, and took a long pull. He wiped his eyes on one blue cotton sleeve, his nose on the other.

"Damn, what a day!" He laughed hollowly. "Let's see, I left here this morning right after breakfast." Plummer frowned. "It was today, wasn't it? Sweet Jesus, it was just today!" He grabbed the bottle and drank again.

"Go on, Joe," O'Keefe said. "What next?"

"Well, the drive home was nothing to talk on. Hell, it was just like any other I made until I come close to the camp. The first thing that bothered me was no smoke. The wind was coming direct to my face, but I couldn't smell no wood smoke. Then there was that other smell." The bottle tipped another time.

"What smell?" Eddy prompted. He saw Plummer's gaze drop.

"You know, a skinning camp don't remind a body of apple blossoms in the spring, but . . ." He paused, groping for the words. "You know what hides is like. Well, what I smelled weren't hides; it was sweeter, more like a carcass. Something inside me said to git, but I shook it off and drove on in." Plummer smiled ruefully. "Guess I shoulda listened, huh? Anyways, I'm in camp, and it's real quiet. Too quiet. Suddenly, I spot Dave on the ground. I run over to him, but the flies and smell tell me what's there. I started hollering Tommy's name and searching the camp.

"Well, boys, I found him. It was a horrible sight. They'd pulled his clothes off, cut out his insides, cut off toes, fingers, ears, and even his nose. Parts of him was burnt, and the damned thing was, they broked open his head, pulled out his brains, and filled it up again with grass. Shit! What kind of a thing is that to do to a body? Answer me that." Plummer drank once more.

Eddy asked, "So what'd you do?"

"After finding the boys, I was casting about trying to decide. I remember pulling my six-shooter and backing to the wagon. Then this buck stands up at the top of this little ridge we camped by and yells at me. Next thing I know, I'm cutting the traces on a mule and hauling balls here.

"I come across the party of surveyors for the railroad. They'd made camp and was cooking supper. I told them what happened, and they went back with me. We buried Dudley and Wallace, stacked what we could in the wagon, and I come in here."

"Where's the surveyors?"

"While we was doing all this work, we saw Injuns watching us. The railroad men decided to head back to Camp Supply. Me, I come on back to the Walls."

Shepherd rose. "Damn, that's a shame, Joe. I'm real sorry about Tommy and Dave. You can sleep over here if you like."

Plummer got shakily to his feet. "Hell, no! If'n you think I'm gonna wait here to be scalped, you're crazier'n shit! I come in to sell my rig and possibles. Then I aim to buy me a horse and head for Dodge. Tonight!" He weaved a path toward the door and exited the saloon.

"George, you think we oughta stop him?" Shepherd asked.

"Why? He's made up his mind. I reckon he'd shoot anybody who interfered."

O'Keefe said, "You think we might should go to Dodge, too?"

Eddy snorted. "No," he answered flatly. "Every year we lose a hunter or two to the Indians. This year's no different. Soon's Joe's gone, things will settle down again, and we can get back to business."

Ten

Eddy opened one eye and cast a glance around the room he shared with Johnson and Langton. The Swede's bed stood vacant; Langton dozed, eyes hidden by a black sleeping mask.

From the other side of the building came the sound of shouting. Eddy sighed deeply. He couldn't understand the words, but recognized William Olds's sharp, staccato bark. In reply came a deeper, melodious voice, its sonorous singsong filling the air as only Hannah could.

"Damn," Eddy muttered. "What are they fighting about now?"

The bookkeeper swung his legs out of bed and rose. He slipped on dungarees, dragging galluses over the shoulders of his long-handles. He pulled on his shoes, and with laces untied, shuffled toward the restaurant, yawning and absently rubbing tousled hair.

Hannah stood at a table, her back to the room. She mercilessly slammed and pounded bread dough. The muscles in her broad back flexed rhythmically as she twisted and tortured the elastic mixture—possibly imagining William's neck in her hands. William paced behind her.

"Hannah, you're being unreasonable! You heard what those savages did. What do you think would happen to you?"

Hannah stopped kneading long enough to favor William with a wilting gaze. "I'm unreasonable? We sold the boardinghouse and virtually everything we owned to move here. If you want to go back to Kansas, git! If my choice is between the whores and killers there and the Indians here, I'll stay."

Johnson and Carlyle were seated at the employees' table, taking great interest in their breakfasts. Eddie decided this was one meal that could wait when he found himself staring directly into William's eyes.

"George," the little clerk said, rushing across the room, "George, you've just got to make her understand."

"Uh, I . . . I—"

"Don't listen to him, George," Hannah said, her back to Eddy. "He's talking foolish."

"Well, I . . . uh—"

"Come on, man," William said. "Tell her how we need to leave before we're attacked and scalped."

"Don't you dare take his side, George Eddy! You're not going back and neither is Andy or Bermuda. Now, you tell him to hush."

Eddy squirmed. "Well, I . . . I believe I'll have a cup of coffee."

Hannah beamed at her husband. "See, William? It's settled."

"What's settled?" Langton stood in the doorway in his nightshirt, the sleep mask pushed up on his forehead. "What's settled?" he repeated, his gaze traveling from face to face.

Eddy recovered first. "Hannah's not leaving."

"Why would she be leaving?"

" 'Cause of the goddam Injuns, you silly-ass—" The remainder of Carlyle's remark was lost as Hannah's slap on his back drove the wind from his lungs.

Langton paled. "Indians?" He nervously looked around the kitchen, then stared at the open back door. "Are they attacking? Shouldn't that door be closed?"

"Relax, James," Eddy said, rising and walking toward the coffeepot. "We ain't in any more danger now than we were yesterday. Joe Plummer showed up at Hanrahan's last night. Seems his partners were killed by Indians."

"Oh, my." Langton sagged against the sod doorsill. "Plummer? I know that name. Wasn't he just here?"

Johnson nodded. *"Ja,* he was, for sure. He done brung in a load a hides a couple days ago."

Carlyle stared at his plate, appetite gone. "Dave Dudley and Tommy Wallace. I knew both them boys. They sure as hell deserved better."

William wrung his hands. "It was just awful. Terrible, really, what happened. I heard from a hunter that they had cut off their—"

"William!" Eddy barked. Then he said more softly, "Spare us the details. That kind of talk ain't decent in mixed company."

Olds nodded. "Of course, of course. My apologies, but now you see, Mr. Langton, we must leave."

Langton straightened and pulled off his mask.

"We'll stay, of course," he said decisively. "Chances are the savages haven't a clue we're here. If worse should come to worst, we have guns, ammunition, and three-foot-thick walls for defense." He turned and left the room.

Carlyle shook his head. "Well, I'll be a son-of-a-bitch! I never expected that."

Eddy decided a change of subject was called for. "By my reckoning, today's June eleventh. Now you figure eight days to Dodge and back, plus a couple to load, and that wagon train ought to be here today, tomorrow latest."

William Olds crossed to the back door and looked out. "You hear that?" He looked at the others. "Do you hear it?"

"Got to be John Webb and his bull team," Carlyle said. "We had a rider come in from Wright Mooar's camp saying they was stuck at the Canadian. John went out to fetch 'em."

The Rath & Company employees, accompanied by Carlyle, filed through the store.

Snorts and lowing filled the air as the team came closer. Soon Eddy saw the first of twenty-four yoked pairs of oxen. The line of animals seemed endless as they plodded past. Terminating the string were two large wagons pulled in tandem. Massive oak wheels, banded in steel and measuring seven feet in diameter, kept each enormous bed four feet off the ground.

As the lead wagon pulled abreast of the group, Carlyle stepped forward. "Hey, John! How'd it go?"

John Webb nodded his grizzled head, teeth glowing through his beard. "Fine, Bermuda. Takes more'n a little river like the Canadian to slow my bulls down."

"Whatcha hauling?"

"Most of Wright's hides. We had to off-load his wagons to get 'em across. I'll see you at the store."

As the teamster drove by, Eddy focused on the wagons following Webb's freighters. The lead vehicle was manned by Wright Mooar and his brother, John. The other was driven by Dave Campbell, with John Hughes riding shotgun. Phillip Sisk and Mart Galloway rode as outriders. All six men carried rifles; all wore side arms.

Eddy knew these hide men. They were killers of animals and Indians alike. Yet they looked frightened. Not the open fear he'd seen on Joe Plummer, but the hollow, sunken-eyed, haunted faces of men fleeing for their lives. It was a look Eddy hadn't seen since the War Between the States. Wright drew his wagon to a halt beside Eddy and the others.

"You look done in, son," the bookkeeper said.

A wry grin spread across Mooar's face. "I've slept better. We got jumped four, maybe five days ago on the Salt Fork of the Red River. Rainstorm saved us then." He pointed over his left shoulder. "Reckon it was the same rain that's got the Canadian back up. I'd sure hate to be the sorry bastard that has to cross that river now."

Dixon looked over the bank and into the boiling red waters of the Canadian River. "Well, shit!"

"Looks pretty wild."

"Yes, sir, Jackson, it do."

"What're we gonna do?"

"Go on. It ain't far to White Deer Creek. They got a wide spot there with lots of sand where we can ford."

The hunter shook the reins, and the mules moved off, paralleling the river. As the men rode, conversation was limited to the condition of the river and Miller's plans after returning to Adobe Walls.

The land started to flatten as they neared White Deer Creek. Soon Dixon saw the delta formed where the creek emptied into the Canadian River. Water stretched across the delta, and while slower, still moved swiftly.

Dixon wiped a hand over his face. "I don't know, Jackson. We could try to float the wagon across, but we're liable to lose her to the current."

"That ain't good."

"No, sir, it's not." The hunter sighed. "On the other hand, we could just unhitch the mules and let them swim over. The water's deep, but not enough to pull a man under—much less a mule. You game?"

Miller nodded.

"That settles it then."

Dixon stepped off the wagon and waded into the river. He braced himself against the current, facing upstream so the water couldn't buckle his knees. Dixon slowly stepped sideways, reading the bottom with his feet. Finally, he felt a toe slip off a ledge.

Afraid he'd be carried off by the current, the hunter slogged ashore.

"See that?" he panted.

"Sure did!"

"I reckon if we swim the mules fifty, sixty yards—"

"Riders, Billy."

"Red?"

"Nope, white and movin' fast."

Dixon walked around the mule named Joe and watched the riders approach. Taking a horse at anything more than a lope along a riverbank was just asking for a broken leg. He waved as they neared.

"Mornin' to ya," he called.

"Hidy, mister," the lead rider returned as he slid the dun gelding to a stop. "You boys headed to the Walls?"

"That we are." Dixon thumbed in Miller's direction. "Got to get my hired man back to his outfit." The hunter watched as the men exchanged glances.

The second rider, a short, dark man with bad teeth on a sorrel mare, said, "What outfit he ride for?"

"Myself," Miller said. "Me and my brother, LeRoy, work together."

"Oh." The first rider removed his dusty brown hat and ran powerful hands through sandy hair. Dixon watched his faded blue eyes as their gaze shifted from him to Miller.

"Hell, Lem, tell the man." This from Rotten Teeth.

"I'm a-fixin' to, Jed. Jesus, man, they could-a been kinfolk. That kind of news—"

"I got no kinfolk," Dixon interrupted.

"Me neither," Miller added. "If'n you don't count LeRoy, that is."

Lem replaced his hat. "Seems they was a couple hunters got themselves killed. One's name was Wallace." He turned to his companion. "Jed, you recall the other?"

"Dave Dudley. They was partners with Joe Plummer."

Dixon shook his head. "Dave and Tommy. Damn, that's a shame. What about Joe?"

"Quit," Jed said flatly.

"Quit?"

"Yes, sir. Sold everything down to his frying pan, took his horse, and lit out for Dodge."

"Where you men headed?" Dixon asked.

"Back to camp," Lem answered. "We still got people up at the head of White Deer Creek. I figure to bring 'em in to the Walls, or maybe head north. You staying at the post?"

Dixon shook his head. "Cain't. The rest of my crew's camped at a creek west of you. Soon's I get Jackson back, I'm headed home."

Lem touched the brim of his hat. "In that case, mister, I wish you the best of luck." He kicked the dun hard and rode off waving.

"Same goes for me, mister," Jed said. He followed his partner. As he moved away, he took off his hat and called, *"Vaya con Dios!"*

"Whatcha think, Billy?" Miller asked, staring at the departing men.

"Don't pay to think too much, Jackson. Every year, we lose some men to the Indians. Comes part and parcel with the buffalo business. Just because Tommy and Dave got killed, don't mean the Indians is on the warpath. We're only about three miles from the Walls, so we'll go on in."

"We leaving the wagon?"

Dixon smiled. "Common sense says to, but if the Indians are on the prod, they'd burn this wagon for the hell of it. Much as I don't want to, we're swimming it across." He looked closely at Miller. "You up for this?"

Miller snorted and grinned. "Hell, yes! I weren't born in the woods to be feared of no owl."

"It ain't being scared I'm concerned about. Traveling in the wilderness, you see danger every day. You turn your back to it, but you never forget it's there. Well, this here river is one thing you got to watch. Streams like this and the Cimarron make up their own rules."

The skinner's smile faded. "Yes, sir. I'll keep a close eye."

"Fair enough." Dixon climbed into the wagon box and grabbed the reins. "Hold on to your hat!"

Dixon slapped the reins down on the mules' backs and the wagon rumbled into the river. In a matter of seconds, water stood at axle level, and the force of the current started pushing the vehicle downstream.

"Pull, Tobe! Pull, Joe!" The hunter knew the smaller hooves of the mules made them no match for horses when it came to traversing quicksand. "Pull, goddammit!"

Joe's head disappeared underwater. When he reappeared, his eyes were huge and round and rolling. Dixon threw the leads to Miller. "I got to tend to the mules," he shouted over the sound of roaring water. "You head for that flat spot on the north side by that big cottonwood."

Dixon dove into the water and climbed on Tobe's back. He reached down, grabbed the mule's bridle, and hauled its head out above the current. Joe, as frightened as his comrade, alternately rose and sank.

As they drove deeper into the stream, Dixon heard a shout. He looked behind just as the wagon, caught in a swell, turned over. Miller flew out of the box and disappeared under the red, rushing river. Presently, his head popped out of the water. He pushed water-plastered hair out of his face and swam for the wagon.

The vehicle slammed into Miller with a jar that made Dixon wince. The skinner said nothing, but grabbed on and made his way hand-over-hand toward Dixon and the mules. No sooner had Miller cleared the wagon than it rolled over again. If the vehicle continued to flip, the mules would drown.

Dixon pulled out his boot knife. "Harness!" he shouted.

Miller's right hand plunged into the water and reappeared holding a ripping knife. Dixon jumped from Tobe to Joe, and nearly fell into the raging water as the hysterical mule reared to throw him off. He clung to the animal's neck, cursing mostly, but occasionally making promises to God.

The wagon flipped again and swung directly into the current. Dixon, Miller, and the mules now found themselves floating backward down the river. Dixon feverishly sawed at the harness with one hand, while clinging to Joe. A quick glance to his left revealed Miller to be doing the same with Tobe.

Dixon looked back and saw the wagon start to drift away, and knew he and Joe were free. He turned the mule toward shore, urging him on, until the water level dropped below the animal's shoulder. He jumped into the river and led Joe by the bridle to dry land. Dixon looked back across the water and saw Miller and Tobe coming ashore.

Miller dropped to his knees, gasping for breath. Dixon sat down heavily. He looked at his hands. They shook. Dixon trembled; Miller trembled; the mules trembled. Suddenly, Joe snorted and fell over.

Miller jumped. "Jesus!" he swore. "What . . . what's th-that all about?"

Dixon crawled to Joe. "Son-of-a-bitch! He's cold as a wagon tire. Christ Almighty!" He felt the white heat of anger rise. "Goddam mule! Stupid, dumb-ass, no-account, piece of shit!" Dixon slapped at the carcass. "Talk about pilin' on the agony. All that work and the ass-wipe goes and hangs up the fiddle on me!" He ran his hand along the matted and sand-covered side and said softly, "Old Joe was a good one. What a waste."

The hunter stood shakily. He spotted the wagon about sixty yards downstream lodged against the bank, and started to walk toward it.

"Where you going?"

Dixon stopped and turned. "Lost my hat. Worse, in case you hadn't noticed, we ain't got a gun—hell, nary a bullet—'tween us."

Miller followed the hunter down the riverbank, each man scouring the vegetation, hoping that Dixon's rifle lay there. Finally, conceding defeat, they gathered Tobe's reins and led the mule toward Adobe Walls.

Conversation was minimal on the trip, the only comment made when they crossed the trail left by Webb's bull train. Both men visibly relaxed when the post came into view.

"I reckon we made it," Miller said.

Dixon nodded. He dreaded the inevitable jokes at his expense when word of his misadventure got around. Still, he knew most of the humor was good-natured, and he'd done his share to other men.

He saw activity in the distance. First a single runner, then a crowd. Getting closer, he recognized Eddy, Swede, Bermuda, and William Olds. There was a stranger with them.

"Billy?" Eddy said. "Is that you under all that dirt?"

White teeth showed through the grime. "Yes, sir, it is."

Eddy smiled back. "Didn't your ma tell you the object of bathing was to leave the dirt *in* the river?"

"It weren't like we wanted in the river," Miller said, scowling.

Dixon sighed. "We heard the red men were on the prod."

"That's right," Miller said. "Then me and Billy decided to float the wagon across so the Injuns couldn't get it. That's when it happened."

In the pause that ensued, Langton shifted his weight

from one foot to the other, then fairly shrieked, "What happened?"

Dixon looked at the man as though seeing him for the first time. Taking in the broadcloth vest, white shirt, and silk handkerchief, he leaned toward Eddy and said softly, "Who's the dainty fellow in the boiled shirt?"

"My boss, Billy," Eddy replied under his breath. "I'll explain later."

Dixon nodded, then addressed Langton. "Well, sir, what happened was we got crossways to the current and lost the wagon. Damn near lost the mules, too."

"Mules?" Johnson said. "I only see the one."

"We *all* swum the river, but that no-account, son-of-a-whore Joe up and drops dead as a can of corned beef."

"At least you boys made it," Eddy said.

"Yeah, but I lost my Sharps and my hat. Wagon hauled up against the bank two, three miles back. You reckon we can maybe see about pulling her out?"

Eddy shrugged. "Maybe when the river drops. Meantime, what you boys need is a *real* bath, a shot of whiskey, and some of Mrs. Olds' fried chicken, biscuits, and gravy."

"You know, Billy," Miller said, grinning widely, "that woman cooks good enough to make it almost worth taking a bath!"

Clean once again and full from Hannah's restaurant, Dixon retired to Hanrahan's for a quiet drink and to contemplate what he'd learned that day.

He stared into the glass of whiskey before him. He watched the image of the flame from the lantern reproduced in the amber liquid. Tapping the glass with his fingernail sent small waves over the liquor's surface, breaking the reflection into hundreds of tiny, white spots. He smiled, remembering how water lap-ping along the banks of the Elk River back in West Virginia had done the same to torchlight.

The hunter frowned and drank his shot. West Virginia was a lifetime ago, when a small boy had a father and mother. Before a sister's birth had taken the mother and sickness had robbed him of the rest of the family. Dixon slammed the glass on the bar and signaled Shepherd for another.

The barkeep silently refilled Dixon's glass and moved off. Dixon respected Shepherd. He valued any man who knew when to talk and when to keep his mouth shut. He ran his hands carelessly through his long, black hair, making the tresses dance on his shoulders.

If the Indians were on the warpath, fewer hides would be harvested. Fewer hides meant less money. Dixon shook his head slowly. What a way to make a living.

He sensed a presence near him and glanced to his right. Tom O'Keefe stood less than a foot away. His face carried a deep scowl, and the twinkle was gone from his brown eyes.

"Hey, Oscar, come over here," O'Keefe called.

Shepherd approached and held a huddled conference with the blacksmith. Strain as he might, Dixon couldn't make out what they were saying.

O'Keefe stood abruptly and said, "I'm going to George's, all right?"

Untying his apron, Shepherd nodded. He looked at Dixon. "You know Anderson Moore?"

Dixon nodded.

"Then you might want to come along, but keep quiet."

Dixon followed the barkeep out of the saloon. A small group of men had gathered near the southeast corner of the Myers and Leonard hide yard. To his right, Dixon saw Eddy and O'Keefe hurrying toward the others.

"You mind telling me what I'm walking into, Oscar?"

"Moore rode in. Said his men had been killed by Indians."

Dixon's stomach churned, and the sour taste of fear rose in his throat. He'd faced Indians before and felt he could handle his own, but George and Frenchy wouldn't know to be alert.

Moore stood quietly, arms by his side. Trembling hands, a slack mouth, and glassy eyes made him look old.

Eddy laid a hand on the hunter's shoulder. "Tom told me what happened. You know for sure it was Indians?"

Though rare, there had been incidents of robbery of hide hunters by white or Mexican bandits.

Moore nodded. "Hell, yes! You should of seen 'em. Jack was tied down, his arms and legs stretched as far as they would go. Then they drove a stake through his middle and pinned him to the ground. Blue Billy got the worst of it, though. He was cut terrible bad, and they cut off his manhood. 'Sides, if it was thieves, they'd took hides, wagons, and all. Only the hosses and mules was gone."

"Sons-of-bitches!" Shepherd swore. "Goddam red niggers! They ain't nothing but animals. Bullet's too good for 'em."

"I suppose we ought to head out to the camp and plant them fellers," Carlyle said.

"Bullshit!" O'Keefe countered. "We don't know what's out there. We heard of four men killed in the last two days. I say we sit tight. If nothing else happens, then we can bury them."

Eddy nodded. "As much as I hate to agree, Tom has a point. If the Indians are on the warpath, we'd best wait. That all right with you, Anderson?"

"Yeah. 'Sides, I got no reason to go back. Injuns burnt me out."

Shepherd took Moore's arm. "C'mon, son, let's go have us a drink."

Without a word, Moore allowed the bartender to lead him away.

Dixon turned to Eddy. "George, I got to get home. My men don't know the Indians are on the prod. I need a horse and a new gun."

"I can't help with the mount, but I got a round-barrel Sharps."

Dixon turned to Carlyle. "How about you, Bermuda?"

The clerk deposited a generous amount of tobacco spit on the soil and shook his head. "Sorry, Billy. Got no long guns, and the riding stock I got I have to keep." He chewed thoughtfully for a moment, then spat again. "Course, that wagon train shoulda been here by now. Why don't you wait for it?"

"What do I do in the meantime?"

O'Keefe draped a muscled arm around the smaller man's shoulders. "What *we* do, Billy—get drunk."

Eleven

Lone Wolf stood quietly in the thicket. He gazed to the northeast where the light of campfires flickered like twinkling stars. He'd chased the men beside those flames for almost two days.

The trail had been easy to follow. The whites made no attempt to conceal their path. Lone Wolf and his men pursued them at a leisurely pace confident they could attack by nightfall. The chief's certainty disappeared with the setting sun, for though the path was clearly marked, he had seen no sign of Buffalo with Holes in His Ears or their quarry.

Darkness obscured the tracks, and Lone Wolf decided to stop rather than risk losing the trail entirely. The night passed in virtual silence. The warriors were subdued, and Lone Wolf withdrew to one side. He spoke to no one, ate little, and slept badly.

At first light, the war party moved again. Riding much harder, they rode past where the whites had slept. The fall of night was threatening to stop the Kiowa again when a familiar figure emerged from a small stand of trees. Buffalo with Holes in His Ears waved and casually walked his horse toward his comrades.

Lone Wolf shouted, "Hello, my friend! Tell me true, are we near the white man's camp?"

The scout grinned. "There is little more than those

trees between us. They have marched long and hard, and so are very tired. I crept close enough to their camp to see many were asleep even as food was cooked."

"Heavy eyes and an empty stomach make for dull senses. Victory should be swift and sweet." Lone Wolf dismounted. "Climb down, and show me where these men are."

Buffalo with Holes in His Ears squatted next to his leader and waited while the others gathered around them. He drew a small circle, then a diagonal line above it running northeast to southwest. "This circle is our trees. Beyond that lies a creek, and the whites are camping here." He poked his finger into the dirt at the northernmost point of the line. "They have three fires, and their horses are grouped to the west."

Lone Wolf stared at the drawing, then stood and nodded. "Here is what we'll do."

Now, he watched his shadow lengthen as the sun set. He was startled when the shade suddenly widened at his feet and began to grow. Turning, he saw a giant, familiar silhouette.

"It is close to time."

Lone Wolf nodded. "Yes, Bear Mountain, it is. Are your warriors ready?"

The massive shoulders shrugged. "As ready as they can be. Most of the young men want to ride with me."

The chief smiled. "They are hungry for coups. Those with me will have no chance for reward; we just hope to survive." He turned. "Let's get started."

They rode slowly toward the camp. Timing was crucial. As the sun finally dipped below the horizon, the Kiowa leader urged his mount into a trot. The distance closed, and he saw more details of the camp. Pots hung over the fires, shapeless lumps huddled near the flames. Lone Wolf raised his rifle above his head, and the war party broke into a gallop.

As they drew closer still, Lone Wolf raised the rifle

and fired. Immediately, the charging band joined in with war calls and gunfire of their own. The white men lunged to their feet and scattered in all directions. The party split. The chief's group charged among the now empty bedrolls firing indiscriminately. Bear Mountain led his men to the white men's tethered horses.

Lone Wolf watched the raid unfold as though in a dream. He felt detached, more a witness than participant. A hat sailed through the air. A warrior rode through a fire trailing sparks and embers like fireflies. Wood smoke filled the chief's nostrils.

A white flower blossomed to his right, then another, and more still from other locations. The angry buzz of bullets surrounded him, followed by the hollow boom of pistols. He choked on the sharp odor of spent gunpowder. He stared into the white, rolling eyes of his enemy. Lone Wolf swept by the terrified figure, casually planting a moccasined foot in the other's chest, sending him reeling.

Nearing the far side of the camp, Lone Wolf risked a look back. Through the smoke and dust, he saw Bear Mountain still at the white men's horses. Then he heard the sharp, flat crack of a rifle. A warrior fell. Unable to stop, he sped out of the camp and allowed the darkness to envelope him.

Lone Wolf kept his horse at a dead run across the clearing and past the headwaters of the creek. Slowing, he allowed the others to catch up. His heart pounded, and his breath came in short, sharp gasps. Other whites they'd raided had panicked or fought ineffectually. These men were different. They'd awakened prepared to fight.

What of the warrior who fell? Lone Wolf would have to wait for Bear Mountain for the answers. He stopped and turned his horse to face his approaching men. The men's features were invisible in the darkness, but he sensed their disappointment. As they closed on him, he slowly turned his horse and walked on. He drew to halt near a small stand of cottonwoods.

"We'll wait here," he said softly. "Someone light a fire. No need to make Bear Mountain search for us."

Soon a fire burned brightly and, as a group, they stared into its flames. Lone Wolf had no idea what the others thought, but he brooded over the sudden reversal of fortune. He'd allowed himself foolishly to underestimate his enemy. Too many easy kills had left him complacent, and his overconfidence had almost ended the raid in disaster.

He stiffened at the sound of riders, but relaxed when the large frame of Bear Mountain emerged from the dark.

The man slowly climbed off his horse and eased to the ground. "That was no fun."

Lone Wolf nodded. "It's my fault."

"No, it isn't."

"I saw someone go down."

Bear Mountain suddenly laughed. "That was Goose. He'd just reached the white men's horses when his horse was shot. He's bruised and embarrassed, but unhurt."

"Good." Lone Wolf turned to his friend and smiled. "Now, tell me, how many more ponies do we have?"

"Two."

"Two?"

Bear Mountain nodded glumly. "That's if you count the horse Goose had to take."

Lone Wolf began to laugh. He laughed loud and long, partly from relief no one was killed, and partly because they had risked life and limb for two horses.

Lone Wolf reined his horse to a stop and sniffed the wind. He smelled wood smoke mingled with the tempting aroma of roasting buffalo meat. Home.

Returning to his village brought mixed feelings. He

relished being able to sleep without the constant fear of attack, yet his lodge would be empty without his son. He returned with scalps and trophies of the people he'd killed, but he still had to face the mother of his son, and tell her he'd failed to retrieve the young man's body.

"It will be good to sleep in my own tipi tonight," Bear Mountain said.

Lone Wolf turned to his lieutenant and smiled at the big man. "I had the same thoughts. We have been gone much longer than I wished. I long for my sleeping robe and my woman."

The warriors prepared for a grand entrance as they neared the village. Several of the young men donned victory paint. Scalps were tied to lances and coup sticks. Captured jewelry adorned necks and ears. Pots, pans, brushes, anything of value hung from the saddles of the warriors. The war party came home conquerors, and a jubilant mood worked its way through the men.

Lone Wolf's mood was sober. While he'd regained his medicine, his original mission, the recovery of Tau-Ankia and Gui-Tain, had failed. He couldn't bring himself to celebrate.

Before the warriors came in sight of the tipis, young women who had been gathering roots called out to them. Occasionally Lone Wolf heard a cry of relief as a brother or uncle was recognized. Two long lines of people met the war party as it entered the village. The young, the old, men, women, and children, all waved and cheered the warriors.

So enthusiastic was the greeting, Lone Wolf felt a surge of pride in his people. He sat straighter on his horse and thrust his chest forward. Holding his chin high, he gazed beyond his admirers. His attitude was stern and aloof as befitted a great war chief. This his people expected; this they deserved. His pony seemed to adopt the same manner, nodding vigorously and whinnying as though to say, "See who rides me!"

Lone Wolf continued past the well-wishers. He glanced back and saw his men reveling in their popularity. He smiled faintly. It was good for the Kiowa to celebrate.

He made his way through the village acknowledging those who had not been in the greeting lines. In front of one tipi stood an old man. Lone Wolf knew him only as Skinny Legs, and he had been old when the war chief was a child.

Skinny Legs stood as erect as his gnarled spine would allow, and leaned heavily on a tall staff, gripping it with an arm that looked as frail and brown as kindling. His entire body, save for that arm, was enshrouded in a red blanket. What little face showed was tortoise skin.

"Lone Wolf," Skinny Legs called in a tumbleweed voice. He watched the warrior dismount and approach. "I see you have returned to us safely."

Lone Wolf laughed. "And I see you are here to greet me as always."

"It will not always be so. I am just an old, dried-up mesquite bean that's too stubborn to fall off the tree. One day a great wind will blow me away."

"That will be a sad day for us all, Skinny Legs."

"Bah! Mourn for yourself. You will be down here fighting the white man while I hunt buffalo with the Great Spirit. While your manhood freezes in the time of the snows, I'll have a new, young wife to keep me warm. It is I who should mourn for you."

A sudden gust threatened to topple the old man, and his other arm shot out from under the blanket to grasp the staff. As the material fell away from his head, Skinny Legs's white hair whipped in the wind. "I really hate being old, Lone Wolf. Even breaking wind makes me fall down."

Lone Wolf shrugged. "You have traded your youth for wisdom, old friend."

Skinny Legs grunted and stared at the war chief

with one eye, the other squinted against the sunlight. "You're a good boy; I always told your father that, too. You listen when the old men speak, not like some of these young rowdies today."

"Who?"

"While you were away, a young Comanche came along and passed the war pipe. The council refused the pipe and he left, but some of the young men went with him."

"Did they say where they were going?"

Skinny Legs shrugged. "The council said no. The matter has no interest for me now." He gathered his blanket about him and turned to the tipi. "I must rest now, Lone Wolf. I'm old, you know."

Lone Wolf watched his friend enter the lodge, and heard him muttering about the lack of respect among the young men for their elders. He smiled. If the Great Spirit allowed, he hoped one day to be a tottering and muttering old man like Skinny Legs.

The old man's rambling about a Comanche visitor interested him. He'd heard tales of a shaman, some said prophet, among the Comanches; one who was supposed to have great powers. Could this have been the one who'd come? And if he did have such power, why had the council refused to join his battle? Lone Wolf pondered these questions while he walked toward his home.

Standing in front of the Lone Wolf's home was another warrior. He was taller and broader than the war chief, but he had Lone Wolf's thin face and lips, and the same aquiline nose.

"Red Otter," Lone Wolf called. "It gladdens my heart to see you again."

"And mine to see you, Brother. You have been gone for too many moons."

"True, and to make it worse, we failed."

Red Otter frowned. "I'm sorry, Lone Wolf. I know how much you wanted to bury your son."

"No more than you yours."

"Could you not find them?"

"Oh, no," the war chief said, stripping the saddle and blanket from his horse. He grasped a handful of dried grass and began to rub down the animal. "On the contrary, we had very good luck. The warriors lay where they fell. We buried all but your son and mine." He paused and stared into the distance replaying the scene in his mind. "On the way home, we were attacked by soldiers. I lost the pack animals." Lone Wolf sighed. "We should have buried our children with their friends."

Red Otter placed a hand on his brother's shoulder and spoke softly. "You did your best. None could have done better, and many would not have tried. I, for one, wish to thank you."

Lone Wolf's shoulders sagged. He took a deep breath and cleared his throat. "I spoke to Old Man Skinny Legs on my way in. He was complaining about some of the young men leaving camp."

"True." Red Otter nodded. "A Comanche came here and tried to get us to join his war party. He said we would sweep the white man out of these lands, and with them gone, the buffalo would return."

"Was he a medicine man?"

"You mean the one called Isatai? No, this one was just a warrior. He said he knew the shaman and had seen him do his magic."

"Skinny Legs said the council decided not to join."

Red Otter laughed. "Why ask me when you seem to know all? The council voted and decided that if we attack the white man, more will come to take his place."

Lone Wolf turned. "And you agree with this?"

"Who's to say? I took the council's decision as my own. Some of the young men went with the warrior. Perhaps I will, too."

"Why would you change your mind?"

"Because . . ." Red Otter started and paused. "Because the old men are old men. They are afraid for all the People. That is good, but sometimes I think they're too cautious. I have heard that this Comanche is going to the Cheyenne camp to pass his pipe."

"When?"

"This very day."

"Hmm." Lone Wolf absently scratched an old scar on his chest. "How would you like to ride to visit our friends the Cheyenne?"

"When do we leave?"

"Shortly, but first I need a fresh horse. I also need to talk to my wife."

Red Otter grunted. "I'll get you a horse, and I'll see if anyone else wishes to accompany us. But as to your other task, I'll leave that to you, Brother."

Lone Wolf smiled grimly. "Today, I'd face a horde of Tejanos and buffalo soldiers sooner than enter my own lodge."

Twelve

Quanah sat quietly as Brown Bull paced the floor of the tipi. Overt actions of anger were rare among the People. They preferred to sit and talk. That Quanah's adopted brother refused to sit demonstrated to the young warrior just how deep Brown Bull's fury ran.

The older warrior stopped. "I can not believe what you did last night."

"But—"

Brown Bull raised his right hand for silence. "Don't interrupt. You will get a chance to speak." He paused to take a deep breath. "You and your medicine man caused much trouble. By walking out, Isatai didn't allow the elders to answer his summons to war."

"They could have spoken after we left."

"They did, and they're unhappy with you."

Quanah bristled. "Me? I merely followed Isatai out of the Sun Dance lodge."

"That's just what I'm talking about, Quanah." Brown Bull sat on the opposite side of the fire. "After Isatai spoke, he was to listen to the response of the others. Leaving as he did told them he had hardened his heart to any discussion. By itself, that wasn't a bad thing. He showed strength and resolution. On the other hand, *your* actions insulted the elders."

The news rocked Quanah. Without the support of

the peace chiefs, gathering a war party of any size would be impossible.

"I don't understand," he said. "Wouldn't it show that I, too, wanted no further discussion? Did it not show strength in me?"

Brown Bull shook his head. "The medicine men work in a world full of spirits and shadows. They are expected to be different. Warriors deal with life in this world. You left the council meeting without listening to the old ones. Now they think that you are too blinded by vengeance to effectively lead a war party.

"I must lead!" Quanah shouted. "It is my family's blood that is to be avenged."

"I know, and I've spoken to the council. You and Isatai are to return to the Sun Dance lodge. This will be your last chance to convince the old men that the path you seek is for the good of the People."

After Brown Bull left, Quanah sat alone in his tipi and brooded. What the old men thought was unfair. After all, it was he and Isatai who had brought the People together for the Sun Dance.

He smiled ruefully. *No,* he thought. *Isatai brought them here. His vision, his promise of the return of the old life, that is why they came. Brown Bull was right. I have been blinded by what I want. It is time for a change.*

His mood lightened, Quanah felt starved. His nostrils flared as the smell of roast buffalo floated through the tipi, and his stomach growled and grumbled like an old bear. He'd always enjoyed the taste of buffalo, especially the liver. The thought of raw liver covered with gall juice brought back fond memories of the hunt.

His eyes narrowed and their gaze hardened. The hunt would be no more if the white man had his way. The soldiers kept the People away from the herds while hunters killed the buffalo for their hides. The thought of such waste ruined his appetite.

Stepping out of the lodge, he saw Isatai squatting near a campfire, chewing a piece of meat and staring into the distance.

"Isatai," he called.

The shaman continued to stare. Quanah crossed to the fire and nudged his friend with his toe.

"Isatai, I've been thinking."

"You are always thinking," Isatai replied, standing slowly.

"This time it's different. Brown Bull says the old ones may not let me lead the war party."

Isatai grunted and started toward the Sun Dance lodge. "We can speak as we walk. The elders cannot stop you, you know that."

"And you know that without them taking the pipe, many men will not join."

Isatai sighed. "What you say is the truth. What is worse, if we can't gather a strong war party, the Kiowa and Cheyenne won't go with us."

"What will we do?"

"Do?" The medicine man grabbed Quanah by the shoulders and gazed intently into his gray eyes. "We are going to make the council see our vision. Remember, the Great Spirit is on our side. He will guide the hearts of the old men."

They entered the lodge and found Chief White Wolf and the other band leaders waiting for them.

White Wolf rose and waved a gnarled hand at them. "Come, young men. Come into the center of the council. We have questions to ask."

Quanah walked with all the dignity he could muster. The old chief remained standing, and looked from Quanah to Isatai and back again.

"To be so young again," White Wolf said with a smile. "I remember well the hunts, the horses, the battles. But that was long ago when our enemies were only the Crow, Navajo, and Tonkawas."

He shuffled forward and turned to eye his audience.

"The white man has done more to end the life of the People than all of our other enemies combined. They take our land and give us paper. They take the buffalo and let us starve. I hate all whites, but the ones I hate the most are the buffalo hunters." White Wolf paused, then turned to Quanah and Isatai. "Tell me why we must fight the soldiers when the hunters are leaving us hungry."

Quanah stepped forward. "The soldiers killed my nephew and Isatai's uncle. They stole my mother and sister from me. Soon they will come here and kill us all. These hunters are few. Once we have dealt with the soldiers, we can destroy them at our leisure."

"What you say is true, but what good will it do to kill the soldiers if the buffalo have all been slaughtered? What do we eat then?" White Wolf sat down again and stared into the fire. "Before you came, we took a vote. We wanted to hear what you had to say, but it will not change the outcome. Quanah, you're a good fighter, but you don't know everything. The hunters are on our land and killing our buffalo. Take the pipe against them. You, Isatai, will lead the war party, and use the gift of the Great Spirit to assure success. Seek your revenge and gladden your hearts. When you return, we will take all the Comanches south to fight the soldiers."

Quanah was sickened by the news. The real enemy lay south, not on the plains.

"I will accept the decision of the council," he said. "But only if you will take the pipe now to fight the soldiers after the hunters are destroyed."

White Wolf nodded. "It is agreeable. I gladly take the pipe, and can't wait for the day when no white man walks the earth."

Quanah entered the Kiowa village on his favorite war pony. He was dressed in the same fine buckskin he'd worn the day of the Sun Dance buffalo hunt. In his right hand, he carried the war pipe. Dismounting near the center of the village, he asked a young warrior where to find the tipi of the chief.

Isatai and Quanah decided the best method of approaching the Kiowa was one warrior alone with the pipe. Quanah would find the chief and convince him to join the cause. The head man would then bring his own warriors.

As he approached the lodge, Quanah wondered if a show of force would have been more appropriate. He circled the tipi to the left, then entered and moved to the back. The chief sat to his right.

"I am Quanah, Comanche warrior of the Quahada."

"Good things are said about the Antelopes. Welcome to my home. Will you eat?"

"Your hospitality honors me, but first, perhaps we could smoke."

"I will smoke, but not from that pipe. You are going to war, and if I smoke, I will have to go."

Quanah frowned. "We need the Kiowa to battle the enemies of all our peoples."

"In that case, speak to the people outside, and let's see what they say."

The chief left the tipi. Once outside, he called together as many people as he could. Quanah watched as warriors, women, and children gathered.

"This warrior is from our friends, the Comanche. Listen to what he says."

With that simple statement, Quanah became the center of attention. He cleared his throat and began his plea.

"I have come to ask the Kiowa to join us on a raid against the buffalo hunters. After that, we will gather the rest of the Comanche and go fight the soldiers in the south. With us is a powerful medicine man who will turn away the bullets of the white rifles. We cannot lose. So I ask, who will take the pipe?"

He raised the instrument over his head, but no one ventured to take it. All present looked to the Kiowa leader. He turned to Quanah.

"I am not afraid of that pipe, but let all the old men hear. If they say this is a good thing, I will smoke."

Quanah visited with the elders. He told them of Isatai's magic and how defeating the whites meant the return of the buffalo. While many heads nodded in agreement, no hands took his pipe. The old ones complained such a war would bring the soldiers down on everybody, and the Kiowa would die. They did offer to talk again after the white hunters were killed.

Quanah nodded and gathered the reins of his horse. "I must return to my tribe. I thank you for your hospitality."

He jumped on the pony's back and rode away. At the edge of the encampment, he was met by a group of braves. They looked like children, but most seemed old enough to fight.

One detached himself from the others. He was slender, but well-muscled. His bearing was proud, yet not arrogant. He looked a natural leader.

"We wish to take the pipe," he said.

"Your elders have spoken against the war."

"The old men do not speak for us. We'll go if you'll have us."

Quanah smiled. He remembered his first war party and how hard it was to gain permission to go.

"If that's what you want, gather your ponies. I will ride east. You will find me by a small creek. There we will smoke and make plans." He kicked his mount into an easy lope and rode off.

Reaching the stream, he hobbled his horse near some tall grass. Soon he had a fire burning, and was loading the pipe when he heard riders approaching. Standing, he waved, and the young warriors charged him at full gallop.

He talked with the young men until late in the day.

He believed their sincerity, and hoped their enthusiasm made up for their serious lack of experience.

In the waning sunlight, he led them to the camp and paraded them before his people. Curious, the Comanche came out and warmly greeted the new arrivals. Many were invited to the tipis, and those that remained pitched camp near Quanah's tipi. All the people brought food. The Kiowa ate, drank, and listened to stories of the Comanche. They then told their own tales, and so the party went into the night.

Quanah excused himself and stepped inside his lodge. He sat in the back, near the fire, and retrieved his newest acquisition. He stroked the rifle's stock as though the weapon lived. It was heavier than the guns he was familiar with, and he remembered the effort required to get it.

He, Brown Bull, and Isatai had ridden into the camp of a Comanchero, a Mexican trader from beyond the Comanche lands. Inside his wagon, the merchant carried pots, pans, knives, guns, mirrors, and a host of other goods available for purchase. The usual medium of exchange was buffalo hides or ponies, though sometimes there was a little money or gold from a raid.

Quanah dismounted and approached the small brown man wearing a very large hat. He remembered they called them *sombreros*. The trader also wore a blanket with a hole in it over his head. He smiled a great deal, his thin black mustache drooping over his upper lip.

Brown Bull approached and picked up a pot. "Do you think Blue Running Water would like this?"

"How many pots does a woman need?" Quanah answered, then turned to the Comanchero. He pointed his fingers like a gun and gestured. *"Armas de fuego?"*

"Sí. Pistolas?"

"No. No." Quanah squeezed his eyes shut trying to remember what little Spanish he knew. *"Carabina."*

The small man smiled and nodded his head. He walked to a long crate, pried off its lid, and removed one of the rifles within.

"Carabina," he said, proudly handing the weapon to Quanah.

The warrior had seen this kind of gun before. Not particularly powerful—which didn't matter since they weren't accurate. Cheaply and poorly made. A trade rifle. He shook his head.

"This won't do. I need a better weapon." He placed crooked fingers on either side of his head. "I want a buffalo gun. Do you understand?"

The trader blinked uncomprehendingly.

"Brown Bull, do you speak this man's language?"

The older warrior set down a mirror he was contemplating and came to Quanah's side. "Some. I hope better than you."

"Good. Tell him I want a buffalo gun."

"Uh, rifle de buffalo?"

The trader fired off a rapid answer.

"I'm not sure, but I think he said buffalo don't need guns."

"Brown Bull, you must make him understand that we wish to buy the same gun used by the buffalo hunters."

"I'll try." He faced the trader. *"Señor, rifle?"* he asked, gesturing as though he held the weapon.

"Sí. Sí." The trader pointed to the box of trade rifles.

"Por favor, rifle por cazador de buffalo. Do you see? *Grandes armas!"* He spread his hands wide.

The Comanchero sat for a moment talking quietly to himself. *"Grandes armas de cazador?"* His eyes widened and he turned to Brown Bull. *"Cazador de buffalo?* Ay-yi-yi-yi-yi!"

The trader broke into an impassioned speech, pacing the ground. Quanah leaned toward his brother.

"What's he saying?"

Brown Bull shrugged. "He's talking about being a poor, honest trader with goods for his red brothers. What business would he have with such a gun? Even if he had one, the price would be very high."

Isatai snorted. "We are wasting our time. I say we kill the Mexican, take his goods to another, and see if he has the hunter's rifle."

The trader stopped talking and looked at his customers. Quanah saw fear in his eyes. Perhaps this man knew the language of the People after all. He continued to watch Quanah and his compatriots warily. Then he spoke quietly and eloquently at length to Brown Bull.

The warrior turned to Quanah. "He says that he may be able to get the gun you want, but the price would be very high. Many buffalo hides; many ponies."

"I don't care." To the Mexican: "*Señor, lo acepto. Entiende?* I want that rifle."

"*Sí, señor.*" The Comanchero again addressed Brown Bull. Quanah understood virtually none of the conversation, but the word *mañana* caught his ear.

"What was that about tomorrow?"

"He says that he will meet us here when the sun is high."

"No!" Quanah faced the trader and spoke slowly. *"No mañana! Hoy!* Listen to me, little man. I want that rifle today. We will gather the hides and horses and be back before nightfall."

Now firelight reflected off the smooth barrel as Quanah sat in council with his warriors. He looked at the eager faces around him. Mere boys. Two faces caught his eye. What were they doing here? Yellowfish was barely old enough to travel; Timbo, younger still.

Quanah stood. He surveyed his men again, pleased to note that none showed signs of drunkenness. Earlier, Quanah and Isatai had had a short and pointed discussion about Quanah's desire for everyone to remain wide awake and alert. He raised the rifle over his head.

"This is why the buffalo hunters must die. It looks like a rifle any of us may own, but it's not. This gun is the end of the buffalo, the People, and the Kiowa." Quanah leaned the weapon against a log. "How many of you carry the white man's rifle?"

Several hands raised.

"One of you throw me a bullet."

Quanah deftly caught the cartridge, then bent and reached into a box at his feet. In one hand he displayed the warrior's bullet. In the other was a three-inch brass missile.

"Look at this. The hunter's bullets are twice as long and wide as ours. The trader I bought this gun from said it could kill a buffalo farther away than you can see."

A voice called out, "Any gun that can kill buffalo can kill whites as easy."

War cries erupted. Warriors brandished axes, knives, and guns.

Quanah raised his hands. "What you say is true. They can also destroy young warriors."

"That is why the Great Spirit gave us the yellow paint!" Isatai shouted. "The white man's guns are useless against us no matter how big his bullets are."

Quanah awoke instantly. He sat up and found himself in an empty lodge. Outside the tipi, he heard the low murmurs of Weckeah and Chony as they prepared breakfast. Quanah stretched, enjoying the feel of moving muscle. He stood, wrapped a blanket around his waist, draping one end over his left shoulder and arm, and stepped into the daylight.

The sun sat low on the eastern horizon. Birds sang to the awakening Comanche camp. A cool breeze blew from the southwest bringing to his nostrils the smells of cooking fires. He watched his wives tending to his morning meal. A long strip of buffalo meat hung over one section of the flames, while a small iron pot bubbled with boiling corn over another.

"Smells good," he said.

Chony looked up from her cooking and smiled. "You will need your strength today for your journey. The food is ready if you are." She smiled again.

Quanah grunted. "Let me piss first."

Chony always smiled and fawned over the warrior. He enjoyed the attention—most of the time. Weckeah was his favorite and also his first wife. Should he decide to change matters, Quanah would tell his wives then.

Bladder relieved, he returned to his home. He sat at his accustomed position in the back. Weckeah entered first carrying the meat on a skewer. She drove the sharpened stick into the dirt close to her husband and settled to his left. Chony walked through the doorway, kettle in hand. She set the pot next to the meat and, using a horn spoon, ladled corn into a small wooden bowl. She then set the vessel within Quanah's comfortable reach and retired to the left of the first wife.

Quanah cut off a piece of rare buffalo and bit in. He relished the warm, bloody juices as they ran over his tongue. Nothing compared to fresh buffalo. He scooped up enough mush to cover his fingers and plopped it into his mouth—even the corn tasted good.

"My wives," he said, as he cut more meat from the strip, "I go to see the Cheyenne. We will feast and talk. Isatai says this is the best time to go. The Sun Dance has ended, their warriors filled with renewed spirit. Many men should take the pipe today. My war party will grow." He beamed at the two women.

Chony and Weckeah exchanged glances, and looked back at Quanah saying nothing. The warrior's smile faded. Why should he have bothered speaking to these women? They knew nothing of war, nothing of the ways of men. Babies and buffalo skins, that's what wives understood. He continued the meal in silence.

Breakfast finished, he dressed quickly, called on Isatai, and rounded up his war party. They left amid cheers from friends and relatives, and rode north into the land of the Cheyenne.

During a quick lunch of jerked buffalo and water, Isatai outlined his plan for the visitation. They stopped almost within sight of the Cheyenne lodges. Quanah told each warrior to paint himself and his horse. Then they waited, and as the sun dropped toward the west, the men lined up abreast and started a slow advance. Within sight of the village they halted.

Quanah nervously rode behind his men ranked across the plain. He looked between the warriors to the Cheyenne encampment, and saw the flickering fires brighten as night crawled across the land.

He worked his way around the end man and continued back up the line, inspecting the warriors carefully. Each wore his best clothes and rode his war pony. He'd instructed the younger men to apply more paint to help conceal their age. Until the Cheyenne agreed to join, Quanah didn't want them to know that many of these warriors were untested in battle.

Halfway through the rank, he saw Isatai. The medicine man sat astride his pony in front of the war party, dressed in a breechclout and red sash. German silver hung on his arms and dangled from his ears. His face bore no paint, and his countenance was of one waiting for dinner.

Quanah wheeled his horse and drew near Isatai. "What are we waiting for?"

"Patience, my friend. The time is at hand. Soon we will charge to the Cheyenne. He will see us pour from the sinking sun like blood from a wounded heart. Appearance is everything."

A frowning Quanah fidgeted on his horse, and moved the big buffalo rifle from his shoulder to his saddle and back again.

The shaman sighed. "Very well, if you can't wait, go tell those men down there to be ready for my signal. I will ride this way and tell the others."

With a shout of joy, Quanah galloped down the rank of warriors, waving his weapon and shouting orders. He turned and rode back to the center, again at Isatai's side.

The shaman turned and smiled. He then waved his right hand in the air. Suddenly, it held a flaming arrow. The sight brought cheers from the war party and made Quanah's heart beat faster.

With a small flourish, Isatai pulled his bow over his head. He nocked the arrow, drew, and sent the missile toward the Cheyenne camp. It streaked through the air like a falling star. Quanah was sure the Cheyenne saw the arrow as well. What would they make of it? Would they know of Isatai's magic? These and many other questions were wiped from Quanah's mind as he saw the flaming arrow begin its final plunge to earth.

The fiery needle struck ground and, as one, the war party charged. Over one hundred hearts pounded in cadence to the ponies' hooves. War cries melded into a single wall of sound that drove ahead of the warriors like a tangible force. Quanah's heart sang as he felt the spirits of all the men intermingle and flow through his body.

He cried and laughed, overcome by a feeling beyond description: more frightening than combat, more powerful than sex. He felt as though the Great Spirit had brushed against him. Perhaps this was what had happened to Isatai. If it was, Quanah easily understood how the experience changed a man.

Again the feeling started. A shudder moved from the base of his spine, up his back, and across his shoulders. He cried out. Tears ran down his face unheeded and unchecked. He felt the presence of all the Comanche warriors from the past riding with him. His father was there, and his grandfather and his grandfather's father. All rode as one. And behind them was the hand of the Great Spirit pressing them forward— unstoppable as the wind that pushes the long grass of the plains.

He heard another sound over the thundering of the horses. Thousands of voices roared as the entire Cheyenne tribe cheered the warriors. But then he was among them, reining hard to avoid injuring anyone. As he slowed, the trailing dust rolled over them in a great tan cloud. He saw shapes moving through the dirt. Comanche and Cheyenne greeted one another. A drum started, faintly at first, but growing louder as the people took up the chant. His vision clearing, he saw the Cheyenne dance and sing their greeting.

The war party was shepherded to the Sun Dance lodge. He knew that until recently the building had been filled with young Cheyenne men tethered to its center post by long strips of rawhide attached to sharpened bones piercing their chest muscles. The men had danced continually, pulling on the leather strips, trying to tear themselves loose. Those that succeeded still bore the fresh wounds of their ordeal.

The warriors gathered just inside the lodge entrance, further movement barred by Dog Soldier guards. Large fires burned brightly on either side of the center pole, lighting most of the building.

He scanned the group of men before him. The Cheyenne Council of Forty-Four consisted of a head chief and forty-three underchiefs. These men decided everything the tribe did. It was the Council he and Isatai must convince.

"Quanah," called a voice at his side. "Look there."

Quanah recognized the young Kiowa speaking to him, but couldn't recall his name. The man pointed.

At the fringe of the Council a warrior intently watched the gathered Comanches.

"That is Lone Wolf. He is one of our greatest war chiefs. If he will join us, so will his men. The huge man next to him is Bear Mountain, another great warrior."

Quanah nodded and passed the information to Isatai, along with a suggestion that they meet with the Kiowa chief after the ceremony. Isatai murmured his agreement.

A Dog Soldier approached. "I am Wolf's Breath. I speak your language, as do many of my people. Your war chief and the shaman will move to the center post." He signaled; the Dog Soldier guards moved aside.

The head Cheyenne chief stood. "We the People greet you Comanche and our friends the Kiowa," he said solemnly, waving his hand toward Lone Wolf. "We have been friends since before the Night the Stars Fell. It is known the Comanche are a good people, almost as good as the Cheyenne. We will listen to what you have to say."

Isatai faded into the shadows, and Quanah found himself the center of attention. He cleared his throat and began:

"I am called Quanah. I am Quahadi Comanche. To the south are white men, worse than the soldiers or the Tejanos. These men kill our buffalo. They slaughter for the hide only. And when we are weak with hunger, the soldiers will come. They come to drive us onto the reservation, killing those who will not go. There we will be slaves of the white chiefs in Washington. We will live on rotten meat until one day there are no more Comanche, Kiowa, or Cheyenne!

"But," he said, raising his right hand, "this does not have to be." Quanah paused and smiled. "As we rode in here tonight, I felt the hand of the Great Spirit push us." The smile vanished. "This same hand will sweep away the white man before us. Then the buffalo will return. Why?" He pointed to the almost invisible figure in the shadows. "Isatai—who predicted drought, and it came to pass. Isatai—who brought flaming arrows out of the air, coughed up bullets, and brought the dead back to life. Isatai—who has been to the home of the Great Spirit and has the power to rid us once and for all of the white plague. Such is the man who comes to speak to you now."

Quanah quickly withdrew from the light and watched as his friend appeared from the other side. The medicine man walked slowly and confidently to the center of the circle. His silver ornaments brightly reflected the firelight. His skin glowed coppery. A small smile played at his lips.

"Quanah makes a good talk," he said. "As he grows old, many children will gather at his lodge to hear the stories of these times."

Low laughter filled the room, and Isatai paused to allow the earlier tension to melt away.

"Yes, Quanah speaks well. More importantly, he fights well. He keeps his wits about him."

The shaman paced slowly, feeling every eye upon him.

"This is a man who thinks all the time. He is always looking for the 'why' in everything. This same man, who was never impressed by anything I have done, has just stood before you and said he felt the hand of the Great Spirit on him." Isatai rubbed a hand over his face. "I am confused. Why Quanah? He is not awed by magic or visions. He is a thinker, but now he has been touched by the Creator. I don't understand why the Great Spirit chose Quanah when *I* was there."

When the laughter subsided, he continued. "Perhaps the Great Spirit touched Quanah to show him that He is with all of us. I have seen Him, felt His presence, heard His word. I have been given the powers and knowledge to defeat the white man."

Isatai waved his right arm, and a burning arrow appeared clutched in his hand. He heard the collective intake of breath from the Council.

"Gaze upon this and know the Great Spirit has empowered me!"

He waved again, and the single arrow became two.

"As the arrows multiply, so do the whites."

Another flourish and his hands were empty.

Isatai coughed, gagged, and spat a cartridge into his hand. He repeated the act until three gleaming brass bullets lay in his palm.

"I can bring forth wagon loads of bullets," he said, rolling the ammunition about his hand, "just as the white men have wagon loads of soldiers."

He raised the shells to his mouth and swallowed them.

"But with magic, they disappear like the arrows before.

"The Great Spirit told me of a special paint. This gift of heaven will turn aside the bullets of the white men! His guns will not fire, and if they do, the bullet will pass through any painted warrior harmlessly! This was the promise made to me by the Great Spirit.

"I will cast a spell to make the buffalo hunters sleep. We will club them to death." Isatai raised his hands toward the sky. "After they are killed, the Comanche, the Kiowa, and the Cheyenne will unite and destroy the whites like a prairie fire, leaving behind cinders! Then the buffalo will return! This, too, was promised me!"

Isatai quickly retreated to the darkness.

The head Cheyenne chief arose and adjusted his blanket.

"We have heard the talks of the two Comanches," he said. "One spoke of war, the other magic. This is a good thing, we think. We prefer to die as warriors rather than slaves to Washington. The Great Spirit is strong in these two men." He pointed to Quanah. "Warrior, if you have brought the war pipe, we will gladly accept it and smoke."

Thirteen

"Hell, Billy, I ain't a-feared of nothin', but a man'd have to be damned stupid to head back south again. We're striking out to the north and west, maybe up to Palo Duro Creek."

Dixon stood quietly at the bar contemplating his beer and the words of Brick Bond. Perhaps the red-headed hunter was right. Why risk a fight with the Indians?

"Maybe so, Brick, but I really like my place on that creek. You were there. Charley and Frenchy didn't even know there was Indians near."

"Yeah, but that was most of five days ago." Bond sighed. "Suit yourself, friend. Me? I'm right partial to my hair."

He emptied his drink in a single swallow.

"I'm to bed," he said, offering his hand. "Good luck, Billy."

Dixon shook hands with Bond and grinned. "I'd rather have a sharp eye than luck any day. Good hunting, Brick."

After Bond left, Dixon ordered another beer and decided to see what card games were available. He turned and walked directly into the chest of a huge man.

"Son-of-a-bitch!" swore the stranger. "You done made me spill my drink."

"Pardon me, friend," Dixon spoke quickly, embarrassed by his own clumsiness.

"Your pardon don't dry my shirt."

"I cain't help on the shirt, but . . ." Dixon faced the bar. "Oscar? Get this man whatever he wants to drink. I'll pay." He gazed at the stranger. "That suit you?"

"Hell, no! I ain't having no goddam midget bumping into me for no cause. I reckon you done it a-purpose. Maybe figure that you being a runt an' all, no real man'd lay a hand on you."

Dixon wasn't sensitive about his height, but this large man was looking for trouble. He replied evenly, "I said I was sorry, friend."

The stranger leered, big yellow teeth showing behind the curled lip. "Yeah, you're sorry, all right. You're a sorry son-of-a-bitch!"

Swinging from the hip, Dixon's fist hit the other man flush in the mouth, splitting his lip and snapping his head back.

The stranger grunted and straightened his neck. He wiped the back of his right hand across his mouth, gazed at the smeared blood, and smiled. "I'm gonna hurt you, little man."

Dixon saw death in that smile. His only advantage had been surprise, and that was gone. As the stranger advanced, the hunter circled to the left.

"Get 'im, Curry. Kick his skinny ass!" a voice shouted from the crowd.

Curry laughed and spat blood from his lip onto the dirt floor. "C'mon, leprechaun. Let's get to it."

The hunter knew his only hope of surviving the fight was to hit Curry hard and often while staying out of the reach of his massive fists. He stepped in and drove two fists quickly into the big man's stomach, then moved back.

Curry grunted, then charged.

Dixon sidestepped the initial attack, but was caught

on the right shoulder by a wildly swung blow. He reeled, his arm numb to the wrist. He clenched and unclenched his fist to force feeling back. Again the two men circled cautiously.

The skinner stepped forward, only to be driven back by a vicious blow to the nose. He howled in pain, blood streaming down his face and dripping onto the floor.

Dixon pressed his advantage and drove a fist deep into his opponent's belly. As Curry doubled over, the hunter clasped his hands together and struck as hard as he could at the other's left kidney.

Curry straightened and swung backward, catching Dixon on the side of the head with an open backhand. The hunter flew across the saloon and struck the bar before falling to his hands and knees on the floor.

The room spun wildly and large black spots danced in front of him. Dixon's eyes focused on a large pair of boots near his hands. Looking upward, he saw Curry, grinning through the split lip and past the blood of his ruined nose. Dixon rose to his knees.

"I ain't whipped yet, Curry."

The skinner laughed again and snorted, spraying blood on Dixon. "Little bastard! I think you broke my nose. When I'm done with you, your nose is gonna be the last thing I break."

Dixon knew Curry meant every word he'd said. Men like him usually did. With every ounce of his remaining strength, he punched straight out, catching Curry in the crotch. The big man's breath whooshed out, and he grabbed himself. Holding his hands between his legs, Curry sank slowly to his knees in front of Dixon. He tried to talk, but failed, and sat sucking wind.

The hunter regained his feet and grabbed Curry's ears. "Nobody calls my momma a bitch," he said, and drove his knee into the other man's face. Curry fell flat on his back.

The skinner slowly sat up and reached for a skinning knife.

"I gonna get me some balls," he hissed, struggling to his feet.

Dixon backed up, reaching for his own knife, prepared for the worst.

Curry suddenly froze. A derringer had appeared, its snub barrel resting behind his ear.

The weapon's owner eased around Curry. Dixon's gaze followed the barrel to the cocked trigger, past the hand holding the pistol, and up the arm to the face of Bat Masterson. Masterson's gray eyes were cool, his features calm, relaxed. A small smile played at his lips.

"I believe this fight's over. Don't you, Mr. Curry?"

The other said nothing. Masterson continued. "Now, I only got two shots, but they are both .41-caliber, and I daresay they'd make an impressive hole even in your head."

Curry sagged, beaten.

The hunter moved to the door, followed by Masterson. Outside, Dixon leaned against the sod wall.

"Thanks, Bat. I sure as hell didn't want to dance with him anymore."

"Judging from the way you look, you shouldn't have danced at all."

Dixon laughed. "That's the truth. Jesus, that man could hit." He grimaced as he rotated his shoulder. "I'll be glad to be shut of this place."

"Where you headed?"

"Back south to my creek. I hired Cranky McCabe on as another skinner. You want to hire on?"

"No, sir. I've had all the skinning I want. I've been thinking of working for Mr. Leonard. I figure I can start here and maybe end up at the big store in Dodge."

"Sounds good. Now, if you'll pardon me, I'm gonna

get me a bottle and nurse myself to sleep. I'll be seeing you, Bat."

"Same to you, Billy. Watch yourself."

Dixon, astride Jack, slowly approached the site of their camp. The black gelding stepped lightly and quietly through the underbrush, seeming to sense his master's tension.

The campsite seemed normal enough. The hides Frenchy had staked out a week ago were still there. Strips of buffalo meat hung from the drying racks. The most reassuring sight was the stack of folded flint hides they'd made ready for shipment and abandoned during their hasty retreat.

The hunter relaxed. Had Indians come across the camp, they would have taken what they could and burned the rest, especially the hides.

Dixon heard the clanking of wagons, and knew his crew was near. The addition of Mike McCabe to the outfit meant Dixon would be able to kill at the same level he had when young Miller was in camp. By tomorrow he'd be back in the routine, and he'd be a rich man come the fall.

Dixon removed his hat and retrieved the photograph of his mother from the crown. "Momma, I'm back again. Here on the prairie amidst the buffalo and Indians. Don't fret now. I heard talk, but ain't seen a feathered head yet. Besides, we done killed all of our buffalo in Kansas. Remember that, Momma? Lord, when we first set eyes on them brutes, they blackened the earth as far as a man could see. Now they're gone, so we come south." He sighed and returned the picture to its resting place. "Yep, killed ours, and now we want the red man's."

He ran his hand through his sweaty hair and started to replace his hat, but stopped short. A gentle breeze blew off the prairie and down the ravine past his campsite. Dixon shuddered and felt a tingling at the nape of his neck.

"Indians," he muttered.

Later that afternoon, Dixon stood atop a hill watching the horizon for any sign of trouble. He watched Armitage climb up the hill toward him. The Englishman looked tired, and his entire body seemed covered in a fine, tan dust. As he neared, Dixon saw darker lines crisscross the skinner's face as sweat mingled with the dirt and produced an effect not unlike war paint.

"How goes the loading, Charley? You looked tuckered."

Armitage waved a hand. "It's not the work I mind; rather, it's this blasted heat. I can't remember the last instance of rain, can you?"

"No, sir, can't rightly say."

Dixon surveyed the horizon. In the distance, billowing clouds towered over the hunter and his crew.

"I've seen clouds," he said. "Big, black ones. Sometimes I hear thunder or maybe see a flash of lightning, but no rain. It's enough to make a body think God's moving all that water to someplace that needs it worse than the prairie."

"Perhaps. As to the loading, we've about finished."

Dixon nodded. "Good. I can't wait to be shut of the place."

"So I assumed. You've been a bit nervous lately."

"Nervous ain't the word. I've been feeling Indian every time we get near here."

The hunter stood and took a final look at the country around him.

"Well, let's get moving."

He started down the hill, followed by Armitage.

"Mike," he called. "I want you to ride your horse

and keep your rifle at the ready. You got a Sharps or a needle gun?"

McCabe shook his head. Long, curly auburn hair whipped back and forth across his collar under the brim of a black Army slouch hat. He fixed clear green eyes on Dixon.

"I aim to carry my Spencer. Eight shots, without no reloading. Sure beats the hell out of them one-shot pieces you carry."

"Suit yourself. Frenchy, you drive the big wagon. Got your weapons?"

Frenchy nodded curtly, his expression hidden by his beard. "Sure do. I got a needle gun, my double-barrel scattergun, and a Colt."

Dixon looked from man to man. "Mike will lead. Frenchy takes the second position. His wagon will set the speed. Charley's third, and I ride drag. When we get to a rough spot, we take the trail one at a time until everybody's through."

"Good God, Billy," Armitage said. "You sound like we're looking for trouble."

"Actually, Charley, trouble's looking for us."

Fourteen

Lone Wolf loved this part of the hunt. Below him was the unwary hunter. His heart thudded with excitement, and his mind raced with questions. Would the quarry be taken by surprise or would he get away? The kill always pleased Lone Wolf, but it was the hunt he lived for.

He watched as Goose worked his way close to the hunter. The snapping twig sounded like a rifle shot across the clearing. The white man leapt to his feet, pulled his revolver, and shot into the brush. Goose dropped immediately.

Stunned by what they'd seen, the others stared as the white man ran and mounted a bareback mule. He'd already started to ride off when Lone Wolf realized his prey might escape.

"Shoot!" he shouted. "Shoot!"

Four arrows flew through the air. Three struck the mule; one landed in the left thigh of the hunter. The mule crashed to the ground, dumping its rider.

The war party charged down the hill on foot.

"Bear Mountain," Lone Wolf ordered, "check on Goose."

The lieutenant nodded his acknowledgment and veered to the left.

The Kiowa quickly surrounded the hunter, who lay on the ground. His face was pale and sweaty, and each breath carried a groan. One hand lay on his injured thigh, the fingers laced around the arrow.

Lone Wolf approached his captive slowly. The need for hurry was over. He hunkered down by the hunter and gazed at him.

"Your face tells me that you are in pain."

He grabbed the arrow's shaft and worked the missile back and forth.

The white man yelled in agony. Grasping the arrow with both hands, he pulled it from Lone Wolf's grip.

The Kiowa chief sank back on his haunches and grunted.

"I see," he said thoughtfully, then looked into the other's wide, frightened eyes. "I'm not a medicine man, but I think your leg hurts because of that arrow."

He smiled as the party members laughed. The white man's gaze shifted from warrior to warrior.

"You don't understand, do you, white man. Maybe you know this: *Hey, white man.*"

"Look at his face," Boy said excitedly. "He knows what you said."

"Of course, he did, Boy. He *is* a white man. Let's see, I know some more. *Hey, white man, you summabitch.* Pretty good, huh?"

"What'd you say to him?" Boy asked. "He looks a little angry and not so scared."

Lone wolf shrugged. "I don't know. I learned some of the words from Comanche, some from Cheyenne. You want me to make him mad? I know something that the Cheyenne said would work good."

"Sure," said Boy.

"Watch. *Hey, white man, you go home, you white shit, bastard, goddam, nigger, son of a whore.*"

The prisoner's eyes narrowed in anger, and he shouted at the Kiowa. The warriors took a step back as their captive changed from a wounded, frightened deer to a pain-maddened bear. He tried to sit up, but

Lone Wolf stuck his foot in the man's chest and pushed him back down.

"I have never seen anything like that before," Buffalo with Holes in His Ears said in awe. "Can you teach me those words?"

Before Lone Wolf could answer, Bear Mountain joined the group.

"Where is Goose?" the chief asked, fearing the worst.

"He's hurt pretty bad. He needs to go home where a real medicine man can care for him."

Lone Wolf again squatted by the hunter. "You're a good shot." He rose. "After we're done with this one, we'll take Goose back. We should still be able to meet Quanah before he reaches the hunters' village."

He looked at his captive.

"White man, I know you are in great pain, but shortly the arrow in your leg will be the least of your worries."

Fifteen

Eddy rose from bed and stretched. Looking out of the small window set in the room's west wall, he saw sunlight strike the tops of the hills and mesas surrounding Adobe Walls. He retrieved his trousers, slipping suspenders over his undershirt, and shuffled toward the restaurant. Langton still slept. Eddy wasn't surprised, any more than by Johnson's empty bed.

Yawning mightily, the bookkeeper walked into the kitchen. Hannah and William Olds were seated at the employees' table.

"Mornin', folks," Eddy said.

"Good morning, George," Hannah answered, rising and walking toward the stove. She returned with a cup of coffee and set it before Eddy. "Steak and eggs?"

"Yes'm, sounds good."

The back door opened, and Andy Johnson stepped into the kitchen. "I tell you de trut', by damn, purty soon we be covered over in buffalo hides." He plopped down in a chair across the table from Eddy. The ends of his massive red handlebar mustache raised as he smiled. "Boy, that feels good." He fixed blue eyes on Eddy. "*Und* how are you this morning, my friend?"

Eddy shrugged. "Tolerable."

"Tolerable," Johnson echoed, then laughed aloud. "*Ja,* is easy for you to say. Last night you again meet with those poker buddies of yours and loose your money and drink too much. Then today"—Johnson raised his hands, palms inward about a foot from each ear—"today you have the big head and dry mouth, *ja?* I am right?"

"I've been better," Eddy conceded. "But last night we talked mostly business. Jim Hanrahan's really worried about the Indian attacks. Thinks it's going to cost us money in the end."

"What about our leader?" Olds asked, dabbing at the corner of his mouth with a napkin. "What's he think?"

Eddy took a long sip of his coffee and contemplated the brown liquid. "Langton's a queer one, all right. He don't gamble or drink or take part in other manly pleasures, but then you get him to talkin' about killing Indians and his eyes change." He paused and looked at the others at the table. "I don't rightly know how to put it, except to say his eyes go empty and bottomless—kinda like you could look in 'em and see clear to hell."

The rest of the morning meal passed in silence, each lost in his or her thoughts. Eddy ate quickly and left. He was more than anxious to get to work. The whole idea of an Indian attack bothered him. He'd never fought redskins before, but he had fought in the War Between the States. He knew killing and wanted no part of it.

Rounding the corner of the store, he quickly stepped to one side as a burly skinner rushed out the restaurant doorway. Hannah Olds filled the open frame, one hand on her hip and the other holding her broom.

"God—" The skinner cowered as Hannah raised her broom. "Dad-blame-it, Mrs. Olds, I'm hongry!"

"And you stink as well. Don't come back until you wash!"

The skinner watched Hannah go back inside the eatery. He turned to Eddy. "I 'bout had my fill of that woman and her warshin'."

Eddy shrugged. "You can always eat at the Myers and Leonard store."

"Billy Keeler's place?" The skinner shuddered slightly, then grinned, yellowed teeth barely visible through a matted brown beard. "I do believe I'll get me a quick rinse in yon crick." He frowned. "Hell, I say I'm gonna go, only I ain't got nary a stone for soap."

Eddy reached into his pants pocket and extracted a small bar of Castile soap.

"Just so happens one of you gentlemen is regularly asked to remove himself from Hannah's restaurant. I've found it helpful to keep a couple of these on my person."

The skinner took the bar and sniffed it suspiciously. "Lilacs. Shit! Goddam lilac soap!"

"It's the best I have to offer. Hannah and her broom have made sure we're all but sold out of any soap. I'll take it back."

"No, sir, it'll do. I'm much obliged for the trouble. I'll settle accounts after breakfast."

Eddy smiled. "No need. Consider it a gift."

Again came the quick smile. "That's right nice of you. Most shopkeepers'd be looking to gimme the little end of the horn." He held out his hand. "Name's Smith. Sam Smith, buffalo hunter, skinner, woodsman."

Eddy shook Smith's hand, noting the strong grip and sandstone feel.

"George Eddy. I'm over at Rath & Company."

"Pleased to make yore acquaintance, George." Smith sighed and gazed at the bar in his hand. "Well, I reckon I best get to it." He looked up again at Eddy. "Whyn't you meet me to Hanrahan's groggery later. I'll stand you a drink, and we can swap lies."

"I'd enjoy that, Sam."

The hunter waved and ambled toward the creek. For

all his bulkiness, Smith moved with the ease and grace of a panther.

Eddy had started away when he heard his name called. The voice was hoarse and so low he'd thought he'd imagined it.

He turned and saw a half-dozen men approaching him quietly. He recognized the leader as one of Hanrahan's skinners, Shorty. "Mornin'," Eddy said. "What's ailin' your voice?"

Shorty's eyes went wide. "Shhhh! Keep quiet!" he whispered. Staring directly at the open restaurant doorway, he asked, "Is Miz Hannah in there?"

"Course she is," Eddy answered, keeping his voice at a conspiratorial level. Then louder: "Whoa! Wait a minute here. You boys ain't about to go back inside the restaurant again, are you?"

"Dammit, George, keep the noise down!"

Shorty stepped closer. The crown of his hat barely reached the bookkeeper's chin. He grabbed Eddy by the elbow and led him toward the east wall of the store.

"C'mon over here, so's we can talk plain."

Once he was among the skinners, their combined stench made Eddy's stomach roil. He tried to move to one side, but they had him effectively encircled.

Breathing through his mouth, he asked, "What the hell's going on?"

Shorty took over and puffed up all five-foot-nothing of his frame.

"You 'member that day Miz Hannah run us outta her shop?" Eddy nodded. "She chased us with that damn broom of hers. Then, just to pile on the agony, she goes and says we stink so bad that some of her highfalutin customers is gettin' sick."

"Do tell," Eddy managed.

"I swear it, George. Now, we ain't the cleanest men here'bouts, but sayin' that hurt our feelin's. We got 'em, too, y'know."

"I don't doubt that for a moment, Shorty," Eddy gasped.

He'd have agreed to virtually anything to shorten the conversation.

Shorty tipped his hat to the back of his head. "Me and the boys got to speculatin' on what put that bee in Miz Hannah's bonnet. Near's we can reckon, it's 'cause she ain't got no young'uns to love and care for. Only natural for a woman to bear fruit, but I reckon her old man don't got the proper root to do the job. So we aim to fix things."

"What!" Eddy fairly shrieked.

"Calm yourself, man," Shorty said quietly. "Ain't good for a body to go and get hisself all wound up. You just fetch Miz Hannah to the door, and we'll take care of the rest."

The thought of fresh air overrode any misgivings Eddy might have had about Shorty's intentions. He fled to the restaurant door and called for Hannah. The cook arrived, wiping her hands on a flour-sack towel.

"Yes, George?" she said. Then she spotted Shorty and the others approaching. "You men bathe yet?"

Shorty stopped a discreet ten feet away and removed his hat. "Not 'xactly, Miz Hannah. We come to—uh—well, we come to . . . to . . . damn!" He turned and shouted, "Junior, come on out!"

A tall, rail-thin man stepped around the store corner. Behind him, tied to a short tether, followed a mustang colt.

Shorty pointed to the baby horse. "We come 'crosst this 'stang colt. Didn't have no momma, so we figured you might like to keep him. He ain't no use to us."

Hannah's eyes rounded in delight. "Oh, my," she said softly. "Just look at you." She faced Eddy. "Look at him, George. He looks like a chestnut."

Shorty smiled, more than pleased with Hannah's re-action to their gift. "Yes'm, he is. Leastwise, part of him's chestnut. He got stockings on his front legs, too, an—"

"And a white blaze on his forehead," Hannah interrupted. "Oh, Shorty, he's beautiful!" She walked through the gathered men and slowly approached the colt. "Hello, baby," she cooed. "Aren't you a pretty baby, now?"

The colt seemed to sense Hannah meant him no harm, and nuzzled her palm. The cook murmured to him gently as she ran labor-roughened hands tenderly over his back. She turned to Shorty, eyes glistening.

"I . . . I don't know how to thank you." She sniffed, blinking rapidly.

Shorty had hoped Hannah would be grateful for the colt, but the sight of that large woman all teary and at loss for words made him uncomfortable. He never could take a crying woman.

Shuffling his feet, he waved his hat in a gesture of dismissal. "Aw, hell . . . I mean, dang, Miz Hannah, it weren't really so much. Y'know, we . . . uh . . ." He could think of nothing to say and let the sentence die.

Hannah laughed and took the rope from Junior. "The least I can do is feed you and your men. Come on in the restaurant. Breakfast is on me."

Shorty and the others cheered and started for the door. Hannah led her colt away.

"George," she called over her shoulder. "Why don't you get some soap for Shorty and his men so they can wash. I'll be right in."

"What?" The word exploded from the diminutive skinner.

He spun in Hannah's direction, but the cook had already disappeared. With a shout, he threw his hat on the ground.

Eddy quickly stepped into the restaurant, grinning at one of the more inspired strings of profanity he'd ever heard.

* * *

The riders crested the edge of the valley at sundown. Fred Leonard watched as one by one they stopped, silhouetted by the setting sun. He counted six men on horseback. The lack of wagons said they were not hunters. Perhaps they were travelers or desperadoes. Considering the location of Adobe Walls, Leonard doubted the former.

Two of the men started down the hill, with the others falling in line until they formed two columns of three. As they neared, Leonard saw the four riders in the back wore uniform coats. Even in the dim light the bright yellow stripes of a sergeant were easy to see. The leaders wore civilian clothes.

That these men wore military clothing was of little comfort to Leonard. He remembered another time a column of men rode in like this. It was during the Civil War, August 21, 1863. He was living in Lawrence, Kansas, when a troop of men appeared at the edge of town. By the time they left, Quantrill and his raiders had killed over a hundred men and burned down parts of the town. Quantrill had called it an act of war on behalf of the Confederate States of America, but Leonard remembered the killing and pillaging. Many of the worst offenders wore uniforms.

Leonard had also heard tales of Indians dressing in the uniforms of slain soldiers to get near settlements undetected before attacking. A surprised enemy was always easier to kill.

He called over his shoulder. "Bermuda, we have company. Would you please bring me a pistol, and get a shotgun for yourself."

Carlyle quickly appeared at Leonard's side and handed him a weapon. He leaned the shotgun against the wall within easy reach. "Injuns?" he asked quietly.

"Don't know. But they are strangers, and they have no wagons."

Carlyle sent a stream of tobacco spit through the doorway as he watched the riders approach. "Looks like soldier boys to me. You reckon they're deserters?"

"I couldn't say, Bermuda. They may be a legitimate military force, but I want to be prepared for the worst."

The group's leaders reined to a stop outside the Myers and Leonard store. The man with the sergeant stripes rode past the others. He was a large man with broad, square shoulders. He removed his wide-brimmed slouch hat and ran fingers through sweaty black hair. In the fading light, his blue eyes seemed to glow from sockets set on either side of a wide nose. A paint-brush-bristle mustache hid most of his mouth, and dark stubble covered his cheeks and strong chin.

The sergeant quietly regarded the men in the store. "Evening. One of you gentlemen the proprietor of this establishment?"

Leonard stepped forward, pistol behind his back. "I'm Frederick Leonard. I own this store."

The soldier nodded and replaced his hat. "All right, Mr. Leonard. I'm Sergeant J. B. Williams, Sixth Cavalry, out of Camp Supply. I've been sent here to deliver a word of warning to you and the others here. Do you have a central location where we can meet?"

Carlyle sent another stream into the dust. "Hanrahan's place'd be good, Mr. Leonard."

Leonard nodded. "Indeed, Bermuda." He addressed the soldier. "There is a sod saloon just east of the compound. I believe it will suit your needs."

"It will suffice, sir. By the way, besides the watering hole, how many other shops are here?"

Leonard hesitated. If these men were deserters, that kind of information would prove useful. On the other hand, a thirty-second ride would also tell them anything they needed to know. "Two," he replied. "The blacksmith shop is between us and the saloon. Beyond Jim Hanrahan's is the Rath & Company store."

Williams nodded. "Good." He turned to his command. "Chapman, you take Logan and tell the smithy to head to the saloon. McAlister, you take Smith and visit that other shop." He looked at Leonard and touched the brim of his hat. "Gentlemen, I trust I will see you shortly."

The bar was crowded with hunters, teamsters, merchants, and their employees. Eddy made his way to a back table. Fred Leonard, Tom O'Keefe, and Jim Hanrahan were already seated. The man who'd told him of this meeting stood next to a big soldier with sergeant stripes.

The sergeant cleared his throat. "My name's Williams. This detail's from Camp Supply, and I'm in charge, but I'm not the man you need to listen to. Standing to my right is Amos Chapman. He's a scout for the Sixth."

"He's a breed," a voice called out.

Chapman stepped forward. He was a small man dressed in fringed buckskins and beaded moccasins. He had high cheekbones, black eyes, and an aquiline nose. To Eddy, he looked like an Indian until one noticed that the lower half of the scout's face was covered with brown hair.

"I don't mind the word 'breed,'" Chapman began in a husky voice. "Hell, I been called worse'n that by my old woman. 'Sides, it's true. Don't mean nothin'. A body cain't rightly choose his parents, can he?" He paused and glanced around the room. "I live with the Cheyenne back in Indian Territory. My wife's the daughter of a chief, so they kind of adopted me, I reckon. We got some young Comanch hotheads brewing a mess. Seems they've got themselves worked up for a fight and talked a passel of Kiowa, Cheyenne, and even some Arapaho, into joinin' up."

"Sounds to me like the Army's got a problem," O'Keefe said.

Chapman shook his head. "No, sir, we don't. For the last couple a weeks, my Cheyenne been telling me that they're comin' to Texas to kill buffalo hunters."

The room fell silent.

"Bullshit!"

Eddy looked around the bar and saw Henry Born making his way through the crowd. Born, called Dutch Henry by friend and foe alike, was a large man known for his hunting prowess. Eddy had heard stories that the hunter might also have been a horse thief, but without proof, a remark like that could get a man shot.

"Bullshit," Born repeated. "That goddam Injun lover don't know shit. Hell, I'll bet he's a spy for them stinkin' red niggers. They probably sent him here to scare us off."

Williams stepped between Born and Chapman. "Hold on, now. We didn't have to come here and warn you."

"That's right," Born replied. "You didn't. So why're you really here? Army ain't gonna send a patrol clean into Texas to warn a bunch of hide men about Injuns."

"Technically, we're searching for two men who stole a couple of mules from the camp. Their trail led this way, and my company commander thought that as long as we're near here, we may as well inform you of what we've learned. From what we can tell, you have two days to prepare or leave. How you choose to act on this information is up to you."

Born laughed. "You hear that, boys? Sarge here says we're horse thieves."

The men booed and yelled at the soldiers. Eddy heard mumbled threats of lynching the patrol, Chapman in particular. The bookkeeper knew some of the men present had highly questionable backgrounds, but buffalo hunting was a dangerous line of work and drew desperate men.

Williams, sensing the mood of the gathered men, leaned over to Hanrahan. "I don't like this one bit. I'm taking my men downstream a bit and camp there. I think I'd be safer among the Indians right now."

"Why don't you head to the old trading post. It's less than a mile away, and the adobe will offer some protection. I'll be along in a while with some beer for yourself and the men."

The sergeant smiled. "Thank you, Mr. Hanrahan. Any kindness is appreciated." The smile disappeared. "When you come, announce yourself. I'd hate to think of a cold beer wasted by a nervous sentry."

Williams led his men outside amid taunts from the hunters. Eddy noticed Chapman was not among them, and looked to the back door to see him slip out with Wright Mooar.

"Let 'em go," Born said. "Son-of-a-bitches don't know what they're talking about. Anyway, even if it's true, we got the best shooters in the world right here in this saloon. My Sharps can blow a hole through a buffalo, much less any Injun."

Eddy listened to the men brag of their conquests and shooting skills. Many hoped the Indians would attack, and treated the matter as a turkey shoot. He sat quietly at the table. If the Indians did attack and the hunters won, there would be stories for a lifetime. But if the Indians won . . . Eddy wondered how bad scalping hurt.

Sixteen

Quanah sat cross-legged and watched the sun slowly rise above the eastern horizon. The Great Spirit lived there, so some elders said. Others insisted the Great Spirit lived beyond all that man knew, that the only way to talk to Him was through the sun.

Honey-colored light poured over the plains and flowed up the bluff where he sat. Eyes closed against the glare, he felt the cold driven from his body. An eagle cried in the distance. His personal medicine spirit bade him good morning. He spread his arms wide, threw his head back, and basked in healing radiance.

He heard the sound of approaching feet and stole a sidelong glance to his right. Brown Bull sat next to him and said nothing, just closed his eyes and seemed content to sit. Again Quanah looked at Brown Bull, and saw a single bead of sweat work its way down the warrior's broad brown cheek.

"You are up early this morning," Brown Bull said without opening his eyes.

Quanah shrugged and dropped his chin to his chest, allowing his neck muscles to stretch. "I couldn't sleep, so I came out here to greet Father Sun and receive his blessing."

"You must be patient, Quanah. You know this."

"I have no use for patience. It is the game of the

buzzard to fly around and around. My blood carries the spirit of the eagle. I must swoop down and kill my prey."

Brown Bull laughed, his rich baritone voice echoing off the surrounding bluffs. "I wish I were your age again, to be so full of life that each passing hour seems a day, each day a lifetime. I envy you, my brother. Still, even the hunter waits and strikes at the right moment lest the prey escape. True?"

Quanah nodded and sighed. "True."

"Good. We make progress already." Brown Bull rose and stretched. He offered his hand to Quanah, and pulled the young warrior to his feet. "Now, tell me about your plans for today."

Brushing the sand from his legs, Quanah said. "We are to go to the Arapaho village."

"All of you?"

"No, just Isatai and me. The older warriors are teaching everything they can to the young ones. Even with the Cheyenne and Lone Wolf and his men, we number less than three hundred."

"Certainly that is enough to kill a few buffalo hunters." Brown Bull carefully kept his expression neutral, but could not prevent his amusement from showing in his eyes.

Quanah looked deeply into Brown Bull's face, then grunted. Maybe the older man sensed Quanah's doubts. Maybe that was why three hundred seemed such a small number. The young warrior wondered if ten times that many would be enough.

"It will work!" he muttered under his breath. "It must!"

Brown Bull nodded. "And so it shall. Come, let's eat."

Quanah followed his brother down the ridge and back to Brown Bull's lodge. Blue Running Water had prepared a meal of boiled buffalo and corn. The warriors ate heartily and long, finally lighting the pipe.

Satisfied and content, Quanah walked home and dressed for the Arapaho. Brown Bull was right. Three hundred warriors were more than enough for the hunters.

He mounted his horse and rode toward the edge of camp. He waved to his wives and Brown Bull. Isatai waited ahead, dressed in leggings and a bright red and yellow serape. A leather bag tied to the pony held the red blanket and German silver he'd wear at the Arapaho village.

"Quanah, my friend," the shaman hailed. "Are you ready to amaze the Arapaho?"

"I suppose, but I'd prefer to be leading all of our warriors like we did at the Cheyenne camp."

Isatai nodded and turned his pony to the north. "I agree, but then again, the Arapaho have spent more years among the whites than we have. They are like the Yaparika, in that that life is now more to their liking."

"Then why do we bother? They are useless!"

"Not quite, Quanah." Isatai adjusted his position on the grass saddle. "Do not underestimate the Arapaho. They are formidable warriors. Just ask any of their enemies. But they have been led to believe that the white man's way is the only way. We must show them what the Great Spirit has in store for them. Also, with the Arapaho and Cheyenne beside us, we have a way to the tribes of the north, like the Lakota. Imagine it, Quanah, all the tribes banded as one great war party!"

Staring into the distance, Quanah paid little attention to Isatai's remarks. "Yes, one great war party. Isatai, look in the direction of the Kiowa camp. Do you see riders?"

The shaman gazed in the direction Quanah indicated. "I see them. Perhaps they are more warriors for our war party."

The party numbered about a dozen men. As the Indians came closer, Isatai recognized Lone Wolf.

The shaman stepped his horse forward. "Greetings, Lone Wolf. How are the Kiowa today?"

"Well enough," came the chief's curt reply. "Where are you going?"

"To see the Arapaho. Would you care to join us?"

Quanah could see Lone Wolf was in a foul mood. The corners of his mouth were turned down, and a deep scowl furrowed his forehead.

"I am tired of meetings and dances, and I grow weary of waiting. How soon before we find the camp of the hunters?"

Quanah edged forward. "We cannot leave until the full moon. The elders have so spoken. I am as anxious as you to begin, but we must wait."

Lone Wolf stared stonily at Quanah, then sighed deeply. "My wife does not come out of our home. She will not eat. Perhaps the scalps of *these* white men will ease her pain. I can't go back home. I am taking my men to the south again, back into Texas."

"It is your decision, Lone Wolf," Quanah said, then added, "We are to leave on the first night of the full moon. From the camp of the Cheyenne, we will ride south as you do."

"Good. Then on the second night, we will come north to meet you. I am looking forward to fighting at your side, Quanah."

"There is much a war chief of the Kiowa can teach me. The honor is mine."

Lone Wolf regarded Isatai coolly. "Magic man," he said, "I leave it to you to supply us with good medicine."

Isatai smiled. "The Great Spirit rides with us. We will prevail."

The war chief laughed. "If that is the case, I hope He carries a big lance."

Lone Wolf signaled to his men and turned to leave.

Watching their backs, Quanah envied the Kiowa. They were attacking the enemy, not waiting for the permission of old men. While he collected reluctant warriors and boys, they collected scalps.

He angrily kicked his horse and galloped across the prairie. Behind him, Isatai shouted for him to slow down and wait, but Quanah ignored the shaman. If he could not fly into battle, he could at least soar over the plains. Such was the eagle.

Just in sight of the camp, they stopped and Isatai changed into his oratory clothes before they made their entrance.

The Arapaho were polite, attentive, and not really interested in what the Comanche had to say. They made the appropriate noises when Isatai brought forth his arrows and bullets, and Quanah saw many heads nod in agreement with the talk.

Then the chief of the Arapaho rose. "You have good magic," he said in a husky, windblown voice. "I am impressed. And you, young warrior, you speak with a fire in your heart that reminds me of myself as a young man. That is good as well.

"We Arapaho are pretty good fighters, too. We have spilled the blood of many enemies over the years." He paused and drew a deep breath. "Now we sit here on land the white man says is ours. It's not as nice as what we had, but we have peace.

"Our numbers grow smaller, and it is our wish to preserve our warriors as long as possible. Perhaps this medicine man is the one who will lead us all against the whites. Perhaps not.

"I say we send those whose hearts he has stirred to watch the battle. If the Comanche and their friends do well, and the other tribes prepare for major war with the soldiers, let the observers tell us, and we will take the pipe."

With that, the chief sat. Two men of the Lance Men society escorted Quanah and Isatai from the elders' tipi. As police for the Arapaho, these men maintained peace in the village.

Frustrated, Quanah waited by his horse for a final word.

Soon a Lance Man approached them. "Six men will arrive at the Cheyenne village on the night of the full moon. With them will be an elder who will pray for your success. I share in your desire to rid our home of the white man and his soldier, but I am bound by the wishes of my chief." He turned and walked back into the lodge.

"I wish . . . I want . . . bah!" Quanah muttered darkly.

"What did you say?"

"Nothing, Isatai. Everyone wants to help, wishes he could help, would help if he could, but no one acts! Do they not understand the Comanche alone cannot free them of the white invaders?"

The medicine man shrugged. "What can I say? People are afraid of the white man. Fear is very powerful. We will do what we can with the men we have. There are not so many hunters, and once they are gone, all of the tribes will join us. Then we will see who has the fear!"

Morning had arrived at last, and a restless Quanah was up with the first light. He dressed quickly, ate without tasting his food, and settled in his tent to apply war paint. Carefully checking his hair in the small mirror, he muttered darkly as first one area of his scalp, then another showed in the glass. How was he to tell if Chony had parted his hair straight, or the line of vermillion went down that part, if he could only see one hair at a time?

He snorted in irritation, then dipped a finger in a bowl of ochre paint. Starting at the top and in the middle of his forehead, he drew a single yellow line down his face, between his eyes, along the center of his nose, and across his lips and chin, to stop at the base of his neck. He gathered more paint on his fingers and covered the entire left side of his face, carefully skirting around his hairline.

Quanah wiped his fingers on a scrap of leather, then dipped them in white paint and drew two horizontal lines under his right eye. Between them, he painted two red lines. He gazed critically at his features in the mirror. The paint looked good. He grimaced, growled, and shouted at his image.

"Hmm," he said to himself. "Almost, but something is missing." He looked over his collection of paints and spied the black.

He set the mirror aside and scooped the charcoal-based paint into his right palm. Using a stick with one flattened edge, he coated the hand evenly from wrist to fingertips. Retrieving the mirror, he carefully placed the blackened hand across the left side of his face, the thumb under his nose, and pressed firmly.

The yellow side of his face was now covered with a raven-colored hand. His right thumb and forefinger had combined to make a lopsided mustache under his nose and up the side of his face, almost touching the left eye. The middle fingers left black trails across his cheek, and the little finger angled down across his jawbone.

Again he made war faces in the mirror.

"Much better," he said happily, wiping his hands clean.

He inspected his ermine-covered pigtails, gently stroking the fur and admiring the red strips of cloth binding them. He rose and checked his war shirt, looking for anything that might distract the eye. His buckskin leggings, decorated with fringe and scalps, were clean, and he wore a new pair of moccasins beaded with porcupine quills in the old way. The white man's colored beads would not do for war clothing.

Stepping out of the tipi, he noticed the sun had fully cleared the horizon. He enjoyed the warmth. Almost as warm were the gazes of his wives. He smiled at them and strutted before the lodge like a pheasant displaying his feathers.

His heart burst with pride in himself and his people. Today was the start of the great war with the whites. Soon all the Comanche dead would have their revenge. So would the Kiowa and Cheyenne. Bonded by war, the combined tribes would again rule this land. Of course, the most important decisions would be made by Comanche chiefs. After all, they were the People.

The war chief mounted his pony, carefully painted to reflect the attributes of both animal and rider. Weckeah handed him a war bonnet made of golden eagle feathers. When worn, the bonnet's twin trails of feathers reached almost the full length of his body. The bonnet was neither earned by heroic deeds, nor was it the property of chiefs. Instead, any seasoned warrior could ask to wear it, the only stipulation being that he must fight bravely and fearlessly as long as it was on.

Chony handed him his lance and coup stick. The spear was covered in ermine matching his hair wraps. Two scalps hung just behind its iron point. The coup stick, bent like a shepherd's crook, was wrapped in red cloth and decorated with eagle feathers and scalps. He took the weapons, nodded to his wives, and rode toward the edge of camp.

He was joined by Isatai, who wore his red sash and breechclout. The German silver bracelets sparkled in the sunlight, and his rattlesnake earrings chattered with each step the horse made. Isatai rode unarmed, and his pony was covered in bright yellow paint.

"Isatai," called Quanah. "You carry no weapons?"

"The Great Spirit protects me this day and all the days we are on the warpath. His magic paint shields my horse. I need no weapons."

Passing the last tipi, the two Comanches were joined by Black Beard, He Bear, Tabananica, Chiefs Stone

Calf and Red Moon of the Cheyenne, Woman's Heart of the Kiowa, and Chief Spotted Wolf of the Arapaho.

The leaders began their journey out onto the plains and south toward Texas. The rest of the war party would leave later. That night there would be a huge fire and dance to celebrate the final liberation of the plains tribes from the white man.

Seventeen

Seventeen

Fred Leonard woke up shivering. He opened his eyes. Low, dark clouds rolled over him like waves breaking on a beach. He sat up, expecting to see the damp gray-green of the English countryside, its colors washed out by the ever-present pall of fog. Instead, he saw a picket wall ten feet high and stacks of dried buffalo hides.

Leonard stood, grabbed boots with one hand, bedroll with the other, and hurried through the back door of the Myers and Leonard store. Dropping the items just inside the doorway, he padded across the floor in stocking feet to the Ben Franklin stove. He reached out as though to embrace the device, and bathed in its radiant warmth. As he turned to take the chill off his backside, he spotted Carlyle quietly gazing at him over the rim of a steaming cup of coffee.

"Good morning, Bermuda," Leonard said.

"Mornin', Boss." Carlyle sipped at his coffee. " 'Pears a mite nippy."

Leonard grunted. He sighed, rubbed his back, then stretched. "Oh, yes, much better. Have you another cup?"

"Yes, sir, been expecting you." Carlyle tossed Leonard a tin coffee cup. "Coffee's right behind you."

The shopkeeper turned, and only then noticed the blue-enameled pot. "Why, so it is."

Leonard poured himself a cup of coffee. "Let us address our current situation as perceived from your outlook."

"Meanin', is the Injuns comin'?"

Leonard nodded.

Carlyle rubbed his face. "I don't know." He raised a hand. "Now, afore you say anything, hear me out. I've met a passel of soldiers in my time, and more'n enough Injuns. That there sergeant seems to me to be a pretty honest fellow. I don't know about the scout. Breeds is hard men to know or understand. Sometimes I think it's the Injun blood what makes 'em so different."

"And the Indians themselves?"

"Hell, Mr. Leonard, I'd as soon try to predict the weather as guess what a redskin will do. But you got to figure, we know there's a shipment of rifles and ammo due any day now. If *they* know, too . . ."

Leonard sat a moment and sipped his coffee while he mulled over Carlyle's suggestion. "Tell me honestly, do you think we can keep them from taking the post?"

"There is only two things I seen that scared the hell out of me. One was a cyclone dancing and skippin' across the prairie, first picking this to kill, then that. No rhyme or reason to it, just a great big twistin' wind sucking the life out of the land."

"And the other?" Leonard asked softly.

"Think of it as a cyclone with feathers in its hair."

Leonard shivered at the idea, then checked his watch. "I'm late, Bermuda. It seems our Mr. Hanrahan has called an emergency meeting of the shop owners this morning."

James Langton arrived first, silk hanky all a-flutter, followed by a groggy, sleepy-eyed George Eddy. Tom O'Keefe walked in next, damp stains under his arms showing he'd already been working. Leonard appeared last, apologizing for his tardiness.

Once the men were seated, Hanrahan had ordered Shepherd to clear the bar. He stationed Mike Welch at the back door and the bartender in the front to keep anyone else out.

Eddy stared at the men before him. Hanrahan looked nervous and irritated, O'Keefe just nervous. Leonard kept his British upper lip stiff, but his eyes flicked back and forth. Only Langton looked calm, as though he suffered from serene boredom. The Rath manager produced his handkerchief and used it like a signal flag.

"Well, before we decide anything, let us review our facts. First"——the hand flipped and the hanky fluttered——"everything I own is invested in the store. If the store goes, I am ruined.

"Second"——another flip and flutter——"we don't *know* the savages are going to attack. After all, we have only the word of a man who is half-savage himself.

"And finally"——flip, flutter, flip——"we have many men here and a great deal of ammunition, not to mention thick earthen walls."

"It's easy for the likes of you," O'Keefe said pensively. "You can hide behind those thick walls, but my shop's got picket walls with no chinking. Them damn redskins got more than enough room to shove a barrel between them boles and shoot me."

He turned to face the rest of the shopkeepers. "Now, what I can't load on a wagon, I can replace in Dodge, but I can't get my scalp back. Staying here is foolhardy at best and liable to be the death of us all!"

Embarrassed by his outburst, the blacksmith stared at the tabletop.

"Anyway," he mumbled, "that's how I feel about it."

"Fair enough, Tom," Hanrahan said. "You're entitled to your opinion. How about you, Fred? You surely have feelings about what's happening."

Leonard sat a moment to gather his thoughts, then took a deep breath. "For the sake of argument, let us consider the threat real. As I see it, we have two avenues available. We can stay and fight, as Mr. Langton suggests, or pack and leave, as per Mr. O'Keefe. Should we stay, there is a chance that we will be overrun. As for you, Tom, you may join us at the store or come here to Jim's saloon.

"On the other hand, if we pack and leave, we may escape. Do bear in mind, though, the scout said the Indians would arrive in two days. One is already under way. Packing would require the rest of this day, and the heathens may be here in the morning. Worse still, finding us gone, they might attack us on the trail where we have little or no protection. On that basis, I fear, there is but one course—stay and fight."

"I believe that's enough discussion," Hanrahan said quickly. "Let's vote. Fred's already cast his ballot. How about you, Langton? Stay or leave?"

"Stay."

"George?"

"Stay."

"I vote stay as well. And you, Tom? Will you make it unanimous?"

"Why the hell not? It ain't likely any of you fools are going to change your mind. If I'm to die, I might as well die among friends."

"Splendid!" cheered Leonard. "What I propose next is to inform the men and pre—"

"Hell, no!" Hanrahan interrupted. "We ain't saying nothing to nobody."

"Are you mad? These men need time to check weapons and pick defensive positions."

Hanrahan sighed. "Can't you see, Fred? They ain't got a thing to lose. You let them goddam worthless son-of-a-bitches think the Indians are really comin', they'll light out quicker'n a nigger at a Klan meeting. If you really want us defenseless, just let word of this get-together out. Before you know it, there'll be just us to hold on to what's ours."

"So what do you propose?" the Englishman asked.

"Chapman said two days. That means tomorrow by my reckoning. Ain't no self-respecting Indian gonna attack us on a day like today. If the weather holds, or it really rains, they can't do anything for at least another day."

"So you plan to wait them out?" Eddy asked.

"Sure. Indians ain't like regular people. They got no stomach for waiting around until next time. If we get past this full moon, they'll like as not see it as a sign from the spirits and attack somebody else."

"Yes, but, Mr. Hanrahan," Langton said, silken square alive and dancing in the air, "what shall we do if tomorrow is cloudless and warm?"

Hanrahan flinched at the question. "Well, Langton, I reckon I'll have to come up with something, but I assure you when—and if—the time comes, we'll be ready."

The rain came as no surprise to Dixon and his men. They had watched its steady progress across the plains toward them. Dixon had hoped to make Adobe Walls before the weather let loose, but fate seemed against them.

Behind him, the wagons rattled and swayed as iron-clad wheels slipped in rain-slick ruts quickly churned into mud. Occasionally, a shout of encouragement or curse came from Armitage and Frenchy as they man-handled the overloaded vehicles. On the whole, though, each of the four men quietly endured soaked clothing and soggy boots.

Fortunately, the Canadian had not yet risen, and their crossing at the mouth of White Deer Creek was uneventful. The sight of the red swirling water reminded Dixon of another crossing and the loss of his rifle and a good mule. His mood soured, he huddled under a buffalo robe to ward off the cold rain, and allowed Jack to set his own pace.

Frenchy shivered as his hat brim buckled and a torrent of water ran down his back. He groped for a half-empty gin bottle, pulled the cork with his teeth, and spat the stopper into the rain. The bottle, quickly drained, followed the cork. As the skinner returned to his driving, he cursed the liquor's lack of effect.

When the rain started, Armitage pulled his old oil-skin coat from beneath the seat. Over the coat he wrapped a buffalo robe. Relatively dry and warm, the Englishman reflected on how much the weather reminded him of home, and contemplated a hot cup of tea at the post.

McCabe followed Dixon and the wagons. Wet and miserable, he'd long ago stopped watching for Indians. Back at work less than a week, he'd yet to skin a buffalo. Worse still, all this talk of war parties made him nervous, but as time passed and nothing happened, anxiety turned to irritability. Now he was mad at the Indians for not showing.

The small wagon train plodded across the valley, finally rounding the corner of the Myers and Leonard compound. Dixon dismounted in front of the main store and handed his reins to McCabe, telling the skinner to stable the horses. McCabe nodded and rode on.

Armitage pulled his wagon around until its tailgate faced the building. He waited patiently as Frenchy climbed down from his own wagon and opened the shop's wide double doors.

"Back!" he ordered, lightly slapping the reins down. "C'mon, mules, back up!"

To reinforce the command, Dixon and Frenchy each took a mule by the halter and pushed the animals backward until the wagon rolled into the store, completely out of the weather. The mules were protected by a narrow porch roof that extended about five feet from the building. Frenchy waved his farewell and ran back into the rain to move his wagon through the gate and into the hide yard.

Carlyle approached the hide men, grinning. "Well, goddam, lookit here!" He laughed. "A finer pair of drowned rats I ain't never seen."

Armitage said, "Thank you. Your keen perception is only exceeded by your rapier wit."

Carlyle chuckled. "I reckon you and Mr. Leonard have got probably the kindest way of callin' a man a asshole as I ever heard. Regular poetry." He spat a brown glob into the wet sand and continued. "Now, gentlemen, what can I do for you?"

Dixon took off his hat and slapped it across his leg, sending out a fine spray of water. "I got some flint hides in here, but I'm worried about the green ones under 'em. You reckon I can unload here and lay them out until the rain quits?"

"Don't see why not. We can throw the flints over by the counter. If'n they ain't too wet, take the greeners and stretch 'em out over the sacks in the back."

Dixon nodded and walked to the back of the wagon. He pulled the pins and lowered the tailgate while Armitage climbed into the bed. Together, they made short work of off-loading the buffalo hides.

"All right, Charley, you dry out a bit. I'm gonna take this rig over to Tom's and have him check the singletree."

"You could wait until the bloody rain is finished."

Dixon shrugged. "Why? I'm already soaked to the bone."

He climbed into the box and drove the wagon out of the store. Once outside, he continued around the end of the stockade and to the blacksmith's shop.

O'Keefe's door stood wide open. Inside, Dixon could see the smith pounding on a piece of metal, producing a shower of red sparks. The hunter reined to a halt just outside the door and hurried in.

"Afternoon, Billy," O'Keefe called. "Must be something mighty important to bring you out on a day like this."

Dixon shook off a new layer of water and gripped O'Keefe's hand. "Hell, I'm wet head-to-foot now, couldn't see where a drop or two more would make no matter. 'Sides," he added with a slow smile, "thought I'd get my bath in early."

O'Keefe smiled and absently brushed a raindrop from his forehead. "You'll get no complaints from me. Between the forge and the summer heat, I feel like I'm making horseshoes in hell." He pointed to the wagon. "Problems?"

"Cain't rightly say, Tom. Charley's been bitchin' about something being jiggered up with the front end."

"Alrighty, I'll look her over. By the way, what do you make of this Indian business?"

"Which?"

"What that scout and them soldiers said last night. Ain't you heard?"

Dixon shook his head. "No, sir, we were out on the plains last night. What'd he say?"

"Nothing much really, just that every goddam Injun in the territory was coming to kill us."

Sheets of water swept across the little valley, pushed by a steady northerly wind. The Rath employees gathered in Hannah's restaurant and huddled close to the stove.

"Never know it was summer," Olds complained, tightly gripping his coffee cup.

"Hallo! *Bist du zum Haus?*"

Andy Johnson jumped to his feet.

"I know dat voice!" he shouted as he ran for the front door.

Eddy followed Johnson through the Rath & Company store, but stopped short of running into the rain.

"Jacob Scheidler, Hertzlich Wilkommen!" Johnson pronounced the first name "Yah-cobe." "Come on down out of the rain."

Scheidler, wrapped head-to-foot in a buffalo robe, had difficulty getting out of the box. Johnson caught him just as he slipped. The big Swede, who stood a head taller than his German friend, picked the hunter up and carried him into the shop.

Eddy watched a huge black head poke out from under the tarpaulin covering the wagon bed. With one booming bark, a Newfoundland dog almost the size of a yearling leapt from the wagon and followed the others in.

Johnson set his bundle down and beamed as Scheidler emerged from beneath the hide. The German was short, but had the same stocky build as Johnson. He had close-cropped blond hair, bright blue eyes, and, something Eddy noticed about all the people he'd met from Sweden, Germany, or Austria, rosy cheeks.

Johnson laughed. "You look well, my friend!"

"Ja, I suppose, but I am . . . how do you say? *Auf die Haut nass."*

"Soaked to the skin."

"Ja, that is true. *Heute ist schlechtes Wetter."*

"Is not so bad. Soon the rain stops, and it is hot again. That is what *I* call nasty weather."

Eddy stepped forward, hand outstretched. "Shorty, it's good to see you again."

"Danke, George. I would not have come, but *meine Brüder ist* supposed to meet me here. I bringed in a load of hide, too. You know, we have the *geld aufbringen*—we have to make the money."

"Und how is Isaac doing?" Johnson asked.

"Real good. He is in Dodge City taking care of family business, but I hope he gets in soon."

"In the meantime," Johnson said, "we will drink some beer and have some fun."

"Sounds good to me, but first, I must have a dry *hemd* . . . uh . . . shirt and new trousers."

"Komm mit mir. We will get you new clothes, and you can change in the back."

"Und meine Hund?"

Johnson glanced at the Newfoundland.

"Him, too." He threw a massive arm around Scheidler's shoulders. "Have you heard the news of the killings?"

The hunter shook his head.

"So far we have lost four men to the Indians. Some soldiers came and said more Indians are coming here."

Leonard stared out the door and wondered if the Indians would pour over them like the rain, unstoppable, flowing into every available space. He sighed and tapped his pipe against a boot heel, dumping tobacco onto the floor. "I believe I will join Mr. Armitage at the cafe for tea."

"Fine by me, Boss," Carlyle answered. "Ain't likely to be no rush of customers today."

"True." Leonard faced his employee. "Bermuda, why do you stay here?"

"It's more comfortable than sleeping on the ground."

"That's not what I meant. You heard that scout. No one would blame you for leaving."

Carlyle waved his hand in dismissal. "Hell, them Comanches ain't gonna attack us. We got nothing they want, unless you count the guns, bullets, whiskey, buffalo hides, and our scalps."

Leonard smiled gently. "In spite of it all, you can

joke. You know, you'd make a good Brit, stiff upper lip and all."

"Now, that could scare a man."

"Oh, I don't—" Leonard paused and cocked his head to one side. "I say, do you hear a noise?"

Carlyle rose and walked to the open door. He stopped and listened. "Sounds like another wagon."

Two mules trudged by, heads hung low. As a second pair passed the door, a voice called out, "Whoa! Hold up now, mules!" The animals ignored the command and continued to plod blindly. "Goddammit, I said hold up now!"

The wagon stopped, its team turning to face the storm. Leonard knew mules were like that. In bad weather, a horse would turn tail to the misery, but mules, contrary by nature, looked the storm in the eye.

Dirty Face Ed Jones jumped from the driver's seat and hurried into the store. Once inside, he pulled off his hat and slapped it against his leg, sending water flying.

"Jesus Sweet Christ A'Mighty! Dumb-ass mules woulda walked clean to Mexico." Jones stopped his tirade to grin at Leonard and Carlyle. "Howdy, boys. How in the goddam name of hell are ya? See them ornery-ass mules walk by? I swear, by God, I truly do. Well, whatcha standing there for? Man comes to see you through the biggest rain since Noah and nary a greetin' for a weary traveler."

Carlyle sent liquid tobacco into the dirt at the teamster's feet. "If'n you'd shut your cake-hole a minute, you might just get a by-the-bye. Howdy, Ed. Good to see you."

The three men shook hands, then Jones moved to the stove.

"Man'd catch his death today," he said, holding his hands toward the Franklin stove.

"Why didn't you stop and wait out the weather?" Leonard asked.

"Hell, no! Ain't you heard? Redskins on the war-path. I done drove the last ninety miles with no sleep. I aim to unload, let the mules rest a mite, and get my sorry ass to home. If'n I was you, I'd go, too."

"Balls!" Carlyle punctuated the remark with an-other stream of spit. "Couple'a men lose their hair, the Nancy-boys is ready to run away! Ain't no Injun trouble for certain."

Jones shrugged. "Suit yourself, son. Your funeral, but I run into Wright Mooar about eight miles out, and he's headed to Dodge. Whyn't ya'll help me un-load these crates so's I can get me some sleep." He suddenly chuckled.

Leonard shot him a quick look. "Something amus-ing, Mr. Jones?"

"I'm haulin' six boxes of Sharps and better'n twenty-five hundred rounds of big-bore ammo. Any red visitors you get are in for one hot howdy-do!"

Hanrahan wiped up the small puddle on the bar with a sodden towel and shifted the pail under the new leak.

"Goddam rain," he muttered.

Eddy looked down the length of the saloon. The bar was lined in buckets, bowls, jars, anything that would hold water.

Hanrahan shouted, "Oscar!"

Shepherd stepped back through the saloon's front door, a hand-rolled cigarette dangling from the corner of his mouth. "Yeah, Boss."

"What's the weather doing?"

The bartender removed the cigarette and spat out a bit of tobacco. "Nothing much. Rain's down to a fine drizzle."

"Good. Grab Mike Welch, and stack some more sod along that ridgepole. Don't look to be leaking any-where else."

Shepherd sighed and flicked the remainder of his cigarette through the doorway. "It's supper time, Jim. Mike's probably at Hannah's place."

"I don't give a shit! All I want is more sod on that goddam roof before nightfall. Understood?"

Shepherd nodded and turned to leave, only to run into Bat Masterson.

"Hey, Bat," he said sourly, and left without further comment.

"Oscar." Masterson watched the bartender walk off. He shrugged and approached the bar. "Evenin', Hanrahan. You tending tonight?"

"Yep. Oscar's got a chore. Drink?"

Masterson nodded. "Beer. Hey, George."

Eddy raised his half-empty beer. "Bat. Miserable weather."

"Yes, sir, it is."

"A beer for the gentleman," Hanrahan said cheerfully, setting a bottle of Kirmeyer's on the bar. "Pickled egg or something?"

"No, sir, don't believe I will. Beer and eggs give me the farts." Masterson looked around the empty saloon. "Mite quiet, ain't it?"

"Supper time for most. I reckon the others are hiding from the rain."

Conversation gave way to companionable silence as Masterson slowly drank his beer. Quiet never bothered Eddy. He often hated to be in the saloon when it was full and noisy.

"What's a man got to do to get a drink around here?" a loud voice called from the saloon's front door.

The speaker came through the doorway slowly and walked to the bar. He was a young man with dark hair and eyes and those chiseled good looks women like. Several days' worth of patchy beard discolored the new arrival's cheeks. His trail clothes were dampened by the rain. A Colt .44 rode low on his hip, its holster tied to his right thigh.

Masterson regarded the other coolly. Then a slow smile spread on his face. "Buy you a beer, Billy?"

The other grinned back. "Thanks, Bat."

Hanrahan opened another bottle of Kirmeyer's and set it on the bar.

"Mr. Hanrahan, George," Masterson said, "I'd like you to meet Billy Tyler."

"Tyler." Hanrahan shook the cowboy's hand. "You wear that hog-leg .44 like you mean business."

"I been jumpy since the Cimarron."

"Why?" Eddy asked sharply.

Tyler offered a half smile and tugged at an ear. "Well, we come across Wright Mooar and his bunch headed for Dodge, and they were looking everywhere but at us. They were real convinced that something awful was about to happen. In fact, one of 'em told me to git back to Dodge 'cause I was going to fall early in this fight."

Masterson frowned. "Hell of a thing to say."

"You're telling me."

"Whatcha gonna do?"

Tyler drank deeply of his beer and covered a belch. "Don't rightly know. I *do* know I ain't settin' foot on the plains for a while."

"Come work for Mr. Leonard then. Hell, we got plenty to do now, and when the hunters go back out, we'll be even busier."

"Reckon so?"

"Sure." Masterson laughed. "Ain't no Indians going to attack us here. You'll be safe as a tick on a old hound dog. Ain't that right, Mr. Hanrahan?"

Hanrahan lied. "Sure, Bat, ain't a Injun within a hundred miles of here."

Eighteen

The wind blew steadily, drawing a low moan from the trees surrounding the war party's camp. Quanah watched the low gray clouds slide by, and felt the heavy wetness of impending rain. He turned to Isatai.

"Two medicine men in the camp, and this is the weather I get?" Quanah spoke softly and evenly. "Was cold, wet rain a part of your prayers, Isatai? Perhaps we should blame the old Arapaho. After all, he prays alone, away from the camp."

Isatai shifted uncomfortably under Quanah's glare. "No one asked me to pray for warm weather, plenty of sunshine, or blue skies. I sought wisdom from the spirits, strength for battle, assurance that the paint would not fail. If you wanted sunny days, too, you should have asked."

"I'm asking now."

"Now? Impossible!" the shaman sputtered. "Weather cannot be changed at a moment's notice. The wind blows; the rain prepares to come. The Great Spirit works hard to make these things happen. I can't say to Him, 'Wait a moment. Save the rain until after the whites are dead.' I mean, what if another medicine man has asked for this rain?"

"Oh, so you can't stop it?"

Isatai fidgeted. Their conversation was drawing a crowd. "I didn't say 'can't.' There is nothing that is not within my powers, but you have to consider the other shaman. If this rain is in answer to a prayer, and I stop it, the spirits will surely tell the other man. Then where would we be? One man asks, another refuses to allow it to happen. Soon nothing gets done as medicine men battle one another instead of getting down to their work."

Quanah sighed. "So what can you do?"

"I will talk to the Great Spirit himself before we leave here. If this weather is in answer to a prayer, it will have to run its course. Whatever happens today, I will ask for warm weather and sunny skies as long as we are on the warpath."

Isatai scowled, wishing the subject was closed.

Quanah turned to Brown Bull, who had come with the others to listen to the two speak. "You heard?"

The older warrior nodded.

"Could it be that these clouds are a message sent to us to return home? That if we kill these hunters the soldiers will fall on us like rain?"

Before Brown Bull could answer, one of the old chiefs, Tabananica, came forward. He raised his hands for silence, and the talk subsided among three hundred men.

"We know why we are here," he said calmly. "The matter has been discussed many times among the chiefs."

He faced south and swept his arm before him.

"Out there lies the enemy. But where?" He turned to Quanah. "Do you know?"

Quanah felt his face flush. In all the excitement, no one had bothered locating the hunters. He looked at Isatai, but the shaman only shrugged.

"Try the Canadian River."

As one, the warriors turned toward the new voice. Ten feet away stood Lone Wolf and his lieutenant, Bear Mountain. Both men had arrived on foot, and had managed to walk up to the camp undetected.

Tabananica recovered quickly. "You know this is true?"

Lone Wolf stepped through the ranks of men until he stood next to the old Comanche chief.

"It is merely a guess, but I have killed several hunters already. Their wagon tracks lead toward the Canadian River; help arrives from the same direction. I say send some men to scout along that river. There you will find your hunters' village."

Tabananica nodded, then addressed the war party. "I know of Lone Wolf. He is a wise warrior, and I trust his judgment. Do any of you disagree with me or the Kiowa chief?" He paused, but received no reply from his audience. "White Wolf, gather seven men and go to the Canadian. Find the houses of the buffalo hunters."

Quanah awoke to the sound of much movement and excitement. A brief question posed to a passing warrior garnered a briefer answer—"Hunting." Quanah ran to Isatai's campsite, and found the medicine man with Tabananica and Lone Wolf.

"We hunt?" Quanah asked the three. "The day before battle, we hunt?"

"Tomorrow will be the first battle for many of these warriors," Tabananica said. "Over and over, we have seen them check their equipment, resharpen sharp knives, and put on war paint just to remove it. They have too much time to sit and think about what the morning will bring."

"So," Isatai broke in, "Lone Wolf thought a buffalo hunt would be just the thing to distract everyone until we move on. I agree with him. If the warriors are tired tonight, they will sleep well and fight better."

Quanah pondered what he'd heard. He had no authority to disband the hunt. Even if he had, what harm could come of it?

"Perhaps you're right," he said, then grinned. "In fact, I think I will hunt as well."

He ran back to his campsite and retrieved the rifle bought from the Comanchero. He mounted his war pony and proceeded out of camp, accompanied by Brown Bull and Lone Wolf.

Nearing the herd, the trio reined to a halt. Quanah opened the rifle's rolling block and inserted a three-inch cartridge.

"What are you planning to do with *that?*" Brown Bull asked, pointing at the rifle.

"Shoot a buffalo," Quanah answered lightly. "This is the gun the whites use. I want to see what's so special about the rifle that will kill all the buffalo."

Lone Wolf adjusted his position and leaned forward. "How are you going to do it?"

"Just like we do now," the young warrior said. How else would he kill a buffalo but ride beside him, point, and shoot?

"Oh." Lone Wolf paused a moment, then continued, "The white hunters I've seen almost always fire while on foot. Many lie down or lean against a tree."

"Bah!" Quanah grinned. "Anything a white man can do on foot can be done better by a Comanche on horseback."

He kicked his mount, and was soon riding beside the now-running herd.

He picked out a large bull and drew his horse nearer, knowing the animal's reflexes would protect them both should the buffalo suddenly turn and charge. Dropping the reins, he gripped the horse's sides tightly with his thighs and knees. He held the rifle in both hands and sighted on the buffalo just behind the left shoulder. Target found, the warrior gently pulled the trigger.

What happened next Quanah would never know first-hand. What he did remember was the deep feeling of self-satisfaction as he prepared to fire. The next sight he saw was a ring of concerned faces looking down at him.

"Are you all right?" Brown Bull asked.

Quanah sat up slowly. He felt no broken bones, could not feel the warm stickiness of flowing blood.

"I think so. What happened? Did the bull charge?"

The warriors laughed. They laughed harder and asked each other if the bull charged. They practically howled as first one, then another, acted out a foolish routine that consisted of standing in one spot, then jumping straight back and landing on his butt.

Quanah struggled to his feet. Peering through the ranks, he saw the herd disappearing in the distance. Scattered here and there were the distinctive black mounds of dead buffalo. He was worried about his warhorse until he spotted the Kiowa, Bear Mountain, riding toward them and leading the pony.

"Now that you all have had a good laugh, maybe someone will tell me what has happened."

Brown Bull wiped tears from his eyes. "You really don't know?"

Quanah shook his head.

"We watched you ride to the herd. Then we saw you take aim on a big bull. Suddenly there was a boom like thunder. The horse went one way; you went the opposite direction, and the herd . . ."

Brown Bull started to laugh again, tears rolling freely down his cheeks.

"And the herd, the *whole* herd, turned and ran over the hill. I have never seen one warrior turn a whole herd before, especially while sailing through the air like a feather in a storm."

The gathered warriors once again broke into laughter. Quanah felt his face redden until he thought he must glow. There was nothing to be done but take the jokes with the best possible face. As the men quieted down, Bear Mountain presented him his mount.

Taking the reins, the young warrior grinned sheepishly. "Perhaps, Bear Mountain, this weapon must be tamed by a man such as you."

"Oh, no, Quanah." Bear Mountain smiled gently. "If the buffalo rifle is powerful enough to unseat a Comanche warrior, it would probably kill this poor Kiowa."

The location White Wolf had chosen as the site of the main camp pleased Lone Wolf. There was a stream for fresh water, trees for relief from the sun, and plenty of grass for the stock. He immediately had Bear Mountain check on each Kiowa warrior.

"Remember," he told Bear Mountain, "I want you to make sure the men only take what is necessary for the battle tomorrow."

"Lone Wolf, do you think we will win this battle?" the lieutenant asked quietly.

"Of course. This fort, village, or whatever the white men call it, will fall quickly. This is the easy fight. But the smoke of this battle will stir the hearts of the whites, making each remaining battle more difficult than the last."

"And we will win them all! Then the soldiers and hunters will leave the plains, and the buffalo will return."

"You've been listening to that yellow Comanche, haven't you?"

Lone Wolf smiled to remove any sting the remark might have carried.

"I hope you're right, but I fear that a long war means the end of all Indians. Many white men's houses will be emptied to pay for the life of my son, but one day, a white man's boots will grind my bones to dust."

* * *

The campfires, small and built from very dry wood, made little smoke. The war party had settled into their final camp for the night.

Some warriors painted themselves with the magic ochre paint provided by Isatai. Others, already painted, dozed. Quanah knew these were the more seasoned warriors. He heard the nervous chatter of the young men. Occasionally laughter erupted as one or another boasted of a deed he'd performed in the past, each embellishing on the other's story until the tale was unbelievable.

Isatai had drawn himself to one side, and was dancing and asking the spirits to shine on them for the next day's battle. He beseeched the Great Spirit to allow the magic paint to perform as promised. As he danced, his German silver ornamentation flashed in the firelight like the muzzle blasts of tiny rifles. Sweat ran down the shaman's cheeks and left long dark trails in his makeup.

In the distance, Quanah heard more chanting, and knew it was the Arapaho medicine man. Since the first day of their journey, the old man had taken himself far away from the camp to talk to his spirits. None among the war party had witnessed what he did, but eventually the shaman would return, drink a little water, and retire to his buffalo-robe bed.

The medicine men were not the only solitary figures that night before battle. Some of the warriors kept away from the others. Perhaps some feared death or the loss of face in front of an enemy. Maybe they were afraid they'd collect no coups or scalps. Whatever their thoughts, Quanah neither desired nor attempted to question these lone soldiers. Each man faced war in his own way.

For Quanah, the time for speculation was past, worries now a thing of another time. The battle would be joined, and the spirits and his personal medicine would determine the outcome for him. His only concern was for his men. Three hundred warriors willing to allow one young man to decide their fate. He had to lead.

To this end, Quanah wandered the camp offering words of encouragement to any who asked. He exuded a confidence he didn't really feel, but knew the men expected. The older warriors understood Quanah's actions, and sounded war cries until the camp rang with their calls.

Reaching the camp he shared with Brown Bull, Quanah sat on a buffalo robe. He pulled a stick from the fire and tore off a piece of half-cooked buffalo meat. Savoring the taste, he felt content.

"The camp sounds good," Brown Bull said, his face cast in deep shadows by the flickering firelight. "There is much optimism in the air."

Quanah nodded. "That is as it should be. Doubts and fears must be left behind. I may curse this battle, lament the death of friends, perhaps lie dead or wounded myself, but that is for after the battle. Now we are invincible. We are the People—unbeaten and unbowed before any enemy!"

Nineteen

Hanrahan's bar was filled to overflowing by the residents and visitors of Adobe Walls. The party was to celebrate the return to hunting. Even the antisocial Langton had joined in.

Dixon sat at a table with Bat Masterson, Charley Armitage, and Frenchy. Though physically present, the latter was so deep in his cups, his head had been down on the table for the last half hour.

"This one will suffer on the morrow," Masterson shouted over the noise, pointing at Frenchy.

Dixon nodded. "True, but he'll be in good company."

He grinned at his friend, the slightly crooked smile the only indication he'd been drinking.

Someone produced a fiddle, and a reel scratched its way across the room. The men pushed and shoved each other for a chance to dance with Hannah Olds, the only woman present, who seemed delighted with all the male attention. William Olds stood at the bar, a frown creasing his pinched face.

Dixon laughed and pointed at Olds. "William seems a mite unhappy over Mrs. Olds's popularity."

"I don't believe it's the popularity that bothers him," Armitage said. "I daresay he's put out by the fact she's enjoying it."

Frenchy sat up unsteadily and looked Armitage in

the face. "Damned Englishman!" he shouted. His eyes rolled whitely, and he crashed to the floor.

"My, oh, my," Armitage clucked. "That was rather uncivil."

Masterson looked at the prostrate form on the floor. "You reckon we oughta move him?"

Dixon sighed. "Sure as we don't, somebody'll trip over him and kill theirselves."

The three men lifted the unconscious Frenchy and deposited him against a saloon wall. Satisfied with a job well done, they returned to their table.

"Oh, shit!" Dixon swore.

"Problem?" Armitage asked.

"Nothing a walk can't cure," Dixon replied, grinning.

The hunter stood and walked unsteadily to the saloon's front door. The night air felt cool and refreshing after the hot, smoke-filled atmosphere inside Hanrahan's. The silence roared in his ears. He took a deep breath and made his way to the side of the building. He fumbled with his pants buttons, muttering to himself.

"Billy?" a voice called. "Billy Dixon, is that you?"

"Hell, yes. Who's that?"

"It's me, Hanrahan. What are you doing?"

"Pissing on your saloon. Why? You wanna watch?"

"Hell, no. I thought we might have us a little talk out here."

"Oh," Dixon said. "All right by me, but I'd appreciate you letting me put myself together. After all, the sight of my manhood has caused women to faint and men to marvel."

Hanrahan chuckled. "Horseshit."

Dixon completed his task and ambled around the saloon's corner. Lighted by a full moon, Hanrahan looked like a scarecrow.

The hunter offered his best lopsided smile. "What can I do for you, friend?"

"I hear you're headed out to the plains tomorrow."

"That I am. I got me three good skinners, a new Sharps, and millions of buffalo. Sorta seemed to me I may as well make use of 'em."

"Hmm," Hanrahan replied, handing Dixon a bottle of Kirmeyer's. "You reckon to keep them three busy?"

"I can keep twice that many hopping."

"How about three times as many?"

"There's enough buffalo out there to keep twenty skinners working day and night."

"Good. What I propose is that we join forces. I will supply you with my six skinners. You shoot, the others skin, and we split the profits fifty-fifty."

Dixon took a long pull on his beer and thought. By forming a partnership with the saloon keeper, there'd be ten men in the hunting party. A group that large would deter most Indian attacks, and the extra hides skinned would bring in a handsome income. He stuck out his hand.

"Done."

Later, a hot and tired Dixon stepped from the saloon. The first thing he noticed was the lack of a breeze. The inside of Hanrahan's had grown hot and stuffy from cigar smoke and gamy from sweating bodies. He'd looked forward to a cooling wind, and the stillness disappointed him.

He walked around the saloon toward O'Keefe's shop. Near the blacksmith's establishment loomed the dark shapes of his wagons and those Hanrahan had supplied.

Jack snorted softly. The horse was tied to the vehicle Armitage would drive in the morning. Dixon ran a hand over the animal's side. He then placed the new Sharps between two blankets to protect it from the dew and rain. Next to his life, Dixon's rifle and horse were his most prized possessions. He didn't intend to lose either one.

He unrolled his bedroll close to his horse and lay

down. Staring at the full moon, he thought about what the morning would bring. His crew now consisted of nine skinners instead of three. With that many men, he'd kill five hundred head a day. At four dollars a hide, he'd be quite wealthy by the end of the season, even after splitting the profits with Hanrahan.

A smile crossed his lips.

"Yes, sir," he murmured, "gonna be a busy, busy day tomorrow."

Dixon sat straight up at the sound of the shot. He slid his hand between the blankets and grabbed his rifle. He saw no Indians, heard nothing else.

Then men ran from both doors of Hanrahan's saloon. Some stumbled and fell, still drunk. All were in some state of undress. Two men grabbed a ladder lying next to the building and propped it against a wall. They climbed to the roof and threw sod onto the ground.

Dixon yawned and stretched. Curious, he slipped on his boots and, rifle in hand, walked to Hanrahan's. He spotted the saloon keeper coming out the back door.

"Hey, Jim. What's going on?"

"Goddam ridgepole cracked! Scared the shit outta me. Thought I'd been shot." He pointed at the roof. "Shepherd, you and Welch make sure you get enough of that off."

Shepherd answered from atop the building. "We wouldn't be here if it weren't for you tellin' us to pile it on in the first place."

"You just watch that mouth of yours before I put a boot upside your sorry butt!" Hanrahan turned back to Dixon. "Damn, Billy, I tell you it was 'most the death of me. You heard them tales of people killed by soddies crashing in on 'em, ain't ya?"

Dixon nodded. Nothing seemed more frightening

than to be trapped under tons of dirt, alone in the dark, slowly suffocating as the very act of breathing robbed you of the air you needed. He shuddered. Better to face a thousand screaming Comanches.

A small party of men appeared and walked across the pasture.

"Hey, you men!" Hanrahan called. "Where are you going?"

"Down to the creek," Hiram Watson answered.

"What you want to do that for?"

"Well, hell, Jim, you said the ridgepole was cracked. We aim to wander down to the water and see if we can fetch us a prop. Won't do no good to shovel the sod off if the pole breaks. Now would it?"

"I reckon," Hanrahan conceded, "but you boys be careful, and keep an eye peeled."

Watson grinned. "Yes, Momma. We'll watch out for them grizzly bears and mean Injuns."

Watching the men leave, Hanrahan muttered, "Lord, what'd I ever do to You that You'd beset me with assholes of all kinds?"

Dixon quickly smothered a smile and cleared his throat. "Anything I can do?"

"If you don't mind going back in, I still got a couple men who won't rouse. One of 'em's your man, Frenchy. I don't know what you poured in him, but I believe it'd be easier to raise the dead."

Twenty

Lone Wolf reined to a stop.

"What is happening?" Bear Mountain asked.

"The Comanches want us to walk the rest of the way. We must be close."

Lone Wolf dismounted and, taking reins in hand, followed the warrior ahead of him. He had no idea how far it was to the hunters' camp, but he trusted the judgment of his allies.

"I hope so," Bear Mountain said, looking at the setting moon. "Soon we'll have nothing but the stars to light our way."

"I feel good, Bear Mountain. Why shouldn't I? I have had sleep, food, and the blessing of the Great Yellow Comanche."

"You shouldn't make fun of Isatai. What will you do if he really is what he says? How will you battle his magic if it's used against you?"

"I have my own medicine. That's all I need. Is the Comanche going to fight with us? No. He will sit astride his pony and pray for our success. I would rather have him in the midst of battle with a gun or lance."

"What of Quanah?"

"He is young, but full of fight. I believe he'll be there when it starts and when it's over. I will even take the children who ride with us over a man who thinks to talk the enemy to death."

"I don't know, Lone Wolf, some medi—"

"Wait," interrupted Lone Wolf.

A voice called softly from the darkness, "Get on your ponies. We are there."

Lone Wolf passed the word to his men and re-mounted. Following the others, he soon heard the sound of splashing and knew they were crossing the Canadian. On the north bank of the river, the war party formed a line abreast until it disappeared from his sight.

He looked across a flat plain and in the distance saw shapes—the hunters' lodges. The village was dark and still.

Perhaps Isatai was right and we will *catch the white men asleep.*

Lone Wolf tightened his grip on his war ax and shook the tension from his shoulders.

Soon the order will come, and we will charge. Then we'll see if the yellow Comanche knows what he's talking about.

Dixon looked at the sky through the open saloon door. As dawn neared, it turned from black to a deep metallic blue. After the roof repair, Hanrahan stood drinks for those who had helped. The hunter accepted a beer to cut through the alcohol-induced haze of the evening's festivities. In another corner of the saloon, Frenchy sat quietly drinking coffee heavily laced with rum. Dixon saw no sight of Armitage or McCabe, and assumed they were still sleeping. Yawning mightily, he envied them their rest.

"How you doing, Billy?" Hanrahan asked, approaching the hunter.

Dixon nodded, turning away from the door. "Tolerable, Jim, but I miss my bedroll."

"Sorry, son. I'd never believed that ridgepole'd let go like that."

"I can imagine," Dixon answered, looking at the offending timber, now sturdily supported by an eight-inch cottonwood trunk. "Must have been a hell of a surprise."

Hanrahan shuddered. "I don't even want to think about it." He squinted at the hunter. "Looks to be daylight soon. You thinkin' to get an early start?"

"Why not? Cain't go back to sleep till nightfall. 'Sides, there's work to be done. I guess I'll ready the wagons, then rouse Charley and Cranky. You let Frenchy know I'll be back for him?"

"Sure, Billy. By the look of him, that fellow's going nowhere right now."

Dixon sighed. "True. I reckon McCabe's going to have to drive his team." He shrugged. "Oh, well, time to git. I'll be seeing you, Jim."

Hanrahan offered his hand to the hunter. "Good luck, Billy."

Quanah's warhorse danced impatiently. He seemed to share the Comanche's excitement at the prospect of battle. The warrior held the reins tight. He looked to the left and right. His wasn't the only mount giving its owner trouble.

The chiefs and Isatai were silhouetted atop a bluff. He Bear gave the first signal, and the massive war party moved as one.

Quanah's heart pounded as it always did before combat. His mind raced, but not with questions of victory, only wonder. How quickly would the whites be beaten? How many scalps were to be his? Would Isatai's magic work? Who would die? Would they be his men?

The tall prairie grass effectively muffled the sounds of the horses' hooves. Its swish against horse and rider sounded like whispering. Quanah smiled tightly. He imagined the white men listening, wondering. *Who is that? Why do they whisper?*

But those men were asleep, their camp quiet. They heard nothing, knew nothing of the war party, and soon would feel nothing.

He Bear signaled again. The pace quickened. Young, inexperienced men, bulletproof in their yellow paint, pushed forward—only to be called back and chided by the elders in hushed tones. The wall of warriors surged across the prairie like floodwater.

Dixon completed his inspection of the wagon and jumped to the ground. He yawned and stretched, then turned as a man approached through the gloom. It was Billy Ogg, one of Hanrahan's skinners.

"Good morning, Mr. Ogg."

"Mornin' your own self, Mr. Dixon."

"You're up a mite early."

Ogg flashed the hunter a quick smile. "Who ain't, Billy? Hanrahan's got me fetching his teams. Want me to get yours, too?"

"I'd be much obliged. If you can get them this far, I'll handle the hitchin'."

Ogg waved his acknowledgment and walked across the plain toward the river. Dixon watched the skinner a moment, then returned to checking the wagons.

He Bear gave the third signal. The warriors on the fastest ponies broke from the group at a full gallop. These men would chase the white hunters' horses through the village, not only depriving the enemy of his horse, but offering another layer of protection for the attacking Indians.

Quanah watched the lead warriors pull away and

longed to join them. His horse strained at its reins, trying to break from a canter to a run.

After what seemed hours, the final signal came. Quanah lightly kicked his mount. The horse's ears flattened and its stride lengthened. Quanah raised the lance over his head and sounded his war cry, his voice blending with three hundred others into a roar meant to paralyze the enemy with fear.

Dixon finished his knot, rose, and tossed the bedroll into the wagon's seat. He turned to pick up his rifle, and glanced in the direction of the horse herd to gauge Ogg's progress.

Movement in the distance caught the hunter's eye—an undulating black mass near a line of timber. Peer as he might, he couldn't tell what the objects were, but as he watched they spread out like a fan. From the mass came a roar that seemed to shake the very ground he stood on. The roar became the thunder of horses' hooves. He heard the cries of individual warriors.

The horses! They're after the horses!

His mind raced. Reflexively, he turned to his mount. The war cries had frightened Jack badly. He lunged and pulled on the stake pin, white showing in his rolling eyes. Dixon knew that should the horse pull free, he'd disappear with the other stampeding animals. He grabbed Jack's reins and tied them securely to the wagon.

He ran, snatched up his rifle, and prepared to get off a few good shots before the Indians had a chance to run away. He stepped forward and froze.

Run away? My God, they're coming in straight as a bullet!

The sight was such that he knew he'd never forget it—if he lived to remember.

Hundreds of men were mounted on their finest

horses. They were armed with guns and lances and carried heavy shields of thick buffalo hide. He saw ochre men, ochre horses. Scalps dangled from bridles. War bonnets fluttered; bright feathers hung from the tails and manes of the animals. Brass and silver jewelry glittered in the early morning light. Behind it all lay the plains, fiery with the rising sun. And from this glow, Indians continued to emerge.

Dixon fired one shot and ran. He hit the saloon door and promptly rebounded.

How'd they lock a door with no proper latch?

Dust kicked up by Dixon's feet.

"Oh, shit!"

He banged on the door.

"Open up! Inside there, open up! It's me, Dixon."

Another round thudded into the sod wall beside him.

"Sweet Mother of God, open up!" he screamed, frantically hitting and kicking.

The door swung open, and he stumbled in. He leaned heavily on a table and glared at Shepherd.

The barkeep shrugged. "Sorry, Billy. We was a bit busy with the proceedings and all."

Shepherd raised his pistol to fire through the doorway, only to dive away as Billy Ogg fairly flew through the opening. The skinner ran almost the entire length of the building before collapsing in a heap on the floor. Immediately on his heels came the heavy drumming of hooves. He had outrun the Indians.

Shepherd whistled. "Son of a bitch! That was one hell of a run, Ogg!"

He turned and raised his pistol again. Each fired round lit his face in bright yellow light. Soon other men joined the barkeep, firing through the open door at targets not yet visible.

After the hunters' horses passed, the front ranks of Indians appeared. Dixon's own pistol joined in the firing, and the combined output from the men split the war party.

"Gents to the right; ladies to the left," Shepherd called, and fired another round before slamming the door shut.

Eddy raised himself on one elbow, trying to figure out what woke him. He heard the soft rustle of bed linens.

Langton muttered. "The very nerve of some people. Banging on the door at all hours of the night. Really, how rude." He continued louder. "Oh, *do* show some patience!"

"You all right, James?"

Langton sighed—a long, drawn-out sound that carried all the weight of a man terribly burdened but bravely carrying on.

"Yes, George, I am. However, there is a barbarian at the gate who demands entrance. I suppose he's one of your buffalo men—drunk."

Eddy sat up in the darkness. "I'll see to him, James."

"No, no, George. I'm up. I'll take care of the gentleman."

Eddy heard the sharp scrape of a match and squinted against the sudden flare of light. As his eyes adjusted to the gentle glow of the oil lamp, he saw his employer leave their room clad only in his long-handle underwear. Eddy rose quickly, for he now heard the pounding. He followed Langton into the store proper, to be met by the Oldses carrying their own lamp.

"What is it, George?" William asked anxiously. "We heard a noise. . . ."

Again the thumping resounded through the heavy wooden door. But this time, the residents of the store could hear a voice.

"Open the door! Indians!"

"Did he . . . he . . . did he say Indians?" William stammered.

"Meine Gott, open the door, Langton, or, by damn, dem redskins is gonna get him!"

Eddy turned and stared at Johnson. The Swede was magnificent in faded red underwear, a pistol strapped about his waist, blue eyes blazing like gaslights, mustache bristling.

Langton opened the front door and Tom O'Keefe fell through, landing on the dirt floor. Shirtless and barefoot, he clutched a blanket in one hand.

"Hold the door!" a voice yelled.

Sam Smith ran in behind O'Keefe, lightly stepping around the prostrate blacksmith. Like Langton, he wore only long underwear, but he had his pistol in one hand and a cartridge belt in the other.

As he ran through the doorway, he called to Langton, "Sonny, I'd be a-shuttin' that door. Them Injuns is close enough to smell."

Langton hurriedly closed the door and threw the crossbar. No sooner had he stepped from the entrance than large splinters exploded from the wood as the Indians' bullets struck. Glass broke in another room.

"To the windows, boys!" Smith shouted.

Eddy ran to his bed and picked up his pistol and holster. After the soldiers had come—he never could decide whether the Indians would attack—he'd kept his handgun and cartridge belt close at hand. He looked up as Johnson ran into the room they shared.

"Meine Gott! You should see the excitement, yessiree! Little Olds run back to his room. That hunter you know, he's in the kitchen. O'Keefe is hollerin' for a gun, and Langton's puking in the corner. *Ja,* is a sight I never forget."

The Swede pointed his pistol at the small window and fired three times. He looked again at Eddy, eyes wide and wild.

"Is a sight for you to see to believe. But you better

look at it quick . . . *ja*, make it a quick one, 'cause we're gonna die!"

He faced the window again and emptied his weapon into the darkness.

Masterson awoke with the sound of the first shot. He sat up and looked into the wide eyes of Fred Leonard.

"Did you hear that?" the shopkeeper asked, looking around the stockade.

"Yeah, but what's that other sound?"

Leonard listened and heard a low rumbling like distant thunder. "Rain?"

"Nope, wrong kind of noise. Maybe buffalo stampeding like when the Indians chase them."

Leonard stared at Masterson and said quietly, "How about horses, Bat? Horses chased by Indians."

"Oh, Christ!" Masterson jumped to his feet, grabbed his holster, and started running across the compound.

"Where the hell are you going?" Leonard shouted.

Masterson stopped and turned back. "The saloon, Fred. My momma didn't raise her boy to be killed in no house of sticks." He spun on his heel and disappeared into O'Keefe's restaurant.

Masterson strapped on his weapon, climbed over a table, and poked his head through an open window. In the dim light he could see the square box that was O'Keefe's blacksmith shop about one hundred feet from his present location. A good fifty feet beyond was the back of the saloon. He looked toward the rising sun.

"If you're going to go, Bat, go now," he muttered.

He climbed through the window and dropped to the ground. Now more shots sounded from the direction of Hanrahan's. He ran for the saloon, but the sound of rushing horses made him veer toward O'Keefe's. He slammed into the back wall of the shop.

Looking around the building's corner, he saw the first of the horses approaching at a gallop. His heart pounded, and he slipped his pistol from its holster.

The first animal raced by; it was riderless. Not only riderless, but also without saddle, bridle, or any kind of gear.

The herd. They're pushing the herd ahead of them.

The horses now passed in a seemingly endless stream too dangerous to cross. He decided to wait and hope for a gap between them and the pursuing Indians.

He heard a voice, and turned to see a warrior yell at the fleeing horses. The Indian rode low in the saddle, his head alongside his mount's neck. His body was covered in yellow paint. The horse was decorated with bright red handprints and zigzag lines like lightning bolts. So intent was the Indian on his charges, he failed to see the white man crouching by the building.

Masterson again looked around the corner. The last of the horses was in sight. He holstered his weapon and started to move out when another Indian rode by—on his side of the shop. Only ten feet away, he, too, was busy with the job at hand, and again Masterson survived unmolested.

The fire from the saloon increased in intensity. He made his break. One quick peek around the corner, and he saw the main war party as it split to either side of the saloon. He knew that if he didn't leave now, he'd be caught and killed.

He ran to the back of the saloon and heaved himself at the back door prepared for it to be bolted, but it gave easily and crashed against the wall. Masterson followed and fell to the floor. He rose quickly only to find himself staring down the barrels of a half-dozen pistols. Never taking his eyes off the guns or the men holding them, he slowly bent and brushed at the dirt on his pants.

"You know," he said with a lopsided grin, "you boys ought to put a bar across that door."

Quanah was surprised at the gunfire coming from the house in the middle of the hunters' village. He knew most of the shots were wild, but enough had come close to make him veer his pony away. The rest of the war party followed his lead, and soon the men rode in two directions, making a wide circle around the lodges.

The older warriors made for a large log house; more went to another building, but Quanah and his men stayed with the middle house. They encircled the building quickly and dismounted. Warriors ran to the doors and beat on them with their rifles and their fists.

Quanah backed his horse to the door and made it kick. The wood refused to yield, though it cracked. Frustrated, he drove the animal backward until its rump pushed into the doorway. Again there was cracking, but no sign of opening.

The warrior moved away, and several men took his place pushing on the stubborn door. A black line showed along its edge, and suddenly there was a six-inch space. Quanah quickly threw his lance into the opening hoping to spear someone in the darkness. The door slammed shut.

Warriors again crowded around to force another opening. Three loud booms sounded, and two of the men flew away from the door. One lay still, but the other rose, blood running blackly through the yellow protective paint Isatai had provided.

The warrior stared in disbelief at the hole in his stomach. He looked at Quanah and started to ask the question that was already in the war chief's mind. He stepped toward his leader. Blood poured from his mouth, and he pitched forward.

Quanah howled. He raged against a worthless medicine man with worthless magic. Isatai was right—there would be a slaughter. The slaughter was to be of his own people.

The war chief shouted orders for the men to withdraw from the doors and windows. He called the men on the building's roof to come down.

He was ignored.

More gunfire—a warrior fell from the roof.

Another blast—another body in the dirt.

Twenty-one

Lone Wolf and Bear Mountain stood on a hill that overlooked the hunters' camp. Below them ochre warriors crawled over the buildings like ants on a grasshopper. But this grasshopper had a sting, and when it stung, Indians fell.

He looked at his pony's mane, absently playing with the hair, and continued. "Look at them. There is no reason behind this. I see no plan, no organization."

"They believe in the war paint."

Lone Wolf spat. "For all the good it is doing."

Unlike his men, he'd refused to cover his body with the Comanche's yellow paint, and it was only after much argument he'd relented and painted his arms.

He pointed down the hill. "Do *they* look bullet-proof to you?"

"What will you do?" Bear Mountain's voice was low.

What a good question, Lone Wolf thought bitterly. What could he do? Abandoning the battle was out of the question. He'd have to leave men behind—something that was not going to happen again.

In the distance, he heard a bugle call. Startled, he wheeled his horse toward the sound.

"Come with me!" he ordered. "I hear the soldiers."

"It is nothing, Lone Wolf," Bear Mountain replied calmly. "The bugler is with the Comanche. I heard some of the others talking that one of the warriors was a buffalo soldier who ran from his army."

The Kiowa chieftain took a deep breath and willed his heart to slow. "Have you ever wondered why a soldier who refused to fight for his own kind will fight with us?"

Bear Mountain shrugged his massive shoulders. "The buffalo soldiers I have seen are not white. Their skin is mud-colored. They have hair like a buffalo, big lips, and flat noses. They don't even look like black white men."

"True," Lone Wolf replied.

Another bugle call sounded across the valley.

"I have watched the soldiers. They wake with a bugle. They eat with a bugle. Sometimes, I think they piss with a bugle. Does this bugler know what he is doing?" He looked at the blank expression on his lieutenant's face and smiled. "Never mind. What I want you to do is to gather our men—carefully. Take them out of rifle range and wait for me."

"What are you going to do?"

Lone Wolf turned his mount slowly and started back down the hill.

"Find Quanah," he called over his shoulder. "Find Quanah and stop this madness before we all die."

Eddy rushed into the main store and shot through the door. Each bullet left a hole on his side of it and sent splinters flying from the other. He'd fired three rounds when he felt a hand against his back.

"Do not waste the bullets, George."

Eddy stared at Johnson. The Swede's eyes had lost their madness.

"Why?" he argued. "I saw you empty your gun through that little window."

"Ja, you did. And it was stupid to waste the bullets. You think maybe I hit one of dem redskins? Oh-ho, I

think not. Nope, now the boiled pork is being fried, and if we don't make it right, we'll sing with the angels tonight while these *Djavels* dance with our hair." He tapped his right temple. "We must think. They cannot shoot through the walls, so we must protect our doors."

Johnson walked to the stored grain and picked up a fifty-pound sack of feed corn. He sidled up to the front door and dropped the bag. He looked at Eddy.

"So? What you think? Maybe you could give me a hand."

Eddy shoved his pistol into the waistband of his pants and joined Johnson at the sacks of feed. He grabbed a bag and placed it atop the corn. The Swede followed suit, and the two men continued until the door was hidden by heavy burlap sacks.

"One more oughta do it, by damn."

Johnson bent and picked up the last sack, grunting under the effort. He walked straight to the wall of feed and threw the bag on top. He smiled, then froze as a spray of corn shot directly into his face.

Eddy jumped, almost screamed. He was sure Johnson was hit, but the Swede just stood there.

"You all right, Andy?" Eddy's voice was barely above a whisper.

Johnson slowly raised a hand to his face, then brought it away again and examined his fingers.

"No blood! Dat ol' bullet go into the bag, but not through."

"Maybe you best move to one side."

"Good idea." Johnson stepped next to the bookkeeper. "I think the door is all right now. I'm going to go help block the other one. You watch the little window."

Eddy started to move toward his bedroom, but was stopped by a low moaning. He looked around the main store and saw Hannah Olds huddled against the wall that separated her bedroom from the store.

"Oh, my God!" he breathed as he rushed to her side. He spoke louder. "Hannah? Can you hear me? Are you hurt? Hannah?"

He reached out and touched her shoulder.

Hannah uncoiled like a rattlesnake and grabbed Eddy. She held him so tightly he feared he felt ribs crack. Then she screamed.

"We're gonna die! Oh, my God—oh, my God—oh, my God! Indians . . . Indians everywhere! They're here! They're here! They're coming through the door!"

Twenty-two

Quanah rode from the middle house to the one that looked as big as an entire village. The scene there was the same. Warriors clambered over the structure, only to be blown away by the white men's gunfire.

Stopping next to a covered wagon parked near the building, he was soon surrounded by other Indians from the three tribes.

"What has happened to the medicine, Comanche?" a Kiowa warrior demanded. "The whites were not asleep. What heads have you knocked in?"

Before Quanah could answer, a Comanche named Cheyenne spoke.

"Why are you asking him? He is a war chief, not a shaman! Maybe you did not believe strongly enough for the magic to work for you."

The Kiowa snorted. "If you believe, charge the camp. Show us that the bullets cannot harm you."

"Wait," Quanah ordered. "Our friend is right, Cheyenne. Something has happened to Isatai's magic paint."

He turned at the sound of an approaching horse. Lone Wolf joined the group at the wagon.

"Have you seen, Quanah? Is this the protection we are given by your medicine man?"

"I know, Lone Wolf. I have tried to gather my men, but they refuse to move away."

The Kiowa chief sneered. "That's because they're bulletproof. Isatai was right about one thing, though—the whites' bullets do pass right through the warriors."

"Perhaps there is something in this wagon we can use to force the doors," Cheyenne said thoughtfully.

"You haven't checked it?" Quanah asked incredulously.

Cheyenne shrugged and walked his horse to a corner of the wagon, lifting one side of the canvas with the tip of his bow. He found himself staring into the twin muzzles of a double-barreled shotgun. The last thing he saw was a bright flash.

The blast of the shotgun startled Quanah; he watched in rapt horror as Cheyenne's nearly decapitated body toppled. The remaining Indians fired into the wagon with bows and rifles until its cover was shredded.

Quanah rode close and buried his lance deep into the chest of one of the men in the wagon. Whether the man was already dead was immaterial. The blow was both coup and punishment for what they had done to one of his men.

The Kiowa who had upbraided Quanah jumped from his horse and made for the wagon. He grabbed for one of the white men's arms. Instead, his hand disappeared inside the mouth of a huge black dog. The warrior screamed and jerked his hand away. Other men dismounted and approached the bodies, but as each neared, the animal would bar his way, teeth bared.

Lone Wolf came forward and leveled his rifle. The bullet passed through the dog's head, and the animal dropped without a sound. The chief then climbed from his horse, drew his knife, and cut a long strip of hide from the carcass. Remounting, he turned to Quanah.

"The dog had the spirit of a warrior. It is only right that he is treated as one."

Quanah nodded. "I don't understand how he escaped injury. I can't count how many times we shot into the wagon."

Lone Wolf shrugged and looked at the dead Comanche. "Unlike your men, his protective coating seems to have worked."

Dixon stabbed at the sod wall with his Bowie knife. Most of the defenders now concentrated on making loopholes through the saloon's thick walls. The rest guarded the entrances, occasionally shooting to remind the Indians that someone was home. The doors were barred, windows shuttered. The air hung thick with acrid gun smoke that teared eyes and left a sulphurous taste on the tongue.

Hanrahan paced the floor, his rifle in the crook of his arm, his pistol tucked into his waistband.

"I knew this would happen," he said. "Goddam, son-of-a-bitch redskins! Yes, sir, I just knew those red niggers would be here. I was right, by God! I was—"

He stopped in midsentence and looked around the room. Those who paid any attention at all stared at him. He walked over to Dixon.

"Well, Billy, I reckon you'll have to call off your hunt today."

Dixon grunted his reply and dug deeper into the dirt wall.

"Course, I suppose you could always go out after this here ruckus is done."

The hunter stared at Hanrahan. "If, and I do mean *if*, we get outta here alive, I'm taking my body elsewhere. There's gotta be seven, eight hundred Indians outside this saloon. I aim to live and leave. You want to hunt, be my guest."

"Hell, Billy, it was just a suggestion. Wasn't like you had to go and get nasty." Hanrahan turned his back on Dixon and walked away.

Dixon shook his head and continued digging. Light began to show where the hole reached through the wall. He quickly cleared an area large enough to accommodate either a pistol or rifle barrel.

A patch of yellow flashed by the hole. He pulled his pistol. Another appeared; he jammed the gun into the rectangular hole, but the Indian moved away before he could fire. He lowered the weapon and waited. Still another appeared. He shoved the weapon into position and fired. The hole cleared, and smoke poured from both ends.

He leaned against the wall—away from the hole. Nothing prevented the Indians from using the loophole against the defenders.

He checked his pistol: two rounds left, a dozen more in the loops of his gunbelt. The new Sharps rifle he'd bought leaned against the wall, useless. He had no ammunition to fit the gun. Cursing silently, he wondered what had possessed him to leave a full case of .44-caliber bullets in the Rath & Company store.

"How you doing, Billy?"

Dixon looked up. "Holding my own right now, Bat. How about you?"

"Ammo's lean."

"Yeah, me, too. Fourteen, fifteen shots from now, we're a gun short."

Masterson grinned. "I don't reckon our red brothers plan to leave any time soon."

"Bat, if there's one thing we ain't runnin' out of, it's Indians."

Eddy struggled with Hannah Olds. Her arms were clamped around his waist, and in her hysteria, she was squeezing the air out of his lungs.

"Hannah!" Eddy's voice was a hoarse whisper. He struggled to suck in more air. "Hannah! Listen to me!"

The woman ignored him. "I can see them, can't you? Lord help us! We're gonna die!"

Eddy could imagine her fear. The tales of white women taken by the Indians were well known. Particularly well known was the fact that their deaths started with rape. To make matters worse, even those who lived were routinely passed from buck to buck.

Hannah's outburst wasn't unexpected, just dangerous. How much harder would the Indians pursue their objectives if they knew a white woman was in the house?

Hannah forced herself to her feet, taking Eddy with her. She pushed toward the door, and he felt himself being carried along. What was she going to do? Open the door? Tear down the wall? Eddy braced himself and pushed hard against the woman's arms. He fell to his knees as she suddenly let go.

Looking up, he saw Langton had Hannah by the shoulders. The shopkeeper spun the large woman and slapped her with a resounding blow.

Hannah shut up, her eyes wide, a hand near her reddening cheek.

"Listen to me, Hannah Olds!" Langton's voice was hard, cold. "You listen good! We have enough trouble here without some crazed woman carrying on. Scream if you like, but load guns, too. Tear cloth for bandages; make breakfast. I truly do not give a good goddam what you do, but if you interfere with the defense of this establishment and the men inside it, *I* will kill you. Understood?"

Hannah nodded quietly, a single tear running down her cheek. Langton sighed, put his arm around his cook, and led the woman back to her bedroom wall.

"I'm really sorry, Hannah. Sorry to have let a woman come here. Sorry to have to make you endure this attack, and sorry to have struck you.

"We need your help. I can't say how the others are faring. I hear shooting, but I don't know from whose guns. They may all be dead; we may die as well." He handed her his pistol. "Take this. I have no intention of losing to the Indians, but if they do get in, William will meet you at Heaven's Gate. Waste no time in joining him."

Twenty-three

Despite the failure of the yellow paint and the morning's losses, Quanah felt heartened at the death of the men in the wagon. He had begun to think that Isatai's medicine had worked in reverse, and the white men were bulletproof.

Still, the battle was a disaster. The warriors, deluded by grand visions of a cost-free victory, had charged into the fight recklessly. They now paid a dear price for such foolish behavior.

Even with overwhelming odds in their favor, the war party had only managed to kill two white men and one dog. They had not been able to breach a single lodge. The ones made of earth were understandable, but the log house should have gone quickly.

He rode over the battlefield, his headdress flowing behind him. He'd decided to gather his men, pull back, and attack the camp one house at a time. As each fell, those inside would be captured if possible, killed otherwise. He could right the mistakes of earlier and win the battle.

He was still contemplating the coming victory when his world went black.

"Hoo-wee, boys! Looka there! I done bagged me a chief!"

Dixon turned at the sound of the voice and saw Hiram Watson, round-eyed with excitement, pointing at his loophole.

Across the saloon, Bermuda Carlyle spat tobacco juice on the dirt floor. "How the hell you know that?"

Watson's expression changed from triumphant to confused to indignant in a matter of seconds.

"Well, goddam, Bermuda, I ain't no tenderfoot. I seen Injuns aplenty, an' I know a chief when I see one. Hell, he had him a train of feathers eight, ten feet long. No pimply faced buck gonna have no head-gear like that."

Carlyle absently scratched his nose and squinted at the buffalo skinner. The lingering cloud of smoke from the morning's gunfire hung in the still air, a blue haze stinging eyes and drying nostrils.

He sighed and spat again. "What I meant was, how'd you know *you* shot him?"

"Jesus, Carlyle, I pointed my rifle at him, shot, and he fell offa his horse. Sounds like I shot him to me."

"Balls! You and a dozen others. I even took a shot at that head full of feathers myself."

"You're just jealous! If he was just another Injun, you wouldn't give no never mind, but let me get a chief, and it's 'How you know he's yor'n?' Well, let me tell you somethin'. When this here fracas is over, we'll just cut the ball outta that Injun. I got me a .44-caliber Springfield here. I know what my loads look like."

"Won't be there," Shepherd said matter-of-factly as he wiped at the accumulated grime on his face. He looked at the blackened areas on his handkerchief and sighed. He felt as though he was just pushing the dirt around.

Watson eyed the bartender suspiciously. "What you mean, Oscar?"

"The others will pick him up."

"Maybe so. And maybe not. I seen it afore."

Shepherd regarded Watson with the weary eyes of a father repeating the same lecture to his son for the tenth time. "Indians are Indians. There ain't no changing that. Niggers is lazy, Mexicans steal, Irishmen drink, and Indians always pick up their dead and wounded."

Quanah cautiously opened an eye. All he saw was grass, tall and yellow-green. A loud buzzing noise attracted his attention, and he slowly shifted his gaze to his right. Next to him was the rotting carcass of a skinned buffalo. The noise was from a dense cloud of flies busy at work.

He felt no pain, and this bothered him, for he knew he must have been shot. He'd known of warriors who'd been shot in the back. They'd felt no pain. They couldn't walk. He wiggled the toes on one foot, then the other, and sighed. His feet still functioned.

He tried to recall the events before he hit the ground, but remembered no sound of rifle fire close to him. For that matter, he didn't remember falling off his horse. He decided to raise himself slightly above the grass to get his bearings.

Fear gripped the chief as he pushed up with his left hand, but saw his right dangle. Panicked, he sat up abruptly, brushing aside the feathered bonnet that had somehow stayed on his head. He poked and prodded his right arm, feeling nothing.

Sliding his knife from its sheath, he lightly stabbed at his skin, again with no sensation. Angrily he pricked himself with the blade's point, and watched in wonder as a thin line of blood trickled down his forearm. He picked up his right hand and dropped it. The numbed appendage flopped to the ground as though it were no longer a part of his body.

A single tear rolled down his nose as he saw his life as a hunter and warrior pass away. What use was a one-armed man? He would be forced to beg food from Brown Bull and depend on the generosity of the peace chiefs. Better he were dead.

At that moment, a lead hornet neatly parted the feathers in his headdress. Quanah snatched off the headgear and pulled himself around until the dead buffalo lay between him and the hunters. On the other hand, he might recover from his wound to fight again.

He peered over the body. Warriors moved away from the houses. Those on foot regained their ponies and began to circle the village. He nodded in approval as his men took the more traditional method of attack.

Taking in his surroundings, he saw he was trapped in the open. Fortunately, the grass was tall, but there was no wind, and any movement he made would attract unwanted attention.

As more warriors joined the circle, they would eventually attack one house en masse. If it was any of them but the log fort, he would try to run for a plum thicket he'd spotted nearby.

He flexed his calf muscles and felt confident he could easily make the run. The only fault with his plan was that he wouldn't really know if he could walk, much less run, until he stood—an easy target.

Yet, he would try. He needed to show his men he lived. He needed to get help from a medicine man. He needed to get back into this battle or die trying.

Lone Wolf watched warriors ride around the white hunters' lodges. Many clung to the far side of their horses, firing their weapons under the ponies' neck. Gunfire from the village had slowed considerably. The occasional boom of a hunter's rifle sometimes took down a warrior, sometimes a horse.

Bear Mountain stood next to his chief, observing the same scene. He leaned in close. "Perhaps we should join the others."

Lone Wolf nodded. "Yes, we should, but I am thinking of the best place to attack. We can't ride circles
around them all day. There is no victory in that."

He pointed to the center of the valley.

"That long building in the middle seems a good
target. It has but two doors and as many windows."
He looked to the south. "But we will attack the big
dirt house. It stands apart from the others. It has many
windows, and best of all, there is one side that cannot
be protected by anyone in the other houses.

"When we charge, I want you to go to the blind
side and try to get into the windows. I will take another group of men and attack the front door. After
the first house falls, the others will go quickly."

Sam Smith ran across the store and stuck his head
through the doorway of Eddy's bedroom. The bookkeeper stood on a small stool, his rifle in the window.
"Hey, George, looks to me like they's a-pullin' back.
Reckon so?"

Eddy peered out the window and watched the yellow-
skinned Indians. Though many remained close to the
store, more seemed to be leaving. "I don't know, Sam.
It kinda looks like they're running off." He looked at
the hunter. "You think we won?"

Smith rubbed his neck and shrugged. "Hell, you
just cain't tell about Injuns. They'd as good as had us
whipped. Who knows? Sometimes them devils just up
and quit for no reason we'd think of."

Hannah Olds raised her head. She'd resumed her
seat on the floor, reloading rifles and pistols and praying to herself.

"Did I hear you right?" Her voice trembled.
"They're going? We've won?"

She got to her feet, still holding a pistol in one hand
and cartridges in the other.

"We're safe? Is that what I'm hearing?" She raised

her hands toward Heaven and shouted, "Praise be to God! We have been delivered from the hands of the Savage!"

Joyous tears coursed down her grimy face, leaving black trails on her cheeks.

Smith raised his hands. "Now, Miz Olds, I didn't say we won. You got to understand about In—"

"Nonsense!" Hannah interrupted. "We've won! The Indians are leaving. Soon we'll be leaving as well. It's back to the civilized world for William and me."

"George! Eddy!" William Olds's voice called from across the store.

The small clerk scampered out of his bedroom door and joined the others.

"You got to come quick!" He grabbed Eddy's arm. "C'mon, George. You got to come now."

"Let go, William." Eddy pulled free of Olds's grip. "What's so damned . . . uh, 'scuse me, Hannah, durned important? Ain't the redskins leaving your side of the building?"

"Actually, they aren't."

Olds's tone of voice was so matter-of-fact, Eddy thought the clerk was trying to play a prank on them.

"William, I enjoy a joke as much as the next man, but your timing leaves something to be desired."

"It's no joke, George. I was watching them run away, then I stuck my head out the window—"

"You did what!" Hannah's voice thundered through the store. "Are you completely out of your mind?"

"Hush, woman! This is man talk."

Eddy quickly smothered a smile as he caught the shocked look on Hannah's face. Her expression would have withered most plants, and he had no intention of becoming a target for her wrath later.

On the other hand, William positively glowed. He'd done his share during the fight. He'd taken the south-west corner of the store and stood his ground armed with two rifles and a pistol. Now he stood his ground again—against his wife.

Olds's back was ramrod straight, his thin chest swelled to its fullest. His nightshirt, always too large and now stained with sweat, soil, and smoke, draped his body like a battle ensign. His hair, mussed and standing straight up, perched above a pinched, grimy, tear-streaked face, its jaw defiantly thrust out.

He looked almost comical until Eddy saw his eyes. They were radiant. Two blue orbs that burned with the fire of a man whose mettle had been tested and tempered in the heat of battle.

Eddy smiled softly and glanced at Smith, who watched Olds with open admiration. Whatever else the tiny clerk had gained from this fight, the one thing that would never be taken from him was the respect he'd earned from his fellow defenders.

The spell was broken as Hannah harrumphed loudly, spun on her heel, and marched back to her spot by the wall. She turned back to her husband, and Eddy watched a small smile play at her lips before she caught him looking at her. She favored the bookkeeper with a glare and slowly slid shells in the pistol's cylinder.

Eddy cleared his throat and returned his attention to Olds. "Now, William, what were you talking about?"

"I took a look to the south and saw a bunch of Indians gathering there on horseback. I noticed the others were starting to ride around the store, but as they neared these first fellows, they stopped. Then I saw more of them. They just sat there like they were waiting for something."

"That ain't good," Smith said quietly. "That ain't good at all."

"Why?" Eddy asked, though he thought he knew the answer.

" 'Cause that means they've gone back to fightin'

reg'lar. Them boys is gonna line up and take us on one shop at a time. From what William's said, I reckon we're the lucky souls who get the first try."

"Oh, God, not again!"

Hannah's hands shook, dropping bullets onto the dirt floor. She quickly plopped down, gathering ammunition and praying.

"Our Father, who art in Heaven, hallowed be thy . . ."

She dropped another cartridge, snatched it up.

"Our F-Father, who art in Heaven . . ."

Still another bullet dropped.

"Shit!" She took a deep breath, brushed tears away from her face with the back of a dirty, trembling hand. "Our . . . our F-F-Father . . ."

A shell fell.

Hannah buried her face in her hands. "Oh, God, please help us!"

Quanah watched the warriors as they gathered near the south side of the large earthen lodge. He pulled himself into a low crouch, thankful his legs seemed unimpaired by his wound. He waited, gently bouncing in anticipation.

The sound of a bugle split the air, and the war party charged. Part of the warriors split from the main group and ran to the back of the house. Another group made for the front door. Almost immediately, gunfire came from the long dirt house. These shots were joined by those of the hunters inside the besieged lodge.

He knew the time was right. Most of the white men would be far too busy to notice him, and those in the fort were too far away for a clear shot. He leapt to his feet and ran toward the plum thicket, holding his right arm tightly against his body with his left. Entering the thicket, he hid behind a tree, leaning on its trunk as he sucked air into his lungs.

He was safe. The feeling washed over him like cool spring water. Until he'd reached the line of trees, he hadn't realized how afraid he'd been. And for what? The white man had shot him, but he lived. His right arm was useless, but his left worked, and he could still run like an antelope.

The chiefs overseeing the battle would have seen his dash for safety, and soon a rider would come for him.

What then?

The battle was going badly for the Comanche and their allies.

Isatai must answer for the failure of his magic. A new, or rather an actual, battle plan needs to be made.

He allowed the tree to hold him up as he breathed deeply and let his thoughts wander. His numbed arm hung limply at his side.

We're not beaten yet. The white man is trapped, and we have many warriors. I can still fight, even with one arm.

He threw himself to the ground as a bullet smashed into the tree trunk near his head. Wide-eyed, he scanned the woods near him. He'd heard no shot. How was this to be? It was as though the hunter's bullet had sniffed him out. He shuddered at the thought. Maybe there *was* magic in the enemy's village. A knot formed in his stomach, and as he pondered this new development, it twisted tight and grew.

Twenty-four

Dixon checked his cartridges again: The count remained the same. Ten. What he'd do once the ammunition was gone, he hadn't any idea, but it seemed ironic that one of the best shots among them should be without a weapon.

Masterson joined Dixon at the loophole. The hunter admired the way the young teamster remained cool under fire. It was as though they were back in the saloon the night of the big fight. Masterson showed no signs of anger or fear, just a determination to get the job done.

"Well, Bat, Rath's certainly had a merry go of it."

"Sure as hell did. I don't think the Indians thought we could cover both the front and back doors."

Dixon smiled. "They know now."

"It's a funny thing, Billy, but I'd swear I heard a bugle just as they run in on 'em. You know, I think they believe we don't know what that call means."

"Could be, Bat. I figure they've seen the Army work. Maybe they got a brave there who wants to time the attacks with the bugle. And then again, maybe that ol' bugler just makes his calls according to what he sees." Dixon ran a hand through his hair. "Shit, I don't know. I'm just ready for this foolishness to end."

In the distance, the bugle sounded. Dixon loaded a round and slid the rifle barrel through the gun port.

"Here we go again," he muttered.

Without a word, Masterson returned to his own loophole just as the others opened fire. Dixon saw a warrior ride into sight and drew a bead.

The real problem with shooting at men on horseback was motion. The intended recipient of the bullet had a bad habit of weaving to avoid being shot. This, coupled with the unpredictable behavior of a horse in combat, led to mixed results.

A head shot was almost impossible, even for a marksman like him, so he aimed low, for the center of the body. The best target was the middle of the chest. A slug in the lungs or the heart was an almost guaranteed kill. Next came the gut shot. He'd seen men with lead buried in their bellies. Most died; all suffered—terribly.

If he could not achieve the first two, he hoped for a shot in the upper leg. He once saw a man die from a thigh wound. The doctor had said there was a big artery in the leg, and if a bullet passes through it, a man would bleed as if his leg had been cut off.

Like as not, though, Dixon would miss the rider and shoot the horse. A good hit was high on the spine, which would break the animal's back, and make it drop like a rock. With any other hit, there was no telling how the horse or rider would react.

All of this flashed through the hunter's mind as he aimed and squeezed the trigger. The rifle slammed into his shoulder and a thick column of white smoke shot through the loophole. He saw both the Indian and his horse go down. Unless the warrior showed himself, Dixon would have no idea whether he'd struck his target.

As he reloaded, he heard steady fire coming from the front of the saloon. He turned and saw Shepherd shooting as quickly as he could chamber another round.

"Oscar!" the hunter called. "Oscar, slow down!"

The bartender stared at Dixon with wild eyes. "Have you seen how many goddam red niggers there is out there?"

Dixon crossed to Shepherd. "Banging around like that ain't gonna get the job done. Why don't you let me take your rifle. You could use a rest."

Shepherd shoved the rifle into Dixon's hands so fast he almost dropped it. The hunter admired his newly acquired weapon.

"Big fifty?" he asked with a smile.

Shepherd nodded. "I got four boxes of shells, too. You're welcome to the lot."

"Thanks, Oscar. I'll do you proud."

The bartender stared at Dixon as though the hunter were mad, and scuttled away. He grabbed a bottle off the bottom shelf and disappeared behind the bar.

Dixon looked out Shepherd's loophole and saw a large force of Indians bearing down on the saloon.

Gunfire from the attackers intensified, with bullets thudding into the sod walls and occasionally coming through a gun port to smash into an inside wall. He peeked past the edge of his loophole. Indians hiding in the grass jumped up and ran under covering fire from their comrades.

Suddenly, a warrior on a white horse charged directly toward Dixon. At the last moment, he wheeled his mount. As he stopped, an Indian came out of the tall grass and leapt on the horse's back.

The horse and riders had started away at full speed when Dixon heard the familiar boom of a Sharps. The horse stumbled and blood poured from a wound in its left rear leg. Immediately, the two warriors beat on the animal's hindquarters, one with his bow, the other barehanded, until it staggered away on three legs, carrying its passengers to safety.

Dixon whistled under his breath. He truly admired the bravery of these red-skinned men to risk their lives trying to rescue their friends. The fact they'd perform the same heroics going after their dead impressed him even more, though he couldn't understand the reasoning behind it.

Still marveling at what he saw, he sighted on a magnificent-looking warrior at the head of the charging party. Sunlight danced off his jewelry. Bright red stripes, painted over yellow ochre on the face, were crowned by a headdress of eagle feathers.

A splendid vision of barbaric beauty, he thought as he squeezed the trigger and calmly put a half-inch slug through the warrior's head.

Twenty-five

Lone Wolf rode into the chaos of the war party's campsite. Wounded men lay everywhere, their yellow paint washed away by blood from wounds that should not have existed. Most of the stricken died. Some went quickly, but many lingered until sickness from the wounds killed them. Those who lived would carry scars they would someday weave into battle tales told to children and grandchildren.

Still others would live with parts of their bodies blown away and bones shattered by the white men's bullets. These men would come to depend on the band for support. Lone Wolf frowned deeply as he thought of yet another burden placed on families already taxed by too little food.

The worst were those who had to be carried back. As medicine men sang and prayed, these men clung desperately to life, only to die or to suffer the living death of paralysis.

This last thought crossed his mind as he neared the edge of the camp and saw Quanah lying facedown on a buffalo robe. The Arapaho shaman knelt beside the Comanche, chanting softly and waving his hands over a huge bruise in the middle of Quanah's back. As Lone Wolf approached, the healer moved away.

"I expected to see your yellow medicine man," Lone Wolf said.

Quanah grunted. "Isatai is talking to the spirits. He wants to know why the Great Spirit's magic paint failed."

"Do you think it ever worked?"

"I don't know. After the way we ran right into the hunter's guns, more of us should be shot. Perhaps the paint worked for some. Maybe it was only meant for Comanches."

"Do you really believe that?"

Quanah rolled over and sat up with a painful groan. "Not enough to test," he gasped.

Lone Wolf squatted next to his ally. "You can move?"

Quanah grinned, pulled up his right arm, and let it drop. "Most of me. My back hurts now, where before there was nothing. Maybe the rest will return."

"I am pleased," Lone Wolf said, smiling. Then his smile faded. "The battle is not going well, Quanah. We have attacked all the houses separately. I even used your buffalo soldier and his bugle so we could all charge together. Nothing works."

"I don't understand. Have we not knocked down doors before? Why is it that we can ride against our enemies anywhere and win, but not here?"

"There is talk the lodges of the whites are protected by magic. Many among my men and the Cheyenne are ready to go home."

Quanah regarded the other closely. "And you, Lone Wolf? Will the war chief of the Kiowa ride away?"

Lone Wolf shrugged.

"Well, I won't!" Quanah snapped. "They have spilled Comanche blood. The dead cry for scalps. I don't even know where my brother is. He may be dead out there in the tall grass.

"No, Lone Wolf, I will not quit. There is magic involved, but not from the white men. We were foolish to believe that a magic paint could do what our personal medicine can't.

"Now we will hold a real war council. I want you to gather the chiefs and older warriors. It's time we started acting like warriors and not old women with sticks." He extended his left hand. "Help me up. We have work to do."

Eddy stepped off the stool and flexed his legs to ease the stiffness. His shoulder ached from repeatedly firing his rifle. He was pleased he'd been able to offer protection to his fellow employees and the others at the Walls—particularly pleased with several long-distance shots he'd made in defense of the saloon and the Leonard stockade. Now the Indians appeared to be moving farther back, out of range. He'd no complaint with this latest course taken by his adversaries.

He felt emotionally drained by panic followed by anger followed by exultation—only to find panic waiting again. He dropped onto the stool and leaned his head against the cool sod wall. Tears and gun smoke had taken their toll. He was dried out as a tumbleweed and too weak to hold his own. He'd have rolled across the room with the slightest puff of air.

From the main part of the store, Eddy heard the quiet, earnest prayers of Hannah Olds. Considering the very real possibility she could have fallen into Indian hands, he wondered whether, had he been a woman, he would have been able to withstand the attacks. Perhaps he'd have taken his own life, as had so many pioneer women, and not a few men, rather than risk the chance of capture.

He envied Hannah's ability to cry unfettered. He'd shed his own tears, as had others that day. But these were often blamed on smoke, soot, dirt—whatever. No *man* cried.

What was worse was the coming posturing. They'd escaped the initial onslaught by the Indians. Soon the tales would begin as, with swollen chest and matching head, each *man* declared he'd been never afraid; had never wept—though he did get smoke in his eyes— and had never doubted the outcome.

"George, you look beat."

Eddy opened one eye and swept Langton's lanky frame. The shopkeeper still wore his underwear, now sullied by combat. His sleep mask had somehow managed to stay perched on his forehead. His face seemed sharper, harder, now, the cheekbones prominent, the chin angular. His lips curled into a thin, though sincere, smile that rode his haggard face up to crisp, blue eyes. The lines and wrinkles surrounding those orbs were packed with grime so they appeared to be drawn on Langton's face with lampblack.

"Why can't we cry, James?"

Langton was taken aback by Eddy's question. "Excuse me?"

Eddy straightened up slowly and shook his head. "Nothing, James. Just a thought that strayed from the corral." He offered a tired smile to his boss. "I am beyond beat, sir. I'm hungry, thirsty, pissed off at the Indians for ruining my morning, and just too tired to give a shit."

Langton chuckled and sat on the edge of his bed. He slid the sleep mask from his head, examined it a moment, and dropped it on the floor. From his right sleeve appeared the silk handkerchief. The manager wiped at the dirt on his face, regarded the cloth briefly, then consigned it to the floor as well.

"I'm filthy," he said. "If I were to die right now, they wouldn't be able to tell me from one of your hunters." He sat a moment, then shrugged. "On the other hand, if I must die, I don't think I'd change the company."

"Thank you, James. I feel—the same."

Much to his amazement, Eddy realized he meant the remark.

The hesitation in Eddy's voice wasn't lost on

Langton. A wry smile crossed his lips. "Surprised, George?"

"I . . . uh . . . that is, I mean . . ." The embarrassed bookkeeper stammered, searching for a reasonable explanation. Failing to think of something clever, he chose the truth. "Hell, James, it's just that you and me are pretty different."

"Don't be deceived by appearances. A wanted man might put on the robes of a priest, thinking the law would not look for a killer in a church."

Eddy smiled. "Or a man might put on the airs of a Nancy-boy after rumors got started about him and a certain well-known, though very married, woman. He allows his reputation to be ruined to save that of the lady. Something like that?"

"Who knows?" Langton answered evenly. "Anything's possible in this world."

"That explains why you'd say that the Indians wouldn't get Hannah unless they went through you first."

"I believe you'd have said as much. Were you not prepared to die to protect her?"

"That's true enough, I suppose, but I recall you telling her that you'd shoot her if she didn't hush up. Would you have?"

"Without a second thought, George," Langton said as he stretched out on the bed and closed his tired eyes.

Dixon moved from loophole to loophole asking for bullet counts and offering words of encouragement. Near the rear door of the saloon, he found a sober, miserable Frenchy.

"You look like you been drug by a bear."

"Couldn't feel no worse. I gotta get me a drink, Billy. My vision's blurry; I got the shakes. My insides is all crawly-feeling."

Desperation was etched deeply into the skinner's face, and his bleary, watering eyes reflected the pain he felt. Dixon had never approved of his employee's drinking habits, but now was not the time for a temperance lecture.

"Hang on. I'll be right back."

He crossed the saloon and leaned over the bar. Seated on the floor, Shepherd looked up, smiled, and saluted the hunter with an almost empty gin bottle.

"You look peaceable," Dixon observed.

"Right you are, my friend. I've had enough of Brother Hanrahan's snake oil to ease my nerves quite well." He lifted his pistol from the dirt floor and waggled the weapon at Dixon. "Course, I'm ready should the heathens broach the doors."

"Good. Say, Oscar, Frenchy's a mite puny. You happen to have a spare bottle?"

"My God, man! This *is* a saloon. We got lotsa hooch." He leaned forward and pulled a bottle off the lower shelf. "Here, give him this. Genuine Kentucky bourbon. Won't find any snake heads in that." He tossed the liquor to Dixon and leaned back against the wall. "Anything else?"

Dixon smiled. "No, sir, this'll do fine. Thanks, Oscar."

He returned to Frenchy's side and gave him the bourbon. The skinner quickly pulled the cork and drank deeply.

A shudder worked its way down Frenchy's spine. He took a deep breath and exhaled slowly.

"Oh, man! Thank you, Billy." He tipped the bottle again, then pointed the half-empty vessel out the open rear door. "See that gray standing out there?"

Dixon found the horse his skinner indicated.

"That one behind Rath's? Don't see nothin' special about it."

"Well, that horse has been standing in that same spot for most of two hours now."

"Really?" Surprised, Dixon gave the animal a closer look. "Why?"

Frenchy shrugged. "Cain't say, but you see them reins? They're taut, like someone's holdin' 'em."

"Injun?"

"Don't know. If it is, he ain't moved. Even with the others charging us, that horse has stayed put. I don't reckon there's a redskin there, 'cause I ain't seen nary a soul approach the gray."

"Sure is strange, huh?"

Frenchy nodded as he drained the bottle and tossed it through the doorway. "Yes, sir, strange, indeed."

"You watch that horse, and holler if you see any movement in the grass. Wouldn't put it past them to try and sneak up on us."

In silence, the pipe passed from hand to hand to open the council meeting. Though this was custom among most of the Indians, judging from the expressions on the warriors' faces, Quanah believed none was inclined to speak.

The Comanche looked pensive, as though embarrassed by the morning's fight. Those Kiowa present looked both angry and worried. He knew the issue of magic on the side of the whites weighed heavily on them. He hoped Lone Wolf would lend his support to continuing the battle.

The Cheyenne were openly hostile. If blame were placed for failure, it would come from these men. Only the Arapaho observers looked serene, if not a bit amused, by the day's events.

Isatai was conspicuous by his absence. There was no way he could not have known of this meeting. What did he hope to accomplish by avoiding the rest of the war party? Perhaps he prayed for intervention by the Great Spirit. Whatever else he was doing, he needed to be here, and Quanah resented having to face the council alone.

The old Comanche chief, White Wolf, rose to speak. "My heart is saddened by what has happened this day. Many young men have shed their blood in battle. The women will weep and cut their hair. There will be much sadness in the villages. We have lost fathers, sons, brothers, uncles." He pointed to Lone Wolf and his men. "Our good friends the Kiowa have fought well." To Stone Calf. "The Cheyenne are brave and true warriors. We Comanche are better for having fought at their side." He pointed to the observers. "You Arapaho will tell the story to everyone. Tell the truth. Say how well these warriors fought."

White Wolf paused. Custom called for the remaining members to hold their silence until he indicated he was through speaking. White Wolf knew this, and used the time to marshal his thoughts.

"Young Quanah came to me. He said he wanted to fight the soldiers down on the Brazos. They had killed his uncle, and he wanted a scalp. Isatai came to me as well. He talked of war against these same white soldiers because they had killed his friend. Both men's hearts were hot with revenge. I told them to come here and kill the hunters to cool their hearts; then we would fight the soldiers. I was wrong."

White Wolf again paused.

"Now we are here. All have lost men. The wounded cry with pain. We must forget the magic of Isatai, and each warrior must use his personal medicine. I am asking the older warriors to gather and plan an attack as we would normally do. We will win this battle. The blood debt will be paid. You will bring this council the hair of all the white men!"

Twenty-six

Eddy crossed the main store, surveying the damage done by the Indians. Goods stacked at window height had been struck by bullets passing through the wooden shutters. Those above or below this level seemed untouched. He was thirsty, but wanted no part of beer or whiskey or any of the other lukewarm offerings they sold. He found Andy Johnson standing guard at the rear door.

"Swede, you doing all right?"

"Ja." Johnson pulled a chair around and sat. "I think maybe the Indians is gone—for now, anyway. *Und* you, George, how is the bookkeeper?"

"I've had better days, but I can't recall a more lively morning."

Johnson laughed. "No argument here." He ran a tongue over dry lips. "I could use a drink."

"My thoughts exactly, Andy," Eddy said. "You dug the well here, right?"

"Ja, I did. Dat water is so close, you stick your thumb in the ground, and it comes out wet."

"You reckon we got water here?"

"Maybe so. You want me to look?"

"Yeah, as long as nothing is happening." Eddy walked to the door and peered through a loophole. "Sure is quiet."

A small movement caught his eye near the edge of

the gun port. He twisted and turned his head to see, but the object remained just out of sight.

"Damn!" he muttered, and moved to one of the loopholes cut through the sod. "Hey, Andy, come here."

Johnson joined Eddy at the wall. He looked through the hole. Standing near a rick of hides was a brown horse. Its bridle sparkled in the sunlight. Red calico was plaited into its mane.

"Dat's an Indian pony."

"What else can you see?"

Johnson scrutinized the scene. "An arm!" he said, suddenly excited. "By damn, I see an arm!"

"Just what I thought," the bookkeeper replied, shoving the barrel of his rifle through the loophole.

He sighted on where he believed the Indian's head would emerge from behind the stack of hides.

"Come on out, redskin," he muttered.

Johnson made his way to the door, and unable to see clearly, opened the portal a crack. He also aimed at the Indian, and waited.

Though the pony occasionally stamped its feet or tossed its head, the hiding warrior seemed content to stay put.

"Andy?" called Eddy. "You got a shot?"

"Nope. All I see is horse. How 'bout you?"

"Well, I can see him move around some behind that pony, but nothing good enough to shoot at."

Johnson took a deep breath and shifted his aim. "Now, George, you shoot right after me."

He squeezed the trigger and put a bullet in the horse's head. The animal screamed and dropped, exposing its rider.

The instant appearance of the Indian, full and unprotected, surprised Eddy. He jerked the rifle's trigger, throwing off his aim and sending the bullet wide. The Indian scampered to the other side of the rick and disappeared.

"Goddam son-of-a-bitch got away!" he shouted angrily. "Jesus Christ! Might just as well give *him* the rifle."

He heard the report of a rifle from the saloon, and the Indian reappeared.

"Well, looky here, Andy. The chief is back."

Dixon watched the Indian disappear. He'd been checking on Frenchy's gray horse when Billy Ogg said he saw another horse acting the same way. Investigating, Dixon heard the shots from the Rath & Company store and saw the horse drop. Then the Indian showed himself. Ogg quickly fired and missed. The warrior ran to the other side.

Another shot from the store. Feathers peeked from behind the rick, and Dixon saw a bare calf and foot. Ogg rammed another round into the rifle and fired again. Another miss. Again the Rath people shot. And once again, feathers peeked from behind the rick.

"Wait a minute," Dixon said.

He raised his Sharps and, watching the feathers, aimed where he thought the Indian was hiding. His shot went through a corner of the rick.

The response from the Indian was instantaneous. He appeared to jump six feet straight up, howling with pain. Then he ran zigzag for about forty yards, yelping with each step. Reaching tall grass, he dropped from sight.

Ogg stared through the loophole. "Jesus, Billy, you really scorched that buck." He started to laugh.

Dixon soon found himself surrounded by others who'd witnessed the event. Rough hands grabbed his arms and slapped him on the back. The shooting broke the tension of the last five hours, and the whole atmosphere inside the saloon relaxed.

He thought it odd that men who'd have said nothing had he killed the warrior seized on the wounding as a moment of levity, and remarked as much to Masterson.

"Oh, I don't know, Billy," the young teamster replied. "It's like what my daddy used to say about drowning men and straws. I reckon these fellows'd laugh at most anything to keep from cryin'."

Dixon rattled the shells in his pocket. "If they knew how short we were getting on ammo, they'd be crying right now."

Twenty-seven

Quanah and Lone Wolf, flanked by Brown Bull and Bear Mountain, stood on a bluff overlooking the battlefield. Before them stretched the small valley and the three houses that had caused them so much trouble.

"They should be burning," Quanah said to Lone Wolf.

"What? The lodges?"

"Yes. The hunters are supposed to be dead, the houses on fire. Is that not what we planned?"

Lone Wolf surveyed the scene and shrugged. "I don't know, Quanah, but we cannot quit now."

Brown Bull stepped forward. "He is right, little brother. The day is still new enough for us to grab victory. We need to destroy one house. The whites will see they can't win and lose heart. A warrior without heart is an easy kill."

"What would you suggest?"

"Take the house in the middle. It will then serve as cover against the remaining lodges."

"We've tried that," Lone Wolf said. "Before we can break down the doors, we are being killed by hunters on either side."

"Not if you do this." Brown Bull squatted and, using his finger, drew three boxes in the dirt.

He quickly outlined his plan, carefully explaining

how the war party was to be divided and what each group was to do.

As he finished, Lone Wolf said to his lieutenant, "Do you understand, Bear Mountain?"

The huge Kiowa nodded.

Lone Wolf looked at Quanah. "My men will follow me. The Cheyenne are also bound by the orders of their chiefs, and Stone Calf will attack if I ask. But what of the Comanche? Your men are free to leave if they wish. Why should they stay?"

"As long as one of us stays, the others will. We do not abandon warriors, and will not leave until all choose to do so."

"In that case, let's go back to the council and tell White Wolf we have a plan to get his scalps."

Eddy and Johnson were still telling the others about the Indian hiding behind the hides when the shots started. The firepower was primarily directed at the north side of the store. The fusillade was so intense, the defenders leaned against the thick sod walls or crowded into Eddy's bedroom. Only Olds refused to take cover, and returned to his southwest window.

Eddy grabbed a mirror, lifted it to the small window, and tried to see what was happening. He saw puffs of smoke as the Indians fired, but their bodies were hidden from view. Just before a bullet shattered the glass, he saw a huge group of Indians charging across the floodplain.

When he first heard the shots coming from the direction of the large dirt house, Quanah signaled his men to prepare to charge. Then came the firing from the fort side. Now was the time to attack.

He kicked his horse into a gallop, the feathered headdress flowing behind him. He was unarmed except for a pistol tightly gripped in his left hand along with the horse's reins. Quanah sounded his war cry and was joined by over a hundred voices. He rode straight toward the middle house, determined to go through the front door and out the back.

Lone Wolf heard the shots, then the sound of Quanah's men attacking. He wheeled his horse, and screaming, made for the back door of the long earth lodge at full gallop. Close behind rode Bear Mountain and the rest of his men as well as many Cheyenne.

As inspiration to the others, he carried no weapon. Instead, he had his coup stick. He'd told the war party that the white man was nothing to fear, and to prove it, he was going to ride into their house and count coup on every man inside. He'd said the hunters would then know the might of the Kiowa and Cheyenne.

He'd said many things to keep his men dedicated to their purpose, but deep inside he believed he would die in this part of the fight. Dying didn't frighten him. He was war chief of the Kiowa. As a warrior, it was his duty to die if necessary.

The saloon defenders ran to the south side of the store. They saw no Indians, but the heavy fire made many speculate the Rath store was soon to be attacked.

Then they heard shooting from the other side and ran to the north side of the saloon. Would the Indians attack Leonard and Rath both? The defenders split, and each shot at the puffs of smoke showing the Indian positions. Masterson looked out the back door and saw a large party of warriors descending on them.

"Here they come, boys!" he shouted, swinging up his weapon.

Shepherd turned at Masterson's voice. He looked left, then right. The fighting seemed to be coming from all sides, yet in the excitement no one manned the front. He ran to his old position and flung open the door.

Indians on horseback completely filled his field of vision. On frothing horses, brightly painted, bejeweled, yellow-skinned savages brandished knives, spears, rifles, and clubs. They screamed like crazed animals and rode straight at him.

Shepherd's knees weakened, and he fell to the floor. His bladder betrayed him. His arms were paralyzed with fear, and he stared at the door, wishing it shut. He would die under the hooves of a charging horse.

Dixon glanced about, and saw Shepherd on his knees in front of the open door. Thinking the bartender was wounded, Dixon ran to his side. He looked up and locked eyes with a Comanche not twenty yards from the door, bearing down on him at full speed.

"Oh, shit!"

Eddy sat in the corner of the room, his rifle trained on the small window. He'd felt the rumble of the Indians' charge, and expected the onslaught at any second. Prepared to shoot anything that showed itself, he hoped an Indian might try to climb through. He'd shoot him and leave the body in place. The thought wasn't pleasant, but at least the dead Indian would help protect the whites. He heard a noise and swung his rifle toward the doorway.

"George? It's me, Sam Smith. I'm coming in, so hold your fire."

Smith walked in to be greeted by a grinning Eddy. "Right polite of you to announce yourself," he said, and laid the rifle in his lap.

"Well, I'd sure as hell'd hate to be shot 'cause I didn't observe my manners. Folks is a mite skittish at the moment. I thought Wild Bill was going to shoot me anyway."

Eddy laughed aloud. "Wild Bill? William sure don't paint me a picture anything like Hickok."

"Nope, he don't," the hunter replied, grinning broadly, "but you got to admit the man has sand. 'Sides, Wild William won't cut it. Maybe somethin' like Wondrous William, Wolverine Will . . . Hell, I cain't think of a good name other than Wild Bill. You?"

The bookkeeper shook his head and frowned with concentration. "No, sir, I can't. Before this morning, I'd thought more along the lines of Winsome Will."

Smith nodded slowly and pursed his lips. "Or maybe Whip-o-Will?"

"Or Will-of-the-Wisp."

The hunter drew a deep breath, thrust out his chest, and declared in a powerful baritone voice, "Look out, stranger. You're talkin' to Will-o'-the-Wisp."

Eddy gawked at the posturing Smith and guffawed. Both giggled and snickered, repeating their invented names, each repetition bringing on fits of laughter and tears.

Finally, Smith held up a hand, wiping his eyes with the other. "Shut the hell up, George!" he ordered. He sniffed and drew a deep shuddering breath. "Goddam, son, people gonna come running in here thinkin' we done lost what little sense we got. Besides, that ain't what I come to see you about."

Relaxed, Eddy regarded his friend. "All right then. What can I do for you?"

"I don't know if you noticed, but even with all this shootin' going on, there ain't many bullets coming our way. I sneaked a peek, and them red gentlemen is all over the saloon."

Fully alert now, Eddy jumped to his feet. "We got to help them, Sam!"

"Haul your reins in. I tried, but them bucks got most near all the gun holes covered. Every time I poked my barrel out, they'd shoot at it."

"What are we going to do?"

"Nothing, George. We're gonna do nothin', 'cept wait our turn."

Instinct saved Dixon's life. No reasons, no thoughts at all, just a gut-level desire to live drove him to his feet. He kicked the door shut, turned, and screamed for the crossbar. A heavy thud. The door slammed into the middle of Dixon's back. He thought he'd been shot. Another thud. The door opened two inches before the hunter's weight drove it back against the jamb.

"Where's that goddam crossbar?" he shouted, trying to be heard over the gunfire.

More blows. Dixon heard a whinny and realized that one of the Indians had backed his horse to the door to kick it in. Again hooves crashed into the door. Dixon heard wood crack.

"I cain't hold this much longer," he cried, his voice breaking with hysteria.

Hanrahan ran across the saloon and picked up the oak crossbar. Moving beside Dixon, he slipped one end of the board into its L-shaped iron slot. "All right, Billy, when I give the word, you move, and I'll drop the other end."

Dixon nodded, then held up his hand as the pressure at his back eased. "Wait a minute. I think they quit." He stepped forward, and Hanrahan let the bar fall into place.

The hunter turned and gazed at the door. Why'd they quit? he wondered. A hole appeared in the wood. The bullet screamed close by his head. Dixon grabbed the still-kneeling Shepherd and yanked him to the side. A sudden flurry followed the first shot, with more bullets striking or passing through the door.

Dixon turned to shout a warning to the others in the saloon, but the firing stopped as quickly as it had begun. Now he heard the thumps and bangs of human hands and feet attempting a breach. He relaxed a bit. The Indians had tried this line of attack before and failed.

Helping Shepherd to his feet, Dixon led the bartender back to his seat. He opened a pint bottle of gin and handed it to the bartender. "Here you go, ol' hoss. A man that comes that close to death deserves a snort."

Shepherd took the vessel with shaking hands. He drank like a man gone two days with no water. He lowered the half-empty bottle and drew a shuddering breath.

Dixon watched Shepherd's hands lose their shake. He saw the barkeep's lips move, but could not hear what he said. "What was that, Oscar?" he asked.

Shepherd looked up. Tears sparkled in his eyes like liquid diamonds. The wet eyes and quivering lip made Dixon decidedly uncomfortable. He didn't care if a man cried when it was called for, but he hoped Shepherd's reaction was to his near demise. Dixon, better than anyone else, knew he'd probably saved the bartender's life, but the last thing he wanted was a half-drunk, sobbing soul promising him eternal friendship and gratitude. Later, Shepherd could stand him a drink.

Shepherd drew himself up and wiped at his eyes. Dixon tensed.

"I said I pissed myself." The bartender's voice was barely above a whisper. He glanced around the room to see if anyone else might have heard his confession.

Dixon felt a rush of relief. "Oh, Jesus, is that all?"

Shepherd flinched as though slapped. "Is that all?" he barked. Then he quickly surveyed the bar again and lowered his voice. "What more do you want, Billy? Hell, I just stood there in that doorway and pissed myself like a baby!"

"Listen, Oscar, it don't mean a thing. You ain't the only man here who wet his drawers, or worse. As for standing in the doorway, why do you think it's called 'scared stiff'? Sometimes a man sees something that his body just cain't handle, so it freezes. Don't make you less a man."

Shepherd grabbed Dixon's arm. "Really, Billy? You don't think I'm a coward?"

"Look around. I see a lot a scared men, but no cowards."

Shepherd relaxed his grip, then patted the hunter on the back. "Thanks, Billy."

"You're welcome, Oscar. Now, I got to get back to fightin' Indians."

"Sure, Billy, you go ahead."

Dixon rose to leave, but turned back at the sound of the bartender's voice.

"I know I owe you for saving me, but if you tell anybody I pissed my pants, I'll shoot you dead."

The hunter laughed as he made his way back to his station. Picking up his rifle, he peered past the edge of the loophole—and came face-to-face with an Indian. The warrior's eyes went wide, and he screamed before ducking out of the way.

Dixon smiled and gently shook his head. "Oscar, my friend," he muttered to himself, "you're gonna have to stand in line."

Twenty-eight

Dixon and Masterson walked over to the bar and accepted a lukewarm beer from Shepherd. Dixon longed for cool water for his parched throat, but the Kirmeyer's worked.

Hanrahan leaned against the bar, sipping on a large tumbler of whiskey. He looked tired. Not beaten, but sorely tired. His face was gaunt, his expression dour, and his eyes were like two bushy-browed holes.

"We're getting low on ammo," Dixon said.

Hanrahan grunted. "The thought *has* crossed my mind."

Dixon and Masterson exchanged glances.

The hunter continued. "Bat and me thought we might make a run to the stores. It'd give us a chance to rearm and catch up on the news."

"Too dangerous."

"Well, then, we need to split up and move to a store."

Hanrahan glowered at the men. "Like hell, you will. I ain't about to leave my liquor stores here unprotected."

"You know that we can't hold off another attack," Masterson said. "If the Indians come back and we run out of bullets, they're going to come in here and take your whiskey and your hair."

"Yeah, and probably my balls, too. Who gives a

shit?" Hanrahan straightened, emptied the tumbler in one swallow, and placed the glass on the bar top. "Where are we going?"

Dixon cleared his throat and set down his beer. "No offense, Jim, but you're a mite old to be dodgin' Indian bullets and runnin' about."

"Bullshit! If there's any foolishness to be done, I aim to be in on it. I figure if I get my ass shot off, I won't care what happens to the saloon. On the other hand, if I live through the run getting there, I know *I'll* come back."

"Damn, Jim, it's most of a hundred yards to the Leonard stockade," Masterson said, shaking his head. "And close to that to Rath's."

"So?"

"Hold on, Bat," Dixon said. "This old coot's mind is set. I plan to head to Rath's. I got me a case of ammo there. Bat's going to Leonard's."

Hanrahan gave the young teamster an appraising look. "Billy's got no cover between here and Rath's store, but at least he's got running room. If you start following that wall at the compound, the Injuns will pin you to it."

Masterson grinned. "I ain't plannin' to go in the front door."

Hanrahan arched a shaggy eyebrow. "And, pray tell, just how do you plan to do it?"

"Same way I come here, Jim, if you and Billy'll give me a five-minute head start."

Masterson slipped out the back door of the saloon and dropped to the ground. He surveyed all the land he could see. No sign of Indians. The area between the saloon and the window at Keeler's restaurant was littered with dead and wounded horses. Some milled about, but most just stood and regarded him with pain-dulled eyes.

He moved from horse to horse, using each as cover, until he reached O'Keefe's blacksmith shop. He lay against a wall, keeping a bay mare between himself and the open valley. Listening intently, he heard no sounds coming from inside the shop, and decided it was safe to move on.

Again using the animals for cover, he crossed to the stockade wall of the Myers and Leonard compound. The shutter had been torn off the window he'd come through earlier. Catching a black wearing a bridle, he slowly walked the horse to the open window. Standing under the animal's chin, the teamster peeked over the sill.

The remaining shutter and both doors had been ripped off. The inside of the eatery was strewn with broken china, spilled flour and cornmeal, and furniture. Seeing no one, he climbed over the sill and dropped inside, wincing at the clattering of cracked crockery.

He drew his pistol and quickly crossed to the north door. He peered at the stables, but saw no signs of life. His eyes scanned the hide yard between the restaurant and the main store. Each rick of hides was tall enough to easily hide a man, especially if he didn't want to be seen. This was the most dangerous area he had to cross.

Stepping through the door, he ran to the first stack of hides. With each step he expected to hear the crash of the rifle, feel the bullet smack into his body—but nothing happened. He walked the length of the rick, looking around the corners at the other piles of hides. Still he saw no Indians.

He ran to another rick and repeated his actions. Nothing. He moved from one stack to another until he was within thirty feet of the store's back door. Here he waited, gauging when best to make his final effort. He wanted to call out, to warn the others he was coming in, but dared not, in case there were Indians hidden nearby. He hoped those inside could see him. More importantly, he hoped they saw him and didn't think he was an Indian.

He was still trying to decide a course of action when the shooting started. At first, there were just sporadic shots, but these soon intensified into the sound of a small war. The firing came from the direction of the saloon, and he guessed Dixon and Hanrahan had made their break.

Knowing the Indians would be preoccupied with the spectacle of the running men, he broke cover and ran for his life. Just as he approached the door, it flew open, and he sailed into the waiting arms of Dutch Henry Born.

Dixon ran as he had never run before. His feet seemed to float above the ground as he weaved his way from a side window in the saloon toward the Rath & Company store. Initially, there had been some argument about who was to cross first and who was to follow, until he pointed out that the lead man was essentially helping the Indians to kill the second. Now they ran together, the long-legged Hanrahan in front, the shorter Dixon not six feet behind.

They'd run almost a third of the way before the first bullet struck, kicking dust between Hanrahan's feet. Acting as a spur, the round forced the saloon keeper from a gallop to a dead run.

The closer they came to the other store, the heavier the firing became. Each bullet that missed sprayed dirt over the men or buzzed by their heads. Dixon was amazed to find himself uninjured. With every passing second, he expected to see Hanrahan fall, expected to feel the sting of a bullet himself. Would he stop for the saloon owner? Would Hanrahan stop for him?

Dixon saw their destination nearing rapidly. The Indians changed their focus from the two men to the door frame of the store. Dixon and Hanrahan hit the door, shouting to be let in. As they waited, bullets rattled about them like hailstones. Dixon had no idea how many Indians were shooting at them, but he couldn't believe so many rounds could be expended without a hit. Whatever else these Indians may be, they were no marksmen.

The door swung open, and Dixon and Hanrahan fell into the store, landing in a heap on the dirt floor.

Johnson pushed the door shut and dropped the crossbar. "Move!" he shouted at the men on the floor. "Move, move, move!"

Eddy came out of his room just as Hanrahan and Dixon scrambled out of the doorway. Bullets continued to slam into, and smash through, the door, and the defenders hugged the dirt walls. After a few minutes, the shooting slackened, then stopped altogether.

"Where the hell did you come from?" the bookkeeper asked.

"Saloon," Hanrahan answered between gasps. "It's a goddam long run over here."

Dixon drew a deep breath and let it out. His heart rate was already returning to normal. "You folks all right?"

Langton appeared from the kitchen. "Well, hello. It's Jim Hanrahan and Mr. Dixon, I believe."

Eddy laughed. "Hell, James, these two braved Indian fire to come over here and see how we're doing."

Langton clucked. "I don't know whether to applaud your courage or decry your foolishness. However, as long as you're here—"

Hanrahan had recovered enough to talk coherently. "This ain't exactly a social call. Naturally, we're concerned about you all over here, but more to the point, we need ammunition."

"You're leaving again?" Hannah asked, still sitting against her bedroom wall.

"Course we are," Hanrahan said. "We need ammo. I mean, we are down to almost nothing to shoot."

"Can't you stay?" Hannah pleaded. "There are so few of us."

"How many's a few?"

"Six and the woman," Langton answered.

Hanrahan grunted. "Hell, Mr. Langton, I got barely nine myself."

"Yes, but most of your men are seasoned hunters. With the exception of Sam Smith, we are city folk, used to city ways. Must both of you leave?"

"I cain't speak for Billy, but I have to get back. That saloon is my livelihood. Those men deserve better than to be deserted now."

Dixon nodded. "Jim's right. I fought with those men, and I cain't leave them like this. We've got to return with the shells."

Hannah stood and approached the hunter. "Does it really take two of you to take the bullets back? It's like Mr. Langton said, most of the men there are hunters. We have no one here, begging Sam's pardon, but what difference would one more gun make to the saloon?"

Eddy cleared his throat. "We have another problem, Hannah. It's not her fault, but if them redskins find out we got a white woman here, they'd stop at nothing to get to her. You know how they are."

Dixon looked at Hanrahan. "What do you think, Jim? Those Indians just might make a real effort to get in here if they find out about Miz Olds."

"Do what you think best, Billy. Me, I got to go back."

"All right." He turned to Langton. "I'll stay. Meantime, we got to get Jim loaded up for his trip back."

"I could use a flour sack or some such," the saloon keeper said.

"And don't forget to get some of the Sharps .44-

caliber ammo as well. That new rifle of mine is still at the saloon."

Over the next ten minutes, the occupants of the Rath & Company store were busy opening crates of ammunition and filling Hanrahan's flour sack. When he gauged he had about all he could carry, he made his way to the back door.

"Don't reckon them fellers will be expecting this," he said, laughing.

Nope, I reckon they won't." Dixon scanned the countryside through the partially open door. "Looks clear to me, Jim. You set?"

"Yes, sir. Now let me get the hell out of here before them sons-of-bitches drink me dry."

As Hanrahan stepped through the doorway, Dixon offered his hand.

"Good luck, Jim. Remember who that shiny new Sharps belongs to. I'll be over presently to collect it."

Hanrahan shook the hunter's hand and said, "I'll be there to give it to you."

The saloon keeper took a deep breath and began his second run of a lifetime.

Rifle resting on the sill, Dixon watched through the restaurant window as Hanrahan made his mad dash. Firing from the Indians was sporadic and, to the hunter, seemed halfhearted. Hanrahan sped across the open terrain and, unscathed, disappeared into the saloon's back door.

Dixon removed the Sharps from the window and leaned the weapon against a sod wall. "That's that," he said to the room at large.

"*Ja,* dat's dat." Johnson turned to Eddy. "George, if you don't mind, I think maybe I'll go see about that well."

The bookkeeper nodded. "Good idea, Swede. I'd enjoy a nice, cool drink of water."

"*Ja,* by damn, dat's not the half of it."

Eddy sat at the employees' table. He tipped the chair

back on two legs, resting his foot against the top. Perched comfortably, he regarded the newest member of their defense force. Though Dixon's posture seemed relaxed, his eyes constantly moved as he scanned the room.

"I'd offer you a cigar, but . . ."

Dixon changed his focus to Eddy. He wondered if he looked as worn-out as the begrimed bookkeeper. "But they're in your other pants?"

Eddy smiled. "Somethin' like that." The grin faded. "I truly appreciate you staying here with us. We can use the help."

"Don't sell yourself short, George. Looks to me like you handled matters well enough. Hell, it's noon and ain't a one of you dead or wounded."

"I suppose." Eddy dropped the chair to the floor and rose. "Where you headed?"

"Cain't rightly say. I thought I'd wander around a bit, take a gander at what you got."

Eddy nodded. "Fair enough. I'm going to see how Andy's comin' with that well. Holler if you need anything."

"Thanks, George, but I got a Sharps, lots of bullets, a good eye, and a passel of Indians to shoot at. What more could a man want?"

Lone Wolf looked across the valley at the bodies of warriors lying with those of dead horses. Were Kiowa not among the others, he'd have gladly put this battle behind him. His gaze narrowed, and he clenched his jaw.

"Do we ride into the white guns to retrieve our dead?" Bear Mountain asked.

Lone Wolf turned to his lieutenant. "We will not abandon a single Kiowa today. We will get ours."

"And the others?"

"If you can pick up a man without getting shot, do so, but only after we have our men."

Bear Mountain nodded and returned to the waiting warriors. He mounted his warhorse and turned to speak. Before the Kiowa could utter a word, one of the Cheyenne grunted and toppled from his mount.

Bear Mountain jumped from his horse and reached the fallen man at the same time as Lone Wolf. Together, they turned over their stricken comrade. Lone Wolf laid a hand on his chest.

"He is dead," he said, awestruck.

"But how?" Bear Mountain asked.

A small trickle of blood ran down the dead warrior's face. Lone Wolf lifted the long black hair away. He found a neat hole in the side of the Cheyenne's head. Looking at the other side, he found a good portion of the man's skull missing.

"He has been shot."

"This cannot be!" another of the Cheyenne declared. "We heard no shot, saw no smoke."

Lone Wolf stood. "Fool! The man has half of his head missing. I have been in enough battles to know a bullet wound."

Bear Mountain stood and nervously peered around himself. "Is it possible the white men have bullets that can sniff us out? What if they can shoot from their log houses and the bullets fly until they find us?"

Lone Wolf looked at his second in command. "It is bad enough that I have a yellow Comanche medicine man telling me what to do. I don't need you to start wailing like an old woman about the magic of the whites." He addressed the gathered warriors. "There is no medicine here to fear. Somewhere out there is a hunter with a rifle. We did not hear the shot because he is downwind. We did not see smoke because it was gone by the time we looked for it."

He turned away from the others and walked to his horse. Mounted, he rode with a straight back. A voice screamed in his head to lie low on the animal, to become one with his horse and cheat the white man of his target. But he wouldn't. His men were unnerved, the Cheyenne and Comanche dispirited. What was needed was a show of a Kiowa war chief's medicine. He rode back to the group.

"You Cheyenne, get your man. We will return to the camp. I will meet with the other leaders and see what can be done about those that have fallen near the hunters' lodges."

Stone Calf's Son remounted his pony and turned to the Kiowa chieftain.

"I tell you true, Lone Wolf. The Comanche shaman is the reason we suffer. His bad medicine has angered the Great Spirit, and now He offers help to our enemies to punish us for following Isatai. Until we are rid of this false prophet, we are doomed. I say this with truth, and my father says it, too. When the time comes, you would do well to choose your friends carefully."

As the party rode off, Lone Wolf held back, giving the Cheyenne breathing room. He started walking his horse slowly toward the war party's main encampment.

Bear Mountain rode next to his leader, with the remaining Kiowa close behind. "The Cheyenne spoke with much anger."

Lone Wolf nodded. "Yes, he did."

"Do you think he will risk war with us just to kill a failed magician?"

Lone Wolf grinned. "He's young, full of fight, as you and I once were. Chief Stone Calf is a wise man. The friendship between the Kiowa and the Cheyenne is more important than the life of one man. If the Cheyenne want to kill the Comanche, I will not stop them unless the Comanche chiefs ask me."

The pair rode in silence for several minutes. Then Bear Mountain spoke again.

"I wonder if it is true. I wonder if we are accursed because of the actions of one man."

"Bear Mountain, my friend, we are accursed by ourselves. Isatai only offered the bitter fruit of foolishness. *We* ate it."

Dixon chewed thoughtfully on a dried apple as he wandered through the Rath & Company store. Though he saw extensive damage, it seemed to be localized to those areas directly facing windows. The building was stuffy from having been shut up and filled several times with gun smoke, but the thick walls kept the interior cool.

Hannah had finished reloading weapons, and now sat quietly reading the Bible. She offered Dixon a warm smile as he passed. He went to the Olds' bedroom to visit William.

The clerk sat on a stool in front of the window, his round-barrel Sharps leaned against the wall, close at hand. He had one pistol tucked into the waistband of his pants and held another. A box of .40-caliber Sharps ammunition rested on the windowsill, and he wore a single bandolier of pistol rounds across his chest. To Dixon, he looked like a miniature Mexican *bandido*.

"William."

"Billy."

"Looks to me like you're loaded for bear."

Olds shrugged. That was when Dixon noticed the change. Gone was the weakness, replaced by a hardness that only a near brush with death can bring. Take away the weapons, and the small clerk would look as he had before this morning, until you saw his eyes. They were clear, sharp. Olds's eyes reflected the changes in his spirit. Dixon knew he was now a man to be counted on in a fight. He clapped the clerk on the shoulder.

"Didn't want nothin'," the hunter said. "Just came to pay my respects and get a lay of the land."

William gazed out his window. "You don't need to worry about my corner."

"That's true, William. Just knowing that you're here at this window makes me feel better. Now, if you'll excuse me, I got some other folks to visit."

Dixon turned to leave, but stopped at Olds's voice. "You know, Billy. I'm glad you decided to stay and help us with Hannah, but I think we could've handled this alone."

The hunter faced the clerk. "I don't doubt that, William. But if Miz Olds feels better by my staying, I don't reckon it's doing any harm. You?"

Olds's tired smile didn't quite reach his eyes. "No, sir, no harm done, and no offense meant," he said.

Dixon started back out of the room. "None taken, William. I'll see you directly."

The hunter made his way back to the main store. He crossed to Eddy's bedroom and stuck his head inside the doorway. Johnson stood up to his knees in a hole while Eddy and Sam Smith watched. The Swede brought up a handful of mud dripping with water. He grinned at Dixon.

Dixon smiled, waved, and moved on. He examined the front door, stacked to the ceiling with sacks of corn, feed, and flour. He looked through several loopholes, but none grabbed him and said, "Use me." Finally, he popped the last bit of apple into his mouth and made his way back to the kitchen.

The west door had been barricaded again after Hanrahan's departure. Dixon's gaze followed the breastwork of feed sacks, but stopped near the ceiling. A transom cut over this door was still open. The hunter climbed up the bags and scanned the land west of the store. Something crawled along the edge of the tall grass.

As curious as he was suspicious, Dixon leveled his

rifle and aimed, resting his body across one knee. He fired. The recoil knocked him off his perch, and he tumbled backward from the barricade. On the way down he dislodged a washtub and several cooking utensils, which made a terrific crash as they landed on the floor around him. The clatter of his Sharps following him down did nothing to lessen the uproar.

As he struggled to regain his feet, Dixon heard the sound of approaching voices. First to peek around the corner was George Eddy. The look on the book-keeper's face was one of concern.

"Oh, my God!" he cried, seeing Dixon lying on the floor amid a jumble of pots and pans. "Are you all right?" He turned to the others, now crowding through the doorway. "I think he's been shot."

Langton pushed his way past. "Are you sure, George?" He saw Dixon lying on the floor. "Oh, my. Speak to me, Billy." He dropped to one knee and leaned over to the hunter. "Speak to me, son. Are you hurt? Are you shot? Where are you hit?"

"He's hit?" Hannah's voice was shrill. "He's hit? What shall we do? Lord Almighty, help us now in the hour of our need!"

William Olds placed a hand in the middle of Hannah's back. "Shush now, woman. This ain't no time to be hysterical." He knelt next to Langton. "You see any blood, James?"

Hannah shrieked. "Blood? Blood? He's dead! I'm sure of it."

Olds sighed and looked up at his wife. "Dammit, don't you have some knittin' or some such to attend to?"

Hannah jerked as though slapped. She sniffed, turned her back, and left the room.

"I ain't shot."

All heads turned to Dixon, who was again struggling to sit up. Langton and Olds regained their feet and helped Dixon to his.

"What do you mean, you're not shot?" Eddy asked.

"Just that, George. I climbed on that stack of feed sacks to look around. I saw somethin' in the grass and took a shot. Damn rifle knocked me clean off my perch."

Olds stared at Dixon. "You ain't hurt at all?"

The hunter grinned. "Not if pride don't count."

"It ain't funny, Billy. You like to scared me to death, not to mention gettin' my missus all riled. It ain't right. Least you could do is get hurt if you're gonna upset folks."

Dixon drew a deep breath and let it out slowly. Before he could answer, Eddy put his arm around the clerk's shoulders and led him back into the main store.

"Now, William, don't fret," the bookkeeper said. "I'm sure Billy meant no harm. I don't think he jumped off that seed on purpose."

"But, George, it just ain't right. I mean . . . it just ain't."

Langton looked from the departing men to Dixon. "Sorry, Billy. William's been under a lot of stress as of late."

"Yeah," Dixon answered dryly. "I reckon what with him the only one gettin' shot at, it'd tend to wear on his nerves."

Langton smiled and refused the bait. "You sure you're not harmed?"

Dixon nodded. "Fine as frog's hair."

"Very good. Then I shall go. Don't hesitate to call if you need help."

Langton had no sooner left the room than Dixon retrieved his rifle and clambered back up the barricade. The object he'd seen earlier was still moving about eight hundred yards to the west. After finding a secure purchase, he aimed again and fired. In dismay, he saw dust rise in front of the target.

"Damn!" he muttered. "That's twice you missed."

He quickly reloaded and drew a third bead. The

third round was true. All movement stopped. Dixon
had no idea what he'd just shot, but the satisfaction
was in the shot itself.

Quanah led a band of Kiowa and Comanche to the
northwest of the log fort. The white men could not
see as well there because they had no windows or
doors in that wall.

He'd gathered the men from areas near the battle
ground. Now regrouped into a small, but deadly, fighting force, they'd decided to use the northwest
approach to attempt another breach.

Each warrior rode low on his horse, avoiding hills
and riding through draws and over low mounds. Topping one such mound, Quanah saw the tall walls of
the fort. He longed to climb those walls. Many scalps
were due his people. He had dead to rescue from the
whites. More than a raid, the attack became a quest
for him to redeem himself in his own eyes for the
abject failure of their initial charge.

Another crest, and the target was closer. Soon they
would reach the edge of the valley. The last part of
the ride was the most dangerous. The path down the
wall of the valley was unprotected.

He topped a final mound, and the lodges were in
plain view. As he dropped into a nearby arroyo, he
heard a grunt, and one of the Kiowa fell from his
horse. Wheeling his own mount, he hurried to the
fallen warrior. Brown Bull already knelt next to the
Kiowa. He rose as Quanah arrived.

"He's dead, little brother."

Quanah was stunned. "How can that be? I heard no
shot. Did anyone hear a shot?"

The remaining warriors kept quiet. He looked from
face to face. He saw fear in many, resignation in others. The one thing he could not find was outrage.
These men acted as though the death of a warrior was

to be expected. As though it was as natural as the setting of the sun.

"What is wrong with you?" he screamed. "These white men have killed another of us. Do you not wish for blood? For scalps? Will you stand about like old women and be cut down?" He sneered. "Maybe you'll slit your own throat, save the white man the effort. Come, Brown Bull, we will go back to camp where the *men* are. There I will find warriors."

"But, Quanah," Brown Bull asked sadly, "how do we fight an enemy who can kill us in or out of sight?"

Twenty-nine

Eddy stood transfixed, watching an Indian on a magnificent white stallion charge directly for the Rath & Company store.

What could the warrior do? Was he looking to get killed? Eddy had heard of some Indians making a suicide run if they'd been shamed. It was the only way to repair their reputation. Faced with the same decision, the bookkeeper thought he'd just as soon move to another town.

"Folks," he called. "We gotta Injun comin' in fast."

Johnson answered from their shared bedroom. "Just shoot him, George."

"I cain't. That buck is weaving and dodging about. Besides, he's here now!"

Eddy watched as a brightly painted young man leapt from his horse and charged the store on foot. He ran straight at Eddy's loophole, and the bookkeeper shrank back against the wall. A pistol appeared inside the hole.

"Jesus Christ, God Almighty, he's got a gun!"

The warrior pulled the trigger, sending a round into the sod wall across from the loophole.

The thumb cocked the piece. The hand twisted and turned. The pistol bucked, and a second round went into the floor.

Cock. Aim. Blam! The third bullet went into the floor as well.

Eddy, barely three feet away, just knew that soon the gun would point his way.

The Indian again twisted the pistol and fired his fourth shot into the ceiling.

With mounting terror, Eddy watched as the warrior turned the pistol his way. Afraid to move, he stared down what looked like a two-inch-wide barrel.

He expected to see his life pass before him or to hear a chorus of angels. Neither happened. As Eddy waited for the bullet to crash into his skull, he was trying to decide whether a two-inch wide pistol barrel was two-hundred-caliber or two-caliber.

Click!

Misfire!

Eddy threw himself to the floor.

Bang!

The last round passed through the space his head had occupied and buried itself into the wall.

The pistol disappeared. A few moments of quiet followed. Then he heard a rifle report coming from the Olds' bedroom. Eddy hurried to see what William was shooting at. He found the little man calmly regaining his seat on the stool he kept near the window.

"What happened, William?"

"I got him."

"Who?"

"That Injun what just shot up our store." Olds stood to act out his story. "I heard you holler. Then I heard all this shootin'. I count rounds and figure no Injun is gonna take the time to reload, so after his last shot, I lean out my window and wait."

"Dammit, William! What'd I tell you about hangin' your skinny butt out like that?"

Olds drew himself up. "Do you want to hear my story or not?"

Eddy sighed. "Sure. Then what happened?"

"Alrighty. Now, here I am, ready to shoot." Olds pantomimed holding a rifle. "Then I see him come runnin' around the corner of the shop like the Devil himself is pokin' him in the butt with that pitchfork. I reckon he thinks that the south wall is good 'cause we don't have loopholes there." Olds started to laugh. "What he didn't figure is that anybody'd be hanging out a window *and* around the corner."

Olds sat, still laughing. "You should have seen his face, George. Eyes like saucers. I think maybe he might of peed himself."

Despite the time it was taking, Eddy was fascinated by Olds's story. He marveled not so much at what the clerk had done, but at his attitude toward the whole event.

"Then what, William?"

Olds shrugged. "Nothin' much. He turned to run, and I plugged him in the back."

"Well, I'll be damned. You kill him?"

"Nope."

Eddy's surprised must have shown on his face, for Olds grinned but said nothing. Apparently, the clerk was enjoying himself and in no hurry to finish his tale.

"All right, William, I'll ask it. Don't you think you ought to finish the job?"

The grin grew wider, and Olds's eyes twinkled merrily. "Nope. You wanna know why?"

Eddy closed his eyes. "I'll bite."

Olds stood and walked to his window. "If you listen, you can hear him hollerin' for help. He ain't goin' anywhere, because I think I busted his back. He just lays against that south wall and calls and calls. I figure sooner or later, someone's gonna come runnin'. Then I'm gonna bag me another one."

Quanah walked his horse to the edge of a bluff overlooking the battleground. He watched the log

ouses below, taking care not to show the fear he felt.
he silent killing of the Kiowa warrior bothered him.
Vorse still was Brown Bull's observation.

How could he maintain the fight if the war party
hought the white men had a more powerful magic?
Comanche warriors were not bound by orders to re-
nain. Each had his own reason for coming, fighting,
nd if he chose, abandoning the fight. Quanah had no
uthority to make them stay.

He heard horses approach, and quickly pulled his
ight arm into his lap. He knew his injury was com-
non knowledge, but this meeting was crucial. He
ould afford no impression of weakness.

White Wolf rode up on his left, Isatai on his right.
he three men sat quietly gazing at the white men's
illage.

"How is your arm?" White Wolf asked, breaking
he silence.

"It is getting better."

"Can you move it?"

Quanah shook his head. "Not really, but some of
he feeling is coming back."

White Wolf made no reply, continuing to stare into
he valley.

Quanah heard more riders, and the three were joined
y Lone Wolf and his shadow, Bear Mountain. Behind
nem rode some of the lesser Cheyenne chieftains.

"Where is Stone Calf?" Quanah asked.

One of the chiefs, an older man with a dour face,
nswered, "He has gone down to the lodges. His son
es wounded against a house."

The information settled in Quanah's stomach like a
ock. What else could possibly go wrong? Perhaps the
iowa were right—it was time to go home. He shook
imself.

"I will not be beaten by frightened men," he mut-
red. Louder he said, "It is time we came together to
ecide what we can do."

"Do?" Dour Face laughed. "What have we not done? We charge as one, and the whites shoot us. We charge as many smaller groups, again we are shot. What would you have us do, Quanah? Attack one by one? Stone Calf's son tried that. Now he is crippled and trapped." He pointed to Isatai. "He has poisoned this fight for all of us. His magic is false, and it works against us."

White Wolf turned and gazed at the Cheyenne spokesman with aged eyes. "Are you saying you intend to leave the fight? To turn and run?"

Dour Face bristled at the thinly veiled insult. "We are afraid of no man! Send the medicine man away, and we will talk of another fight."

White Wolf's face wrinkled into a frown, and he pursed his lips. "Is the presence of one man the cause of failure? I think not. We have allowed ourselves to act foolishly and to believe in promises. I promise you nothing but that the Comanche will continue the fight. We ask that you join us."

"Look into the valley, White Wolf," Dour Face said. "See how far we ride to hold council? We move away, the whites shoot us. We move farther away, they still kill us. The Comanche shaman has angered the Great Spirit, and we are to be punished as long as he is allowed a part in this battle. Send him away. Send him—"

Suddenly the dour-faced chief's eyes went wide. Mouth open, but soundless, he rolled backward off his horse and fell to the ground. Before any of the others could react, Isatai's warhorse screamed once and dropped, tumbling the medicine man into the dirt. Quanah turned his horse and rode for cover. From concealing brush, they looked at those left behind.

Isatai slowly raised his head and looked around. Unhurt, he jumped to his feet and ran to Quanah's side.

"Did you see that?" he asked, wide-eyed and gasping for breath.

Quanah looked at Isatai as though the medicine man had lost his mind. "How was I not to see it? Soon we will be on the reservation trying to hide from their bullets."

A Cheyenne chief dismounted. "Come with me," he ordered his companions. "We must gather our dead."

As a unit, the Cheyenne warriors ran out on the bluff. Quanah, Isatai, and Lone Wolf followed, but made for the shaman's horse.

"The bullet went right into the blaze on his forehead," Lone Wolf said. "Tell me, medicine man, why did you not paint all of the horse's head?"

"See? There is the proof. They couldn't kill my horse, except by shooting the only spot on his body not covered by my paint."

"If you ask the Cheyenne, they would say the hunters could not see the unpainted blaze. That the Great Spirit carried the bullet up here and placed it in the only spot not covered by your paint. They would say He did this to show His displeasure with you and those of us who have followed you." Lone Wolf stood and absently scratched his chest. "I don't believe I'll mock them anymore."

Lone Wolf rode into camp, deep in thought. The death of Isatai's horse made the accusations of the Cheyenne all the more believable. Though he asked Bear Mountain to say nothing to the others, he wasn't sure the huge warrior would keep quiet.

Perhaps it was just as well. The fight had not gone as promised by the Comanche. No scalps hung from his lance except for that of the dog. How many men had died for three scalps? If they stayed, how many more would die?

The Kiowa war chief sighed and stopped at his campsite. He dismounted and sat, prepared to rest until a decision was made by the others.

He heard hoofbeats. Stone Calf galloped into camp.

The Cheyenne veered neither right nor left, but rushed at Isatai, who cowered away from the charging horse.

"You!" Stone Calf yelled. "You, shaman. I have listened to your speeches of what you have done, where you have gone. I heard the tale of the magic yellow paint." He pointed to the sky. "A gift from the Great Spirit, you said. You have been to His lodge, you said." Stone Calf pointed at Isatai. "I challenge you. Prove to me that the Great Spirit protects you. My son is wounded. He cannot walk, and lies against the hunters' lodge. Go to him."

Isatai kept his gaze on the ground. "I can't. I have no magic to heal a paralyzing wound."

Stone Calf laughed, a hollow mocking sound to Lone Wolf's ears.

"Heal him? I would not let your tainted magic near him! I want you to bring him to me. The paint that covers your body will protect you. Is that not what you say? Bring him to me. If the magic is real, you will do as I ask."

Isatai said nothing. His shoulders sagged. He was a beaten man. Lone Wolf almost felt sorry for the Comanche—until he remembered how many of his own men were dead or wounded.

Stone Calf sneered, then spat on the shaman. "Bah! You are as useless as an old woman. Worse. An old woman knows her place. If you believe nothing else, Isatai, believe this: If my son dies, you will die!"

Dixon climbed down from the sack barricade and crossed to Eddy's bedroom. He heard the cries of the wounded Indian. There was pain and desperation in the voice.

"Damn, George, we got to listen to that caterwaulin' all night?" he snapped.

Eddy's eyes widened in surprise. "Feel free to step outside and shut him up," he replied tersely, angered by Dixon's insinuation that he had some control over the situation.

As though on cue, a low moan came from outside. The sound rose to a wail and a chattering in a language no one inside the store understood.

Dixon frowned. "Listen to that, George. What the hell is that all about?"

"Perhaps he's calling to Jesus," Hannah said quietly.

Sam Smith snorted. "Ain't likely, Miz Olds. He's a heathern. They don't believe in no Jesus, God, or nothing you an' me'd know. Most likely, he hollerin' for his old man to rescue him."

"He's right," Dixon said. "Long as that buck's drawing air, none of the Indians are leaving. They don't like leaving dead behind. They sure as hell ain't gonna desert this fellow."

Langton rose from his bed. "What shall we do, Mr. Dixon? We can't leave here to drag him in. We daren't allow the other Indians to come to his aid. What are we to do?"

Dixon thought about his reply a moment as he grasped the significance of Langton's question. Even in the midst of the fight for his life, the shopkeeper clung to his ideas of civilized behavior.

"Actually, Mr. Langton," Dixon started slowly, "it ain't a question of what's to be done, but who's to do it."

"I'm confused," Langton said, running grimy hands through his hair. "I thought we'd agreed it was too dangerous to go outside. Even if we could, I daresay there is little care we could give him. I am no physician, and I know of no one here with any medical skills."

Smith guffawed, slapping his knee. "Well, I'll be dipped in buffalo sh—" He cast a quick glance in Hannah's direction. "I mean, that's plumb amazin'. You think we aim to doctor that redskin? No, sir. We're deciding who's gonna kill him."

Langton paled. "You mean shoot him in cold blood?"

Smith grinned. "Yep. Shoot him like the red dog he is."

Langton turned to Eddy. "George, are you a party to this . . . to this . . . murder?"

"Murder, James?" Eddy was shocked at the notion of killing the wounded Indian out of hand, but he was equally surprised by his boss's attitude. "As I recall, he was trying to kill me earlier."

"Yes, but as decent Christian folk, we are obliged to help him."

Dixon gazed narrowly at the thin shopkeeper as though seeing him for the first time.

"You know, Langton," he said, "you sure picked a mighty peculiar time to be showing us your sanctimonious side."

"Not really, Billy. I just—"

"Hold on there," Dixon ordered, raising a hand for silence. "Even if I agreed with anything you said, that only applies to Christians. That copper-skinned gentleman out there believes in many things. The Lord ain't among them. Besides, if the tables was turned, the only act of charity he'd show you was to wait until you were dead to take your hair."

"What's all the fuss about?" William Olds stepped through the doorway.

"William," Langton said, "you're a reasonable man." He pointed at the others in the room. "These men want to murder that helpless savage outside."

Olds stared from face to face. "Why?"

"You can hear him," Dixon said. "Sooner or later, help is gonna come his way."

"I know."

"You know?"

Eddy stepped forward. "William told me that he let the Indian live hoping to use him as bait to draw in others."

Smith nodded. "That's pretty good thinkin', Wild Bill. Bait always works."

Dixon shook his head. "I'm a gambler. Sometimes I play for money; sometimes I wager my life. The Indians have been charging us since dawn. Each run, the odds move more into their favor. Now, you stack these odds with something really motivating, like the buck out yonder, and we're liable to come up short." He turned to Langton. "So I'll put the decision to you, shopkeeper. Do we kill the Indian or take a chance on another raid?"

Langton stared into the dirt floor. "Put that way, I suppose there is really only one answer." He looked around the room. "But who will do the deed?"

"Ain't no decision to make," Olds said, walking back toward the doorway. "I shot him. I'll finish the job."

The room fell silent, each man lost in thought. Watching his companions, Eddy saw emotions run from dread to satisfaction. He was looking at Langton's expression when the shot came. The shopkeeper jumped.

Shortly, Olds returned, his face wrinkled in thought. "Damnedest thing I ever saw," he said, shaking his head.

Hannah snorted from her position on the floor. "William, really, such language."

Olds ignored his wife. "Goddamnedest thing I ever saw."

"What, William?" Eddy asked.

"Well, I went to shoot that Injun. I leaned out my window, just like before. He sees me about the time I draw a good bead, and raises his pistol. Then, before I get my shot off, he puts a bullet in his own head. Don't that beat all? He had a loaded gun, and rather than shoot me, he killed himself."

* * *

Quanah felt the pounding of running horses before he heard them. Six horsemen rounded the edge of a butte and galloped straight for the campsite. He recognized the man on the lead animal as Stone Calf. The others were also Cheyenne. Trailing at a respectable distance, and a more leisurely pace, were the Kiowas Lone Wolf and Bear Mountain.

The party rode straight to Isatai's camp. Stone Calf leapt from his horse before the animal could completely stop and charged into the medicine man's tipi.

"Brown Bull," Quanah called to his sleeping brother. "Brown Bull, wake up."

"Leave me alone. I was having a dream about my wife."

"This is much more important," Quanah insisted.

Brown Bull opened one eye and regarded the young war chief. "What can be more important than sporting with a young wife?"

"I just saw Stone Calf going into Isatai's lodge and . . . Look, Brown Bull, they are coming out!"

The Cheyenne chief emerged from the tipi, dragging the hapless shaman. The other Cheyenne warriors gathered in a circle, and Isatai was thrust in the center. Each shouted at the medicine man and shook knives and tomahawks in his face. Isatai looked terrified and constantly cringed or ducked to avoid being struck.

Quanah and Brown Bull raced to the circle, and arrived just as White Wolf appeared. Behind the old Comanche chief was Tabananica. Lone Wolf and other Kiowa chieftains had also arrived.

"What is this all about?" demanded White Wolf. "We are all friends here. Why has Stone Calf attacked my medicine man?"

"My son is dead, old man!" Stone Calf shouted. Seeing the Comanche chief bristle, he quickly lowered his voice. "Forgive me, White Wolf. My fight is not with you, but with this medicine man who makes warriors throw away their lives."

White Wolf saw the anguish on the Cheyenne's face. The loss of any warrior hurt, but the death of a child could never be understood except by others who had suffered the same fate. He reached out and placed his hand on Stone Calf's shoulder.

"My heart cries for your loss. I know no words to act as a balm for your wounds. But for all this, why have you come to Isatai for vengeance? Should you not make the whites pay?"

"I have watched many brave men die today. Not as warriors in battle, but like buffalo running over a cliff. And why?" He pointed at Isatai, who tried to shrink away. "Because of him. He made these men believe they could not be killed. He made these men charge into the guns of the hunters to be slaughtered. He made my son attack the village single-handed with a pistol!"

Stone Calf turned and addressed the crowd. "Is it not enough that he has made fools of us all? Look at yourselves. All of you, painted yellow like prairie flowers. Is this how a warrior appears? Where is the magic the Great Spirit gave each of you? I see no signs of bear medicine or eagle medicine. You, Quanah, where is your medicine bag?"

Quanah was stunned the chief would ask so personal a question. Medicine pouches and their contents were something not open for discussion. Before he could speak, Stone Calf continued.

"Do not answer that, my friend." The Cheyenne chief's voice was calmer now. "I know that among the Comanche personal medicine is left between you and the Great Spirit. We have been duped by a failed magician. For this he must die!"

White Wolf turned and conferred quickly with Tabananica. He then faced Isatai. "Shaman, you have heard the accusations of the great Cheyenne chieftain, Stone Calf. Do you have anything to say?"

Isatai glanced at the men around him. His gaze

didn't linger on any face. Every countenance wore tl
same expression, even those of the Comanches he
known for years. He was in deep trouble.

"White Wolf," he began, then stopped.

His voice quavered. This would never do. Isat
drew a deep breath and let it out while he straighten
his posture.

"White Wolf," he began again, sounding muc
more confident than he felt, "let me begin by tellii
the esteemed war chief of the Cheyenne that I a
grieved by his loss. I will pray to the Great Spi
to make the young man's passage to the next wor
effortless.

"I, too, am shocked and disheartened at the failu
of the ochre paint. Stone Calf is right. I am responsib
for the deaths and injuries of our men. I cannot sa
otherwise. It is true that I told of the things I saw
the house of the Great Spirit. I was given the pai
and I used it. Was not my own horse slain by
hunter?" Isatai paused and looked at his audienc
"But he was shot in the only place on his body n
covered by paint. Some of you say the Great Spiri
hand carried the bullet that killed my horse. Perha
so. Yet, if the paint did not work, why put the bull
in an unprotected area?"

Isatai saw the impact his last statement had mad
Some of the faces registered surprise; others remaine
hostile. Encouraged that he at least had their attentio
he continued. "I say the death of my warhorse was
sign that the magic itself did not fail. I searched tl
edges of the battleground. What did I find? A skun
A dead skunk."

Impatient with the medicine man's speech, Stor
Calf broke in. "A skunk? This is what you offer us?

"Please, Stone Calf," White Wolf said. "Let hi
finish. Then you may answer."

Isatai said, "There is but one way to destroy tl

magic I possess, and that is to kill a skunk on the way to battle."

Stone Calf snorted, but said nothing.

Isatai ignored him. "It is easy for those who do not understand of magic to scoff, but I know this to be true. Not only that, but the animal was trampled to death by a Cheyenne horse."

"No more!" cried Stone Calf. "I say no more of this foolishness. He is stinking up the air with his stories of skunks. And now he tells us my own men ruined his magic. Next, he will say I caused my own son's death."

"But it is so!" Isatai argued. "I found the animal in the area where the Cheyenne made their charge. As to blame, it is not only for the Cheyenne. No matter who killed the skunk, the charge was doomed from the start."

Stone Calf flung his hands into the air. "I surrender, shaman. Just stop talking. White Wolf, if we can't kill him, can we whip him soundly?"

The ancient Comanche shrugged thin shoulders. "Will it make things better?"

Stone Calf let a hard smile cross his face. "No, but it would gladden my heart."

Tabananica spoke for the first time. "There is no need to punish this fellow further. He is disgraced among the Comanche. He is a medicine man with no medicine. Let him go, Stone Calf. Mourn your son as his father and chief. Leave Isatai to us."

Stone Calf glared a final time at Isatai before spinning on his heel and stalking away.

One of the departing Cheyenne warriors turned back to the shaman. "I know what's wrong with your medicine. You have skunk medicine."

The warrior's companions laughed and held their noses as they passed Isatai.

Quanah let go of a breath he hadn't realized he was holding. His heart sank. With the Cheyenne angry at

Isatai, how long before they went home? How soon would the Kiowa join them? "The Arapaho observers will have many funny stories for their fires," he muttered darkly. "And at our expense."

Thirty

Carlyle walked toward the front door. The clerk looked through cracks between the planks, then lifted the crossbar.

"What are you doing, Bermuda?" Hanrahan asked.

"Nothin' much. I saw something sparkling out there."

"And?"

"And I aim to fetch it."

Hanrahan quickly rose to feet. "Have you lost your goddam mind?"

"Aw, hell, Jim, we ain't heard nary a sound for a couple of hours now. I cain't see any movement at all, and what I want is close by."

With the doorway cleared, Carlyle opened the portal a fraction and scrutinized the area. Satisfied no Indians were hiding nearby, he stepped out and walked into the valley.

He breathed deeply, savoring the first bit of fresh air he'd had since dawn. Moving quickly, he scampered to the object he'd seen, scooped up the piece of jewelry, and ran back to the saloon.

Safely inside, he looked at his find, turning it over in a shaft of sunlight from a loophole. It was obviously something for decoration. Slightly smaller than his hand, it consisted of a leather band covered in intricate and colorful beadwork. Mixed with the beads were small pieces of silver. Light reflecting off the metal had caught Carlyle's eye.

Hanrahan looked over the clerk's shoulder. "What is it?"

"Cain't rightly say. Maybe a bracelet or armband kind of thing. Fancy, though, eh?"

"Not fancy enough to risk your neck over."

"Weren't no risk. You hear a shot? We've whupped those redskins for now." Carlyle pocketed the trinket and walked back to the door. "I'm going to get me something else."

On his second trip, Carlyle strolled, taking his time to carefully examine each artifact before claiming it.

Dixon glanced out the restaurant window and saw figures moving in the distance. Instantly suspicious, he looked closer and realized they were white men. One of the men faced his direction, shouted, and waved his arms. Though the hunter couldn't understand what was being said, he understood the message.

"They're comin' out!" he shouted, and he made his way to the store's front door. He poked his head through Eddy's doorway. "Hear me? I said, they're coming out. We've won, boys!"

Eddy quickly followed Dixon and helped him remove the stacks of seed. The hunter threw the door open and raced outside. Eddy turned to shout the news, and was almost run down by the rest of the defenders hurrying to get out of the store. Langton brought up the rear.

"Well, George, we seem to have vanquished our foes."

Eddy laughed. "Ain't it the truth?" He breathed deeply. "Isn't that air wonderful? I may just sleep out here."

Dixon watched his companions celebrate with much

laughter and back-slapping, but he was on a mission. He rounded the store and made for the spot where they'd seen the gray horse, curious as to why the animal had stayed still until he was shot by the Indians.

Reaching the spot, Dixon found his answer. Lying next to the horse was a dead Indian who had fallen in such a way that the reins had caught beneath his body, effectively tethering his mount. Examining the horse, Dixon saw it wore a silver-mounted bridle. Using a buffalo bone, he pried open the animal's mouth and removed the bridle. He also picked up a rawhide lariat lying nearby.

Attached to the bridle, a foot from the bit, he found a scalp. It had apparently come from a white woman. It was fifteen inches long, the hair dark brown. The scalp was lined with cloth and edged in beadwork.

Crossing back toward the Rath & Company store, he walked to the sod outhouse. Sitting on the far side was an Indian. Dixon jumped back, his heart pounding. He pulled his pistol and peeked around the corner. The Indian just sat there. Cautiously, the hunter stepped closer.

The warrior sat perfectly upright with his legs crossed. His head was turned to one side and he looked asleep. But he didn't breathe! Dixon decided he must have broken his neck in a fall and died instantly.

What they had been shooting at earlier was a lance. It stuck in the ground, adorned with black feathers spaced six inches apart. The feathers had whipped in the wind until a bullet cut the shaft in two. The upper part lay across the dead Indian's legs. Dixon took the lance.

Finally, he had to know what he'd shot in the tall grass. Walking the half mile, he wondered why the Indians had quit the fight. From experience, he knew the red man's reasons and motivations were often a mystery. Maybe they just got tired of waiting. Maybe one of their medicine men told them to pack up and go home.

Once in the tall grass, he found the body of another Indian lying flat on his stomach. He wore only a breechclout, but had a pistol in his belt. Looking closer, Dixon saw he'd been shot through the middle of the body, and the size of the hole told the hunter it was a Sharps that had killed him. The Indian also had a shattered knee.

A blood trail wound its way through the grass. He followed it. Dixon soon came across a shot pouch containing fifteen cartridges and a powder horn. A few steps further, he found a .50-caliber Springfield needle gun. Next to the rifle lay the warrior's bow and quiver. Dixon gathered up everything and headed back to the store.

As he deposited his war prizes on a restaurant table, Dixon saw Hannah Olds sitting alone crying. "Problem, Miz Olds?"

Hannah nodded and noisily blew her nose. "They killed Ike and Shorty and that young boy, Billy Tyler."

"Oh." Dixon was saddened that the men had died, but at least there had been only three. He wondered if Hannah knew how close they had come to all dying. "That's awful. Who told you?"

"Sam Smith. He was over at the saloon when Bat Masterson brought them the news. Isn't it just terrible?" Hannah started to cry again. "Just terrible."

Crying women made Dixon uncomfortable, and he hurried away. Back outside, he decided to check his own wagons.

Still tied to a wagon lay Jack. Dixon felt a lump rise in his throat as he looked at the horse that had served him so well for so long. He cursed the Indians for the senseless slaughter of his horse and the other horses that littered the battleground. He decided to leave the animal for now and check on his friends.

Moving across to the saloon, he spied the small

body of Hannah Olds's colt. The tiny horse lay on its side, an arrow sticking out of its back. If he had ever seen a truly unnecessary act, killing the baby mustang was one. Cursing loudly and fluently, he walked to the saloon.

"Well, goddam, look what come in!" Hanrahan shouted as Dixon entered the saloon. "Get your sorry little ass over here, Billy. Drinks are on me."

Dixon nodded his thanks and leaned on the bar. Hanrahan poured him a generous amount of whiskey in a tumbler. The hunter drained the glass without comment or pause. Hanrahan refilled it. This time Dixon sipped.

"Hell of a fight, son," the saloon keeper said, taking a drink from the bottle. He stared at the floor and took another, deeper pull. "Hell of a fight."

Fred Leonard entered next, followed by Bermuda Carlyle and Charley Armitage. The English shop-keeper accepted a beer and took his place next to Dixon.

Armitage slapped the hunter on the back. "God, but it's good to see you, Billy. It wasn't until now that I even knew whether you were alive."

Dixon grinned. "Alive and well, Charley." The smile faded. "Course that don't hold for Tyler and the Scheidlers."

"True. Too true." Armitage lifted his glass and shouted. "A drink." He waited for the voices to still. "I offer a toast to our fallen comrades. May God watch over the souls of Billy Tyler, Isaac and Jacob Scheidler."

"Hear, hear," called Leonard.

After the toast, Armitage threw his glass into the wall, shattering it. Others joined in, and soon glass objects of various types flew through the air to smash against walls, the bar, and unwary hunters.

"Hey!" yelled Hanrahan. "Hey, hey, hey! Hold up, now. Them glasses are expensive."

"Bugger yourself," Armitage said.

Hanrahan reddened as men started to laugh. "Kiss my rosy red ass, limey," he countered, and stalked to the far end of the bar.

"Did you see all the dead horses we have?" Leonard asked Dixon.

The hunter nodded. "Yeah. I counted twenty head between here and the Rath place."

"My God. I counted thirty-six from my store to here. That is fifty-six dead horses."

"Most of what I saw were war ponies. I only saw two of ours, mine and Miz Olds' colt."

"Hmm," Leonard said, stroking his face as he tried to recall what horses he had seen. "Let's see, now. Five were shot in the corral, including that mare that liked to kick. I remember three more lying near the south stockade wall. Including what you saw, I make it ten animals we lost."

"That's dead horses. Ain't no telling where the others run off to."

"They also killed all the oxen the Scheidlers had."

"Jesus," Dixon swore. "Why shoot a dumb ol' ox? Sometimes, I think Indians are just crazy."

O'Keefe walked into the saloon and approached Hanrahan. They had a quick, quiet discussion. Hanrahan pounded the bar top with his pistol butt for attention.

"Listen up, boys. Tom's brought up something important. We know we can move around pretty good right now, but dark's comin' on, and we don't know if them red son-of-a-bitches are gonna come back. So Tom thinks we ought to bury our dead while we can."

"Sounds good to me," Dixon said. "I'll help."

Every man in the saloon volunteered for burial duty. They split into three parties. One would take care of Tyler; Masterson offered to dig the grave.

"Bat," Hanrahan said gently, "I know Tyler was your friend, but we need to hurry. You can help, but

want several men digging a big grave. Make it deep
nough to hold all three men. You all right with that,
at?"

Masterson nodded and left the saloon, trailed by a
alf-dozen helpers. The remaining men set out to
ather the dead. The bodies were wrapped in blankets
nd carried to the northwest corner of the stockade,
ear where the Scheidlers had met their fate. The
rave ready, they gently laid the three together.

After the hole was covered, Leonard cleared his
roat. "Boys, I wish we had time to say the proper
ords, but that will have to wait until later. For now,
lease bow your heads." Leonard took a breath. "Lord,
e commend the bodies of these men to the ground
nd their souls unto You. Take good care of them.
.men."

After a few mumbled "amens," the burial detail
urried away for the safety of the buildings. They de-
ided to abandon the saloon and divide themselves
etween the main post stores. Alarmed by what they
aw as inadequate protection, most left Leonard's and
an to the safety of Rath's thick sod walls.

Leonard chose to remain at his store. Carlyle joined
im, as did Old Man Keeler. He also managed to talk
ree of his employees into staying, until his group
umbered six men.

Carlyle approached his boss in the gathering gloom,
is cheek bulging with tobacco. "I got to tell you, Mr.
eonard, this ain't what I call an unbeatable defense."

"We shall get by, Bermuda. Have no fear."

"I ain't worried about gettin' by. That damn Swede
old me we was gonna die over here tonight, and it's
ust the notion that he might get proved right that galls
ne."

Thirty-one

Dixon felt the charge before he heard it. The ground rumbled and shook underfoot. Then he heard the wild screams of the Indians, the thundering of the horses' hooves. He searched for his rifle, but it was gone, lost in the gloom of the dark room. Looking at the others in the saloon, he realized they still slept. He ran from man to man, shaking them.

"Wake up!" he screamed. "Can't you hear 'em? Wake up!"

He lit a match and rolled Frenchy over. "Get up! The Indians are coming again."

The skinner stared at him wide-eyed, but made no move. Dixon grabbed him and shook. The match flared and he saw the raw wound where the scalp had been lifted, the cut throat. He cried out as the match burned his fingers.

"This can't be," he moaned, and reached for another match. "No, no, no. This just can't happen."

He struck the second match and grabbed the nearest form. Again the empty stare, the gash in the neck. He made his way through the saloon. Not a man breathed except him.

His own breaths came in short, sharp pants. He felt them, could hear himself clearly. Then he caught his breath. How could he hear himself over the sound of the attacking Indians?

Silence roared.

He turned and stared at the saloon's front door—
standing open. The match fluttered as it neared his
fingers, and in its fading light, Dixon saw the yellow
ochre arm reach for him.

Quanah awoke with a start. He rolled over, grab-
bing his knife as he rose to his feet.

The camp was quiet, except for the low moans of
the wounded. Glancing left, then right, the war chief
held his breath, feeling his heart pound as though it
would burst from his body.

"Quanah?"

The voice startled him, and he spun, prepared to
attack.

"Quanah, it's Brown Bull. There is no enemy. You
were dreaming." Brown Bull moved slowly into the
light of the campfire. "See? It's only me. You can put
the knife down."

"But the vision was so clear. I saw the hunters here,
in the camp, killing us. I tried to fight, but I could
not move my arms or legs." He looked down at the
knife, its blade reflecting flames. He loosened his grip
and let the weapon fall to the ground. "Do you think
it was a sign, Brown Bull?" He looked at his brother.
"Should we abandon this fight?"

Brown Bull shook his head. "Not yet. You did not
have a vision. It was a dream, nothing more. The same
thing happened to me on a raid that went badly. The
medicine man told me that I was punishing myself in
the dream world because I led a failed attack. He told
me it would pass."

"Did it?" Quanah asked, rubbing his still-numb arm.

"In time. Now, let's eat something. Then we go back
out to kill your hunters."

* * *

"Hey, lookit over to the east."

Eddy ran to the nearest loophole and peered outsid In the distance, he saw a small group of Indians atc a bluff. He slid his rifle through the gun port. "Let give 'em something to think about."

All the men on the east wall of the Rath & Compar store opened fire.

"Damn," Johnson swore. "Dey's too far away hit."

White puffs of smoke came from the Indians, an the bookkeeper realized they were returning fire. H quickly moved away from the hole and waited to hea the familiar sound of bullets slamming into the so wall. No sound came, so he peeked back through th loophole.

"Well, I'll be damned. They can't hit us either." H leaned the rifle against the wall.

"What're you doing, George?" Olds asked. "Ain ya gonna kill 'em?"

Eddy looked at his clerk and marveled at how th little man's entire speech patterns had changed ove night. He sounded more and more like Sam Smith "No, William, I'm not. They can't hurt us, and I don want to waste the ammo." He went to his bedroo for a drink of water.

Langton sat on the edge of his bed reading. H looked up as Eddy entered. "Hello, George."

Eddy nodded. "James. How are you this morning?

"All right, I suppose. I had vivid dreams last nigh and many nightmares."

"Who didn't?" the bookkeeper replied, dippin water out of a bucket.

Langton watched his employee drink, and decide to change the subject. "Do you remember the bastion over at Fred's store?"

Eddy nodded.

"I was thinking we might do something simila

ere. Nothing fancy, mind you, but still a lookout ower or some such."

"You want a tower like Fred's?"

Langton shook his head. "Not at all, George. I was hinking we might cut a hole in the roof and build a small structure on top of the store. Visibility would be greatly increased."

Eddy thought a moment, then nodded. "That could work. That way, if the Injuns attack again, we'd have more warning. Yeah, that could work real good. I'll get the Swede on it."

Dixon quietly examined the remaining gin in his bottle, then turned the vessel slowly around to read the label for the tenth time in as many minutes. Through the clear glass he saw a distorted Hanrahan approach.

"Pretty quiet today, wasn't it?" the saloon keeper asked.

"I reckon. If you don't count ol' George Bellfield, that is."

Hanrahan chuckled. "He did come in lickety-split, didn't he? I'd a swore there was a passel of redskins on his tail. You know what spooked him?"

"The flag?"

Earlier in the day, Johnson had made a black flag to warn approaching hunters of the danger.

Hanrahan shook his head. "Nope. It was all them dead horses. George said he thought we was funnin' him with the flag, but when he saw the horses . . . well, that scared the shit out of him."

"Didn't he think all the dark-skinned men with feathers were a worry?"

"He says he didn't see nary a Injun, even when he got close. No, sir, just them dead horses."

Dixon emptied the bottle and tossed it across the room. "Speaking of which, the smell's pretty rank."

"You're probably right."

Dixon grinned. "Course I am. Now, if you will pardon me, I have just enough gin in me to sleep real tight. If the Injuns attack again, you will wake me, won't you?"

"You can count on it, Billy."

Hanrahan watched the other man's eyes close and his breathing become even. He regarded the dozing hunter, then pulled his own bottle of gin from a pocket.

"Here's to you, son," he said quietly, and withdrew the cork and drank deeply. "Maybe tonight, the ghosts'll leave both of us alone."

Thirty-two

Dixon wandered back into the Rath & Company store, hot, thirsty, and not a little nauseous. The entire day had been spent disposing of bodies. The horses, bloated from the heat, threatened to explode and spray the men with maggots and gore.

At one spot, twelve animals lay together. Rather than attempting to drag the carcasses away, they'd dug a pit and rolled the bodies in one at a time. As the first horse hit bottom, it split and the stench sent the hunters reeling. Wearing handkerchiefs over their mouths or holding their breaths, the men finally managed to complete the gruesome chore.

Dixon ran his tongue over dry lips and grimaced as he tasted the smell of rotting flesh. "Christ Almighty! Somebody get me a beer!"

Without comment, Hannah handed the hunter a Kirmeyer's. Dixon nodded his thanks and moved away. He took a swig of his beer, swished it around his mouth, and spat it on the floor. The second mouthful tasted better.

Eddy came into the store next, his face pale and drawn. More than once, Dixon had seen the bookkeeper retch. Eddy also asked for and received a beer. He sat down next to Dixon and took a drink.

"Sweet Jesus," he said, making a face. "This is awful."

"Rinse your mouth out with a swallow," Dixon offered. "It cuts through the crap."

Eddy set the beer bottle between his crossed legs. "What a day."

"That ain't no lie."

"How many animals you reckon we buried or dragged off?"

"Shit. Who knows, George? Too many." Dixon pointed at the roof. "I see Langton's got his watchtower built."

Eddy nodded. "Yeah, he did. Looks to me like Andy done a fair job."

Dixon nodded and returned to his beer.

Both men looked up as William Olds clattered down the outpost's ladder, slipping on one of the rungs and nearly falling.

"There's a bunch of Injuns on a bluff to the east."

"Dammit, William!" Eddy yelled. "You got to be more careful comin' down that ladder. You'll fall and break your fool neck. I don't want to have to tell Hannah that you done a stupid thing like that, so be more careful."

"Sure, George, but what about them Injuns?"

"Aw, hell, William, who gives a . . ." Eddy saw the injured look on the clerk's face and gave up. "Come on, Billy, let's have us a look at William's redskins."

Eddy got to his feet and helped Dixon to his. Together they peered through the open door. In the distance, a group of silhouettes lined the sky.

"What you think, Billy?" the bookkeeper asked.

"Injuns for sure, George."

Olds appeared next to the two men. "What do you think they're doin' up there?"

"Looking," Dixon said.

"At what?"

Eddy turned back into the store. "At the heads, I reckon."

Olds followed the bookkeeper. "What heads?"

"Well, William, while we was handling animals, some of the new men took care of the dead Indians. They scalped them, cut off the heads, and stuck them on the crosspiece of Fred's corral gate."

"Oh, my," Olds said quietly, involuntarily raising a hand to his throat. "How'd they do it?"

"Do what?"

"You know, get 'em on that gate."

"They put them on the wooden pegs that hold the rocks Fred uses for a counterbalance. Yep, there they are, thirteen heads all with their mouths open like they're laughing. Makes for quite a sight."

Olds shuddered. "It ain't one I aim to see," he said, and left for his room.

Eddy chuckled and walked back out the front door.

"You know, George," Dixon said. "It just plumb provokes me that they're just standing up there gawking at us. Makes me of a mind to shoot one of 'em."

"Damn, Billy, that bluff's got be most of a mile away."

Dixon nodded, went back into the store, and returned with his Sharps Big Fifty. "I make it fourteen, maybe fifteen hundred yards." He grinned at Eddy. "Won't hurt to try."

The hunter raised his rifle and sighted carefully. He chose the largest Indian he could see, adjusted for distance and wind, and squeezed the trigger.

Quanah, Lone Wolf, and Stone Calf stood on a bluff overlooking the battlefield. They were surrounded by a dozen warriors including Brown Bull and Bear Mountain.

"We are so far away, I can barely see the houses," Lone Wolf complained. "How can we plan strategy if we cannot see our enemy?"

"What would you have us do?" Quanah countered. "Every time we get closer, they kill us."

Lone Wolf sighed. "I think it is time for the Kiowa to go home."

"I will not leave my son behind," Stone Calf said.

Lone Wolf laid a hand on the Cheyenne chief's shoulder. "I know the pain you feel. I lost my son—twice. But you can't fight the whites if you die down there. This place has only bad medicine for all of us."

"Leave if you will, Kiowa," Stone Calf said, shrugging off Lone Wolf's Hand, "but the Cheyenne are not so easily beaten. And you, Quanah, what will the Comanche do?"

"Against the wishes of many, I want to stay and fight. Even if I must do so by myself."

Quanah glanced at Brown Bull. The older warrior had made it clear that he was ready to go home.

"We cannot fight them near or far," Brown Bull had argued. "We cannot breach their doors, windows, or roofs. All we do is attack and die."

Many in the war party had agreed, but Quanah had persuaded most to stay. Again he looked at his brother.

Brown Bull opened his mouth to speak. Then he suddenly grabbed his chest and fell flat on his back. Like so many of the other shootings, there had been no sound, no smoke from the lodges.

Quanah and the others ran and hid behind a stand of bushes.

"How do they do that?" he asked.

Lone Wolf shook his head slowly. "It is as I said, we are accursed at this place."

"You are right, Lone Wolf. We are accursed." Quanah stared at his brother's body. "But it is not the white man who's to blame. It's my fault."

"How can you say that? You could not know of the rifles that shoot today and kill tomorrow. If any is to blame, it's your yellow medicine man."

Quanah shook his head. "No! I am war chief. I ignored the wisdom of the eagle spirit, my big brother, and the old men. I knew better." He paused and ran hand over his face. Weariness slumped his shoulders. The white man took all I had—father, mother, sister, and brother. I hate him for that, but in my anger I turned my back on everything Comanche. I acted like a white man with whiskey. I wore a Cheyenne head-dress and danced a Kiowa Sun Dance. Now the price has been paid."

The young war chief started across the bluff toward Brown Bull.

"Are you crazy?" Lone Wolf shouted.

Quanah stopped and faced the others. "They will not shoot. Don't you see? We have ten times their number, but we can't kill them. In defying the spirits, I have brought the wrath of the Great Spirit upon us. He protected the hunters, and now has slain my brother. It is my punishment. It is done."

Lone Wolf stared at his ally, then sighed. "Perhaps you're right. If so, we all share in the guilt. I wore the paint, as did my men. We fought like you."

"It is so," Stone Calf added. "We all have paid heavily. I came here though I believe that to fight the white man means the destruction of us all. I believe it more now. I am weary, and I miss my son. The Cheyenne are going home while there are still Cheyenne left to go home."

Lone Wolf walked out on the bluff. "Come, Quanah, I will help you rescue the body of your brother, but then the Kiowa leave, too."

Quanah nodded, and the two ran out on the bluff. Each grabbed one of Brown Bull's arms, and they dragged him back to the bushes. A large, angry, red mark was in the middle of his chest, but the bullet did not break the skin. Brown Bull's eyes fluttered open.

"See, little brother," he whispered hoarsely. "The spirits let the hunter shoot me, but they did not let him kill me—this time. But how long before all the young men are dead? Is this not enough sign for you?"

Quanah stood and regarded his brother. He looked over the battlefield, and as he did so, a single tear rolled down his cheek. "Yes, Brown Bull, we will leave. But not to the reservation. From now on we fight as Comanche led by the eagle, bear, and wolf spirits. Before it is over, they will come to know and fear the name of Quanah!"

Thirty-three

For the first time since the initial Indian attack, Dixon awoke feeling rested. It was the fifth day of waiting, and more than a hundred hunters had taken shelter in the camp. No Indian activity had been seen since the day he made the long shot, and most believed the siege was over.

He walked into the main store just as Eddy came out of his bedroom. Both men watched Hannah Olds come out of the restaurant.

"Good morning, gentlemen," she said with a smile. "Breakfast's ready." She walked up to the outpost's ladder. "William?"

No answer came from the watchtower.

"William Olds, can you hear me up there?"

"Yes, I can, Hannah."

"Well, come on down before your breakfast gets cold."

"All right, all right, just a minute. I think I see . . ." His voice trailed off. "Injuns!" he shouted. "There's more Injuns!"

Eddy heard Olds's feet shuffle excitedly overhead. "William," he called, "you best be careful. You hear?"

The warning fell on deaf ears as the clerk clambered down the ladder. On his third step, his foot slid off a rung.

In Dixon's mind, it was as if everything slowed to

a dreamlike quality. He saw Olds's face, eyes wide with excitement. The clerk rushed down the steps. Then he looked concerned as he slipped. He grabbed for a rail to keep from falling, losing his grip on his rifle. The Sharps .50-caliber fell to the last rung of the ladder and discharged when its butt struck.

Olds' face disappeared in a pink mist of blood and brains. His lifeless body fell, to lie crumpled at the foot of the ladder not three feet from his wife.

Hannah stared at the body at her feet, blood pouring from what remained of the head. She screamed, then screamed again, and collapsed to her knees, arms outstretched.

Eddy blanched. His legs failed him, and he leaned against a wall for support.

No one moved or spoke. Hannah's screams fell to sobbing. She was beyond the reach of anyone there.

Dixon stared in shock and horror. The hunter had seen death in many forms, had brought an end of life with his own hand. But that was killing buffalo or Indians. It had a point.

This was something else. The quiet clerk, who never harmed a soul before this damnable siege—who had found his real courage in the past few days—he didn't need to die. It was senseless, pointless.

Dixon's vision blurred. He didn't try to hide the tears or the lump in his throat. They could all cry now, for Hannah, for William, Billy Tyler, and the rest who had lost their lives during the fight. For those already gone, and for those who were yet to die.

Dixon wiped away his tears, but something remained. A sick feeling deep inside him. No more! No more hunting. No more death for profit. Let the red man have his buffalo.

The hunter smiled, a rueful smile. Others within the Walls, he was willing to bet, felt the same. The Indians didn't know it yet, but they had destroyed Adobe Walls.

Epilogue

Today the site of Adobe Walls lies on the Turkey Track Ranch, bisected by a county road and barbed-wire fence. Cattle feed where buffalo roamed. Not much is left of the post, except the remains of a 1975 archaeological dig and three stone markers.

The first of these was erected in 1924 to commemorate the fiftieth anniversary of the fight. It lists the twenty-nine white participants. In 1929, the second stone was placed as Billy Dixon's body was moved to the site. Finally, the Indians came again in 1941 and erected their monument listing the names of thirteen Comanche and Cheyenne warriors killed.

After The Battle

Quanah kept his word. He and his warriors terror
ized the Llano Estacado until June of 1875, when h
surrendered rather than lead his people to their deaths

After his surrender to General Nelson A. Miles, th
U.S. Government, perhaps realizing the influence h
could exert over his people, made Quanah chief of th
Comanche. By the end of the nineteenth century
Quanah, young war chief of the Adobe Walls fight
had become the legendary Quanah Parker. He died i
February 23, 1911.

Billy Dixon left the buffalo range and never agai
hunted the animals for profit. He joined the Army a
a scout for General Miles, and earned a Congressiona
Medal Of Honor while serving in the Red River Wa
In 1883, Dixon returned to civilian life as a ranche
postmaster, and sheriff, before retiring to quiet countr
life in Beaver County, Oklahoma. He died of pneu
monia on March 9, 1913.

Bat Masterson left the Texas plains and joined Dixo
as an Army scout. He later returned to Dodge City an

chieved fame as a sheriff. After Dodge, he left the West together and moved to New York City, where he worked as a journalist until his death in 1921.

James Langton left Adobe Walls and moved back Kansas to ranch. He returned to merchandising in 877, buying partnerships in several profitable businesses. In 1889, he settled in Salt Lake City, where e founded the Langton Lime and Cement Company nd became a wealthy man. In 1913, he crashed his ar near a highway bridge and died instantly.

James Hanrahan returned to Dodge City, only to move to Lake City, Colorado, where he was elected heriff in 1877. He resigned in April of 1879, and did ot surface again until 1895, when he was elected to represent Custer County in the third legislature of the ate of Idaho. He retired to Blackfoot, Idaho, and died ound 1918.

Fred Leonard went back to Dodge City and opened highly successful restaurant. He moved to Salt Lake ity in 1883. He sold stocks and bonds, real estate, rved as a county tax collector, was a mining broker, nd finally, managed the Cullen Hotel. He died in 928.

Andy Johnson remained at Adobe Walls for a month ter the fight. Back in Dodge City, he worked as a lacksmith, with forays into the restaurant business, tail liquor sales, and other occupations. He returned Adobe Walls in 1922, and again in 1924 to celebrate e fiftieth anniversary of the fight. He died in June 925.

* * *

The following people are thought to have been participants in the fight. Their lives after Adobe Wall are unknown—

Charley Armitage	Dixon skinner
Frenchy	Dixon skinner and cook
Mike McCabe	Dixon skinner
George Eddy	Rath & Company bookkeeper
Hannah Olds	Rath & Company cook
Oscar Shepherd	Hanrahan bartender
Billy Ogg	Hanrahan skinner
Mike Welch	Hanrahan skinner
Bermuda Carlyle	Myers and Leonard employee
Old Man Keeler	Myers and Leonard cook
Frank Smith	Myers and Leonard employee
James Campbell	possible Myers and Leonard employee
Fred Myers	possible Myers and Leonard employee
Edward Trevor	possible Myers and Leonard employee
Thomas O'Keefe	blacksmith
Henry Born	buffalo hunter
Sam Smith	buffalo hunter
Seth Hathaway	buffalo hunter
Henry Lease	buffalo hunter
Hiram Watson	possible teamster
James McKinley	unknown

There is no way to be sure of the actual number of Indians who took part in the battle. In their text *Adobe Walls: The History and Archeology of the 187 rading Post,* T. Lindsay Baker and Billy R. Harrison believe about three hundred warriors to be an accurate estimate based on their knowledge and research into the Comanche, Kiowa, and Cheyenne tribes.

In a 1995 interview, Melvin Kerchee, of the Comanche tribe, said the tribes would have been hard-pressed to field a large war party. He also said the Comanche were split about whether to even participate in Quanah and Isatai's war on the white hunters, effectively reducing the number of warriors available.

On July 7, 1874, Lieutenant Colonel J. W. Davidson reported he'd heard from scouts and interpreters that the war party had numbered less than three hundred.

Quanah and Isatai are undisputed Comanche participants, as are White Wolf, Tabananica, Black Beard, Yellowfish, Timbo, Cheyenne, the black bugler, Co-hy-yah, Co-bay, Esa-que, So-ta-do, Best Son-in-Law, and Tasa-va-te.

Lone Wolf's raiding party consisted of himself, High Forehead, Boy, White Goose, Teeth, Good Talk, Wise, Kicking, Buffalo with Holes in His Ears, Man Who Walks above the Ground, and Bear Mountain. It probable these men accompanied him to Adobe Walls.

Cheyenne thought to have fought included Chief Stone Calf, Stone Calf's Son, White Shield, Red Moon, Serpent Scales, Spotted Feather, Horse Chief, Coyote, Stone Teeth, and Soft Foot.

ACKNOWLEDGMENTS

Any writer can tell you that to complete a novel requires hard work, determination, and the support of those around you. Any work that involves actual historical events depends on research, and good research depends on people. I have been fortunate in all circumstances revolving about this book, and I think it only fitting that I thank those who made it all possible. These folks are listed in chronological order:

Charles Simmons—I can honestly say that all of this is his fault. Several years ago he told me I should write a book. Well, Charles, here it is.

Melvin Kerchee, Sr.—When I first approached this Comanche elder with the idea of writing the story of Adobe Wall from both the red and white points of view, he said, "It is time for the truth to be told." In that respect, I've tried to present the events of 1874 as clear as I can. I hope I got it right.

Melvin Kerchee, Jr.—I first met Melvin Jr. at a pow-wow. He was dressed in full Comanche regalia holding a Styrofoam cup of coffee in one hand and a cigarette in another. He told me of the political situation among the Comanche in 1874 and how hard-pressed they would have been to field more than thre hundred warriors for the battle.

DeWanna Pace—This lady is both writer and agen having penned many romance novels. Dee gave m Karen Haas's number at Kensington and said I shoul call her.

Karen Haas—Karen is my editor at Kensington Without her, the book would not exist. What else ca I say?

Throughout the writing of *Blood Red River,* I hav had help from the reference desk at Amarillo Publi Library and the research library at Panhandle Plair Historical Museum in Canyon, Texas. These fine folk showed me the way and provided the rare documen and books to help me tell the story.

A special thank-you goes to the Write Stuff Critiqu Group. These are my guys. While they made my lif miserable, the book got better and better. Member have come and gone, but we're still here. Thank Carol, Charles, Jimmy, Judy, Karen, Susan, Suzann and Tom.

Finally, to my wife and children, thank you. Withou your support, I would have never been able to com plete this book. The good news is *Blood Red River* i done. The bad news is there are more to come.

William W. Johnstone
The *Mountain Man* Series

toll free **1-888-345-BOOK** to order by phone or use
coupon to order by mail.

...e _____

...ress _____

_____ State _____ Zip _____

...se send me the books I have checked above.

...enclosing $_____

...postage and handling* $_____

...tax (in New York and Tennessee only) $_____

...amount enclosed $_____

...d $2.50 for the first book and $.50 for each additional book.

...check or money order (no cash or CODs) to:

...ington Publishing Corp., 850 Third Avenue, New York, NY 10022

...s and Numbers subject to change without notice.

...rders subject to availability.

...k out our website at **www.kensingtonbooks.com**